THE
WISTERIA SOCIETY
OF
LADY SCOUNDRELS

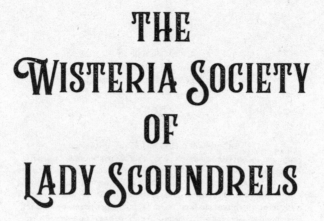

THE
WISTERIA SOCIETY
OF
LADY SCOUNDRELS

✴

INDIA HOLTON

JOVE

New York

A JOVE BOOK
Published by Berkley
An imprint of Penguin Random House LLC
penguinrandomhouse.com

Library of Congress Cataloging-in-Publication Data

Names: Holton, India, author.
Title: The Wisteria Society of Lady Scoundrels / India Holton.
Description: First edition. | New York: Jove, 2021.
Identifiers: LCCN 2020043100 (print) | LCCN 2020043101 (ebook) |
ISBN 9780593200162 (trade paperback) | ISBN 9780593200179 (ebook)
Subjects: LCSH: Female offenders—Fiction. | Thieves—Fiction. |
Great Britain—History—Victoria, 1837–1901—Fiction. |
GSAFD: Historical fiction. | LCGFT: Romance fiction.
Classification: LCC PR9639.4.H66 W57 2021 (print) |
LCC PR9639.4.H66 (ebook) | DDC 823/.914—dc23
LC record available at https://lccn.loc.gov/2020043100
LC ebook record available at https://lccn.loc.gov/2020043101

First Edition: June 2021

Printed in the United States of America
4th Printing

Book design by Laura K. Corless

For Amaya
and Julie
I love you to the edge of the universe and back

TABLE OF SIGNIFICANT CHARACTERS

- In Order of Appearance -

Cecilia Bassingthwaite . . . a plucky young lady

Miss Darlington . . . Cecilia's great-aunt

Cilla . . . a dolorous memory

Pleasance . . . a housemaid and several ghosts

Eduardo de Luca . . . an Italian assassin

Ned Lightbourne . . . a charming pirate in league with the enemy

Isabella Armitage . . . a lady nemesis

Alexander O'Riley . . . a dangerous Irish pirate (and concerned chum)

Patrick Morvath . . . a villainous poet; the aforementioned enemy

Constantinopla Brown . . . a girl just home from boarding school

Assorted scoundrels

Jane Fairweather . . . a spinster

Tom Eames . . . a misled youth

Various ruffians

Teddy Luxe . . . a fencing master with provocative hips

Captain Smith . . . an agent with Her Majesty's secret police brigade

Unnamed brigands

Lady Victoria and Lord Albert . . . pseudonymous hotel guests

Cecilia's wits . . . a costumed company

Jacobsen . . . a determined pursuer

Queen Victoria . . . England's monarch

Prince Albert . . . deceased

Frederick Bassingthwaite . . . an earnest fellow; Cecilia's cousin

Duarte Leveport of Valando . . . a Portuguese baron

The ghost of Emily Brontë . . . alleged

Charles Darwin . . . a rival

Major Candent . . . an officer in Her Majesty's service

Miscellaneous princes

Dr. Lumes . . . a proficient dancer

1

AN UNEXPECTED CALLER—THE PLIGHT OF THE AUK—
SEMANTICS—THE LEVEL MOON—NOT THE LEVEL MOON—
THE CALLER RETURNS—A DISCUSSION OF CHOLERA—
AN EXPLOSION—LUNCHEON IS SERVED

There was no possibility of walking to the library that day. Morning rain had blanched the air, and Miss Darlington feared that if Cecilia ventured out she would develop a cough and be dead within the week. Therefore Cecilia was at home, sitting with her aunt in a room ten degrees colder than the streets of London, and reading aloud *The Song of Hiawatha* by "that American rogue, Mr. Longfellow," when the strange gentleman knocked at their door.

As the sound barged through the house, interrupting Cecilia's recitation mid-rhyme, she looked inquiringly at her aunt. But Miss Darlington's own gaze went to the mantel clock, which was ticking sedately toward a quarter to one. The old lady frowned.

"It is an abomination the way people these days knock at any wild, unseemly hour," she said in much the same tone the prime minister had used in Parliament recently to decry the London rioters. "I do declare—!"

Cecilia waited, but Miss Darlington's only declaration came in the form of sipping her tea pointedly, by which Cecilia understood that the abominable caller was to be ignored. She returned to *Hiawatha* and had just begun proceeding "toward the land of the Pearl-Feather" when the knocking came again with increased force, silencing her and causing Miss Darlington to set her teacup into its saucer with a *clink*. Tea splashed, and Cecilia hastily laid down the poetry book before things really got out of hand.

"I shall see who it is," she said, smoothing her dress as she rose and touching the red-gold hair at her temples, although there was no crease in the muslin nor a single strand out of place in her coiffure.

"Do be careful, dear," Miss Darlington admonished. "Anyone attempting to visit at this time of day is obviously some kind of hooligan."

"Fear not, Aunty." Cecilia took up a bone-handled letter opener from the small table beside her chair. "They will not trouble me."

Miss Darlington harrumphed. "We are buying no subscriptions today," she called out as Cecilia left the room.

In fact they had never bought subscriptions, so this was an unnecessary injunction, although typical of Miss Darlington, who persisted in seeing her ward as the reckless tomboy who had entered her care ten years before: prone to climbing trees, fashioning cloaks from tablecloths, and making unauthorized doorstep purchases whenever the fancy took her. But a decade's proper education had wrought wonders, and now Cecilia walked the hall quite calmly, her French heels tapping against the polished marble floor, her intentions aimed in no way toward the taking of a subscription. She opened the door.

"Yes?" she asked.

"Good afternoon," said the man on the step. "May I interest you in a brochure on the plight of the endangered North Atlantic auk?"

Cecilia blinked from his pleasant smile to the brochure he was holding out in a black-gloved hand. She noticed at once the scandalous lack of hat upon his blond hair and the embroidery trimming his black

2

frock coat. He wore neither sideburns nor mustache, his boots were tall and buckled, and a silver hoop hung from one ear. She looked again at his smile, which quirked in response.

"No," she said, and closed the door.

And bolted it.

Ned remained for a moment longer with the brochure extended as his brain waited for his body to catch up with events. He considered what he had seen of the woman who had stood so briefly in the shadows of the doorway, but he could not recall the exact color of the sash that waisted her soft white dress, nor whether it had been pearls or stars in her hair, nor even how deeply winter dreamed in her lovely eyes. He held only a general impression of "beauty so rare and face so fair"— and implacability so terrifying in such a young woman.

And then his body made pace, and he grinned.

Miss Darlington was pouring herself another cup of tea when Cecilia returned to the parlor. "Who was it?" she asked without looking up.

"A pirate, I believe," Cecilia said as she sat and, taking the little book of poetry, began sliding a finger down a page to relocate the line at which she'd been interrupted.

Miss Darlington set the teapot down. With a delicate pair of tongs fashioned like a sea monster, she began loading sugar cubes into her cup. "What made you think that?"

Cecilia was quiet a moment as she recollected the man. He had been handsome in a rather dangerous way, despite the ridiculous coat. A light in his eyes had suggested he'd known his brochure would not fool her, but he'd entertained himself with the pose anyway. She predicted his hair would fall over his brow if a breeze went through it, and that the slight bulge in his trousers had been in case she was not happy to see him—a dagger, or perhaps a gun.

"Well?" her aunt prompted, and Cecilia blinked herself back into focus.

"He had a tattoo of an anchor on his wrist," she said. "Part of it was visible from beneath his sleeve. But he did not offer me a secret handshake, nor invite himself in for tea, as anyone of decent piratic society would have done, so I took him for a rogue and shut him out."

"A rogue pirate! At our door!" Miss Darlington made a small, disapproving noise behind pursed lips. "How reprehensible. Think of the germs he might have had. I wonder what he was after."

Cecilia shrugged. Had Hiawatha confronted the magician yet? She could not remember. Her finger, three-quarters of the way down the page, moved up again. "The Scope diamond, perhaps," she said. "Or Lady Askew's necklace."

Miss Darlington clanked a teaspoon around her cup in a manner that made Cecilia wince. "Imagine if you had been out as you planned, Cecilia dear. What would I have done, had he broken in?"

"Shot him?" Cecilia suggested.

Miss Darlington arched two vehemently plucked eyebrows toward the ringlets on her brow. "Good heavens, child, what do you take me for, a maniac? Think of the damage a ricocheting bullet would do in this room."

"Stabbed him, then?"

"And get blood all over the rug? It's a sixteenth-century Persian antique, you know, part of the royal collection. It took a great deal of effort to acquire."

"Steal," Cecilia murmured.

"Obtain by private means."

"Well," Cecilia said, abandoning a losing battle in favor of the original topic of conversation. "It was indeed fortunate I was here. 'The level moon stared at him—' "

"The moon? Is it up already?" Miss Darlington glared at the wall as if she might see through its swarm of framed pictures, its wallpaper and wood, to the celestial orb beyond, and therefore convey her disgust at its diurnal shenanigans.

"No, it stared at Hiawatha," Cecilia explained. "In the poem."

"Oh. Carry on, then."

" 'In his face stared pale and haggard—' "

"Repetitive fellow, isn't he?"

"Poets do tend to—"

Miss Darlington waved a hand irritably. "I don't mean the poet, girl. The pirate. Look, he's now trying to climb in the window."

Cecilia glanced up to see the man from the doorstep tugging on the wooden frame of the parlor window. Although his face was obscured by the lace curtain, she fancied she could see him muttering with exasperation. Sighing, she laid down the book once more, rose gracefully, and made her way through a clutter of furniture, statuettes, vases bearing long-stemmed roses from the garden (the neighbor's garden, to be precise), and various priceless (which is to say purloined) goods, to part the curtain, unlatch the window, and slide it up.

"Yes?" she asked in the same tone she had used at the doorstep.

The man seemed rather startled by her appearance. His hair had fallen exactly as she had supposed it would, and his shadowed eyes held a more sober mood than before.

"If you ask again for my interest in the great North Atlantic auk," Cecilia said, "I will be obliged to tell you the bird has in fact been extinct for almost fifty years."

"I could have sworn this window opened to a bedroom," he said, brushing his hair back to reveal a mild frown.

"We are not common rabble, to sleep on the ground floor. I don't know your name, for you have not done us the courtesy of leaving a calling card, but I assume it would in any case be a *nom de pirata*. I am all too aware of your kind."

"No doubt," he replied, "since you are also my kind."

Cecilia gasped. "How dare you, sir!"

"Do you deny that you and your aunt belong to the Wisteria Society and so are among the most notorious pirates in England?"

"I don't deny it, but that is my exact point. We are far superior to your kind. Furthermore, these are not appropriate business hours. We are ten minutes away from taking luncheon, and you have inconvenienced us twice now. Please remove yourself from the premises."

"But—"

"I am prepared to use a greater force of persuasion if required." She held up the bone-handled letter opener, and he laughed.

"Oh no, please don't prick me," he said mockingly.

Cecilia flicked a minuscule latch on the letter opener's handle. In an instant, with a hiss of steel, the letter opener extended to the extremely effective length of a rapier.

The man stepped back. "I say, there's no need for such violence. I only wanted to warn you that Lady Armitage has taken out a contract on your life."

From across the room came Miss Darlington's dry, brusque laugh. Cecilia herself merely smiled, and even then with only one side of her mouth.

"That is hardly cause for breaking and entering. Lady Armitage has been trying to kill my aunt for years now."

"Not your aunt," he said. "You."

A delicate flush wafted briefly over Cecilia's face. "I'm flattered. She has actually employed an assassin?"

"Yes," the man said in a dire tone.

"And does this assassin have a name?"

"Eduardo de Luca."

"Italian," Cecilia said, disappointment withering each syllable.

"You need to be a bit older before you can attract a proper assassin, my dear," Miss Darlington advised from the interior.

The man frowned. "Eduardo de Luca is a proper assassin."

"Ha." Miss Darlington sat back in her chair and crossed her ankles in an uncharacteristically dissolute fashion. "I venture to guess Signor de Luca has never yet killed any creature greater than a fly."

"And why would you say that, madam?" the man demanded.

She looked down her nose at him, quite a feat considering she was some distance away. "A real assassin would hire a sensible tailor. And a barber. And would not attempt to murder someone five minutes before luncheon. Close the window, Cecilia, you'll catch consumption from that icy draft."

"Wait," the man said, holding out a hand, but Cecilia closed the window, turned the latch, and drew together the heavy velvet drapes.

"Do you think Pleasance might be ready soon with our meal?" she asked as she moved across the room—not to her chair, but to the door leading into the hall.

"Sit down, Cecilia," Miss Darlington ordered. "A lady does not pace in this restless manner."

Cecilia did as she was bidden but upon taking up her book laid it down again without a glance. She brushed at a speck of dust on her sleeve.

"Fidgeting." Miss Darlington snapped out the observation and Cecilia hastily placed both hands together on her lap.

"Maybe there will be chicken today," she said. "Pleasance usually roasts a chicken on Tuesdays."

7

"Indeed she does," Miss Darlington agreed. "However, today is Thursday. Where are your wits, girl? Surely you are not in such hysterics over a mere contract of assassination?"

"No," Cecilia said. But she bit her lip and dared a glance at Miss Darlington. The old lady looked back at her with a trace of sympathy so faint it might have existed only in Cecilia's imagination, were Cecilia to have such a thing.

"The assassin won't actually be Italian," she assured her niece. "Armitage doesn't have the blunt to employ a foreigner. It will be some jumped-up Johnny from the Tilbury Docks."

This did not improve Cecilia's spirits. She tugged unconsciously on the silver locket that hung from a black ribbon around her neck. Seeing this, Miss Darlington sighed with impatience. Her own locket of similar forlorn aspect rode the gray crinoline swathing her bosom, and she wished for a moment that she might speak once more with the woman whose portrait and lock of golden hair rested within. But then, Cilla would have even less patience for a sulking maiden.

"Lamb," she said with an effort at gentleness. Cecilia blinked, her eyes darkening to a wistful orphan blue. Miss Darlington frowned. "If it's Thursday," she elaborated, "luncheon will be lamb, with mint sauce and boiled potatoes."

"Yes, you're right," Cecilia said, pulling herself together. "Also peas."

Miss Darlington nodded. It was a satisfactory end to the matter, and she could have left it there. After all, one does not want to encourage the younger generation too much, lest they lose sight of their proper place: under one's thumb. She decided, however, to take pity on the girl, having herself once been as high-spirited. "Perhaps tomorrow the weather will be better fit for some perambulation," she said. "You might go to the library, and afterward get a bun from Sally Lunn's."

"But isn't that in Bath?"

"I thought a change of scenery might do us good. Mayfair is be-

coming altogether too rowdy. We shall fly the house down this afternoon. It will be a chance to give Pleasance a refresher course on the
flight incantation's last stanza. Her vowels are still too flat. Approaching the ground with one's front door at a thirty-degree angle is rather
more excitement than one likes for an afternoon. And yes, I can see
from your expression you still think I shouldn't have shared the incantation's secret with her, but Pleasance can be trusted. Granted, she did
fly that bookshop into the Serpentine when they told her they didn't
stock any Dickens novels, but that only shows a praiseworthy enthusiasm for literature. She'll get us safely to Bath, and then you can take a
nice stroll among the shops. Maybe you can buy some pretty lace ribbons or a new dagger before getting your iced bun."

"Thank you, Aunty," Cecilia answered, just as she was supposed
to. In fact she would rather have gone to Oxford, or even just across the
park to visit the Natural History Museum, but to suggest either would
risk Miss Darlington reversing her decision altogether. So she simply
smiled and obeyed. There followed a moment's pleasant quiet.

"Although eat only half the bun, mind you," Miss Darlington said
as Cecilia took up *Hiawatha* and tried yet again to find her place among
the reeds and water lilies. "We don't want you falling ill with cholera."

"That is a disease of contaminated water, Aunty."

Miss Darlington sniffed, not liking to be corrected. "A baker uses
water I'm sure to make his wares. One can never be too careful, dear."

"Yes, Aunty. 'The level moon stared at him, in his face stared pale
and haggard, 'til—' "

Crash!

The two women looked over at the window as it shattered. A grenade tumbled onto the carpet.

Cecilia expelled a sigh of tedium. She snapped the book shut,
wended her way through the furnishings, pulled back the drapes, and
deposited the grenade through the broken windowpane onto the ter-

race, where it exploded in a flash of burning light, brick shards, and fluttering lavender buds.

"Ahem."

Cecilia turned to see Pleasance standing in the drawing room doorway, plucking a glass splinter from one of the dark curls that habitually escaped her white lace cap.

"Excuse the interruption, misses, but I have news," she declared in the portentous tones of a young woman who spent too much time reading lurid Gothic fiction and consorting with the figments of her melodramatic imagination. "Luncheon is served."

Miss Darlington pushed herself up from the chair. "Please arrange for a glazier to come as soon as possible, Pleasance. We shall have to use the Lilac Drawing Room this afternoon, although I prefer to keep it for entertaining guests. The risk from that broken window is simply too great to bear. My own dear cousin nearly died of pneumonia under similar circumstances, as you know."

Cecilia murmured an agreement, although she recalled that Cousin Alathea's illness, contracted while attempting to fly a cottage in a hurricane, had little real consequence other than the loss of a chimney (and five crew members)—Alathea continuing on in robust health to maraud the coastline for several more years before losing a skirmish with Lord Vesbry's pet alligator while holidaying in the South of France.

Miss Darlington tapped a path across the room with her mahogany cane, but Cecilia paused, twitching the drapes slightly so as to peer through jagged glass and smoke at the garden. The assassin was leaning back against the iron railings of the house across the street. He noticed Cecilia and touched one finger to his temple in salutation. Cecilia frowned.

"Don't dawdle, girl," Miss Darlington chastised. Cecilia lowered the curtain, adjusting it slightly so it hung straight, and then followed her aunt toward the dining room and their Thursday lamb roast.

❧ 2 ❧

THE LADY ANTICIPATES HER CALLER—A DISAPPOINTMENT—
THE PLIGHT OF CECILIA'S DIGITS—ANOTHER EXPLOSION (FIGURATIVE)—
WHISKEY AT WHITE'S—BARBAROUS O'RILEY—THE LOOMING ABBEY—
TWO CAPTAINS CONFER—BETRAYAL IS EXPOSED

Isabella Armitage was no bird-brained girl; and no police force had ensnared her, despite their efforts over the years. Lately, however, she had found herself tempted to do something that would almost certainly see her imprisoned, regardless of her wealth and degree.

The outrage of that Darlington woman displaying herself in plain view (that is, to anyone with binoculars) in such a noble district as Mayfair, when she was no better than a common fingersmith! Lady Armitage could not abide it.

Granted, such outrages had been occurring for a decade, but familiarity was no impediment to Lady Armitage's wrath. As a daughter of the Hollister family from York, none of whom had knowingly spoken to any denizen of Lancashire in the four centuries since the Wars of the Roses, she felt no difficulty sustaining a mere ten years' indignation.

Even so, she'd tried all she could to smooth troubled waters. But Darlington had rudely persisted in avoiding the knife (and gun, poison, rabid dog, fall from a great height, garrote, flaming arrow). The time had come for different tactics. As a daughter of the Fairley clan on her distaff side, Lady Armitage had all the wit and flexibility that had seen her ancestors survive the civil war by deftly switching sides, religions, and marriages, whenever circumstances required. She needn't try a seventeenth time to exterminate the Darlington woman. She would transition promptly to a new plan.

Killing Cecilia.

The pirate had promised to help. "Just rest, and I'll assassinate her for you," he had said, smiling in a lithe, melting way that reminded Lady Armitage of her second husband before the slow-acting poison began bloating his tongue. She'd been wary about hiring an outsider, but within five minutes of their meeting, the pirate had filled her with murderous excitement. They'd sipped wine, exchanged a few jokes about poison, before getting down to business, and she'd felt deep in her heart (or at least somewhere) that he was the one for the job.

"How would you like it done?" he'd asked. "Gun, garrote?"

Lady Armitage had shrugged. "I leave that up to your artistic discretion, Signor de Luca. But killing only. Nothing impolite. I am an ethical woman, and Cecilia is after all innocent."

He'd raised an eyebrow in dispute of anyone's innocence, and Lady Armitage had felt so gently chided, so tenderly assumed to be naive, just like a sweet and adorable woman, that she had actually blushed for the first time in seventy years. Murdering three husbands (and misplacing a fourth) tended to inure a woman to masculine charm, and yet as this man had looked at her over the rim of his wineglass, she'd found herself unexpectedly aflutter and trying to remember dizzily where she'd stored her wedding ring.

"Miss Darlington will be prostrate with grief at the loss of her niece," she'd said. "It's even better than killing the woman herself. And then of course I'll kill her too, but Cecilia's death will soften her up for assassination."

"It's an interesting plan," the signor had agreed. "Tell me about Cecilia. What do I need to know?"

"Oh, she's a dear girl." She'd sighed, remembering a quiet, somber child who called her Aunty Army and was fascinated by her dagger collection. That was back in the good old days, down at the docks and along the golden shores, when the Wisteria Society still met regularly to discuss knitting patterns and the latest explosives catalog. How long ago had it been? Long enough that little Cecilia was all grown up and eligible for assassination.

Thinking of it, Lady Armitage had sighed again, melancholic. And Signor de Luca had reached over, one strand of hair falling across his eye roguishly, and patted her hand with gentle sympathy.

"Do it," she'd said, staring at his long, swooping lashes, his curving lips. "Kill the girl. And then we'll deal with Darlington."

He'd laughed and drunk a toast to her brilliance, and she'd spent that evening sewing rosettes onto a garter and dreaming of the Italian hills bright with summer's sun as she toured them on her (fifth) honeymoon.

The very next day, he'd set her plan into action. And it worked! Lady Armitage watched with bated breath, but after the dust of the explosion settled, she could discern no movement from the Darlington drawing room. Maybe a twitch of the drapes, but that would only be natural considering the great rush of air. On the street, neighbors were gathering in a state of panic, not so much from the explosion as from the realization that there were two pirate houses in their midst, but Lady Armitage had no interest in them. After all, pirates did the civic thing by displaying a black flag from their roof whilst going about pillaging and blowing things apart. If the public failed to look up, whose fault was that?

She turned away from the window, allowing herself a satisfied nod. Poor Cecilia, dead so young. And yet, the chit had been half a ghost already, pallid and quiet: a faint remembrance of her mother.

The thought tossed a memory up with it, a vision of bright billowing hair, flashing eyes . . . and a sword-pierced breast soaked in blood. Lady Armitage shuddered.

Then smiled. This was no time to be maudlin. She'd just killed a girl! Already the air seemed brighter (if literally darker, due to smoke from the bomb). Sweeping herself down upon a pink velvet divan, she reclined sensuously to await Signor de Luca's arrival.

A moment later she sat up to be sure her stockings were taut before easing back once more. With a careful hand, she smoothed the high plume of her snow-colored hair (it is entirely possible snow in parts of the north country could be gray) and settled her expression into elegance.

Several minutes passed without action. Lady Armitage was yawning, scratching at an itch within her ear, when her butler, Whittaker, finally ushered in the pirate.

"What took you so long to get here?" she demanded querulously.

He bowed. "I beg your pardon. I had to climb a drainpipe to reach the front door. It seems your house is currently sitting atop the roof of another."

"We are experiencing minor technical difficulties."

Ever since her lady's maid had thrown all good sense to the wind and run away to become a librarian, Lady Armitage had been forced to fly the house herself. Clearly, however, her brilliant mind overpowered the ancient flight incantation. Last month, she'd bunny hopped the house into the Avon River and had to replace all her carpets; this week she'd aimed for Chesterfield Street and ended up on a rooftop instead. Alas, the perils of genius. A town house was simply too light; no doubt some castle or cathedral would better contain the forces of her great intellect. Besides, she'd always fancied having one of those portcully thingies at her front door.

She ought to train one of her other servants to fly the house, but they were all men, and Lady Armitage doubted their mental strength. Oh, they looked robust enough in their elegant livery, but could they keep it up all night? In her experience, they could not. At least two of her husbands had put it into quagmires, and a third landed it on Queen Victoria's head (the head of the royal statue in Exeter, that is). Lady Armitage thought she was better off managing things herself, and if that meant perching on the occasional rooftop—well, she could simply call it a penthouse.

"Besides," she said to Signor de Luca, "I should imagine climbing is no problem for an Italian."

His expression went momentarily blank as he tried to parse this logic. Then he smiled again. "Half-Italian, ma'am."

"Never mind your preposterous heritage, is the deed done?"

"Yes," he said, and her spirits rose so high they burst forth as a smile from her thin, creased lips.

"That is to say," he added, and her spirits drooped again, as did her mouth. "Not quite yet, my lady. But we have them on the run."

Lady Armitage smacked her hand against the mahogany rim of the divan and tried not to wince as pain shot through her bones. "On the run? On the run? The house is still standing right there!" She gestured to the window, through which the Darlington house could be seen if one walked over and looked out (and down).

"I meant their blood, ma'am," he answered smoothly. Lady Armitage began to suspect his pretty smile was mocking her. "Their pulses will be racing with fear."

"Ha. That is no accomplishment. You might have as easily sneezed in Darlington's direction and achieved the same result. I do not want them running; I want that girl lying still, motionless, dead, and Darlington destroyed by a grief that will end only when I literally destroy her. You have failed me, Signor de Luca!"

She would have swooned in despair, but the divan was rather narrow and she did not trust that a faint wouldn't see her toppling onto the floor.

"Ma'am, I assure you not," the man said. He took a step toward her, his smile rising at one tip in much the same way a shark's might when trailing its prey. Lady Armitage watched warily as he knelt on one knee beside the divan and grasped her hand. It was the left hand, with its pale band around the third finger where her ring had been (the same ring with each marriage, for while husbands were easily discarded, a really nice ring, flattering to the finger, was not). He kissed it, then gazed up at her over her knuckles, through his eyelashes. She almost slid right off the velvet into his lap; only her corset, which was too tightly laced for sudden movements, saved her.

"I will admit I like to play a little with my quarry," he said in a wry, murmuring voice. "As you know, a pirate's life can be tedious, and we take our fun where we can."

She sighed. "Eduardo, Eduardo, what shall I do with you?"

"Oh, anything you like, ma'am," he answered, grinning.

She snatched back her hand and scrambled off the divan before she really did find herself in a compromising position. After all, it was nice to dream, but there remained some legal doubt about the vitality of her lost fourth husband, and she could hardly point to the particular heap in the dust-yard that would settle the matter once and for all.

Behind her back, Ned rolled his eyes, but when Lady Armitage glanced his way again he was smiling sweetly as he got to his feet.

Charming boy, she thought. *Far too charming for anyone's good. Probably best not to look at him.* "Well now," she said briskly, pacing the room, pausing here and there to stroke a stuffed peacock, stare at a portrait of a noble ancestor, shift a chimpanzee's skull slightly on its doily. "I appreciate your jovial manner, Eduardo, but I do so want the girl dead. Perhaps you could, for me, try a little solemnity? A little stabbing, or suffocating her in her—um, chair? Not in her bed, of course, that would be scandalous. And no more incendiary devices. There are treasures in that house to be scavenged once Darlington is dead, and a bomb might damage them. When you have completed your task, bring me the girl's smallest finger, or perhaps a toe or two, and I will pay you our agreed amount."

She risked another glance, and her pulse faltered as she saw a sudden coldness in his eyes. But the next moment, without even blinking, he was returning her gaze with pleasant equanimity.

"Her smallest finger," he said, and bowed. If he was down there a touch longer than ordinary, Lady Armitage thought nothing of it, except perhaps that he meant to show her respect. When he straightened, his hair had slipped down, and he seemed younger—yet more dangerous to her heart, both in terms of sentiment and in regard to its inability to function with a knife impaled in it.

"I shall retire to Lyme Regis. When you have killed the girl, you will find me situated on Marine Parade. I have a mind to walk the Cobb and feel the sea breeze through my tresses."

His gaze flicked to the erect fan of her hair, but otherwise his expression did not alter. "That will be a long journey from London. You might have to wait awhile for your *digitus truncatum.*"

"Oh yes, I forgot you lost your house and are reduced to traveling by mere horse. Poor boy, less a pirate these days than a highwayman."

He said nothing in quite the most disturbing manner, and Lady Armitage found herself reaching for the locket she kept on a fob chain at her waist. Its cool gold surface always eased her thoughts, despite the heated memory it contained. *Oh, Cilla,* she thought, *what has the world come to, without you in it? Pretty boys with provocative smiles, sweet girls who will not die. It is almost more than a poor, frail woman can bear!*

She turned to look again at the assassin. "I want her dead, do you understand? Dead. And I want proof. You have seven days."

"Your wish is my command."

She extended her long white hand, fingers draping from their bones, rings glinting in the light of the chandelier above. She applied the steely will of her Thorvaldson heritage (from her grandmother on her father's side) and absolutely did not allow the hand to tremble, no matter what her heart was doing within its secret cage.

He crossed the room, took her hand—but then unexpectedly lowered it, and, leaning closer, he kissed her mouth instead.

It was as if he had tossed another of his bombs; heat wishes and desiccated flowers exploded in her brain. Shifting back, he gave her a thoroughly piratical grin, then departed the room without further word.

"Well," Lady Armitage said, fanning herself. "Outrageous!"

Falling onto the divan, she laid a hand against her brow. She felt decidedly hot and bothered. But being a Thorvaldson made her kin to Vikings, who had brutalized half the known world, and she had practiced her own piracy ruthlessly, successfully (indeed, Vikingly), for decades before that boy had even been born. No one kissed Lady Isabella Armitage and got away with it for long.

While she awaited the luncheon bell, she pondered whom she might employ to assassinate the assassin.

For the rest of that afternoon Ned sat in White's club for gentlemen, drinking whiskey to cleanse the taste of Lady Armitage from his mouth. He had stopped off at Henry Poole & Co. along the way and outfitted himself in the best suit counterfeit money could buy, for he always honored the club's dress code, even if he was not, legally speaking, a member. He had finally succeeded in ridding himself of the old lady's tang and was contemplating where he might sleep that night when a dark-haired man dropped abruptly into the chair opposite him.

Damn. It was Alex O'Riley—pirate, smuggler, general rogue about town, and just who Ned least wanted to see right now. Without a word, the man slouched back in the chair, his long black coat falling open to reveal a shirt bereft of either tie or waistcoat. He rested his boots upon the mahogany table as if he was in a local pub and pushed a hand against one dark blue eye, squinting at Ned with the other as if he'd just come from *another* local pub and still had the hangover to prove it.

Ned frowned. Alex was the sort who gave pirates a bad—that is to say, an even worse—name; one almost expected him to shout, *Ahoy!* while pushing people off a plank from his sitting room into shark-infested waters far below. He was also Ned's favorite person in the world. They had swindled lords together, got drunk together more times than either could remember, and once they forced Alex's ramshackle house to its limits making the London-Cashel run in less than twelve hours, although they did lose a few windowpanes along the way. Ned counted him as something greater than a brother: a true friend.

"Go away," he muttered, drinking the last of his whiskey in one swallow.

"Charming," Alex replied lightly. He crossed one ankle over the other, his boot buckles imperiling the table's polish and causing a nearby gentleman to gasp in outrage. "You look miserable. What have you been doing, handing out free food or something?"

Ned poured more whiskey from a crystal decanter. "Worse. Why am I looking at your ugly face, O'Riley? Aren't you supposed to be in Ireland?" He made an offering gesture with the decanter.

"Cheers," Alex said, taking it and drinking without any intervention of glass or good manners. The neighboring gentleman gasped more pointedly; even Ned raised an eyebrow. "Don't mind me," Alex said with a crooked smile. "I was indeed in Ireland, so I need all the alcohol I can get."

"Your father?"

The decanter came down on the table with a thud. "Let's not talk about it. What brings you to White's on this fine day?"

"I'm meeting someone you don't want to. Hence, go away."

"Who?"

Ned answered with no more than a long, cold stare, and Alex stopped smiling. He swung his feet down from the table. "Not—"

"Yes. Have I mentioned, go away?"

Alex leaned forward, somber. "Damn, Ned, are you sure you should be doing that? I know he—"

"I'm sure."

"Can't I help you to—"

"No. I don't need any help."

"Everyone needs help sometimes."

Ned scowled. Cilla had said those same words to him once, and her ghost had whispered them through the years ever since, reminding him of dark promises he had yet to keep. His scowl shifted into a grim smile. "I'm better off on my own, O'Riley. You can help by leaving before he gets here."

"Look," Alex said, uncharacteristically serious. "I know we've done some wild things in our day, but this is more dangerous than even I'd want to contemplate, and that's saying something. I think you've gone mad."

Ned laughed. "No doubt. Now, stop talking. He just walked in. If you value our friendship, go steal something—seduce someone—just go."

"All right." Alex stood, but he lingered a moment longer, frowning down at Ned. "I'll leave, but know that I'm in London if you need me."

"I won't need you."

Alex reluctantly left, slipping the neighboring gentleman's gold cigarette case from the table into his coat pocket along the way. Ned would have whispered, *I don't need anyone at all,* but at that moment a shadow fell over him, a coolness, a great dragging silence like the empty dark chambers of an ancient abbey. Ned sighed into his whiskey glass.

"Captain Morvath," he said as the man slid into a chair. This one didn't slouch or put up his feet. This one held himself like a cocked weapon.

"Edward Lightbourne." It was a soft voice, typical of those who long had spoken with great power; a voice that could whisper death in a tower room and far below a man would be strangled among the garden roses.

"You should say Captain Lightbourne," Ned replied.

"Captain of what? Your house fell off a cliff. Captain of a horse, perchance? Or a rented carriage?"

Ned said nothing, swallowed whiskey. He looked sidelong at the sleek, gray-haired man, seeing only angles like a scimitar, eyes like char, cruel suggestions in the shadows. Behind him, at the far end of the room, Alex was glancing back worriedly. The whiskey burned in Ned's throat.

"I've been looking for you," Morvath said ominously.

Ned shrugged. "I was busy with a personal matter."

"You have no personal matters until you get my job done. Who was that man you were just talking to?"

"Some idiot trying to sell me on an investment idea."

"I hope you didn't listen to him. Believe me when I tell you people can't be trusted. Which reminds me, there was an explosion in Chesterfield Street earlier. If you were the one responsible . . ."

"I wasn't," Ned lied complacently.

"I want the girl brought to me safe and sound, Lightbourne. No explosions. Do you understand?"

"I understand." In fact he was only too well aware of the writhing depths of Morvath's psyche, where a bastard heritage the captain could never properly claim lurked like an aquatic monster, rearing now in a moment of narcissism, now in a moment of abject worthlessness. Morvath was riding that monster with the intention of destroying anyone who had offended him, but his plan for Cecilia seemed in some ways worse than destruction.

Ned tried not to think about it. "You can count on me," he said.

The captain expelled a hissing laugh, and Ned understood he was not counted on beyond the merest fraction. It came as a relief. People whom Patrick Morvath relied upon tended to end up facedown beneath the roses.

"Anyone tries to assassinate her, you kill them," Morvath said, and Ned tried not to smirk. "Darlington house is on the move. I heard it from over on Curzon Street. Someone is making a real hash of the spell's unmooring phrase."

"Interesting." Ned drank whiskey again and wished he could unmoor himself and fly away to some cozy hearth fire miles from here, where the drink was warm milk and the company not a homicidal maniac.

"Follow them," Morvath ordered. "Steal a house or, I don't know, a wheelbarrow for all I care. And no more distractions with 'personal matters' if you don't want me to start docking you."

"You haven't paid me any wages at all yet," Ned reminded him.

"I wasn't talking about docking wages," Morvath said, and stared pointedly at Ned's ear. "Time is running out. Everything must be in place before the Queen's Jubilee Banquet. All the other elements of my plan are coming together like the lines of an exquisite poem. My spies are ready, my artillery complete. It's beautiful, Edward, the best plan that's ever been made. Only this last thing remains. If you fail me with it, or betray me, you'll be sorry. 'In the next world I could not be worse than I am in this.' "

Ned nodded. There was really nothing to say when the captain began quoting his ill-fated birth father. At least it was better than when he began quoting his own poetry. Ned tried not to shudder at the very thought. Glancing over the man's shoulder, he saw that Alex had finally left. Something spiky moved in his heart. Damn that anyone should take a pirate at his word. But he'd gone into this venture alone, and really a friend would only get in the way. He looked back at Morvath coolly.

"What about Miss Darlington?"

Morvath's face darkened. "I don't care about her," he growled. "Just Cecilia. Understand?"

Ned set down his whiskey and turned a smile—hard, sharp, uncompromised by humor—to the older man. "Your servant, sir."

"Excellent," Morvath said. "Soon, Edward, very soon, England will burn. It's going to be a beautiful thing."

❊ 3 ❊

A BOTANICAL ADVENTURE—THE INFLUENCE OF GHOSTS—
THE WISTERIA LADIES' SOCIETY—MISS DARLINGTON SURRENDERS—
PREVENTATIVE MEASURES—A BANDIT, A SKYLARK—
A VERBAL SALLY—MISS BASSINGTHWAITE—THE HALFPENNY
BRIDGE—ANOTHER SALLY: LUNN—CECILIA APPROACHES THE LIBRARY

It was not the thorn bending to the honeysuckles that was the cause of Cecilia's annoyance that morning, but the honeysuckles embracing her ankles as she tried to walk through the field. Flowers were altogether charming things, giving her hours of occupation as she arranged them in vases and pressed them in poetry books, but this indiscreet manner in which hedges overflowed and rambled all through the grass was decidedly uncouth.

Of course, she would not be trudging through them had the house gone into the actual city of Bath as it was meant. Pleasance could not explain what had happened.

"The compass was accurate," she had averred. "The incantation was incantateded just right. I did all the math forward and back. It came out perfect."

And yet here they were in a field of cows and feral flowers, half a mile from the city.

Pleasance had dismantled the wheel, searching for a cause, which was pointless since the steering array was not attached to anything mechanical, merely serving as a conduit for the spell to provide direction. She had inspected the navigation tools. She had also held a conference with the old ghosts and villains who plagued her penny-dreadful consciousness, demanding they leave her in peace while she was flying.

Cecilia was privately inclined to believe therein lay the problem and could not understand why Miss Darlington persisted in allowing Pleasance the helm. But she also could not understand why she herself, and indeed all young pirates of her acquaintance, were forced through a long training regime—studying thaumaturgical physics, writing essays, taking countless elocution lessons, running a mile in full bustled gown—before being allowed their wings, and yet servants were just handed a copy of the highly secret, highly powerful spell and told to have it memorized by the end of the week.

She did not argue, however, because if the matter was examined too closely other questions regarding servants might arise, such as *Why don't you wash your own dishes?* and *Why don't you dress yourself for parties?*, and Cecilia was careful not to be too clever for her own good.

Besides, her elders knew what they were doing. After all, they had managed to keep control over the incantation for almost two hundred years, ever since Black Beryl introduced it to England.

Beryl had not originally been a pirate. She'd been the hardy young wife of Jeremiah Black, failed explorer—the failure being illuminated when he smashed their ship into an island in the Indian Ocean while seeking passage from London to Mexico. But on the shore of that island Beryl had found an old washed-up bottle containing a Latin poem. When she realized speaking the poem aloud created a magic that could move objects, regardless of weight, the possibilities had become readily apparent to her in a way they were not to her husband (mainly on account of him having been bashed to death with a compass by "persons unknown"). She'd commandeered a local's hut and flown back to England, where she shared the incantation with the ladies in her book club. They had turned from casual literary criticism to piracy with remarkable ease, establishing a class of magnificent women in flying mansions, thus causing a collapse in the hot-air-balloon picnicking industry—and a whole new meaning to the phrase "groundless fears."

Cecilia had grown up on stories about those exciting days. Miss Darlington's history lessons had been full of gunfire and brimstone. And villains had abounded, such as the book club members who found a devious use for the incantation, surreptitiously moving people and things rather than buildings, thereby committing vulgar witchcraft. The more honorable members had been forced to separate themselves from these degenerates by forming the Wisteria Society, a noble coterie of ladies who were virtuously open about their crimes.

"Two roads diverged in a yellow-wallpapered room, and we pirates took the better one," Miss Darlington had told ten-year-old Cecilia, brandishing the dagger she liked to use to direct her lessons. "Anyone who dislikes pirates needs to blame those wicked witches in the first place!"

Then there had been the army. If His Majesty's troops had not responded to the advent of airborne crime by trying to put the Wisteria Society back in their proper place—i.e., on the ground and preferably in the kitchen—the ladies would never have learned how to fight. Thus weaponized piracy was clearly the army's fault.

"The war ended over a hundred years ago," Miss Darlington had explained to Cecilia when the little girl had offered to rush out and join the battle. "Land-based guns were useless against flying houses, and the army finally gave up. But we can never relax. Anti-smuggling patrols and arrest warrants for minor infractions like armed bank robbery are only some of the indignities the government continues to perpetrate against us. It is nothing more than misogynistic bullying!"

But the worst villains of all were the insurance companies and bodyguard services who made a fortune off an anxious public. And none of this even began to touch upon real estate agents. A nefarious lot, they were forever trying to steal the flight incantation so they could sell houses based on "location, location, *and* location."

Miss Darlington had shaken her head sadly at it all. "Black Beryl would be horrified at how her incantation corrupted the hearts of men everywhere. But we Wisteria Society ladies must rise above it."

"In our flying houses!" Cecilia had added excitedly.

"In our noble hearts. But that's enough history for today. Come and learn how to kill someone with a teaspoon."

As an adult now, Cecilia felt glad she had missed the war. It seemed a messy kind of venture, involving far too much irregularity for comfort. Even the sight of Darlington House's steering array in a jumble of pieces on the cockpit floor disturbed her enough. Miss Darlington, on the other hand, was entirely unbothered by the disorder Pleasance had created. In fact, when Cecilia had suggested they reassemble the wheel and fly to a location nearer the Bath library, she'd spurned the idea. She rather liked the rural view and had decided to paint some cows (which is to say, their likeness, not their bodies) since several of the species were grazing near the house. It was, she'd declared, a nice change of pace from the rigors of entertaining society in Mayfair, and the cows were more interesting conversationalists.

"You did say I might go to the library," Cecilia had argued gently.

"I did? Goodness, that doesn't sound like me. Oh, my dear, do stay safe at home, at least until Pleasance has ascertained there are no evil spirits in our navigation system. The countryside is rife with scurvy."

"That is caused by fruit deprivation, Aunty."

"Precisely! Do you see any orchards out there?"

Cecilia could make no sensible reply to this. But her eyes spoke volumes—specifically, of anguished poetry in which heroines meet a sad end. By the third day, Miss Darlington had relented. Despite the risk to ankles, lungs, and fair complexion, Cecilia was given leave to walk into town and visit the library.

She'd donned a long-sleeved, high-collared dress, boots, gloves, and wide-brimmed hat, thereby leaving no part of her exposed to the evils of sunlight. Then, having selected a book to read along the way, she'd raised her parasol, promised her aunt she would be on the alert for bad air, and at last set out across the waste.

Nothing more dire than honeysuckle and cowpats troubled her, and she made it quite intact to the edge of the field. Pausing, she looked back at the house.

It was a somber edifice, pale and narrow, with three stories and two modestly haunted attics: the sort of building that would sigh mournfully into its handkerchief before proceeding to scold you for fifteen minutes for holding your teacup incorrectly. A building after Miss Darlington's own heart, or perhaps vice versa; Cecilia had never been able to decide which.

The circular window in its gable, curtained with lace that had been spun by a convent of elderly Irish nuns made mad by the haunting pagan song of selkies, could dilate open for the deployment of cannons without affecting the window box of petunias set beneath.

From that window Cecilia now glimpsed a flash of light and knew it reflected off the telescope through which Miss Darlington was watching her progress. She waved a hand in reassurance. The house moved toward her slightly, as if wanting to wrap a scarf about her neck or make her don a coat, but then shifted back again and settled on its foundations with a shrug. Miss Darlington was apparently going to be brave.

Relieved, Cecilia turned away, entering a lane that meandered between brambleberry hedges toward Bath. Soon after, a bandit attempted her purse. She disabled him with an application of elbow then fist, which did not require her to pause in her stride, although she did skip a vital sentence in her book and had to reread the whole page to make sense of it. Then the bandit, collapsing in the dirt, moaned so wretchedly that she felt obliged to return and provide him with a handkerchief, after which she was able to continue on in peace.

The countryside offered more to her sensitive spirit than Mayfair had. She noticed a skylark springing from the earth, although it looked less like a "cloud of fire" the poet Shelley would have her anticipate and more like a flying clod of dirt. She breathed in the fragrance of sun-warmed dust with no thought of lung contamination. She even lifted her face to the gentle breeze. It was altogether so pleasant that by the time she reached the city she was prepared to call herself happy indeed.

And then she saw the pirate.

He loitered near the river, hatless once again and indecently dressed: he wore no tie, his waistcoat was secured with *pewter* buttons, and his trousers were far too tight. The way he had his sword belt slung low around his hips inexplicably disturbed Cecilia.

She had long been hoping to attract an assassination attempt. It was a significant development in her career. That it had been provisioned by Lady Armitage disappointed her only slightly, for there would always be the lingering suspicion that the real target was Miss Darlington; besides, she remembered the lady teaching her many years ago how to use a sextant (for both navigation and dismembering purposes) and always considered her a mentor, not a murderer. But at least Aunty Army had employed a pirate and not just some street thug—although Cecilia did consider tipping him a little money to buy himself a decent suit. She nodded across the street to him as she passed.

Suddenly, he was at her side. Cecilia sighed, lowering her book and looking at him sidelong beneath an arched eyebrow. She did not know how to more clearly convey her disdain, but he just grinned in response.

"Fancy meeting you here," he said.

"I hope you are not intending to do me the discourtesy of assassinating me in the street, Signor de Luca," she replied.

"Call me Ned." He nudged her with an elbow as if they were old friends.

"I shall do no such thing. Your manners are dreadful and your cologne cheap. Go away."

"I declare, for a woman of such delicacy, you have a remarkably firm tone, Miss Darlington."

"And for an Italian you have a remarkably Etonian accent. Also, 'Miss Darlington' is my aunt." He opened his mouth and she held up a hand to forestall any reply. "No, you may not be informed as to how to address me. You may leave."

"Miss Bassingthwaite," he said, "you are being unnecessarily mysterious. I have seen your birth notice; I know the name written there." Noting that she grew even more pale than usual, he shrugged. "Do you think I would undertake (pardon me) to assassinate a stranger, Miss Cecilia M——who is generally known as Miss Darlington junior but prefers to be called her mother's maiden name, Bassingthwaite, by her friends?"

"Of whom you are not one."

"Yet."

She tipped her parasol slightly to better thwart the sun and not inconsequentially angle its hidden blade toward his heart. "When do you propose we become friends? Before or after you murder me?"

"Please, assassinate. After all, we're not corsairs."

"We are exactly that, Signor. Corsairs, robbers, pirates. I, however, am also a bibliophile, and you are impeding my visit to the library. So either *assassinate* me now and get it over with, or kindly step aside."

"Do you have a ha'penny?"

"I should think if you're killing someone it is on you to provide the coin for Charon."

He laughed. "No, I meant for the bridge. There's a toll."

"Oh." She stopped, frowning at the narrow, green-fenced bridge that lay across the Avon River ahead. "I did not realize."

The young man put his hands in his coat pockets and smiled at her impishly. "You could always bludgeon the tollbooth attendant with your book and walk across for free, what with being a corsair and all."

"Certainly not," Cecilia replied, as if he had suggested she dunk a gingerbread biscuit into tea. Noticing his attention on the open pages of her book, she closed it and tucked it into her crocheted purse before he realized what she had been reading.

"I could pay for you," he suggested.

Her eyes narrowed as she regarded him. "Pay my toll?"

"We can make it a loan if you prefer. You can repay me later with a coin or a kiss."

"Over my dead body!" She knew she sounded like Lady Armitage, gasping with outrage, but it could not be helped.

"Well . . ." He grinned, shrugging.

Cecilia again shifted her parasol so that it leaned over her left shoulder, blocking the sight of him. This exposed her to the freckle-causing sunlight, but it was a risk she was willing to take. She almost strode away but recollected herself in time and continued at a sedate, ladylike pace toward the bridge.

"Come now, Miss Bassingthwaite, don't be so harsh with me," the aggravating man went on, strolling beside her. "After all, our souls are made of the same thing, yours and mine."

She shifted the parasol once more so as to stare at him, aghast. "Are you paraphrasing *Wuthering Heights*?"

"Are you reading *Wuthering Heights*?" he retorted with a smirk.

She went on staring for a moment, then realized her face was flushed (no doubt from all the sun exposure) and turned away. "I am returning it to the library on behalf of my maid," she said. "I merely had it open to ascertain the condition in which she'd left it, as she had an unfortunate education and therefore tends to dog-ear pages."

"Liar," he said genially. "I wonder what your aunt would say if she knew you were reading that novel?"

"She would ask me why I did not cut the throat of the man with whom I had this conversation."

"You know, the attendant might let you across the bridge for free if you smile at him. Most men are susceptible to a pretty face. Are you able to smile, Miss Bassingthwaite?"

"Go away."

"Although in truth one such as yourself need not smile to charm a man. Take me, for example. I really ought to be stabbing you right now, but am too enchanted by your lovely—"

"Signor de Luca. If I let you pay my toll, will you leave me alone?"

"Of course."

She nodded, held out her hand for the coin, and waited.

"That is," he said, "once I have seen you to the other side. Of the bridge, I mean," he added, winking.

She closed her hand, drew it back, and continued walking. "You seriously think I would cross a bridge in the company of a man hired to kill me?"

"Madam," he said in an aggrieved tone. "I merely wish to ensure your safety so that when I come into your bedroom—"

"Signor!"

"For the purpose of smothering you with your pillow—that was all I meant. No need for such alarm. And please do call me Ned."

"I will not."

"Then Captain Lightbourne, at least. I'm only Italian in my paternal ancestry, and it's fair to say that was most likely a fantasy of my mother's."

"Lightbourne? As in the Dreaded Captain Lightbourne of Leeds?"

"That's right," he said with pride.

"The same Captain Lightbourne whose house fell off a cliff?"

He scowled briefly. "It was pushed."

"I see."

"And that's beside the point."

"Which is, exactly—?"

"That I'd like to take you to morning tea, Miss Bassingthwaite. I happen to know a charming teahouse near the Parade Gardens."

She glanced at him narrowly. "You refer of course to Sally Lunn's."

"Indeed." His smile was so dazzling, she actually hesitated. What harm could there be in half an hour's chatting over tea with a fellow buccaneer (unless he poisoned the tea, in which case there would be a great deal of it)? Miss Darlington would not approve, but perhaps Cecilia might represent it to her as an information-gathering session—or not represent it at all. She was an adult, after all, and could take tea with whomever she chose. What Miss Darlington did not know would not hurt her (again, unless he poisoned the tea).

Cecilia almost said yes. It lay like a sugared rose petal on her tongue, small yet delicious. She opened her mouth to speak it aloud.

But in that moment she realized they were halfway across the footbridge, with the river tossing glints like sharp blades beneath and the pirate watching her with an alarming stillness in his eyes. Her heart leaped, and she closed her mouth, swallowing what felt now like a thorn.

He must have tossed a coin to the tollbooth attendant when she was not looking. It worried her that she'd been so inattentive. And it proved he was a dangerous man to be around. Not that she needed proof further than the fact that he was intending to murder her, but the flaws of others could be more readily excused than her own. Cecilia did not like making mistakes. And she had made a bad one in almost relenting to this man.

"I beg your pardon, Captain Lightbourne, but I'm afraid I cannot be diverted from my schedule. Thank you for your consideration, however, and if you'll just return my bracelet I'll bid you good day."

"What bracelet?" he asked, all innocence. Cecilia pursed her lips and held out her hand, and he grinned as he laid the loop of gold and pearl in her gloved palm.

"Thank you," she said. "Please do pass on my compliments to Lady Armitage."

She turned to depart, but he took a large step alongside, and it was clear he would stop her if necessary. So she paused and looked at him impatiently.

"My fountain pen, if you don't mind," he said.

Cecilia sighed. She tipped the pen out of her sleeve, handed it over.

For a moment he just looked at her, his smile still and his eyes intense, making the whole world seem to stop even while her heart fluttered as if he was thieving something from beneath it. Her blood began to race—

And then he blinked. "Thank you," he said, bowing. "Tell your aunt I send my best wishes."

"I shall," Cecilia replied calmly, as if tiny bombs weren't exploding inside her body. "Farewell, Captain Lightbourne."

"See you next time, Miss Bassingthwaite."

No you won't, she thought as she left the footbridge and proceeded into the city center: *I shall be nothing more overt than a silence, a shifting of the air perhaps gently scented with lilacs, when I come again into your presence. You will see only the knife I leave in your rib cage. Just who shall assassinate whom, Captain Charming Ned Flirting Light-bourne?*

Smiling at this thought, she nodded to a passing woman, veered away from some children scampering with a puppy, and called briefly in to Sally Lunn's for an iced bun before continuing on to the library.

❊ 4 ❊

A GHOSTLY DISTRACTION—WHEN ONE DOOR OPENS—
CECILIA LOSES HER PARASOL—A MYSTERIOUS ENVELOPE—
TROUBLE IS AFOOT—MISS DARLINGTON TAKES THE WHEEL—
MEASLES AND PERTUSSIS—TEA AND BISCUITS—ONWARD!

There is nothing like the active employment of literature to console the afflicted, and so as Cecilia walked through Bath she gently restored the peace of her mind, which Captain Lightbourne had disturbed, by reading Mr. Lockwood's encounter with the screaming ghost of Cathy Earnshaw. She was not particularly enjoying the novel, but her father had loved it with all the fervor he bore for his Brontë heritage, and so she studied it assiduously under the guise of being entertained. If Heathcliff and Cathy could give her any insight into the tragedy of Patrick and Cilla, her benighted parents, it was worth the toil. That she had to keep it secret from Miss Darlington only added a pleasant frisson of danger.

"You shouldn't be asking questions about your father," Miss Darlington said every time Cecilia attempted to do so. "He is not a subject fit for young ladies' ears."

"But—" Cecilia would argue, since she could not think of how she might track down the man if she knew nothing more about him than what she recollected from her childhood.

"But me no buts," Miss Darlington replied, and there the conversation ended every time. So Cecilia had turned to literature instead.

The Tenant of Wildfell Hall provided some food for thought. *Jane Eyre* she found tolerable (although she herself would have bashed Mr. Rochester over the head with his pipe), and she recognized in Thornfield what had clearly been the inspiration for furnishing her dour childhood home, Northangerland Abbey. But the madness of *Wuthering Heights* informed her best of all the Brontë novels. She became so drawn into its pages as she walked up North Parade that she did not see Darlington House standing in the middle of road, black pirate flag waving proudly from the roof, until she was almost upon its threshold.

People were inching a way around the house and then striding on as fast as their fashionable clothing would allow—not running, mind you, in case the house chased them.

"Be careful, miss!" a man called to her. "Best turn back! It's a pirate house!"

Cecilia thanked him with a nod, but secretly she sighed. She did not understand landlubbers. They were polite enough until you mentioned you were a pirate, or swooped down in your weaponized house, or creatively acquired some little knickknack of theirs that they couldn't possibly care about. Then they blanched or cried, called the police, or insisted you sit where they could see you at the tea party or opera. Cecilia had tried making friends among their ranks but ultimately came away with nothing more than a bruised heart, an arrest warrant, and several pretty bracelets.

Did they not understand that pirates only stole from the rich to give to the—er, to themselves? Not once had she or Miss Darlington used the house to attack a civilian. It simply wouldn't be ladylike. Although they might insist upon acquiring the elegant cameo that young woman in green was wearing, Cecilia thought, eyeing it from beneath the shadow of her hat as the woman approached . . .

Just then, Darlington House began to clatter and creak. Cecilia abandoned thoughts of the brooch. Closing her parasol, slipping Cathy's ghost away into her purse, she stepped up to the door, opened it, and walked through. She had barely made it into the hall when the house began rising.

"Good heavens," Cecilia murmured with surprise at such precipitousness. She glanced at the plasterwork ceiling with its ornate rose, on the other side of which she knew her aunt would be standing at the wheel, feet apart and hairpins erect as she guided her domicile up over Bath.

"Aereo rapido!"

Miss Darlington's voice echoed through the house. A large oil portrait of Beryl Black, hanging on the foyer's east wall, suddenly went askew. Darlington House was banking so sharply, the stabilizing magic faltered.

Cecilia grasped a nearby console table to no avail: the table and its cargo of mail, stacked on a tray, slid westerly, and she went with it. A vase of lilies fell shattering to the floor, and on a sideboard at the far side of the hall a heavy crystal bowl began edging perilously forward. Cecilia recalled that the bowl had previously belonged to the Duke of Kent (and strictly speaking still did) and that its value was in the hundreds of pounds. Letting go of the console table, tucking her parasol beneath her arm lest it open indoors and cause bad luck, Cecilia laid a hand against the wall for balance and began hauling herself up toward the sideboard as quickly as possible before the bowl toppled. The door swung before her and, grasping its handle, she tried to push it shut.

At that inopportune moment the house lurched, the doormat slid beneath her feet, and Cecilia staggered. She found herself tilting out the open door, saved from falling only by means of both hands around the door handle. With annoyance she watched as her parasol plummeted to the road below, where it shattered.

"Doors!" Miss Darlington shouted from somewhere on the first floor. Running footsteps echoed through the house; a door slammed shut. The building shook, and Bath's rooftops seemed to sway beneath it. Cecilia feared the iced bun she'd eaten earlier might at any moment return to the city from whence it came. Footsteps sounded again, moving closer, and then Pleasance had her arms around Cecilia's waist and was pulling her back from the doorway, into the safety of the hall.

"Good heavens, miss!" Pleasance cried, kicking the door shut. The house eased into a horizontal position once more. "I'm ever so sorry, it were all my fault! I was reading *The Mysteries of Udolpho*, and what with my weeping and gasping forgot to close the kitchen door." She shook her head fretfully and curls sprung from their clips. "Because of me, you were about sent falling to your tragical death hundreds of feet below!"

"Not at all, my dear," Cecilia replied, smiling with reassurance. "It was ninety feet at the most."

She returned to the console table, avoiding lilies and the shattered vase as she did so. Taking up the envelope at the top of the mail stack, she considered its originating address with some interest.

"Did you say soup for supper?" she asked.

"Yes, miss," Pleasance said, bending to straighten the mat. "And fresh eggs from the farm what we were camped in. I thought I might make an omelet."

"Lovely," Cecilia murmured. The purple seal of the envelope had already been broken, and a suggestion of fragrance wafted from inside. Cecilia frowned. She laid her purse on the console table and, retaining possession of the envelope, walked upstairs.

"We have a letter from the Wisteria Society," she said as she entered the wheelroom.

This was her favorite place in all the house, for it contained not only the wheel and navigation array but the modest Darlington book collection. Many were the afternoons as a child she had tucked herself up in a plump velvet armchair beside the fire, reading dictionaries and old tales of derring-do while Miss Darlington flew across the countryside in pursuit of treasure. When she had her own house, she would fill every room with books.

As always, she paused now inside the chamber to inhale its musty, papery smell. Some of the books had tipped off their shelves, despite the net barriers that prevented most such accidents, and Cecilia itched to pick them up and restore them to their precise alphabetized positions. But clearly trouble was afoot and there was no time for fun.

Miss Darlington stood stiff-backed at the great oak wheel, staring out across rooftops. She had finished the phrases for *momentum automatica*, and the air itself seemed to whisper with ongoing magic as she moved the wheel to direct their course south over the city. "What were you doing all the way out here?" she asked without turning around.

"Attempting to visit the library," Cecilia replied. "It was a walk of only two miles, and on such—"

"Two miles!" The house lurched as Miss Darlington threw Cecilia an alarmed stare. "Sit down, girl, before your heart gives out!"

"I assure you, I am well," Cecilia said soothingly. "I can see there is trouble and surmise this letter has something to do with it?"

Miss Darlington glanced at the envelope Cecilia held forth. "Yes. An emergency meeting of the Society has been called."

"Goodness," Cecilia murmured. "I can't remember the last time that occurred."

"Eighteen seventy-seven, after your mother was—after she died."

Cecilia blinked away a vision of light flaring against steel as a sword plunged down. In years past it would have made her weep or wince, but now she simply looked at the envelope, wishing she could take out the letter and read it herself. But such a right remained exclusive to senior members, and while Cecilia had been waiting months for her induction to the high tea table, always there seemed some excuse to deny her promotion.

Being a Wisteria Society matron was the highest honor in the criminal world, and Cecilia had never imagined another goal for herself. She'd been born to the great privilege of piracy, and with that came great responsibility. She could not simply turn away to become a governess, a philanthropist, or even a two-bit thief in a shack that could barely fly a mile: she was obliged to be ambitious, if not for her own sake then for the sake of her foremothers. After all, they had sacrificed much to establish the Society (for example, long afternoons reading old hairdressing magazines and taking naps), so that whenever a lady felt depleted by the endless slog of plundering and marauding, she had someone with whom to share a cup of tea, a nice chat, and an invigorating mutual assassination attempt.

The early Society matrons, showing an aptitude for piratic ruthlessness, had quickly turned their social support network into an endless competition among themselves, and this had become so codified over the years that, by the time Cecilia entered, there was a complex system of promotions, demotions, demolitions, and tests to navigate before one was even allowed a biscuit from the tea table. Cecilia had passed all these tests. She had robbed several banks, blackmailed a marchioness, flown the Channel, and even gone dress shopping with Bloodhound Bess, who could take three hours in one store alone. Still they hadn't raised her from the junior women's division. But she was determined to succeed, even if that meant stealing the tea table itself to prove her worth.

Other possessors of Beryl's incantation did exist outside the Wisteria Society, of course. Witches. Introverted women. Men. But for Cecilia, the Society was her whole world. She would rise in their ranks if it killed her.

Which of course was always a possibility with pirates.

"What's happened?" she asked as she watched her aunt read the letter. "Mrs. Rotunder didn't blow up Hampton Court again, did she? Or has piracy been made a capital crime? Don't say Mrs. Etterly's pet tiger ate the Queen!"

"Worse," Miss Darlington intoned direly. "Muriel Fairweather's butler absconded!"

She widened her eyes in horror, then had to focus once more on steering as the house nearly collided with a church steeple.

"Well, that is unfortunate," Cecilia said, "but not what one would usually suppose an emergency."

"He absconded—with her house!"

"Oh dear." A pirate's house was her psyche made corporeal.

"I know they said the butler did it," Miss Darlington continued, "but it seems unlikely he'd be so brazen. A more powerful hand is behind this, mark my words."

"But surely a Wisteria Society member would not go so far as to steal the house of another?"

"We have only three laws in our Society, Cecilia. No killing civilians. Pour the tea before the milk. And no stealing each other's houses. Anyone breaking those laws is cast out—literally, and in most cases from a very significant height."

"So who might it be?"

She already knew the likely answer. Maliciously acquiring houses was a theme of *Wuthering Heights*, after all. But not daring to speak this aloud, she merely looked coolly at Miss Darlington, who replied with a cool look of her own.

Perhaps tracking down her father had just become easier than she'd anticipated.

Suddenly the house swooped, causing a dictionary to topple, its pages creasing appallingly against the floor. Cecilia stepped forward to lay a gentle hand on her aunt's arm. "Why don't I drive for a while?" she suggested. "You are understandably upset. Sit down, have a cup of tea." She eased the elderly lady away from the wheel, supplied her with her cane, and then took the wheel herself. She murmured the pilot phrase, and the magic seemed to grow warm as it adjusted to her mental presence. "Miss Fairweather's territory is Devon, I believe?"

"Yes, Ottery St. Mary. The coordinates are all mapped out." She sank into the fireside chair and laid a hand against her brow. "I cannot believe it," she murmured fretfully. "Two miles, and in the bright sun!"

Cecilia scrutinized the chart that lay on the shelf angled between wheel and window. She saw at once that her aunt had plotted a rather circuitous route so as to avoid the Blackdown Hills and she said nothing, only smiled a little to herself at her aunt's old-fashioned attitude to navigation. The idea that air currents over that region were disturbed by fairies, and forlorn ghosts of people who had seen those fairies, had long been put to rest by rational thinking. Nevertheless, Miss Darlington remained stoutly antiquated. Cecilia reached for the sextant.

"You could have twisted an ankle!" Miss Darlington persisted from the fireside. "Or become suntanned!"

"I am quite all right, Aunty," Cecilia said, aligning the sextant with the horizon and making mental calculations. Her mind, however, kept slipping back to thoughts of Captain Lightbourne. Would he seek her in Ottery St. Mary? What if he lost track of her and they never met again? The prospect of that was miserable—for the sake of her career, of course, and not at all because of his tight trousers and smiling blue eyes.

Clearly, revealing their tête-à-tête to her aunt was out of the question. Never mind his being a wicked piratical assassin; he might have been infected with measles or whooping cough, and Miss Darlington would know no peace for weeks. Besides, a brief exchange with a fellow pirate was inconsequential compared to this stolen-house business. Cecilia would look silly if she mentioned it. Thus she managed quite thoroughly to convince herself that remaining silent on the matter was her only recourse.

"Shall I call Pleasance to bring tea?" she asked.

There was no need. The maid appeared that very moment bearing a tray laden with tea and digestive biscuits, after the consumption of which Miss Darlington snoozed. Cecilia flew them on peacefully toward Ottery St. Mary, watching out for bird strikes, wondering if the village would have a public library, not at all thinking about the provocative blond pirate whose fingertip had slipped briefly, gently, across her wrist when he returned her bracelet in an inconsequential moment that in no way made her feel electrified.

She was gazing at the horizon and thus not thinking, Miss Darlington was challenging someone to pistols at dawn in her sleep, and Pleasance in the kitchen below was hunched in a corner, peeling turnips and chatting with her great-great-grandmother, who liked to call in on her for a pleasant half hour of haunting every week or so; therefore, the great spiked shadow pursuing them over the villages and fields of southwest England went unnoticed by all.

✺ 5 ✺

STEALING O'ER THE FADING SKY IN SHADOWY FLIGHT—
GUNFIRE—THE END OF *WUTHERING HEIGHTS*—
CECILIA IS SHOT, SUPPER IS POSTPONED—THE TROUSERED GIRL—
A LOST TIGER—UNEXPECTED MOUNTAINS

It was foolish to wish for beauty, at least in Miss Darlington's opinion. She had a well-cultivated mind, a well-disposed heart, and tinted goggles that kept out the brightness of the sun; anything else was extravagance. The soft fields and purpling woodland shadows of Devon offered her no more than navigational points. The elegiac light of late afternoon, love-colored and quiet, caressing the wheelroom window, was a hazard that made her squint. When a white swan glided like a tender poem into her path, she considered ramming it, and only the swan's swiftness kept it from being added to Pleasance's soup pot. As Ottery St. Mary came into view beneath, she orated the descent stanza of the flight incantation, turned the wheel to port, and aimed her front door toward a cluster of houses set incongruously in a field beyond the village.

"Coming in to land," she roared into the brass trumpet beside the wheel. Pleasance, in the kitchen, hastily tossed loose cutlery into the sink. Cecilia, reading in the parlor after having spent several hours at the wheel herself, rose and went to the window to see the view. With *Wuthering Heights* held closed against her heart, she reached out to shift the curtain—

Crash!

The window cracked violently and Cecilia was thrown back off her feet. Pain shot through her. She crawled to shelter behind a sofa and then stared at her book, lying where it had fallen from her hand. It bore a gaping black bullet hole.

"That was my only copy," she said aloud in irritation. She then checked her bodice. A seared rip marked where the bullet had ricocheted off her metal corset stay. The lace was ruined and she would have a bruise to be sure. Peering carefully over the back of the sofa, she saw that the window, which they'd only just had repaired, was now shattered again.

"Shots fired!" came Miss Darlington's belated observation, echoing through the parlor trumpet. "Cecilia, secure our landing zone!"

Cecilia swung into action. She rid herself of her dress, and then, clad only in knee-length chemise, petticoat, long lace-trimmed drawers, corset, stockings, and slippers, she hastened from the parlor. Another shot smashed through what remained of the window, rebounded off Lady Askew's silver samovar, and whistled so close past Cecilia's head that her hair seemed to flutter in its passing. It flew through the open parlor door and embedded itself in the grim, painted face of Black Beryl, making her as one-eyed as, well, a pirate.

"Everything all right, miss?" Pleasance asked, glancing out from the dining room.

"Perfectly fine," Cecilia answered, taking a rifle from the umbrella stand in the foyer. She spun it on her index finger to cock it. "Would you open the back door for me, please?"

"Of course." Pleasance jogged down the hall.

"We may be a little late for supper," Cecilia called after her. "I hope you will not be inconvenienced."

"Not at all, miss," Pleasance said, opening the door and glancing out. "Four feet," she called, standing aside.

Cecilia kicked off her slippers, then sprinted the length of the hall and threw herself out the door into the cool dusk air.

Flipping in midair, she landed neatly on the grass. Without a pause she ran along the breadth of the house in her stockinged feet and, rounding the corner, came upon a convenient hedge that provided further shelter. Miss Darlington must have been watching through one of their several rear- and side-view mirrors, for as Cecilia disappeared behind the hedge, the house swerved in the opposite direction, drawing fire away from her position. Cecilia could see a young woman standing behind a tree with a Winchester rifle in her hands. She crept toward her.

It was not easy to be surreptitious when wearing all white, but the shooter was focused on her target, and Cecilia managed to get behind her without being seen. As Miss Darlington swooped the house to avoid another broken window, Cecilia set the muzzle of her gun to the girl's neck.

"Lower your weapon, if you would be so kind," she said. "I'd be most dismayed at having to kill you."

The girl dropped the rifle and spread her hands into view.

"Thank you. Step forward, please."

"You—"

"I beg your pardon, but I must ask you to remain quiet for now. My aunt will wish to hear anything you have to say."

"But who—"

"I am Miss Cecilia Bassingthwaite. It's a pleasure to make your acquaintance. Another word and I shall have to kill you."

"You won't."

"Excuse me?"

"I know of Cecilia Bassingthwaite. Despite your blighted parent-age, you have a reputation for gentle, ladylike refinement. You won't kill me."

Cecilia considered this. She did not mind so much her parents be-ing cast as blighted, since it could hardly be disputed; *gentle*, however, sounded like an insult. "Perhaps not kill you," she agreed. "But I will happily render you unconscious and then sell you back to your family for an exorbitant ransom."

"Fair enough," the girl conceded, and they walked together in si-lence toward the front door of Darlington House.

As they approached, the house came to rest on the grass, and a moment later Pleasance opened the door.

"Good evening, miss," she said with a curtsy, as if Cecilia had re-turned from an afternoon stroll with a lady of the *haut ton*.

Cecilia prodded the girl with her rifle. "Do go in. Wipe your feet on the mat."

"But—"

"I would rather you just did as I asked."

The girl sighed, and Cecilia got the sense she was rolling her eyes with exasperation. She appeared to be two or three years younger than Cecilia herself, and her hair was worn down. An extravagant black bow secured it in a ponytail and rather got in the way of Cecilia's gun. But the girl was also wearing trousers and a man's shirt, by which Ce-cilia understood her to be either a pirate or a farmer's plucky young daughter fed up with houses landing on her father's strawberry fields.

They entered the house, utilizing the mat as they did, and Cecilia was glad to see no bowls or vases had been damaged in the maneuver-ing. Miss Darlington appeared at the top of the stairs and began a stately descent. The girl watched her wide-eyed, mouth slightly ajar.

Miss Darlington had been known in her youth as a hearty lass, but seventy years of battle and enthusiastic ballroom dancing had rendered her dependent on both a cane and the handrail. Her piratical majesty was undinted, however, and her black bombazine dress billowed slightly in the manner of a brigantine's flag as she took the stairs.

The girl curtsied. "Miss Darlington," she said in reverent tones.

"Who are you?" Miss Darlington demanded.

"Constantinopla Brown, ma'am."

Miss Darlington frowned in the severe manner that indicated she was feeling pleasantly surprised. "Not Anne Brown's granddaughter?"

"The same, ma'am."

"The last time I saw you was at the Scottish border. Your mother was helping me dispatch a gang of ruffians. She had you in a sling and at one point you reached out with your wee little hand and grabbed a fellow's blunderbuss. In his surprise, he pulled the trigger, shot dead his captain, and lost his balance from the kick of the gun. Fell into quicksand. Most distressing. It took me three days to get the splashes of muck washed out of my dress. But you helped us win that skirmish, young lady. Good job."

The girl blushed at this praise. Cecilia raised one eloquent eyebrow but hastily lowered it again before anyone noticed.

"I never thought I'd see the day when little Constantinopla would be shooting out the windows of my house. Cecilia!" she snapped without shifting her gaze from the trousered girl, "put down that rifle at once. Ladies do not point guns at friends. At least, not on happy occasions such as these."

"I'm sorry I shot," Constantinopla said, "but you were advised beforehand."

"Advised?"

"Yes, ma'am, in the letter you were sent. It contained a post-script . . ."

Miss Darlington drew the letter from her waistband and opened it. Her lips moved as she perused the contents. "The only postscript is PCAP."

"Yes, ma'am." Constantinopla nodded vigorously, causing her hair bow to waggle. "As you can see, I had no choice but to shoot."

"PCAP," Miss Darlington repeated. "Please contribute a plate. It's standard practice when the Society meets. Pleasance has been making mushroom and shrimp canapés all afternoon."

Constantinopla's blush deepened. "Oh no, ma'am. Provide code at perimeter. Morse code, with your lantern or curtains, so we know you're not with the enemy."

"The enemy?" Miss Darlington was aghast. "No one has accused me of being their enemy in—in—"

"Two weeks, Aunty," Cecilia supplied. "Lady Espiner."

"Espiner? Thin woman, ruby necklace?"

"Yes, Aunty."

Miss Darlington scoffed. "I wasn't her enemy; I was doing her a favor. Imagine wearing rubies in summer! They are an autumn jewel. And I never would have thought my own Society would shoot at me."

"You shot at Mrs. Eames last month, Aunty," Cecilia reminded her. "And Miss Coatwallis shot at us in Greenwich over Eastertide. And Lady Armitage—"

"*Nevertheless*," Miss Darlington said. "I did not expect such a poor welcome."

An answer issued from the open doorway: "We have to be careful, with houses being snatched right from under our noses."

Everyone turned to see a woman step across the threshold. She was dressed in a voluminous black gown, with a black lace cape about her shoulders secured by a brooch of skull and crossbones. Her head was glazed with thin black hair and featured round pallid eyes, thin pallid lips, and a nose so pallid that it seemed more like an insinuation of a nose than actual nasal cavities. If Death had a governess, she would look like this woman.

"Anne," Miss Darlington said in greeting.

"Jemima," the woman replied. She stepped forward, extending a hand in a businesslike manner. Miss Darlington eyed it warily.

"Have you sanitized your hands before coming here?"

"I'm wearing gloves."

Miss Darlington shuddered. "Cecilia, shake hands with Miss Brown on my behalf."

Cecilia set down her rifle and politely shook Miss Brown's small gloved hand. "How do you do?"

"Cilla Bassingthwaite's daughter?" Miss Brown asked, throwing Miss Darlington a complex look.

"Yes," Miss Darlington replied.

"Interesting." She regarded Cecilia more closely, as if mentally measuring the depth of lace on her petticoat and drawers, assessing her posture, and judging her against the memory of a woman far superior to that which stood here now. "With that hair, she looks more like her father. How old is she?"

"Seventeen."

"Nineteen," Cecilia corrected demurely.

Miss Darlington waved this away with an impatient hand. "What's happening about the house theft?"

"Why don't you come over to Gertrude's," Miss Brown said, "and we'll tell you the news. Everyone's there."

"Everyone?" Miss Darlington was surprised.

"Everyone who's currently in the country and out of jail. Only Issy Armitage hasn't come, but we all know how antisocial she can be. I myself flew down from Newcastle for Constantinopla's graduation, only to be waylaid by these events. Rather decent of the Fairweathers to provide some entertainment for my first visit south in ten years."

Her bland countenance did not alter, but she nevertheless managed to exude the impression that she was smirking. "You're the last to arrive, Jem. Better late than never, aye?"

Miss Darlington lifted her chin. "One does like to make an entrance. Pleasance, bring the canapés. Cecilia, fetch my cloak."

"Which one, Aunty?"

"The black velvet that Madame Yurovsky would have gifted me on the opening night of the opera, had she been in the room at the time."

"Yes, Aunty." Cecilia began to walk down the hall, toward the cloakroom.

"And put on a dress. And shoes. And coat, scarf, beret. It will be nightfall soon, and you don't want to develop bronchitis."

"Yes, Aunty," Cecilia replied, brushing gunpowder residue from her chemise as she went.

"This is ever so exciting!" Constantinopla declared. "The Wisteria Ladies' Society, reunited at last!"

Miss Darlington frowned. "Several of us were together in April for Lavinia's bridal shower."

"I hosted a gathering myself only three weeks ago," Miss Brown added. "Olivia lost her tiger on the beach and it was great fun watching the landlubbers run screaming."

"I don't recall receiving an invitation to that," Miss Darlington said frostily.

"Yes, I've been meaning to be in touch ever since you framed me for the Marlborough House robbery twelve years ago. But you know how it is, busy, busy. I've quite lost count of all my heists and husbands. And now this little one is getting her wings." She patted Constantinopla's arm.

"Finally!" Constantinopla added fervently.

"Oply's ever so gifted. With her excellent grades and just a touch of blackmail, she graduated three months early from Mrs. Higglestone's School of Music and Martial Arts."

"School," Miss Darlington said, her tone the verbal equivalent of cold, unsugared tea. "How modern of you."

Miss Brown smiled.

Miss Darlington smiled.

Constantinopla edged away.

They were at the point of showing their teeth when Cecilia returned. Constantinopla huddled in the doorway, and Pleasance, holding a large tray of canapés, was quivering so much that shrimps leaped to the floor. Cecilia sighed.

"Your cloak, Aunty," she said, stepping between the two women to drape the cloak over Miss Darlington's shoulders. The pleasantness cracked and ebbed away. Anne Brown frowned, Miss Darlington scowled, and Constantinopla took a deep breath of relief. Pleasance began picking up shrimps off the floor and replacing them in their canapés.

"Shall we join the others?" Miss Brown suggested.

"Delightful," Miss Darlington said.

They made a dainty, feminine procession into the deepening night.

Cecilia, taking the tray from Pleasance and stepping outside, glanced eastward over the field. In the distance beyond, sharp towers of darkness jutted into the moonless sky. Cecilia frowned, trying unsuccessfully to recall the jagged peaks of East Devon. She would have to consult an atlas tomorrow.

She turned to hasten after the other ladies, therefore missed seeing a light come on in a window of those distant peaks as Captain Morvath lit a lantern with which to inspect his cannons.

❊ 6 ❊

THE WISTERIA SOCIETY MOTTO—THE WISTERIA SOCIETY ITSELF—
ASSASSINATION BY PARROT—SEATING ARRANGEMENTS—
FENCING WITH FLYING BUTLERS—ILL MET BY MOONLIGHT—
A RISK OF MATRIMONY (OR MURDER)—
THE WISTERIA SOCIETY MOTTO, JUNIOR DIVISION—
A SPEEDING HOUSE CHASE—NED MAKES A VOW

I t is violence that best overcomes hate, vengeance that most certainly
heals injury, and a good cup of tea that soothes the most anguished
soul"; thus ran the motto of the Wisteria Society of Lady Scoundrels.
Therefore, by the time Miss Darlington and her niece joined the gathering of ladies in Gertrude Rotunder's dining room, plans had already
been made to chase down the thieving butler and have him hung,
drawn, and quartered, with his remains displayed in Hyde Park as a
warning to others. The ladies, seated around a lace-clothed table laden
with cakes and delicate savories, paused in their conversation as Cecilia and Miss Darlington entered.

It was like walking into a tropical garden in which several flocks of
rare birds had exploded. Feathers jutted in all directions from silk-
flowered hats and bosoms. Entire wings swooped up from some heads;
on others, taxidermied robins nested among swathes of lace. The

gowns below were a hysteria of colors that would have sent any painter mad. Such an array of jewels glinted in the chandelier light that the air was thick with rainbow fragments.

Twelve ladies altogether attended the meeting. The youngest was Essie Smith, who had barely made her début before her parents were killed by the curse of the Black Diamond; she'd inherited their Palladian town house and had spent the next five years looting the northern counties before settling down to motherhood. The oldest was Verisimilitude Jones, known as Millie the Monster, blight of the Cornish coast: so old was she that rumor had it she'd once stolen a cake from Marie Antoinette. She piloted a quaint, thatch-roofed cottage despite being rich enough to own a castle, and had taught Cecilia how to use a cutlass.

No men sat at the table, having been left at home to mind the children, guard the treasure, or quite frankly just stay out of the way of women's business.

Cecilia's heart warmed as she looked upon the ladies. She suspected that, no matter how old she became, she'd always feel a rush of comfort when she entered their company. The motherless child she'd been, hiding behind their skirts, listening to their madcap bedtime stories, and absolutely trusting that they'd keep her safe from her father, could never imagine anyone so powerful, or so magnificent, as the Wisteria Society ladies.

Now she was eligible to become one of them herself. They could not deny it since another Society member wanted her dead. Surely today would be the day of her induction!

Why, how unexpected! she reminded herself to say when they pulled out the chair. She'd probably be placed down at the end of the table by the condiments, but even so. *You are too kind; I am not worthy,* she would murmur as she lowered herself onto the cushioned seat, back straight, head high albeit hatless, while a maid poured her tea.

Envisioning it, she tried not to smile or rock on her heels like an excited little girl.

"Jemima," said Gertrude Rotunder, rising in a flurry of blue lace, ribbons, feathers, and flounces to greet her latest guest. "How lovely to see you. And in such good health, too."

(Mrs. Rotunder had recently failed in an attempt to have Miss Darlington assassinated by means of trained parrot, unaware of Miss Darlington's belief that parrots carried syphilis and were therefore to be scrupulously avoided. This had been in retaliation for Miss Darlington's theft of Mr. Rotunder's leg, which was said to be inlaid with wood from the True Cross, and yet only fetched five hundred pounds on the Catholic black market. Mr. Rotunder—a thin, anemic gentleman who'd never been quite right since a mad doctor sawed off two of his limbs only moments before rescue arrived—had been willing to let the matter go and live out his days in a rocking chair, writing letters to newspaper editors with his one remaining hand and sighing mournfully every now and again, but his wife would have none of that. When the assassination attempt failed, she took solace in stealing Miss Darlington's favorite mahogany cabinet, from which a new leg was made for Mr. Rotunder, and thereafter all was well again between the ladies.)

"Gertrude," Miss Darlington replied. "How suited you are to that headdress. Parrot feathers, I take it?"

"Ha ha ha," Mrs. Rotunder said. "Snowy egret, in fact. Won't you have a seat? Cecilia dear, perhaps you would be most comfortable by the fire?"

Cecilia blinked. She felt her pleasant expression slip and hastily drew it back up into a smile. "Mrs. Rotunder," she dared to say, heart pounding, "may I venture to share my latest news? Lady Armitage has employed an assassin against me."

Mrs. Rotunder raised one pruned silver eyebrow. Behind her, the other ladies exchanged glances. Cecilia was fluent in the language of those looks; she did not require a conversation to know even assassination had failed to win her a promotion. Her heart clenched. Was it that they deemed her inherently inadequate? Or did they care too much for Miss Darlington's nerves? She could not ask. Nor would she sigh, for she had her dignity, but deep inside her heart lay back and moaned into a handkerchief.

"Yes, I had heard," Mrs. Rotunder said pleasantly. "How nice for you, dear. Oh look, I see your friend Jane is over there, and Constantinopla too."

Cecilia curtsied, then retreated without further word to the domain of the junior women: the sofas near the fireplace.

"An assassin!" Constantinopla said with gratifying enthusiasm as Cecilia sat beside her. "Is she fierce and cunning?"

"Something like that," Cecilia murmured in reply. She looked across at the delicate, tight-haired young woman seated opposite. "Jane, lovely to see you."

Jane peered over the rim of her spectacles, nodded sharply, then returned to reading a book of classic war poems that lay across her bony hand. Cecilia suppressed a grimace. She and Miss Fairweather Junior had been chums a long time ago when they shared riding lessons, learning to saddle their horses, trot elegantly, and swing from the pommel with a knife in their teeth. But a dispute had risen between them as to the value of Wordsworth's poetry, and they had not spoken for years. They would not begin again now.

Constantinopla leaned closer to Cecilia. "I don't think Jane likes me," she whispered ostentatiously. "Why isn't she sitting at the main table? Surely she's old enough?"

Cecilia's heart wailed and flapped its handkerchief. She managed, however, to smile. "Jane débuted three years ago," she explained quietly, "but has not yet robbed a bank."

She contrived to fit several volumes of opinion into that one sentence. Jane, having heard it, as intended, turned a page in her book with such vehemence that the edge tore. Cecilia could not help but gasp, and Jane flung her a look like a dagger before tossing the torn paper to the floor. Cecilia felt sure one day she would be thwarting assassination attempts from the lesser Miss Fairweather.

"I plan to rob a bank just as soon as I get my wings," Constantinopla declared.

"Some of us," Jane said pointedly, smacking back another page, "think that a girl shouldn't fly until she's putting her hair up and lowering her skirt hems—or actually wearing skirts like a proper lady ought." She looked down her nose at Constantinopla's trousers, and the girl flushed.

"I'm proper, only in a different way," Constantinopla said. "And I've completed all the theoreticals, I just have my practicum to go."

"How exciting," Cecilia said with an encouraging smile. "It does take *some* girls a few tries before they pass—"

Now Jane was the one flushing.

"—but I'm sure you'll do well."

A maid brought tea and a selection of food to the young ladies, and they partook of these while Jane read, Constantinopla talked about her school experience, and Cecilia tried to hear what the seniors at the table were saying.

"Jane and I had gone out to buy arsenic," Muriel Fairweather explained.

"My fencing master's mustache," Constantinopla sighed dreamily.

"Such a shock, to see my own house overhead—"

"Curled with a Hungarian pomade—"

"Well, that's what you get for trusting—"

"Men—"

"Servants—"

"Pink prancers."

Cecilia, frowning slightly, turned to Constantinopla, who giggled. "I know, who names their shoes?" the girl said. "But he's awfully proud of them, and I do admit they let him move ever so well—"

"Last seen over Bodmin Moor—"

"Dancing a tango—"

"We'll get it back—"

"And then into a dip—"

"We'll beat him with—"

"Kid gloves—"

"Hear! Hear!"

"Hair like spun gold, even with the wax—"

"And leather whips—"

"All hot and melting—"

"And then we'll cut off his—"

"And you can eat it with—"

"Lady Armitage."

Cecilia froze, with her teacup almost to her lips, as she listened even more determinedly to what was being said about her assassinatrix. But Constantinopla had worked herself into quite a passion about her fencing master, and any useful information was so jumbled with descriptions of the master's manliness that Cecilia's resulting impression was of Lady Armitage undulating her hips in skintight breeches while conspiring with the butler to thrust and twirl in Miss Fairweather's cockpit—at which point her brain, not to mention her modesty, threatened to implode.

She set her teacup on the table and rose. "I beg your pardon," she said, "but I might just visit the powder room."

"You do look a little heated," Constantinopla remarked. "Why don't you go outside for some fresh air?"

"But it's dark," Jane said, shocked into joining the conversation.

"I don't mind that," Cecilia said. "It's a good idea. If my aunt asks, would you tell her I've gone to powder my nose?"

The two other girls hesitated at the thought of lying to Miss Darlington, who was infamous for evicting a maid from her service just for saying there were no crumpets when there was in fact one remaining, green and stiff with age, at the back of the pantry—evicting her, that is, while the house was one hundred and twenty feet above Oxford Street. Had the maid's hooped petticoat not served as a parachute, her termination might have proved terminal. But both girls were scoundrels born and bred and ultimately could not resist a deception.

"Of course," Constantinopla said, grinning. "Take your time." She bounced her eyebrows suggestively, as if Cecilia was going outdoors to smoke a cigar or give money away to charity.

"It's your funeral," Jane said, with a tint of hope in her voice, and went back to reading.

The senior ladies were too engrossed in their discussion to notice Cecilia slip from the room. She took the hallway unseen (other than by a maid, two footmen, and the butler) and stepped out into the night with a sigh of relief. The butler offered to fetch her coat but she declined, and as he closed the door behind her with a punctilious click of the latch, she inhaled the dark quiet of evening.

Goose bumps rose on her arms and she rubbed them complacently. The cold was restorative. The several houses surrounding her were lit here and there as husbands or servants went about their gentle evening occupations. Only one seemed to flare, then darken, then flare again, as if the occupants were rushing about with lanterns. Cecilia felt a sense of peace.

She wandered away from Mrs. Rotunder's door and stood gazing

east at the mountains she had noticed earlier. They spiked an allur-
ingly secretive horizon. One day she'd fly her own house into such a
horizon, chasing adventure, stealing treasure, hunting down her father
to murder him, dancing on the unfettered winds. The Wisteria Society ladies could not deny her promotion forever.

She looked west, but then frowned and turned back to stare again
at the mountains. How unusual they were—all blocks and heavy
spires, quite unlike the plump hills she was accustomed to seeing
around southern England. Her heart tossed up melancholy images of
towers from her childhood home. How miserable she had been in those
dark days, huddled in a corner reading while her father stalked the
halls raving about poetry and pain, her mother wept, and the old abbey
ghosts moaned dutifully. Then her mind, not to be outdone, joined in
with visions of *Jane Eyre*'s Thornfield Hall, and Cecilia gasped, clutching instinctively at her locket. She understood now what exactly it was
she was seeing against that eastern horizon.

She would have returned at once to Mrs. Rotunder's drawing room
but suddenly someone was behind her, wrapping their arm around her
waist and pressing a knife to her throat.

"Good evening, Miss Bassingthwaite."

"Captain Lightbourne," she replied frostily, recognizing not so
much his voice but the smirk beneath it. "As we are still not formally
acquainted, I must insist you step back."

"But I am concerned for your health, Miss Bassingthwaite. You
have come outside without coat or shawl. You might catch a chill. I
consider it my duty to warm you with a frisson of fear."

"I am fine, thank you, and would appreciate not being assassinated
in a field like some yeoman. Perhaps we could make an appointment
for the next time I am in town?"

He smiled against her hair. And although Cecilia was not afraid,
inexplicably she began to warm.

"A gentleman does not trouble a lady by pinpointing the time of her murder," he said.

"A gentleman also does not accost a lady at night unless he intends to assassinate her at that moment or marry her."

"I'm not going to assassinate you at this moment," he murmured in her ear.

She shivered at the hot tickling of his breath. Then she frowned. "What on earth is going on in Miss Dole's house?" The rush of lights had settled in an upper front room that Cecilia supposed to be the cockpit, and she could sense the trembling aura of old flight magic.

"We are stealing it," Captain Lightbourne said. "I'm afraid I shall have to render you unconscious so that you do not raise the alarm. Would you prefer a brisk tap on the head or the application of chloroform? The latter is less painful, but some people consider it rather flirtatious, and as you are a very proper lady, I—"

She moved abruptly, inserting her arm beneath his, angling to grasp his coat, and then bent to flip him over her shoulder. He fell with a grunt at her feet, and she turned at once to depart.

She had taken only half a step when he caught the hem of her dress and tugged, causing her to stumble and fall. Within a moment he was rolling her over and sitting astride her waist in a most ungentlemanly manner indeed. He grabbed her wrists, pinning them to the ground, and grinned down at her through the tumble of his hair.

"Sir," she said coolly. "Unhand me at once. You are not wearing gloves."

"Miss Bassingthwaite," he replied, "I humbly beg your pardon, but I am not at liberty to—er, set you at liberty. And yet, I cannot feel too apologetic for imprisoning your soft hand, or wanting to rave about your peerless eyes—"

"Really, sir!" Cecilia was entirely shocked. "You misquote Keats in the most appalling fashion. Furthermore, your dagger hilt is pressing into my—my midsection."

"Dagger hilt?" He contrived a slight, confused frown, which melted into a grin so wicked that Cecilia blushed. They stared at each other for a long, silent moment. His grin faded, her heart began rushing, he bent as if to kiss her, and she kneed him in the groin.

"Urgh," he said.

She shoved him off and hastened to her feet. As he coiled into himself, groaning, she gathered up her skirts. "Excuse me," she said, and ran toward Mrs. Rotunder's door.

Ned was up again even as she reached it, but he did not give chase; instead, he ran rather awkwardly across the field to Petunia Dole's house. Cecilia applied a fist to the Rotunder door, but it was in vain. By the time the butler opened the door, and the ladies were alerted, and all rushed out with swords and pistols drawn, the Dole manor was sailing eastward under billowing enchantment.

"Well, I never!" Miss Darlington exclaimed, taking in Cecilia's disordered hair and flushed face. "What has been happening here?"

"My house!" Petunia Dole wailed.

"It was Captain Lightbourne," Cecilia explained.

"What, the homeless man?" Gertrude Rotunder asked with surprise.

"Who more likely to steal a house?" Essie reasoned.

"I believe he's working for someone else," Cecilia said. "There's another house beyond the woods—a large building—" She pointed, despite knowing that it was rude to do so. Everyone turned to stare as the great spiked shadow rose out of the distance, one light blazing from a high window. Miss Dole's manor flew toward it.

"Northangerland Abbey!" Gertrude exclaimed.

"Captain Morvath!" Essie gasped.

A grim murmur went through the group. Several of the women glanced with narrowed eyes at Cecilia, but as she did not begin shrieking in fear at the sudden appearance of her evil father's monstrous Gothic lair, they looked at one another instead. A wordless code traveled through their gazes.

"To your wheels, ladies!" Anne cried, lifting her sword high. "We must give chase!"

"Tally ho!" someone hollered.

"Hurrah!" someone else shouted—and then: "Oh, sorry, Petunia, it's really not exciting at all."

And the ladies ran for their battlehouses.

Cecilia turned to hurry home, but Miss Darlington caught her by the arm. "We cannot leave without our coats," she said, and hauled Cecilia into the Rotunder foyer with a strength belied by her cane and her frequent claims of being too infirm to fetch anything for herself, even from a table within reach.

"Good man," she said, snapping her fingers at the butler, who was directing staff to action stations. He bowed and went at once, with a butler's instinctual understanding, to retrieve the ladies' outdoorswear.

Mrs. Rotunder had already dashed up to her wheelroom, and servants began running about closing windows and dousing candles. Miss Darlington, still possessed of Cecilia's arm, eyed her closely.

"You encountered this Lightbourne fellow, or merely saw him entering Pet's house?" she asked in a stern tone.

"We had a brief conversation," Cecilia confessed.

"A rather athletic one, from the looks of you," Miss Darlington said, and Cecilia blushed.

"There was some exchange of stances."

"I see." The short phrase seemed to ring with bells—church bells, to be precise, and Cecilia held her breath. She was disinclined to marry her assassin, regardless of how charming his smile might be. But Miss Darlington's eyes gleamed with unexpected humor. "Who won?"

"I would say that I did," Cecilia replied, "but as he is currently getting away with Miss Dole's house, I fear that would be an exaggeration."

"Pish!" Miss Darlington said. "Pet should have locked her door better. Where is that man with my cloak? We shall have to jump for it if he does not—ah, finally," she said as the butler arrived. "Hurry now, Cecilia, there is not a minute to lose."

They took their clothing and exited the house. All around them, buildings were rising into the night. Even as Miss Darlington and Cecilia stood putting on cloak and coat (and scarves, beret, gloves), Mrs. Rotunder's house groaned aloft. Miss Darlington lifted a disapproving gaze to the wheelroom window.

"It sounds like someone mispronounced the second rhyme," she said. "Cecilia Patricia Bassingthwaite, your tonsils are quite exposed. Wrap your scarf again properly."

Cecilia did this and then also rearranged her beret to Miss Darlington's satisfaction, whereupon her aunt said urgently, "Come along, dear, let us make haste."

They walked beneath manors, town houses, and cottages to their own house, where Pleasance was waiting with a tomahawk at the door. "If any burglar tries to get past me, miss," she said as they approached, "I'll make him into a ghost. He can help the White Lady haunt the guest bedroom."

"Well done," Miss Darlington replied, closing the door behind her and proceeding to unlace and remove the cloak she had one minute before so carefully donned. "Now we must rush to join the chase. All hands on deck! Cecilia, I want you to check windows and doors are closed, then put on the kettle. Tea is vital at a time like this. And,

Pleasance, polish the sextant and telescope. We cannot venture forth with dirty instruments."

Cecilia and Pleasance exchanged a brief glance.

"Ain't we in a hurry, miss?" Pleasance dared to ask.

"Absolutely!" Miss Darlington replied in a strident tone. "Every moment counts! Plenty of sugar with the tea, Cecilia. And bring it to me in the parlor. I shall just rest my eyes before setting off. Many's the accident that's been had due to eyestrain, you know."

"Yes, Aunty," Cecilia murmured. She knew Miss Darlington was trying to protect her, not having been appraised of Cecilia's long-held intention to run her father down and put a sword through him. However, she also knew that, if her aunt became aware of this scheme, no buts would be butted, and Cecilia would be thereafter lucky to fly her own armchair, let alone her own house. So she went without argument to do as she was told. (After all, the Wisteria Ladies' Junior Division motto was: "Ours not to reason why, ours but to do and hopefully the other person dies.")

"Also bring biscuits," Miss Darlington called after her. "The ginger ones. I could not eat a thing at Gertrude's table—you never know whether people clean their kitchens properly or not. The dangers of an upset stomach are not to be underestimated!"

Ned sighed dreamily as he limped through Miss Dole's downstairs rooms, filling his pockets with small valuable items and trying to ignore the pain in a certain part of his anatomy. If Cecilia Bassingthwaite hadn't injured him, he would be having quite the opposite reaction to their meeting. So much for implacability! So much for delicate pallor! Fire ran through her veins! He'd felt it in her throat, pulsing against his knife. He'd felt it in her breath beneath him. She had witchcraft in her lips!—and hands, and knees.

Definitely in her knees, he thought, wincing.

Lady Armitage was right to want such a woman blotted out, although right for all the wrong reasons. Lady Armitage thought her only a means to an end. But Ned was beginning to suspect Cecilia was the heart of everything.

One of the lackeys ran into the room, gasping. "They're following us, Captain!"

Ned smirked, picking up a small, onyx-framed portrait from a table. "Of course they are," he said. The portrait was done in oils, and its artist had possessed enough talent to capture the wildness of the woman's smile, but not enough for the sadness in her sky-colored eyes. Ned remembered those eyes, although it had been a decade since he'd seen them. He doubted anyone could forget them. Cecilia's eyes were a softer color, like the calm heart of a storm.

Except tonight, for but a moment, as he bent toward her and she considered not stopping him. Then she'd looked like her mother—a princess of pirates, all girlish wickedness and wild.

Ned tucked the framed portrait in a secret pocket of his coat. "They won't catch us," he said to the lackey. "But get someone to prepare the house gun, just in case."

"You want us to shoot at ladies?"

Ned laughed incredulously. "Where did Morvath find you?"

"On the docks, sir. Navy gunner, but the captain offered better pay."

"Navy. Well, that's about as useful as a feather duster in a sword fight. I'll do the guns; you go make sure the servants are comfortable."

"Comfortable as in—?"

Ned frowned. "We do not kill servants, man. Not on my watch. Comfortable as in not restrained somewhere that heavy items might fall on them if the house swerves. Go. Now."

The man fled toward the kitchen, and Ned, taking a lantern, jogged upstairs in search of the gun turret. He did not particularly want to shoot at ladies—it would inspire them to shoot back, and some of them had excellent aim, what with having been engaged in battles since long before he was born. But he would not fly undefended, either.

He found Miss Dole's artillery in a room with rose-covered wallpaper and a clutter of sofas and tea tables. After trying at first to navigate the maze of them, he simply climbed over instead. He opened the pink window shutters, cranked the window to full dilation, and wheeled the multibarreled rapid-fire gun into position. Lights were flashing in the distance: town houses, manors, and what looked like a plump, vine-swathed cottage, in hot pursuit above the Devonshire fields.

Ned checked the gun's hopper and saw it was only half-loaded. By the light of his lantern he rummaged about on nearby shelves before locating more ammunition in a box encrusted with seashells and ribbon. He loaded the hopper and turned the crank, letting off a few rounds as a warning. Smoke billowed everywhere. Coughing, cursing, Ned stepped back. He spied a painted lace fan on the shelves and applied it before his face. Moments later, when the smoke had dispersed, he peered through the window.

The ladies were gaining on them.

"Damn," he said, and tossed the fan aside. Aiming for chimneys, he fired again, and as bricks exploded in the night there was a battery of return fire. The house banked to avoid it, and Ned clung to the gunwheel so he did not go skidding. Nothing fell—at least the place had good stabilizing magic—but then the house veered in the opposite direction, and he grimaced.

Airsickness was a very unfortunate tendency for a pirate.

"One of these days," he vowed as he set his teeth and began aiming the gun once more, "I am going to steal a nice little cottage and cruise the Lake District, fishing for blackbirds and—" He had a sudden vision of Cecilia Bassingthwaite in the kitchen of that cottage, dressed in white with a rosy tumble of hair, a blackbird pie in her hands, calling him in to supper. "More lovely and more tempestuous than a summer's day," he said dreamily, and as the house swooped again he dropped to his knees and vomited.

Suddenly, a force of stone and shadow reverberated up through the floors. The house went still, but the sensation of movement continued, and Ned realized they had landed on Northangerland Abbey's roof. From below came explosions as the abbey cannons fired. Wiping his mouth with the back of his hand, he got up and looked out the window.

One house, its roof aflame, was sinking toward the ground. Two others followed it, grappling hooks flying from their windows in an effort to catch the house and slow its descent. The remaining pursuers were falling back, and Ned sighed with relief.

A bell chimed melodiously as Miss Dole's front door opened. Ned closed his eyes, knowing what would come next—

"Lightbourne!"

Captain Morvath was on board.

Clambering back over sofas, making his way around tea tables, he went down to meet the pirates' pirate.

Morvath stood in the Dole foyer, dressed in black like a vampire or an opera singer; he held a gilded marble egg up to his eye.

"Terrible work," he said.

"I beg your pardon," Ned replied, bowing in apology.

Morvath sneered. "I meant the egg. It will look good enough to the undiscerning eye, but is in fact a mere replica of Fabergé's genius. You got the house here intact. Well done."

"Thank you."

"And Cecilia?"

"She escaped my clutches."

"Your clutches, hey?" Morvath looked at him; Ned returned the stare without blinking. A taut moment followed.

Then Morvath laughed. He tossed up the egg, allowing it to fall on the polished floor. The supposed marble shattered into clay pieces.

"Cheap lies. Nothing but 'snares and wiles of the tempter, to lure the thoughtless to their own destruction.' Branwell Brontë said that, you know." (The fact that actually Anne Brontë said it tells you pretty much all you need to know about Patrick Morvath.) "He had wisdom to fit every occasion. That I inherited his brilliance proves God is on my side and that my mission of restoring England to men's superior rule is a divine one."

Stepping on the shards with his booted feet, he approached Ned, reaching into his coat as he came. Ned did not move, although his mind was racing to calculate the last moment at which he could draw the knife from his sleeve and stab Morvath if necessary.

But Morvath only produced a locket, which he showed Ned while at the same time laying an arm across his shoulders. "See this? Know who it is?"

Ned studied the miniature portrait of the woman. It matched that which he had found in Miss Dole's sitting room and carried now in his own coat pocket. "Yes," he said.

"My beautiful Cilla. She was the most perfect example of woman-hood, and mine—all mine." His breath reeked of whiskey, but Ned did not dare move away. When drunk, the Captain became even more ego-centric in his attitude toward reality, and more than one man had died for taking a step in what Morvath deemed the wrong direction. Ned was still not sure how someone with such a twisted mind managed to handle a building as big as the abbey in flight when even simple truths seemed beyond him.

"I'll never forgive those Wisteria women for my loss," Morvath went on, unconsciously proving Ned's point. "If they hadn't turned Cilla's heart against me with their poisonous ideas about women's rights and dignity, I know she'd never have left me. But it's not only them. Even my own mother thought she could treat me like a nobody and just discard me, although I have the blood of genius running through my veins. Genius! You know, you've read my poems."

"Indeed."

"Women took my name, my heart, my love, from me. Well, by the time we're finished, the Wisteria Society, the Queen, every damned Englishwoman, will have nothing left except what I deign to give them."

"Yes, sir," Ned responded as he was supposed to.

"Or you'll die trying."

"Understood," Ned replied.

Morvath laughed, slapping him on the back. "Good. Now, on to stage three of our plan. Are you ready?"

"More than you can know," Ned answered—thinking, *You bastard.*

Literally as well as vulgarly, he added, and tried not to smile.

Morvath snapped shut the locket and held it to his breast. "Oh, Cilla," he moaned. "Forever my dearest ghost. It hurts unbearably to be parted from you!"

Then you probably shouldn't have killed her, Ned commented silently.

"Come on, lad," Morvath said, tucking the locket away again. "Let's go burn the world."

7

If a woman drank tea with all the powers of her puny being, she couldn't drink as much in eighty years as Miss Darlington did in the following week. There was the everyday routine to be upheld—tea, and tea-with-biscuits, and a quick cup, and medicinal tea, and tea-before-bed, et cetera; but there was also an endless round of tea drunk in various houses with other ladies of the Wisteria Society as they strategized their response to Morvath's piracy. Friday afternoon they even went into Ottery St. Mary to have tea in a little teahouse where the tablecloths were pink and the spoons were stealworthy.

On this occasion, Miss Darlington, Cecilia, and Pleasance walked into the village with Olivia Etterly, a lady of forty years' age (and some more she did not acknowledge) who was infamous for having once made Lord Byron cry. Miss Darlington took the journey seated beneath a parasol in a wheeled wicker peacock chair pushed by Pleasance. As they went, she fanned herself so as to protect her lungs from the diseases exuded by hedgery, and at regular intervals warned Cecilia about the breeze ("don't breathe too much, it will chill your heart"), a passing sparrow ("they're wingèd mice, you know"), and the perils of walking faster than a gentle stroll ("alack, slow down, you will break your ankle at that intemperate pace, my dear!"). Pleasance kept glancing back, for she was anxious leaving the house. In fact, before setting out there had been a fervent discussion about it between her, the pirate ladies, and the monsters in her head.

"It will be stolen!" Pleasance had wept, her hair unraveling, her hands clinging to the balustrade as the ladies tried to convince her to come along.

"Morvath wouldn't dare take my house," Miss Darlington had retorted.

"The ghost of the Blood Countess is warning me otherwise!"

"Ghosts aren't real," Olivia Etterly had assured her with the authority of a woman who had killed enough people to know.

"The countess told me you'd say that!" Pleasance wailed.

Olivia glanced at Miss Darlington, who shrugged. "She's a fantastic cook," Miss Darlington explained. "It's worth putting up with a few histrionics for the sake of her roast chicken."

Olivia patted Pleasance's arm. "Your passion is a credit to your employer, dear girl. I will send my husband over to be a guard. He was a pirate of some disgrace before he retired, and will keep your house safe."

"But what about your own house?" Miss Darlington asked (mostly concerned that Mr. Etterly might cough on her furniture or drink from her favorite cup).

"Anyone who can get past my pet tiger deserves to steal it," Olivia said.

And so Mr. Etterly came across in his slippers and smoking jacket, equipped with scrapbooking supplies to while away the afternoon while the ladies took their outing. Miss Darlington had brooked no further disagreement. An excursion was vital for Pleasance's mental health. Besides, someone needed to carry the coats, parasols, medicines, spare daggers, coins, handkerchiefs, and smelling salts that a lady required for any afternoon's stroll. In addition to pushing the wheeled chair, Pleasance was so laden that, although her mental health may have benefited from the excursion, her physical health was now in significant peril.

Some way down the lane, they encountered Miss Fairweather and Miss Jane Fairweather, also heading into the village for tea. Both were dressed plainly, for being homeless they had been forced to borrow clothes from the other Society ladies until they could steal some of their own. Miss Fairweather's gown bore only five gold fringes on its bodice, and the bustle was no more than four feet wide. Jane was in brown. In contrast to Cecilia's fashionable ensemble of pale blue and cream, she looked positively dreary.

Cecilia would rather have worn plain brown herself, but Miss Darlington liked her in elegant clothes "for the sake of the starving children in Bethnal Green," who presumably would get emotional nourishment (almost as filling as soup and porridge) from Cecilia's style, if only they could see it.

"Such a good idea of yours to have tea in the village," Olivia said to the senior Miss Fairweather.

"Yes, although I hope none of the locals have typhoid," Miss Darlington added.

The senior women fell into the sort of pleasant conversation about enteric fever and other rigors of farming life that only wealthy urban ladies can have. Jane and Cecilia glanced at each other, whereupon Jane brought out her book of battle poems and read in pointed silence.

Cecilia smiled. She did not particularly want to talk with Jane anyway. She was too preoccupied with her own thoughts. Over and again she strove to analyze her last meeting with Captain Lightbourne. The mere recollection of his ungloved hands gripping her wrists caused the same rush of blood, even all these days later. Had he somehow infected her with a malaise through his touch? And why had he, ostensibly Lady Armitage's hired assassin, been stealing houses on behalf of Captain Morvath? That question made her frown in bemusement, and she hastily tipped her parasol to act as a shield, for a proper lady did not make such an exceedingly vulgar display of emotions in public.

"Hello there," came a woman's voice, and they all looked over to see Anne Brown emerge from behind a hedge, rearranging her skirts as she did so. "I've just been going to see my aunt," she explained, and everyone lowered their gaze politely in the face of this bald euphemism.

"Are you walking alone?" Olivia asked.

"Oply ran on ahead with Tom Eames, mad keen to experience the village graveyard 'for literary reasons'—something about Mary Shelley, who is a lady author, they tell me. It sounded like a wholesome enough activity, so I allowed them to go unchaperoned. Perhaps you'd like to join them there, Cecilia?"

Cecilia, guessing how Mary Shelley's example might inspire a boy and girl to visit a graveyard without adult supervision, but not wishing to enlighten the girl's grandmother, quietly demurred. The group continued toward the village.

"How is Mrs. Eames going with repairs to her house after that dreadful Lightbourne shot it down?" Miss Darlington asked.

"Steadily," Miss Brown replied. "The roof has been patched, and the house managed to float about four feet off the ground this morning, traveling half a mile closer to us until it was stopped by a recalcitrant cow. The biggest problem remains in Thomasina having lost her voice due to all the smoke, for the house responds only to her."

"Pleasance has a honey and ginger remedy for throat damage, don't you, dear?" Miss Darlington said.

"Actually it's a skin cream to thwart vampires from the necks of innocent maidens," Pleasance said, "but Mrs. Eames is welcome to try it if she wants."

An uncomfortable silence followed, broken by Olivia saying to Miss Brown, "It's very Christian of you to accommodate Thomasina's son at this time."

"One does like to do one's duty whenever possible. And Tom's a good boy. He and Oply get on like—well, like a house on fire, ha ha."

"Ha ha."

"Yesterday he offered to help with her math lessons. They spent all afternoon shut up in the library, toiling over multiplication. And last night I thought I heard Oply cry out, and so went to her room, only to find Tom in his nightshirt at the door. He'd also heard the noise, he said, and rushed to see if she was safe. He must have run dreadfully fast to get there before I did, considering his room is upstairs. Indeed, the effort was apparent in his flushed face. Such a fine, upstanding young man."

"Good heavens, Cecilia, are you all right?" Miss Darlington asked with alarm as Cecilia began coughing.

"Yes, thank you, Aunty," Cecilia managed to say through her coughs. "I must have swallowed a speck of dust."

Miss Darlington frowned. "I knew it was a bad idea for you to walk so far."

"I'm fine, truly," Cecilia said, but Miss Darlington was having none of it.

"Cecilia is very delicate," she explained.

The Fairweathers, Olivia, and Miss Brown assessed this with their own eyes. Cecilia stood impassively as they looked her up and down. Growing up with a dozen honorary aunties inures a girl to such inspections.

"Not much like her mother," Miss Fairweather said in a pursed voice.

Out of the corner of her eye, Cecilia saw Olivia and Miss Brown make the sign of the cross.

"I was relieved to see you not joining the chase toward Northangerland Abbey, Jem," Miss Brown added. "Imagine if Morvath got hold of her!"

Jane emitted a small sound that could not have been a snigger, for when Cecilia glanced at her she was once again occupied closely with her book. It occurred to Cecilia that, if Captain Lightbourne turned out not to be a double-crossing henchman of her father, but merely an innocent assassin after all, she could hire him to bash Jane Fairweather to death with that little book of battle poems.

"Cecilia will never fall into Morvath's hands," Miss Darlington declared, snapping her fan shut. "Nor will she be like her mother, who succumbed to the dubious charms of a handsome and mysterious pirate simply because he had a fancy sword and quoted poetry to her. Are we going for tea or not?"

Pleasance began propelling the wheeled chair fiercely along the road, stirring up enough road dust to make them all cough if they were so inclined. Olivia and Miss Brown stared with unfocused eyes into the middle distance, no doubt imagining fancy swords; Miss Fairweather kept looking over her shoulder as if expecting Morvath to leap out at any moment; Jane read; and Cecilia for her part was so bent on not recollecting Captain Lightbourne's handsome face and enchanting smile that the company was at The Ancient Mariner, the teahouse at the heart of Ottery St. Mary village, before she even realized.

On the footpath outside they met with Essie and her husband, Lysander, each of whom was carrying a child on their back. They had been introduced a few years ago while tunneling out of a Turkish prison and were known to be the happiest married couple in the Society, to the regret of many who felt fine-boned, black-haired Essie would be particularly suited to an elegant suit of widow's weeds.

" 'The guests are met, the feast is set,' " Lysander welcomed them, eliciting a smile from Cecilia. The other ladies stared blankly, not being acquainted with Samuel Coleridge's most famous poem. Lysander winked at Cecilia (for he dimly remembered being Lysander the Lout beneath the polish of marriage, fatherhood, and routine villainy). "We have been exploring and are now regathering our breath before we enter the fray."

At this, the children, being well-brought-up young pirates, shouted, "Weigh anchor!" and brandished small wooden swords in exuberant fashion. Miss Brown, never one to shirk an educational opportunity, promptly drew her own sword from the scabbard half-hidden among her skirts.

"En garde!" she cried, much to the horror of Miss Darlington's sensibilities—"A lady should not use French on the street," she admonished Cecilia, although Cecilia herself had said nothing—and a mock skirmish began. The children, directing their parents like battle-houses, giggled with delight. Olivia tried to confound them with the flapping of her fan, Miss Fairweather called out directions, and Miss Darlington, frowning, furled her parasol and jabbed it like a lace-swathed bayonet at the legs of the participants.

Pleasance took this opportunity to lean close to Cecilia and whisper, "Are you all right, miss?"

"Perfectly fine, dear," Cecilia said. "It was only a bit of dust."

"I meant about your murdered mother and hideous, evil father," Pleasance said, and then flushed as she watched Cecilia's eyes widen. "Beg pardon, miss, I said the wrong thing, didn't I? I'm ever so sorry, sometimes bad spirits possess my voice and I just can't stop them. I meant, 'your dearly departed' mother."

"That's quite all right," Cecilia murmured and, glancing up, caught Jane scowling at her a moment before returning to her book.

Cecilia shifted to open the teahouse door. A little bell sounded, and the smell of freshly baked scones wafted from within. Cecilia looked in at what appeared to be an Impressionist's fever dream. Ruffles, ruches, bows, feathers, laces, furs, faux flowers (and the blanched faces of the teahouse staff) informed her that the rest of the Wisteria Society were already present.

"Aunty," she said, standing aside and gesturing so that Miss Darlington might precede her. The group entered the teahouse.

Which is to say, they closed parasols, sheathed swords, disembarked parents, determined precedence, angled, then reangled the wheeled chair, pardoned one another for any inconvenience, thanked one another for any assistance, and then entered the teahouse.

"Ahoy!" the children shouted.

"Ahoy!" the crowd cheered back. Teacups, cake forks, and pistols were uplifted in greeting. The staff cowered.

"Cecilia dear," Miss Darlington said as she waited for Essie's husband to obtain her a seat at the long table, "why don't you see if the teahouse has a library? I'm sure you will find the chitchat of old ladies tedious—it will be all about firming lotions and bulletproof eyeglasses and the best guns to use when you have arthritis. Pleasance can attend to my needs."

"A library in a village teahouse?"

"It's worth investigating. Perhaps they have scintillating novels about—er, Victoria sponges. This is not really an occasion for young people."

Cecilia watched the children clamber onto chairs so as to better reach a plate of cakes. Jane Fairweather was pouring tea for her grandmother. Clearly Miss Darlington wanted to be rid of her for the duration of the meeting and was snatching at the merest excuse.

Cecilia felt unsurprised. Every time someone had tried to discuss Morvath this week, Miss Darlington had sent her from the room on a spurious errand. Cecilia had fetched more handkerchiefs, cups of tea, cursed goblets, snuffboxes, and shawls than she even knew existed in Darlington House. More than once she'd heard the ladies whisper, *"Don't talk about him in front of the poor girl, she'll be disturbed,"* and she'd struggled to repress a smile.

Actually, she rather appreciated being kept in the dark, for that meant the ladies were themselves blind to her own scheming. In a secret copy of *Agnes Grey*, tucked beneath her bed's mattress, she had written notes on her various plans for patricide. Every night she read them through, added ideas, sketched diagrams, and tried not to remember a sword falling, a woman screaming—

"Run!"

—until her pen became a dagger slicing through several pages of the book.

Once Morvath was dead, the Wisteria Society would no longer whisper protectively or send her from the room so she wouldn't be disturbed. They would give her the best seat at the tea table.

Besides, nothing ever really disturbed her . . . except that charming and handsome—er, which is to say *cheeky and utterly deplorable—* Captain Lightbourne.

And maybe Jane Fairweather's smirk, which was presently being directed at her again. Cecilia drew herself out of contemplation to stare coldly back at the other woman.

"Why doesn't Cecilia visit the village library?" Jane suggested.

"Oh no, dear," the senior Miss Fairweather said. "She couldn't go walking alone and"—her tone dropped into darkness—"unchaperoned."

Miss Darlington waved a hand at this concern. "Cecilia is twenty-one, quite old enough to go out and about alone."

Cecilia opened her mouth to remind her aunt she was nineteen, then closed it again in silence. She had been told Chanters House in Ottery St. Mary had a magnificent private library, from which perhaps she could procure a new copy of *Wuthering Heights*. The only defect in this plan was that she might come upon Constantinopla and Tom imitating Mary Shelley in the graveyard. A lady did not want her sensibilities ruffled whilst on her way to burgle a library.

"Only if you are certain," she replied with all due hesitance, but her feet were already carrying her back toward the door.

"Absolutely certain," Miss Darlington assured her. Jane nodded encouragement, despite Miss Fairweather's frown. Cecilia noticed from the corner of her eye Anne Brown laying a sketch of Northangerland Abbey on the table among plates of tiny sandwiches and asparagus rolls. Someone embedded their dagger in it. Cecilia took another step back.

"You look very pale," Jane said. "Do go out, get some sun."

"But—" Miss Fairweather began.

"Excellent idea," Miss Darlington interjected. "Only keep your hat on, and use your parasol, and don't, whatever you do, remove your gloves. Remember the Great Peril, dear."

At that phrase, half the company went silent—including Millie the Monster, who had a quizzing glass up to her unpatched eye, and Bloodhound Bess, whose grin seemed to extend almost to her left ear by reason of a scar obtained when she tried to steal a fur from a Russian tsarina. Cecilia felt like a child being tested on her lessons.

"Freckles," she recited, and the ladies nodded with satisfaction.

Thus it was that Cecilia found herself entirely at liberty on a temperate afternoon within walking distance of a public library, a famed private library, two cake shops, and a museum. That she had Jane Fairweather to thank for this was the most extraordinary part. But Cecilia did not look a gift horse in the mouth (although she'd read enough history that she ought to have known better). Raising her parasol, she crossed the street—

And then paused, overcome with freedom. Where might she go first?

A woman in black walked past with a wrapped object approximately the length of a butter churn or rifle. "Excuse me," Cecilia said, and the woman paused. "Would you be able to direct me toward Chanters House?"

"Sorry," the woman replied. "Not from around here." Without further word, she hoisted her parcel against her shoulder and crossed the street toward the teahouse.

"I think it's that direction," said a gentleman passerby, tipping his head toward the northwest. Cecilia was caught between gratitude, alarm that a male stranger had addressed her, and bewilderment that he was carrying a steering wheel beneath one arm.

"Thank you," she said, and he lifted his hat politely before crossing the street.

She looked in the direction the gentleman had indicated, wondering if it might be wiser to ask for more specific guidance from a shopkeeper. Her immediate options were limited: a gentlemen's tailor, a butchery, and a purveyor of popular magazines. Clearly the only shop she might enter without damage to her reputation was the butchery, but she disliked the atmosphere of violence within such a place. She was turning to see what might exist further along the street when a woman almost collided with her. Cecilia instinctively reached for her concealed pistol before remembering she was surrounded by innocent civilians.

"Watch where you're going," the woman scolded, then hurried across the street, drawing a long knife from her sleeve as she went. Another woman with a cutlass met up with her and they nodded to each other before continuing toward the teahouse. Cecilia turned back to the shops, thinking that she could visit the bakery farther along, where she might ask for directions and purchase some shortbread at the same time.

Three large men in black coats, each carrying guns, strode down the center of the street. Pedestrians began hurrying away. Cecilia checked her fob watch. Half past one. She might even have enough time to tour the village museum on her way back from the library. She had been on the lookout lately for a small silver dish in which to keep her earrings, and museums often had fine, inadequately guarded specimens of these.

Pleased with this plan, she replaced her fob watch, straightened her gloves, closed her parasol, withdrew her pistol from a lace-trimmed pocket, and turned sharply on her heel.

With two quick shots she felled one of the men in the middle of the street and sent the others running. She then spun back to embed her parasol's blade in the arm of a woman hurrying up behind her with a sword. The butcher slammed his door shut, the tailor pulled down his blinds, and as Cecilia began striding toward the teahouse she noted with relief that the civilian population had fled. There was nothing worse than having to shout at people to run—most indelicate indeed.

Tossing aside her blood-soaked parasol, she pulled a small revolver from her waistband and shot it and the pistol at the remaining two men just as they reached the teahouse's door. A bullet skimmed one's arm, but it was too late—The Ancient Mariner was beginning to levitate. Both men leaped up through the open door and slammed it shut behind them, and the building rose sharply.

Cecilia considered shooting at the windows to destabilize the magic but decided the risk to the innocent pirates within would be too great. She could do nothing but stand helplessly in the street, laden with guns and regret, as the hijacked teahouse was maneuvered up and away from Ottery St. Mary.

The entire Wisteria Society had been kidnapped over tea and scones!

"Bother," Cecilia muttered. It appeared that she'd have no chance of getting to the Chanters House library anytime soon.

"Arrrghh!" screamed someone furiously behind her. Turning, she shot the sword-wielding woman who was attempting once again to rush at her. The bullet struck the woman's leg and sent her sprawling in the dusty street. Cecilia watched her for a moment as she cried and writhed in pain, then went to knock at the butchery door.

"Go away!" the butcher shouted from within. "I have knives and I'm not afraid to use them!"

"That is exactly what I need," Cecilia replied. "May I beg your service? There are two people bearing gunshot wounds out here. Neither is fatally hurt but they require medical treatment. Would you be so kind as to assist them? I must hurry away myself."

"What? You want me to what?"

"I believe butchers have surgical skills? Thank you, sir, for helping, it is very neighborly of you."

"But that's just a myth about butchers! I can't even saw the cow bones neatly!"

"And yet I notice you have fine premises here, so you must be intelligent and industrious. I'll leave the injured in your capable hands."

"You want me to save the lives of two pirates that you shot?"

"Yes. I'm terribly grateful." She stepped away, then, upon further thought, returned to the door. "Just perhaps don't wear any valuables while helping them. Good day, sir, and my regards to your wife—er, if you have one, that is."

Holstering her guns and gathering up her skirts, she hastened back through the village and along the hedge-rimmed lanes toward that distant field where the Wisteria Society battlehouses stood waiting for mistresses who would now be long in returning—if they ever did.

✹ 8 ✹

GRAND THEFT DOMICILE—MANNA FROM HEAVEN—
CAPTAIN MORVATH DEFINES CAPTAINCY TO CAPTAIN LIGHTBOURNE—
A SNIVELING JELLYFISH—GHOSTS OF CECILIA'S PAST—MORE MANNA—
HOT-AIR BALLOONS—THEY MEET AGAIN—
CAPTAIN LIGHTBOURNE IS UNMASKED (TWICE)—
A DUEL ENDING IN AN EXPLOSION—CECILIA QUITS THE FIELD

Gentleness! How far more potent is it than force! Captain Morvath
knew this to be so and calculated that, while the Wisteria Society
could resist his wrath if he went into the field with all guns blazing,
they would grow pliant under his surreptitious breaking and entering.
Therefore, while The Ancient Mariner was being hijacked in swift and
dramatic fashion, back at the strawberry field the gentlemen, servants,
and tiger, on alert for frontal attack, were unaware that Morvath's
henchmen were picking their door and window locks, slipping in un-
observed, and whispering the flight incantation beneath stairs and behind drapes. By the time the households realized they had been
abducted, there was little they could do.

Mr. Rotunder and his crack troop of chambermaids did attempt to
overcome their foes, but this resulted in the house crashing into a cow
byre near Buckerell. Morvath's crew were defeated but the house was

on its side and Mr. Rotunder in need of a glass eye and several wooden teeth to add to his collection of replacement body parts. Therefore the household played no further role in the coming drama and instead had their own spin-off, wherein they reoriented their house with much hilarity, fixed the byre, dallied with the local gentlemen in humorous fashion, thwarted the robbery of the local tavern (and then robbed it themselves), and enjoyed bacon and eggs every morning thanks to the obliging farmer and his wife, who had been saying only the day before that the byre needed a new roof, and took these events as the generosity of the heavens.

The other households wisely surrendered and were transported unharmed to Morvath's secret domain deep within the Blackdown Hills.

Ned watched the piracy from beneath an oak tree where he had established himself as supervisor of events, and where he sat drinking wine from a bottle and laughing every now and again to himself. It had all been too easy. Considering these people were professional thieves, they had pathetically inadequate defenses against theft.

Ned would rather have been involved in hijacking The Ancient Mariner, to ensure it went safely, but Morvath assured him his mole within the Wisteria Society would have everything in hand—subduing the ladies with a sleeping potion in their tea, securing the premises, removing the premises—and the more Ned argued, the more suspicious Morvath became.

"Are you not employed by me?" the captain asked. "Is not your role to do whatever I require?"

"Of course," Ned lied smoothly. "But as regards to your daughter, I thought—"

"You thought."

"—that I was meant to—"

"Get her to me long before now. Yes. I grew tired of waiting. So now I have her, and the entire Wisteria Society as well, in one foul swoop. That is how a real captain does it."

"I'm a real—"

"I mean a captain with an abbey, not a house currently at the bottom of the sea."

"Actually, it's still on the beach."

"Broken into pieces. As you will be if you don't obey me, Edward. But I am not cruel. I am not vicious. After I've tortured and killed the Wisteria ladies, I'm more than happy to give you one of their houses as a reward for your service."

"Thank you," Ned said with appropriate gratitude.

"And you will receive the honor of an invitation to Cecilia's wedding, although you'll need to hire a decent tailor."

"Cecilia is to be married?" Ned inspected a smudge on his thumbnail as if it was of more consequence to him than the answer to that question.

"Indeed. I have in my house the Bassingthwaite heir—"

"Her cousin?"

"Yes. Frederick is a sniveling jellyfish, but upon marrying him Cecilia will become mistress of Starkthorn Castle, the greatest man-o'-war in England, not counting my own abbey, of course."

Ned worked to smile in response. He knew the stories about Starkthorn Castle. Its owners, the merchant family Bassingthwaite, had been on the up and up (i.e., the British definition: "becoming successful," not the American one: "honest and sincere") even before they learned how to fly their premises. No haberdashers were more elegant or more ruthlessly ambitious; piracy was almost an easing back of operations for them.

He'd also heard endlessly from Morvath about how Cecilia

Bassingthwaite's mother, also named Cecilia, ran from that castle one night into Morvath's arms, escaping her repressive mother Cess (Cecilia) and grandmother Sissy (Cecilia), renaming herself Cilla, and swearing she would not return to Starkthorn again unless to burn the place down.

And he'd heard from everyone else how Morvath found her in the garden that night and snatched her away against her will.

Ned guessed something between those versions was true. Cilla had ever been an enigmatic figure. She had renounced her proud pirate heritage to marry a man whose only crime up until then had been the composition of a novel so bad publishers had him threatened with legal action if he ever submitted to them again. But by the time Cilla left him, Morvath had gone from dreaming about literary fame to amassing a Gothic abbey, a great stockpile of weapons, and several notebooks filled with plans to destroy England.

Ned was unsure if Cilla had encouraged Morvath's decline or if she had merely been one of the treasures he'd always intended to capture along the way. After all, she was a Darlington on her mother's side, and Morvath hated that family with a passion. Eloping with her had been the perfect way to hurt them.

But as a Bassingthwaite on her father's side, Cilla was practically a pirate princess. Ned could not help but wonder—although Cilla was universally mourned as Morvath's victim, just who had taught him the flying spell and where to get a good deal on machine guns?

It was all as melodramatic as a Brontë story, and it certainly involved as many ghosts. Cilla and her foremothers, Morvath's adoptive parents (who had perished in a mysterious fire while punting on the Avon River), and all the other people he had gone on to kill. Thinking about it, Ned's smile flattened, and he had to glance away before the captain noticed.

In truth, Morvath probably would have become an evil mastermind regardless of who his parents or wife had been. There was a madness in him that need not be traced any farther back than his own broken mind. And now he had a full fleet of battlehouses at his command. He could move forward with his dream to burn down Parliament, seize the throne, and usher in a new age of tyranny, awful poetry, and boring fashions.

All with Ned as his trusted right-hand man.

There was only one apparent flaw in this plan—and it was currently running down the lane in a light blue dress, hat askew and face bared recklessly to the elements.

"Well, well, well," Ned murmured to himself with a smile as he got to his feet. "If it isn't the best Cecilia of them all, falling like manna from heaven right into my hands."

Cecilia had seen the houses rising like hot-air balloons over the trees— albeit rectangular, rigid, and less colorful, without flames beneath, so in fact nothing like hot-air balloons, but a failure of simile was the least of her problems at this moment. She actually resorted to running down the lane, skirts hoisted to her knees, stockings exposed. But there was no one to see her disgraceful behavior. There was no one at all.

Only a lady's bonnet tumbled over the grass in the magic-stirred breeze, ribbons fluttering wistfully.

Cecilia stopped in the middle of the field, staring at its emptiness. The houses were dwindling into the northeast distance. The silence was like a slap, leaving her dazed.

"Goodness gracious," she said, and took off her hat.

"There's no need to be quite so dramatic."

Cecilia sighed. Aggravation clenched around her—and yet it felt almost pleasant, a sense of relief. She was not alone in the world after all.

Flicking her hat to unsheath the blades in its brim, she spun on her heel—only to find a pistol pointed at her. Behind it, Captain Lightbourne smiled affably. He reached out with his free hand, took her hat, and tossed it as far as a disk of straw decorated with ribbons and a feather would go—which is to say, about one and a half feet, before boomeranging back so that he had to step aside before its blades sliced him.

"We meet again, Miss Bassingthwaite."

"Captain Lightbourne," Cecilia replied. "I seem to have been mistaken in my impression that you serve Lady Armitage. Clearly you are Captain Morvath's lackey."

"Not at all."

Cecilia frowned. "What do you mean, sir? Which of those are you not?"

"Both."

Her frown deepened. "You are being most annoyingly ungrammatical. And I have a ladies' society to rescue. So if you will excuse me—"

She went to turn but he cocked the hammer of his gun, and she froze.

"You wouldn't shoot me."

His smile tilted. "I am employed to assassinate you, madam."

"And yet you have proven slow to do so."

"That is because I am employed to protect you."

For the first time in her life, Cecilia went so far as to scowl. "You are a very aggravating man."

"Thank you. I do my best under difficult circumstances. It's an honor to have provoked your anger, although I'm still hoping to make you smile."

"I do not smile at murderers."

"But I haven't murdered anyone, Miss Bassingthwaite."

"So my aunt was correct in her evaluation of your skill, or rather lack thereof."

His own smile tilted in the other direction, then collapsed completely. "No. That is, I mean to say—I could have murdered someone, had I chosen to do so. Just as I could murder you right now."

"Except you won't. Kindly put down the gun and let me be on my way."

"I can't do that. For you see, madam, regardless of how I was employed, my real mission is to keep you from your father. I see in your eye a determination to head in his direction so as to rescue the Wisteria Society, and I am obliged to stop you."

"Why?" Cecilia almost put her hands on her hips before recollecting her dignity. "Exactly who are you?"

He shrugged. "It depends on whom you ask. To Lady Armitage, I am Eduardo de Luca, Italian mercenary, hired to kill the beautiful ward of her archnemesis. To Captain Morvath, I am Edward Lightbourne, a pirate just wanting new premises and willing to do whatever it takes to get them. Which means stealing houses and returning Morvath's long-lost daughter safely to his care. (This is where you shudder with fear.)"

"I am not frightened, Mr. Lightbourne."

"Captain."

"So you say."

"But it's true. For I am also known to Her Majesty as Ned Smith, a captain of the royal secret service, charged among other things with keeping Miss Cecilia Morvath out of her father's hands. And I am—"

"You!" came a shout.

Ned sighed. Grabbing Cecilia by the arm, he pulled her against him and held the gun to her temple, as Constantinopla and Tom came racing across the field.

"Fiend!" Constantinopla yelled. "Blighter! Rogue!"

"Hello, Oply," Ned said wearily.

"Where have all the houses gone?" Tom asked in bewilderment.

"Hijacked by Captain Morvath," Cecilia said. "This fellow helped orchestrate it."

"I'm not surprised!" Constantinopla declared. "Unscrupulous! Traitor! Rake!"

"You are acquainted?" Cecilia asked.

"This is Teddy Luxe!" Constantinopla shouted, her face as pink as her hair bow. "My fencing master!"

"Oh." Cecilia recalled Constantinopla's descriptions of hot, melting wax and undulating hips and tried with sudden urgency to pull herself from Captain Lightbourne's grip. It only resulted in him drawing her even tighter against him. "But he has no mustache," she said rather inanely.

"It was horsehair," Ned confessed. "Itched like crazy."

"Horsehair?!" Constantinopla's face progressed from pink straight through red to a violent purple. "As false as your seductive words! You said you would see us in Monday's class, but by the end of the weekend you had vanished, leaving not even a stray button or lock of hair to entertain our forlorn hopes!"

"I am sorry for the deception, Miss Brown. But at least you are now proficient in fencing and tango dancing."

"Is that all you taught her?" Cecilia asked.

"Good God, madam, what do you take me for?"

"A pirate. A thief. A devious assassin double-crossing everyone . . ."

"Yes, but she is a mere child," Ned replied, waving his gun briefly, expressively, at Constantinopla. "Of course I didn't—"

"I'm not a child," Constantinopla retorted, and would have said further but Tom took sudden hold of her and pulled her around to face him.

"What does he mean?" the young man demanded. "You told me you were nineteen."

"I am nineteen!" Constantinopla replied; then, catching the eye of both Ned and Cecilia, she ducked her head. "In my heart, at least."

"Your heart," Tom echoed flatly. "I see. And what age is your mouth? And your . . . other physical features?"

Constantinopla muttered something, but Tom clearly heard, for he repeated it in a horrified shout. Constantinopla, falling back on her training as a lady and a pirate, looked up with a flash of anger and a tut-tutting of the tongue.

"Thomas Eames, we have been in the same society for years. If you can't count, the blame hardly rests with me."

Tom debated this in a heated tone, to which Constantinopla replied furiously, and in less than a minute they had swords drawn and were proceeding to duel over their mutually stolen honor. Ned stepped back, releasing Cecilia, and they exchanged a blank look. They then edged away from the angry couple.

"You have to admit," Ned said, "she shows good form with a sword. Oply," he called out. "Lift your hand more."

"Why were you working as a fencing master at her school?" Cecilia inquired.

"It was the premier educational facility for children of the high-flying set—in other words, pirate girls. We supposed you would attend."

"No, Aunty believes too much education corrupts the delicate mind of young ladies. I received only the basic instruction at home— reading, writing, horse riding, navigation, weapons handling, piano, harp, the principles of burglary, geography, arithmetic, anatomy, metal-work, confidence trickery, history, battle tactics, dining etiquette."

"Do you ever feel the loss of a thorough education?"

"Sometimes. I should like to know how to cook, and to embroider my own gun wipers. She really does have good form. Oply dear, move your foot back a little. And thrust on a steeper incline if you're trying to gut him."

"I'm aiming for something lower than his gut," Constantinopla replied.

"Understandable. So what is your real name, Captain Lightbourne?"

"God knows, Miss Bassingthwaite. I invite you to call me Ned. We are surely well enough acquainted by now."

"I don't know . . ."

He turned, catching her by the arm, smiling at her with the full power of his charm. "Madam—my dear—Cecilia—"

"Miss Bassingthwaite."

"Really?"

"Yes." She tugged her arm from his grip. "Or nothing at all, if you please, for we must end our association today. I will be attending to the rescue of my aunt and her friends, and you—well, that is not my business."

"But it is," he said, following her as she began to stride across the field in the direction the houses had flown. "The Queen herself ordered me to protect you—"

"Protect me," she repeated dubiously, not looking back.

"Well, her exact word might have been *neutralized*, but—"

Cecilia frowned sidelong at him. "Neutralized? Why? What have I done to offend her? Apart from rob some of her institutions, but that is hardly a capital offense."

"She and her advisers fear you may become like your father, and it was deemed prudent to forestall that by, um, disempowering you."

A sudden thought burned through her mind: Was this also why

she'd not been given a seat at the senior table? Was the Wisteria Society keeping her disempowered?

"I see," she said coldly, both to Ned and to the absent pirate women. Her stomach lurched, but she simply walked faster, as if she could out-race the sick feeling. Ned hurried to keep up.

"But you are nothing like your father, Sissy, and so you need protecting, not neutralizing. Please just let me take you to Windsor, where you will be safe."

"For a secret service agent, you don't listen very well," she said. "Once again, my name is Miss Bassingthwaite. I am not, and never will be, Sissy. And I have no interest in being safe. Wait!" She stopped abruptly, and hope lit Ned's countenance. But she only turned and began walking back. "I forgot my hat."

"Never mind your hat." He followed her with exasperation. "You will come with me."

"No, I won't."

"Yes."

"No."

He stepped in front of her, forcing her to stop, and pointed his gun once again at her face. Instantly Cecilia drew her own gun and held it in parallel to his.

"I cannot leave my aunt in Morvath's clutches. He has caused her to suffer enough for one lifetime."

"I understand. But walking into Northangerland Abbey alone is insane."

"It was my"—she paused to shuffle away from the dueling couple, who were dancing around each other, swords clashing—"my childhood home. I know all the secret doors and passageways."

"And so does Morvath. You will be captured within—Oply, lift your hand more—within minutes. The Queen will send a squad—"

"And you know how that will end. But one person, trained in stealth, could slip in and do all kinds of damage before she was noticed. Tom, be careful not to step on my hat."

"If I take you to Windsor—"

"I will escape."

"Yes, you undoubtedly will. Very well, madam, I shall take you to Lady Armitage instead."

Cecilia elevated one eyebrow. "I beg your pardon?"

They lifted their guns to the sky as Constantinopla shoved Tom through the space between them. The boy staggered but regained his balance and rushed back to re-engage the fight. Cecilia and Ned aimed their guns once more at each other's faces.

"Lady Armitage has the last remaining Society battlehouse," Ned explained. "It's fully equipped with cannons and a well-stocked armory, and I know where to find it. We can steal it, use it as a base."

"What about Starkthorn Castle?"

"Morvath stole its entire load of weapons. It's nothing now but a big stone house with emptied attics and bored ghosts."

"Oh." Her expression wilted.

"I'm sorry, I know it was your maternal family home."

"Actually I've never set foot there. I was only thinking of the loss of all that cannon."

"I do have a friend who would loan me his house, but there's no time to track him down. Lady Armitage is our only resource."

"So you will help me?"

He shrugged. "You're giving me no other choice. I'm honor-bound by royal order to keep you safe. Or, you know, kill you, but I hope it doesn't come to that, Sissy."

"Cecilia. I mean, Miss Bassingthwaite. Where is Lady Armitage located? We have no time to lose."

"Lyme Regis. I'll steal a carriage; we can be there tomorrow."

"No, I'll steal a carriage."

"As you wish."

They stared at each other for a moment longer, then withdrew their guns, holstering them. Ned stepped into the duel, taking the sword from Constantinopla's hand.

"Watch," he said to her. "Right hand up, left foot back, and so—" He thrust the sword to block Tom's, then gave a sharp twist, and Tom stumbled back as his sword was jolted from his grip. It landed on Cecilia's hat, which exploded in a puff of smoke and feathers.

Everyone stared at it.

"Oh dear," Constantinopla said after a shocked moment. "What will you do, Cecilia? You're now exposed to the Great Peril."

"I'll protect her from it," Ned said promptly.

Constantinopla gave him a bewildered look. "From the sun?"

"I—er— Listen, no peril is greater now than Captain Morvath, who will destroy the very foundation of our peaceful civilization if we don't take quick action!"

"Maybe," Constantinopla said, "but have you ever tried to get rid of freckles? Not all the lemon juice and bicarbonate in the world is effective."

Ned blinked. He glanced at Tom Eames, who shrugged helplessly, and then at Cecilia, who stood impassive, emblazoned by the lowering light. Her hair was only barely secured in its braided crown, long, fine strands falling over her shoulders; her face gleamed like polished, unfreckled marble. Suddenly, Ned realized he was the one in peril. He was "a young man and his love lay not truly in his heart but in his eyes"—er, no, the other way around. Then Cecilia's impassivity slipped a little into suspiciousness as she looked back at him, and he realized he was staring.

"Right," he said, raising his hand to brush back his hair—unfortunately, the hand that was holding Constantinopla's sword, thereby nearly eviscerating Tom. "For God's sake, boy, be more careful where you stand. We shall get on our way. Cecilia, you and I will find a carriage. These two—"

"She can't go off with you unless she has a chaperone," Constantinopla interjected.

"Nonsense," Ned replied. "I am an agent of Her Majesty the Queen. I have the highest morals. She will be entirely safe."

"Regardless, I must accompany her, for the sake of appearances."

Ned sighed. "Now, see here, Oply, you are too young for battle. Take lodgings in the village, and I'll send someone to fetch you."

"I'm not too young! I'm only three years below Cecilia." (Tom groaned at this reminder.) "Besides, I've trained all my life!"

"I know, I've seen what you can do. You're going to make a fine pirate one day. But not this day."

"This is discrimination due to my age!"

"Yes."

"I am outraged!"

"No doubt."

"Cecilia doesn't even have her own house. Why should she get to have all the fun while I'm stuck in a little village?"

Tom cleared his voice, wanting to join the discussion, but they ignored him.

"Because she is the daughter of Morvath himself—"

"Don't think any of us have forgotten that. We are all too aware she grew up in the enemy's house."

"—and it's not that she'll be having an adventure, but rather traveling with me for her safety. She cannot be left alone."

"Excuse me," Tom murmured.

"Not now," Ned said, waving a dismissive hand in his direction. "Oply, without supervision Miss Bassingthwaite is liable to be assassinated or kidnapped for ransom or seized by Morvath's henchmen. You are a strong and resourceful young woman, but she is vulnerable, and must be protected at all times."

"Um," Tom said, and Ned turned to him with a scowl.

"What is it?" he demanded.

Tom did not reply, merely pointed toward the edge of the field. Ned and Constantinopla turned to see Cecilia standing in the lane, hijacking a carriage at gunpoint.

"Oh," Ned said. "Right. You two, go to the village and stay there." He tossed down the sword and began to run, calling behind him as he went, "I'll send someone to take you to Windsor. Don't move until then. Miss Bassingthwaite, wait for me!"

Tom and Constantinopla watched in silence as Ned caught up with Cecilia and assisted her in evicting two ladies, a gentleman, and a driver from the carriage.

They crossed their arms, fascinated, as the two pirates argued over who should take the reins.

They waved and called out farewells as Cecilia drove away with Ned at her side pointing out a right turn, which she did not take.

Then they glanced at each other.

"Sixteen," Tom said darkly.

Constantinopla shrugged. "Give or take a month."

"I'm going to have to marry you."

"Oh dear, how unexpected."

"Seriously?"

"The ring I want is in Collingwood & Co. I've cased the joint and marked the display; it should be easy enough for you to get it. And we'll be honeymooning in Whippingham, where Princess Beatrice was married, just as soon as the seamstress has finished making my dress."

"I suppose," Tom said reluctantly. And as the breeze picked up Cecilia's mangled hat, he thought in a daze that its scorched ribbons were his life flashing past his eyes.

"Now we must be on our way," Constantinopla said, picking up her sword.

"Yes," Tom agreed, blinking himself back to the present. He lifted his own sword, pointing it northward. "To the village!"

Constantinopla scoffed. "Of course not to the village. You don't think I'm going to obey Teddy Luxe, do you? Hurry up, we have work to do."

✺ 9 ✺

DRIVING INTO THE SUNSET—HIGHWAY ROBBERY—
WORDSWORTH IS DEVOURED—CAPTAIN LIGHTBOURNE INSISTS—
DISGUISE—CECILIA MAKES A FATEFUL DECISION—
POETRY (INTERRUPTED)—A SICK COACHMAN (INVENTED)—
THE KNOWLE HOTEL

Captain Lightbourne had not breathed a word for miles, or dropped one hint of tenderness or affection, and so Cecilia had been supremely happy. To be near him, and to not have to hear him talk, was enough for her appreciation. She did not feel him particularly worthy to be spoken to—incapable of understanding, in fact, and therefore she encouraged the silence with her own.

The lane ambled through Devon's soft fields toward the fat, dipping sun. Cecilia did not drive the horses fast, although their pace frustrated her, for she knew if they tired it would only slow the journey more. She considered unhitching them, leaving the carriage behind. But the animals had probably never been ridden before, and even if they had, the carriage contained no tack. Furthermore, Cecilia was dressed in colors and therefore could not possibly be seen on horseback.

They entered an oak wood, and the world became a poem of luminous foliage and gentle, glimmering shadows. Ned had some time ago climbed into the carriage to rest from the strain of enduring Cecilia's disdainful silence. The horses trudged on incuriously, allowing Cecilia to focus on seething. So the Wisteria Society thought she might become like Morvath, did they? Disempower her, must they? Treat her like she was a witless girl unable to defy her heritage and make a destiny of her own choosing, including vengeance for Cilla and the frightened grieving child she herself had been, ultimately claiming her rightful place at the senior table, with her own house—er, would they?

Well, she'd show them. After all, who had been kidnapped and who was in this carriage rushing (all right, plodding) to the rescue? By the time Cecilia was finished, the Wisteria Society ladies would be returned safely to their own houses, Morvath would be dead, and Gertrude Rotunder would be serving her tea while Jane looked on jealously from the junior ladies' sofa.

Thus resolved, Cecilia brought out the emergency book she kept in a secret pocket of her dress, and read to calm her nerves while every now and again checking the road. So it was that a small but deadly band of highwaymen were delighted by the ease with which they were able to accost the carriage.

"Stand and deliver!" they shouted as they leaped from the bushes, swords raised and rifles pointed at the sweet young woman looking up wide-eyed from her volume of Wordsworth to behold their terrifying sight.

"Oh dear," she said. "Are you sure?"

"Sure I'll find treasures under your skirts," the brigand chief replied with a leer.

"How uncouth," Cecilia remarked. "But I am in a hurry, so if you apologize I'll let you go with no further trouble."

The brigands had a good laugh at that. Which was quite nice, actually, for in the weeks to come they could barely speak, let alone chuckle.

"It's a shame about your book," Ned said to Cecilia as they drove from the woods into the sumptuous golden glory of sunset over East Devon. "I don't think stuffing its pages down the throat of that brigand chief was likely to make him more eloquent."

"One can only try," Cecilia replied. "Besides, it was just Wordsworth."

"Ah, no great loss, then. Although I should give the man some credit, he did compose the beautiful line 'I wandered lonely as a cloud.'"

"Unless you believe the rumor that he actually wrote 'lonely as a cow' and his sister made him change it."

They shared an amused glance, and suddenly Cecilia wondered what it would be like to be friendly with him. Chat lightly. Shake his hand. Have him reach out, take hold of her chin, and kiss her until she could no longer see straight. The thought shocked a hot blush through her, and she looked away in haste. Oblivious, Ned flicked the horses' reins gently.

"You're being too rough with them," Cecilia snapped.

"They're fine," Ned answered.

"They're noble beasts who don't deserve whipping."

"It's a light touch of the reins. I do know how to handle horses."

"I'm not so sure. I'm only allowing you to have a turn because there are no cliffs hereabouts that you can drive us over."

"Ha ha. I must remind you, madam, that you are in my custody. I am the one who will do any allowing, should it be required."

"It is endearing how you delude yourself."

"I can tie you up if you'd like, to prove the point."

"You can try."

He gave her a speculative look, and again Cecilia imagined their conversation turning more direct. Would he have gentle lips? Or would he kiss her with a bruising passion, his hand tangling in her hair, his tongue tangling in—

She choked on her breath, and Ned grinned as if he knew exactly what she'd been thinking.

There followed a taut silence, during which no glancing at each other (and no kissing) took place. Eventually Ned frowned at the darkening horizon.

"We'll have to find a place to stop soon."

"We can drive right through the night," Cecilia argued.

"The horses need rest."

"We'll steal new horses."

"We need rest."

She frowned at him, but he looked back quite seriously. Cecilia had not imagined he could appear so cool-eyed and sober. A thrill sparked her blood—the effects of a sudden cold breeze, she decided, and wished she'd not left her coat with Pleasance.

Dear, mad Pleasance, who had predicted events correctly after all. What would she make of Northangerland Abbey's bloodthirsty ghosts? How long before she was gibbering their bleak memories and wind-like moans?

"I cannot rest," she said. "I must rush to their aid as fast as I'm able."

"But you don't want to be exhausted when you face Lady Armitage," Ned argued. "And certainly not when you get to Northangerland Abbey. You wouldn't take a blunt sword into battle, would you? It's the same with your own body."

"That is true," she conceded. "But I'll thank you not to speak of my—you know."

He grinned at her sidelong. "Your body?"

"If you are going to be crude, please leave my presence. Go back to

104

sitting in the carriage. I'll call you if there are any more inquiries about our possessions."

"Very well. But do you know where you're going?"

"East."

"Actually, we're headed south at the moment. We're not far from Sidmouth. Make sure you follow this road, keep left, and you should come across a hotel called the Knowle where we can stay tonight."

Cecilia was not unsuspicious. "How do you know this?"

"I did my fair share of smuggling, back before my house was *deliberately pushed* off a cliff. I know Sidmouth."

His innocent explanation only partly eased her mind. "This hotel is reputable?"

He laughed as he climbed down from the seat. "It will suffice."

Cecilia envisioned a beer-stained bar, salty ruffians, and tiny rooms that smelled of mice, but conceded there was no choice. Already, she felt weariness drag at her. At least they would be parted for the night. Lying alone in bed, she would no longer be troubled by thoughts of Captain Lightbourne, his strong hands pulling back the sheets, his smile lowering itself to her bare skin—

She flicked the reins, absolutely in no way similar to how Ned had done, and hoped the hotel was not too far away.

Ned spent the next while inside the carriage. Cecilia heard some clattering about in there, some opening and closing of the door, which would have piqued her curiosity if she allowed it to. The outskirts of Sidmouth began appearing around her—farms, cottages, a public hall. As the daylight faded to shadows, Ned reappeared, clambering up on the seat beside her. He was dressed in a handsome black evening suit and even wore a hat, which he lifted off his head to salute her. Cecilia was troubled once again by that sudden breeze that made her tremble within and yet feel inexplicably hot.

"I found some luggage at the back," he said, "and had a look through it. There are ladies' clothes if you would like to get changed into something more—less—er, different."

"Why should I change?"

"The Knowle is slightly more than a roadside inn. If we are to go in through the front door, we want to present ourselves as well as possible."

"Couldn't we simply climb in a window?"

"Yes, but this will be more fun."

They stopped the horses so Cecilia could climb down and enter the carriage. Then, as Ned drove on, she sat inside, contemplating the luggage piled on the seats around her. The previous occupants of the carriage must have been traveling to a house party, such was the array of silk, satin, lace, velvet. Even in the twilight, Cecilia discerned the fine workmanship of the clothing and regretted momentarily that she had not taken the time to rob the persons of the travelers before taking their carriage. No doubt she had missed out on some decent jewels. Sorting through the clothes, she selected a blue dress with long ruched sleeves and high neckline trimmed with fur—

And then tossed it aside, reaching instead for a gown that would cause her aunt to faint, were she present. "You'll perish immediately of cold!" Miss Darlington would certainly declare.

Now, Cecilia was a dutiful niece, but even the most responsible, sensible lady would be unable to resist lustrous silvery silk faille embroidered with roses, its scooped bodice trimmed with pearl-encrusted lace, its sleeves small and puffed in a fashion Cecilia had never before encountered but immediately wanted to experience. She wrangled herself out of her day dress and into the silk, managing to close most of the buttons at the back. It did not quite fit, but Cecilia decided she had no need to adequately breathe that evening.

She unbraided her mussed hair, brushed it through with her fingers, then coiled it into a knot at the back of her head. She cleaned her face as well as she could with a petticoat she found in the luggage. There were no toiletries, so she had to remain content with her natural scent, which was not entirely pleasant after all the exercise of the day. But the gown itself smelled of old roses, and that would have to suffice.

After transferring her gun to her garter belt and checking that her knives were in place, she still felt only half-dressed. There were long satin evening gloves to match the gown, but they left a two-inch gap of exposed skin between glove and sleeve. Cecilia lost courage, and she was turning back to the voluminous blue dress when the carriage stopped.

Looking out the window, Cecilia saw a large, elegant building set on a trim lawn above the drive where they had stopped. Its dozens of windows gleamed merrily, and gas lamps along the driveway led a shimmering route up to the majestic front door.

"Oh," Cecilia said. This was not the modest roadside hotel she had been envisioning.

There was no time to change her dress now. The carriage door opened and Ned lowered the step, then held out his hand to assist her exit. Responding automatically from a decade's rigorous training, Cecilia laid her hand upon his, lifted her skirt's hem, and alighted gracefully to the pebbled drive.

"Miss Bassingthwaite," he said in a low voice, bowing before her. "You look exquisite."

Cecilia lifted her chin disdainfully. "I will brook no pleasantries from a scoundrel," she said, and then winced as she heard her aunt's tone in her own voice. "You look quite reasonable yourself," she relented. "Would you help me with my buttons?"

She turned her back to him. There was a long moment of silence, and then Ned cleared his throat. "Of course," he said, and began slipping pearls into their related holes. His fingers at no point touched her skin, and yet they seemed to stir the same breeze she had experienced on the road, cool yet electrifying. Cecilia swallowed dryly. Perhaps she was coming down with a cold. Miss Darlington was going to be furious.

"I didn't drive us to the door," he said as he finished his task, leaving her feeling oddly disappointed. "It would look strange for us to have no coachman. Can you stand a walk?"

"I am well equipped for it," Cecilia said, drawing up her hem to reveal her walking boots. "But what about the poor horses?"

"I'll send someone down for them. My lady." He offered his arm. Cecilia hesitated. "It's only for the sake of appearances," he explained, and so reluctantly she took it.

"There will be no Sissy-ing," she said as they walked across the drive to a set of wide marble steps, trying not to notice the strength of the muscle beneath her gloved hand. "No shambolic poetry. And give me back my earrings."

"Madam?" he said in an innocent tone.

She stopped walking, and after a moment he grinned and handed her the pearl drops. Cecilia replaced them in her ears, and they continued on up the steps.

"You need no such adornment," Ned murmured. "You are beauty without—"

"I said no poetry."

"But you are a poem, and so—"

She stopped again. "Do you want to sleep in the carriage, Mr. Lightbourne?"

"Captain."

She merely raised an eyebrow and waited.

Eventually he bowed. "Prose it shall be, Miss Bassingthwaite."

"Thank you."

They finished the steps, crossed the upper driveway, and approached the entrance. The doorman, in a red frock coat, nodded respectfully as he opened the door.

"Good man," Ned said in a lofty tone, "our coachman fell ill and is even now inspecting the contents of his stomach in the bushes beyond the lawn. Would you send someone to stable our carriage and tend the horses?" He slipped a coin to the doorman, who bowed.

"Consider it done, sir."

They swept into the hotel foyer.

✷ 10 ✷

LORD ALBERT AND LADY VICTORIA—FREE WINE!—
A FAIR-WEATHER FRIEND—CECILIA IS DISARMED—
FLYING FISH, WAYWARD SPIRITS, BARE ARMS, AND
OTHER SCANDALS—CECILIA IS DISROBED—A BAD IDEA

Cecilia never lacked common sense, not even when taken by surprise. So although she had not expected such a grand inn as the Knowle, she entered it complacently. After all, she had patronized many grand establishments during her life as ward of the wealthy Miss Darlington and was not overcome by the grandeur of the Knowle, its polished marble surfaces and polished ferns, its elegant furniture, and the stylish people who loitered ostentatiously in lamplit corners. She was tired, however, and hungry, and felt pleased to be in such an excellent place rather than the rustic tavern serving only beer and the hearty stew that, as a reader of novels, she had anticipated.

They did not approach the desk but proceeded directly, and with a calm air of belonging, through the foyer into the lounge, then the dining room beyond. "I'm famished," Ned said. "Shall we eat before taking a room?"

"That would be sensible," Cecilia replied.

The maître d' took their names—Lord Albert, the Viscount Lumines, and his wife, Lady Victoria, who were not on the guest list by some unforgivable error for which the maître d' was most apologetic, and would they please accept a complimentary bottle of wine in lieu of complaining to the management? Lord Albert was most displeased, but Lady Victoria persuaded him to forgive, and after he handed over his hat they were ushered to a white-clothed table beside a window overlooking the park. A menu was brought, and the wine, and Lord Albert ordered two servings of cod with oyster sauce, followed by a Russian salad, duck, lemon sorbet, and assorted cheeses, while his wife gazed out the window at the moon rising over the dark gardens.

"Something to remember," Ned said after the waiter had left, "is that the Wisteria Society are not any regular women and men. They are strong, smart, dangerous. I wouldn't want to be the one trying to manage them."

"How did he even succeed in capturing them?" Cecilia asked, still staring at the moon as if it was a great white house she could hijack and fly to her aunt's rescue.

Ned took a breadstick from a basket at the center of the table. "Trickery. Afternoon tea in the village, away from the houses. A sleeping draft in the tea. All organized by a traitor in the Society's ranks."

"A traitor? Impossible."

Ned shrugged. "Nothing's impossible if you can pay enough."

"No one would help steal the houses of their fellow Society members," Cecilia insisted.

He gave her an amused frown. "Why not? Half of you are trying to assassinate the other half."

"That's different."

Ned was quiet, trying to work out the difference on his own, then gave up and took a bite of bread.

"Who was the traitor?" she asked.

Ned chewed his mouthful, and she watched him impatiently. He rolled his eyes, trying to eat faster, and nearly choked on the swallow. Coughing, drinking wine, attracting disapproving attention from the neighboring diners, he finally managed to say, "Miss Fairweather."

"I knew it!" Cecilia took a breadstick of her own and snapped it in half. Crumbs flew. Ned stared wide-eyed, then set down his wineglass carefully, as if any sudden movement might set her off. "Jane always was a sneak," she said. "Her poor grandmother."

"I don't—"

"When is the food coming?" She frowned toward the kitchen door.

"We only just ordered. I appreciate it's hard to wait until tomorrow, but at least know that Morvath doesn't plan to kill the ladies." *Not right away*, he added silently. "Why don't you have a drink, try to relax?"

"I am relaxed," Cecilia said, snapping the breadstick again. But then she laid it down on her plate and began brushing the crumbs from the tablecloth into her hand. "He told you he would not kill them?"

"Absolutely," Ned lied.

She sighed and tipped the crumbs onto her plate, then laid her hands together on her lap. "Please excuse my shocking behavior. It has been a most exerting day."

Ned smiled. Their gazes met, and a tremulous moment passed before Cecilia looked down, rearranging a fork on the table ever so slightly, and Ned's smile deepened. "I've seen nothing shocking," he assured her. "Do try the wine; it's not bad."

Cecilia hesitated. She'd never taken alcohol before and was unsure it was wise to do so now. Miss Darlington would not even let her drink Communion wine, believing it the surest way to catch rabies. But a young woman in the company of an urbane gentleman did not want to look unsophisticated; therefore, Cecilia lifted her glass and sipped.

Dry sweetness burst in her mouth. The taste was strong but not unpleasant. She took another sip and failed to dislike it. The sweetness fizzed down her throat. After a moment, she sipped again. Her lips tingled. The room seemed to soften with a mild heat. *They must have lit a fire*, she thought, and looked around to see it, without success.

"What do you think?" Ned asked. "Pretty reasonable for free wine, yes?"

"Yes," she agreed, and took another, more protracted, swallow.

"Sissy," Ned said—

"Please don't call me that. I am not a Sissy."

He looked at her a moment (his face swaying in the most peculiar fashion) and then smiled. "I believe you're right. And you are not a Cilla either. Perhaps Ceelee?"

"No."

"Leelee?"

"Certainly not. Not." She drank the last from her glass before setting it down. Then setting it down again as the table leaped beneath it. Ned watched her hand move slowly away from the glass to touch the breadstick, then the spoons, then tap the table, before resting again in her lap. Then he looked into her eyes, holding her steady with his warm, smiling gaze.

"No," he said. "Not Leelee but a lily. Pale and delicate and sometimes poisonous. As William Blake said, 'the Lily white shall in love delight, nor a thorn nor a threat stain her beauty bright.'"

She eyed him narrowly. "I do believe that was accurately recited!"

He gave her a sly, knowing grin. Her stomach, and her understanding of him, both flipped. She lifted her glass to sip more wine as a cover for her confusion, but it was empty. He poured her more.

"A lily," she said, wrinkling her nose. As soon as the glass was full, she took it and drank. "I don't know. Thornless doesn't seem quite right for a pirate."

"Trust me," he said, and she laughed.

113

Ned sat back in his chair, watching her laugh, utterly charmed. She clearly could not hold even the smallest amount of liquor, and the consequence was a loosening of her reserve that not only brought her to laughter but made her eyes turn dark beneath their long lashes and her face soften so that she seemed at once older and yet more vulnerable; gentler and yet more deadly to his heart. She laughed in the same way she did everything else, with innate consideration—quietly, so as to not disturb the other diners, but spirited enough that it honored his joke.

Although he hadn't been joking. She *was* delicate, and dangerous, and the fact that he was completely seduced by it was going to make things very difficult indeed when the time came to throw her into jail.

Or out of a high window.

Whichever came first.

Leaning forward, he poured more wine into her glass. She might as well have one good night. "Drink up," he said, smiling, watching her try to blink him into focus, and then sat back again contentedly as the waiter brought their fish. This was going to be fun.

They ate in quiet, commenting only now and again about the excellence of the food or the heat of the room, and Cecilia remained calm, impassive, undisturbed by fears for her aunt or disgust for her dinner companion. Some other woman in the room kept laughing, then weeping, dropping cutlery, then almost falling out of the chair trying to retrieve it, and at one point flinging a piece of duck off her fork halfway across the room while arguing a point about *Hiawatha*. Cecilia paid her no attention. It would be unladylike to stare. She simply sipped her wine, ate her dinner, and conversed occasionally with Captain Lightbourne, maintaining her usual dignified manner.

When the cheese was finished and it was time to seek a room for the night, she was dismayed by how the hotel lurched as they crossed the dining room. Obviously there was a problem with its stabilizing magic. Perhaps someone was saying the incantation wrong. Cecilia suggested to Captain Lightbourne that they go up to offer their assistance, but he assured her it was unnecessary. Taking her arm, he helped her across the room while other diners watched them in clear admiration of their youth, elegance, and beautiful clothes. Cecilia imagined how amusing it would be to turn at the doorway and wave to them, and Captain Lightbourne laughed as if he had somehow heard her thought and envisioned it too.

"Well, I never!" a woman gasped. Cecilia looked around for her aunt but did not see her. At least, though, it proved Miss Darlington was safe, no doubt enjoying a cup of tea beside the dining room hearth, and Cecilia felt happy to go to bed knowing she need not worry about dear Aunty after all.

Lord Albert's hat was returned to him, and they proceeded upstairs. Alas, the elevator was haunted by the ghosts of smugglers long lost on storm-tossed seas, and as they traveled up—and down—and sideways for a while—Cecilia tried to recall spells Pleasance used to mutter to ward off troublesome spirits. "Lady Victoria is unwell," Captain Lightbourne explained to the elevator attendant, which didn't sound much like a spell, but Cecilia repeated it anyway. Doing so only aggravated the ghosts, however. They shoved her against Captain Lightbourne, and he put his arm around her protectively. Charming man, shame she would have to assassinate him one day soon.

Suddenly the ghosts cried out and the elevator door opened, and Captain Lightbourne guided her to the relative steadiness of the corridor. "Good night," she said in a mild, pleasant voice to the elevator attendant, who muttered something she did not quite hear (no doubt the correct warding spell) and closed the door behind them.

"Do you know," Cecilia said as they stood for a moment, trying to decide which way to go, "I can barely breathe in this dress." She tugged at the bodice and waist, writhing with discomfort. "I should have stolen one bigger."

"Sh," the captain said, and Cecilia rolled her eyes at his rudeness. A woman passing by also appeared aghast, as any woman would in response to a man publicly shushing his wife.

Wait. *Wife?*

Cecilia frowned, trying to remember that part. But she could not, and so she shrugged. The movement tightened the gown even further, and she abruptly reached the end of her tolerance. "No," she said. "I cannot wear it one minute longer." She began slipping the bodice down.

Captain Lightbourne caught her hand, to which she responded by pulling the glove from it, dislodging his grip, before continuing to undress. He countered by lifting her into his arms and carrying her along the corridor. Cecilia removed her other glove and slapped his face with it. He winced but did not stop.

"This is scandalous," she declared, tossing her gloves to the ground in emphasis.

"I shouldn't worry if I were you," he replied. "It will get lost among all the other scandals of the evening."

"And now I am gloveless and might fall victim at any moment to the Great Peril."

"Ah yes, freckles. Well thank goodness there's no risk of that tonight."

"Nevertheless, I insist you put me down at once!"

"Don't be anxious, Lady Victoria. It's not wrong for your husband to carry you."

"Oh. True. Very well, then, Lord Albert, but move a little more gently if you please, I'm becoming rather queasy."

He paused beside several doors along the corridor, listening at each, attempting a handle here and there. Finally he opened one and stepped through into a dark room.

"This should do," he said, and set Cecilia on her feet. She swayed alarmingly but managed not to fall. The captain tossed his hat onto a sideboard and moved about turning on the gas lamps. As the room blossomed into view, Cecilia saw a wide, plump bed draped in gold satin (and some other furniture she barely noticed due to the presence of The Bed). All at once she felt a torrid heat press against her skin from within.

"That's a—*bed*." She whispered the word as if it was lewd.

Captain Lightbourne glanced over his shoulder. "Yes," he agreed.

"I mean, there is only one of it."

"Of course. Have you ever heard of an unmarried couple who have to stay at an inn being presented with separate beds?"

Her wits dragged themselves up, shoving arms into jackets, slapping helmets on heads, coming more or less to attention. "This room will suit me," she said. It sounded good and gave her wits the confidence to stand even straighter, gripping the pommels of their swords; one even saluted. "Will you take another nearby?"

"No," the captain replied. "I don't trust you not to climb out the window and run away."

"I wouldn't do that," Cecilia retorted, and her wits nodded vigorously, although this was not such a good idea—her stomach looked up with a green countenance and moaned.

"You wouldn't?" the captain asked with a skeptical grin.

"Of course not. I'd leave through the door."

"Ha. I'm staying. Nobody knows Cecilia Bassingthwaite is here, and Lady Victoria doesn't exist, so your reputation will be safe."

Her wits looked at each other blankly, then shrugged and wandered off again, leaving Cecilia alone. The bed was shimmering so prettily in the light. Music played somewhere in the distance, and the light began to sway as if it was dancing, a lithe golden ballerina on a plush golden stage, as Cecilia once had a childhood dream to do herself, ballerining through Europe, dressed in tulle and what was the question again?

"Will you please get into bed before you fall down?" Captain Lightbourne said. "I'll turn my back whilst you disrobe."

"A gentleman doesn't talk about disrobing," Cecilia said archly, and then had to fan herself with a hand. Did the gas lamps exude heat as well as light? Perhaps she should ask the captain to open a window. But he had turned away, facing the wall, and so instead she hurried to unbutton her dress. She got as far as slapping her hands against her back a few times before giving up with a sigh. "The buttons keep moving. I need your help, Lord Albert. If you would kindly disrobe me— but you're not to speak of it; that would be scandalous."

Captain Lightbourne turned and considered the situation warily. "Are you sure?"

"I cannot answer that with the ladylike vocabulary available to me. Half of what I'm wearing is unmentionable. Suffice it to say, if you were dressed as a woman, you would understand the impossibility of going to bed in your clothes."

He hesitated, brushing the hair back from his face. "I don't know. Your aunt would kill me. *You* would kill me if you weren't so drunk."

"I am not drunk, sir. I am in full possession of my flaccidities."

He raised an eyebrow. "Your faculties?"

"As I said. Come now, a gentleman would help."

"But not mention that he was helping?"

"Essact—Ezast—Yes."

He shrugged, then came over to stand behind her and unbutton the dress. While she waited, Cecilia began to sway along with the ballerina light, and Captain Lightbourne placed a hand on her shoulder to still her. "Don't touch me," she murmured, and the hand slipped across the naked nape of her neck before moving away. She swallowed a shuddering breath.

"All done." He stepped back.

"Wait." She pulled the dress down. "My *corset.*" She winced as she whispered this word, sure that the entire hotel must have heard her. "Without help, I am trapped, utterly trapped, unable to breathe, doomed to a lifetime of—"

"All right," he said. "But how do you normally—"

"Don't say it."

"I beg your pardon."

"Pleasance helps me."

"Ah."

"You needn't recite the prayer to guard me against flesh-devouring spirits of the blighted netherworld. Pleasance is overcautious, and I'm sure I'll be safe for one night. Just, er, you-know-what with the thingamies. Do you understand?"

"I've done it before."

She glanced over her shoulder at him. "You've worn a *corset?*"

"No," he said, and grinned.

"Well, I never!" Cecilia gasped in outrage, but her face reddened and she turned away.

He unlaced the corset, and Cecilia exhaled with relief as it eased away from her bones. Then he reached around and began releasing the hooks at the front. She inhaled again sharply.

His body rested against hers. His breath stroked the skin behind her ear. "Um," she said.

"Yes?"

The question was a smiling whisper that made her toes curl and her wits duck for cover. But if she answered, telling him in no uncertain words to stop what he was doing, she'd be utterly, linguistically compromised and would have to marry him.

"Nothing," she muttered.

The corset came away; he dropped it to the floor. Blood rushed through her body, stoking the heat of it until she felt she would erupt. She ran her hands down her midriff, trying to calm herself, and Captain Lightbourne cleared his throat.

"And now my hair," she said.

"Oh God, really?"

"Unless you want me to be stabbed to death by my hairpins in the middle of the night."

"It would be a swifter, less painful death than the one you're putting me through."

She laughed, and he caught her arms, turned her around.

"Sir!"

"Forgive me, but I want to see you laugh."

She smiled, and he caught his breath. Reaching up, he drew a pin from her hair. He expected a sensuous unfurling of red-gold glory and steeled himself, but in fact the coiffure was so well established that he had to remove three more pins before it fell, all of a sudden, sending her hair in a luscious deluge almost to her waist. She brushed away strands from her face, blinking as they caught on her long, thick lashes.

"Oh God," he said again in a strangled voice, stumbling back. "Go to bed. Quickly. And pull the blankets up high, and fall asleep at once."

She laughed, perplexed, and he closed his eyes. "Just—bed."

"But I need to make use of the powder room," she said, and he groaned.

"This was a bad idea. Very bad."

"We should have slept in the carriage?"

He envisioned it, which was another bad idea, for given that slight encouragement his imagination began to run wild. "No," he said. "No, absolutely, definitely not. Powder room. Bed. I shall—I know, open this window, take a breath of cold night air. Yes. This, now, this was an excellent plan. So cold. Refreshing—no, *repressing*, that's the word. Ice-cold, all through me, like a winter's river—no, like Lady Armitage's cold, thin face. Perfect, Ned. Just keep thinking about Lady Armitage and everything will be fine. Lady Armitage reclining on her sofa. Lady Armitage's mouth. No, you want to be calm, not queasy. Lady Armitage telling me to bring her a finger."

"What are you talking about?" Cecilia asked. He turned, jaw clenched, and almost leaped out of the window to see her standing close by him. She smelled of wine and roses, and a little of sweat that made him think as vehemently as possible of Lady Armitage throwing ice-cold water at him. Her breath stirred beneath her fine lawn chemise, stirring him as well. Lady Armitage put down the water buckets and shrugged.

"What?" he said stupidly, trying not to stare.

"Never mind." Slipping past him, she leaned on the windowsill, inhaling the dark air. "Night is like the underskin of a poem, don't you think, Mr. Lightbourne?"

"Captain," he answered, for want of anything more sensible.

She sighed, and her face softened, and as Ned watched anxiously, tears filled her eyes.

"You need to go to bed," he reiterated, for if there was one thing that truly terrified him, it was a crying woman. He had not thought this one capable of it.

"I love a horizon," she said, leaning farther out the window. "That feeling of longing, of mystery and distant magic, pulls always on my soul. I suppose that's where my mother must be. Roaming through the afterlight, stealing heaven . . ."

She lifted a hand as if to reach for Cilla, and Ned caught her before she tumbled out.

"Come on," he said, guiding her firmly away from the longing horizon toward the solid, safe bed. When they got there, she crawled over the quilt and burrowed in like a child.

"Will you be comfortable sleeping on the floor?" she asked, looking at him with big eyes. But her gaze was unfocused and he knew she didn't quite see him.

"Of course," he lied. "Go to sleep. I'll turn the lights down."

"Not yet." She shook her head, and her eyes seemed to go on swerving even after she stopped. "I can't sleep without reading first."

"Darling, I don't think you're going to have that problem tonight." He walked around the bed, feeling braver now, for she was more like a lost girl than a beautiful half-dressed woman, and his only desire was to ensure she went to sleep without vomiting all over the sheets. He arranged the blankets around her. Finally she closed her eyes—then flung them open again. He smiled in sheer self-defense.

"You said you'd assassinate me in my bedchamber," she recalled. "How will you do it? Will you suffocate me with the pillow?"

"Maybe," he said, drawing a loose strand of hair away from her face. "What do you think, would that be all right?"

"Tiring," she said. "It apparently takes more effort than you'd think. What about a knife to the heart?"

"No, too messy. This is a very nice quilt and I wouldn't want to ruin it. Poison?"

"Do you have any with you?"

He shook his head. She was so lovely, "pale as the dustiest lily's leaf." He rather thought his heart beat sighs, not blood, looking down upon her.

"Well then, that won't work," she said, her voice fading. "You'll just have to strangle me." She closed her eyes again, muttered something about rope burns, and drifted to sleep.

Ned watched her breathe for a while longer, then went about the room, turning off the lamps, removing his coat and boots, almost tripping over her corset, before approaching the bed. There was enough space that she'd never realize he slept beside her, and in the morning he could rise before she woke. Granted, this was rather unprincipled logic, but after all, he reasoned, what else could one expect from a pirate?

He turned back the quilt . . . then abruptly reversed the action, took a pillow, and tossed it on the floor. With a rug beneath him and his coat as a blanket, he made a bed that turned out to be as uncomfortable and intractable as his honor unexpectedly was. Up on the actual bed, cozy and warm, Cecilia muttered about dynamite, obviously having a pleasant dream. Listening to her, Ned felt his heart soften. He would keep her safe, he vowed—including from himself. Even if it left him with bruises and good grief was that a nail beneath his hip?

Shifting from side to side, trying without success to get comfortable, he finally sighed and went frustrated, noble, like a gentleman, to sleep.

⤜ 11 ⤛

A SUDDEN AWAKENING—CECILIA DISAPPEARS—
THE SENSELESSNESS AND INSENSIBILITY OF READING
WUTHERING HEIGHTS—FLACCID FACULTIES—
THEY ARE INTRODUCED—THE DANGER OF HAIR COMBS—
WHISPERS IN THE DARK—THE HERALD OF THE DAWN

The feeling was not like a gas explosion, but it was quite as sharp, as strange, as startling: it acted on Ned's torpid senses and forced him awake. He did not wait for the sense of alarm to ease into understanding before he reached beneath his pillow for the knife he always kept there. He found nothing. Instantly rolling to his knees, he groped under the rug for a gun that was also absent, before realizing that he wasn't under attack—he'd simply forgotten to arrange his weapons the night before. Considering he woke every morning in the same manner (an occupational hazard, since pirates, secret policemen, and traitorous henchmen of mad poetic tyrants were all at risk even when fully conscious and not bleary-eyed and, ugh, drooling a little), it was remarkable he'd not prepared his comfort knife as usual. And then he remembered.

Cecilia Bassingthwaite.

He stood up, pushing the tangled hair from his face, and looked at her sleeping in the bed. Except she wasn't—sleeping, or in the bed.

She was gone.

"Damn," he said.

Striding across the room, he noticed her gown was no longer on the floor, although the corset was, like the shell of propriety she had discarded last night. Ned stepped around it and knocked on the bathroom door.

"Madam? Are you in there?"

Silence.

Opening the door, he ascertained that she was not inside, and swore again.

Language, chimed half a dozen female voices in his head, but he ignored them.

The sun was only now emerging, its tentative light barely illuminating the room. Hopefully this meant she'd left not too long ago. He checked the pockets of his own clothes and found money, switchblade knives, the maître d's fob watch. So she hadn't paused for robbery. Did that leave her under-resourced, or were her pretty lacy drawers already weighted down with coins and secret weapons? He should have checked last night. For that matter, he should have tied her to the bed.

That thought, mingling with memories of her drawers, and the bare calves beneath them, made him groan. He hastily pulled on his clothes, wondering what was the best plan for chasing after her. Would she continue to Lyme Regis with the hope of stealing Lady Armitage's house on her own? Or would she ride back toward Blackdown Hills? If Ned guessed wrongly, he would be heading in the opposite direction while Cecilia got herself into more danger than even a girl trained by Jemima Darlington could handle.

"Let's think about this clearly," he said aloud as he sat on the end of the bed to put on his boots. "She'll suppose that I'll expect her to try for the Armitage house, and so she'll go north instead—but she'll know I'll figure that out, so she'll try to trick me by riding to Lyme Regis—unless she realizes I'll guess that too, in which case she'll be halfway to Blackdown Hills by now—and yet surely she'll know that I know that she knows she can't trust me, which means she's heading for Armitage—although on the other hand—"

"Coffee?" she asked.

"No, thanks, I only drink tea."

His brain laughed at him. Looking up, he found Cecilia in front of him with a mug in one hand, a book in the other, all her lovely hair bound neatly again, and no hint of emotion on her pale, beautiful face.

"I thought so," she said, passing him the mug. He took it numbly and stared into the steaming milky tea. Well, damn.

"How did you walk in here so silently?" he asked.

"If ever I can't open a door without being heard, I'll quit piracy in shame, retire to the countryside, and take up a gentle lifestyle of raising poultry and blackmailing village parsons."

"Fair enough." He sipped tea, trying to regain some equilibrium. "Where did you go? I was a little disconcerted."

"I needed a book in case of emergencies."

"You mean like being attacked by foul-mouthed highwaymen?"

"No, I mean those moments when nothing important is happening, such as during travel. After supper. Before sleeping. Or whilst one's opponent reloads their gun."

"Ah. So you were in the hotel library?"

"Can you believe they don't have one?" She shook her head incredulously, and Ned sipped tea again to hide his smile.

"Shocking," he murmured.

"Indeed. Luckily, the local Young Women's Christian Association has a reading room. It carries only religious tracts, but when I accidentally knocked over a stack of Bibles, I found this hiding behind them. Who would have thought young women in a small town would be interested in Gothic scenes of wild, dark passion?"

She held out the book for him to see, and Ned raised his eyebrows.

"*Wuthering Heights* again. Are you really sure you want to be reading that?"

"Of course." She held it protectively against her breast. He registered then that she was dressed in a brown riding ensemble and wondered if the Young Women's Christian Association had a wardrobe attached to it, or if she'd been elsewhere that morning. "Why shouldn't I read it?" she asked.

"Because your father is planning to go to war on the basis of it?"

"Surely not. It is only a book."

"A Brontë book. It represents the bastard heritage that drives all he does. You know if Branwell Brontë hadn't fooled around with—"

"How dare you speak like that to me!" Her outrage was so strong, she rocked with the force of it.

"—or even if he'd married her, then Morvath would have grown up with a secure sense of identity and no need to prove himself. Almost certainly we would have been saved his many crimes and the war he intends to bring upon us now. Heathcliff is a moody child compared to your father."

"'Almost certainly' is an oxymoron," she said, and turned away, the long brown feather on her hat flicking the air disdainfully. She opened a small door in the sideboard, rummaging within for something to steal. "Moreover, what would a mere henchman know about anything?"

"Is there ever any point in me saying 'Captain'?"

"No."

"And I know because I've had to listen to Morvath read aloud from his memoirs and poems. He did not inherit his aunts' talent, I can tell you that. He did, however, inherit their overwrought sense of drama: 'Woe is me, I was adopted out, therefore shall burn down the world in revenge!' Besides, my mother—that is, I met your mother."

She went very still. "Did you indeed? Well. Are you almost ready to leave? I would like to be in Lyme Regis as soon as possible."

"Jemima Darlington would have seven fits if she knew you were reading a Brontë novel."

"The many things Aunt Darlington doesn't know about me would kill her outright, I'm sure. Besides, the Brontës are my heritage too."

"Only partly. The rest is a respectable line of pirates tracing back to—"

"Thank you, sir, but I do not need a lecture on my own history from a man who goes by seventeen different names." She closed her eyes, pressing a hand over her mouth. Ned watched her anxiously. He should not have said anything. But to hear Patrick Morvath's daughter speak in such defensive tones of her paternity made Ned shudder. Cecilia was beautiful, beguiling, but if she bore even the merest sympathy for her father, then she would have to be taken out of play, regardless of Ned's personal feelings.

"Let's go," he said, putting the tea mug down on the bed and straightening his black dress coat. "Dining room first for breakfast."

"I'm not hungry. However, I took the liberty of acquiring some food from the hotel kitchen for your sake. I've packed it in the saddle-bags."

"Saddlebags?"

She turned toward him, although her gaze did not meet his eyes. She seemed rather green, and he worried as to just how upset she was. "I have selected two horses from the stables that will transport us more efficiently than the carriage," she said. Her cool, emotionless voice reassured him—and yet, there was a wind-colored silence in her eyes, like a sky over moorlands, that made him believe she might one day cast aside reason and run into the wilds, dragging everyone else behind her until the world was a wrecked heart.

The thought should have terrified him. It certainly should have convinced him to bind her wrists, put her in a carriage, and transport her immediately to secure premises. But apparently some other part of his anatomy had overriden the authority of his brain—namely (and less naughtily than one might be thinking), his heart. He wanted her to be good. He wanted her to be trustworthy.

Hell, he just wanted her.

Would she kiss with that same secret storminess? Or would she be polite, her mouth closed, her inhibitions making a defense he'd have to work at with his lips and teeth and tongue until she was melting in his arms? How soon could he find out?

Not now, certainly. She looked really rather distressed indeed.

"Cecilia, I'm sorry." He made a helpless step toward her. "I should not have taken such liberties with the conversation."

"Apology accepted," she replied. "And kindly address me as Miss Bathingsway—er, Bassethwing—"

"Are you all right?"

"I'm fine." She lifted her chin in fine Darlington style—and possibly Brontë style too; God, what a thought. But Ned wasn't fooled, noticing the shadows beneath her eyes. And then it occurred to him what actually was the problem, and he almost laughed.

"No headache?" he asked. "No thirst?"

"No," she replied. "Which is to say, my head does seem to be possessed by shrieking dervishes, and those dervishes are letting off fireworks, but it is of no consequence. As for thirst, I have had some tea this morning. Also some water. And a little juice. And when I came back in from the stables, I took another cup of tea from the breakfast buffet, along with a glass of lemon water. I remain only a little parched, but nothing out of the ordinary."

"I see." He repressed what threatened to be a very dangerous grin should she see it. "So, no nausea or dizziness, then?"

"None. Why do you ask? I will mention, though, while I think of it, that this town must be set on unstable ground. Have you noticed the way the floors shift when you walk on them? And the walls keep tilting."

"I'm not certain that you should be riding a horse today. Why don't we take the carriage? I'll drive."

"I assure you I am in excellent health," she replied. And tipped abruptly to starboard.

"Oh dear," he said, catching her. "You seem to have a hangover."

"Nonsense," she said, pulling away. He watched the world spin in her eyes for a moment before she sagged again. He put an arm around her once more. "I've been poisoned!" she declared, glaring at him with black suspicion.

"You really haven't."

"Then what is this 'hangover' of which you speak?"

"An illness caught from eating seafood."

She gasped. "We had seafood for dinner!"

"We did!" he said as if suddenly remembering.

"But you are not unwell."

Ned shrugged. "After several bouts of hangover in my youth, I've developed an immunity."

She sighed. "It matters not. I must rescue my aunt, regardless of how I feel. Now, unhand me, sir. You may quote my family history all you like, but you forget we have still not been properly introduced."

He frowned in amusement. "We shared a bedroom last night. After I undressed you. We've been on speaking terms for several days. You have stolen many small items belonging to me"—*including my heart*, he added silently—"and furthermore you are in my official custody."

"Even so."

"Fine." He stepped back, releasing her, and performed a deep bow. "Miss Bassingthwaite, may I beg the honor of introducing myself?"

"You may," she said, rocking slightly and pressing a hand against her brow. "Only do it quietly."

He grinned. "Ned Lightbourne, Miss Bassingthwaite. Captain of Her Majesty's secret police brigade, at your service."

"So you say."

He blinked, taken aback. "You don't believe me?"

"Of course not," she replied with a dry laugh.

"Very well." He bowed again. "Ned Lightbourne, Miss Bassingthwaite. Tired man trying to do the right thing."

Cecilia acknowledged him with a nod. "Captain Lightbourne, I have heard so much about you. It is a pleasure to"—she held up her hand, and they both waited while her stomach contemplated whether it wished to join in the conversation—"to make your acquaintance," she concluded, and turned to vomit over her corset on the floor.

(As a feminist statement, it was ambiguous at best.)

"Oh dear," Ned said sympathetically. "Why don't you go back to bed?"

"I am fine," she averred, wiping her mouth with her gloved hand, and then departed for the bathroom. Ned heard water running and teeth being scrubbed to within an inch of their lives. Several minutes later she returned, fresh albeit gloveless. She waved a hand at Ned. "Hurry up, stop this loitering, we must be on our way at once!"

Ned opened his mouth to argue, then smiled instead. "Surely a decorous lady cannot go out in public with neither corset nor gloves?"

Irritation and disdain formed an unlikely union in her countenance. "Another word, sir, and you shall go out in public without teeth."

(Whereas that went more to the point.)

And there it was. She might have a shady heritage of Romantic intellectualism, but she'd been raised pure pirate. Ned bowed to her again, smirking, and then followed her to the door. She opened it, and they stared at the distinguished couple and porter standing on the other side of the threshold.

Ned immediately placed his hat upon his head. "We were sent to the wrong room," he pronounced in Lord Albert's ostentatious voice before anyone else could speak.

"This one is a travesty," Cecilia added, sounding eerily like her aunt. "Someone has made an appalling mess which has been left uncleaned. We are going downstairs now to complain to management."

"Um," said the dumbstruck porter.

"Out of the way," Ned demanded, and the porter shuffled back.

"I will not be recommending this hotel to my good friend the Duchess of Leinster," Cecilia said as they marched through the doorway and along the corridor. "Do you remember, my dear, how Hermione was talking of her wish to come to Sidmouth?"

"I do indeed, my dear," Ned replied. "But this place will not suit at all." He didn't need to glance back to know they were being watched. And then—

"Oh my heavens!" cried the lady, obviously having looked into the room.

Ned placed his hand on Cecilia's elbow and they increased their pace so as to reach the stairs a moment later and disappear from view.

"Do you really know the Duchess of Leinster?" Ned asked as they hurried down the stairs.

"Of course," Cecilia said. "That is, we would have been introduced had she not been engrossed in the opera while I was relieving her of an emerald hair comb. The weight of such jewelry causes terrible headaches in women, you know."

"So kind of you to help her in that way. How is your own headache?"

"It will surely kill me." They turned off the stairs and into a corridor leading toward the kitchen. "But as long as it does so after I have rescued the Society, I cannot complain."

"Brave girl," he said, and shoved her into a broom closet.

"Well I n—"

He slapped a hand over her mouth and, pushing his own way into the small space between brooms, buckets, and mops, closed the door silently behind them.

"Jacobsen," he whispered in her ear.

Cecilia's heart leaped, for she did not recognize the name, but Ned's breath, so warm and heavy in the darkness, ignited something a great deal warmer, farther down her body. They listened for a while as footsteps sounded along the corridor, dwindling finally into silence.

"My apologies," Ned whispered, lowering his hand. "That was one of Morvath's men. I didn't expect to see him here."

"We must have been traced."

"Obviously Morvath doesn't trust me after all."

"Does anyone?"

He did not reply, and Cecilia's heart unexpectedly cringed with regret at having asked. She certainly did not trust him, whoever he was. She remained in his company only to keep him where she could see him—not that she was *looking* at him, mind you, noticing the bunching of muscles beneath his skin, the slow glide of his eyelashes when he blinked so purposefully at her, the way he cocked his gun, the strong—er, which is to say, *no trust there at all*. Nevertheless, his silence seemed almost wounded, and reminded her that beneath his several names, he was a real person, just as beneath his shirt and trousers he was—

She shoved the thought away, but too late. Her wits held up several illustrations of it, some of which were animated. Thank goodness for the darkness within the closet, because she felt herself blush scarlet.

"Don't worry, Cecilia," he whispered. His voice grazed her mouth.

"I know," she answered, trying to keep her voice steady. "We can easily evade this Jackersen fellow."

"I didn't mean that." He set a hand on the wall beside her head. Which was reasonable, she supposed, since the space was very small.

"I am not frightened my father will capture me," she added. "If he does, I will be better located to save the Society."

"I didn't mean that either." He leaned toward her, which she allowed as a practicality, for with their whispering he might not be hearing her well.

"And I am unconcerned about Lady Armitage, whose house should prove easily obtainable."

He sighed, leaving her bemused. "I confess myself at a loss as to what you did mean," she said.

"I meant," he whispered, "that when I kiss you for the first time, it will be in a drawing room or a garden, someplace much finer than this."

"Oh." Her pulse trembled—no doubt a normal physiological reaction to being shut up in a narrow closet. But then she frowned. "Why?"

There was a small moment of silence. "Why what?"

"Why a drawing room or garden? How is a fine place relevant in such matters?"

He chuckled. "Shall I kiss you now, in that case?"

She gasped and slapped his cheek, although in the darkness she missed and slapped his ear instead.

"Ow," he said, sounding more amused than pained. Turning away, he opened the door and peered out. "I think it's safe to leave."

"Oh. Well, excellent. I'm certainly glad you're not going to kiss me. Yes, indeed, goodness me."

Ned closed the door, turned back, caught her face in his hands, and pressed his lips against hers with a sudden intensity that startled a sound into her throat. Immediately he softened the kiss, easing his passion into tenderness, feeling his heart sink into her warmth as she gentled beneath him. He was surprised to discover she didn't kiss like a storm after all, nor even with prudishness. She welcomed him, her hands clutching at his coat sleeves, pulling him closer, but her mouth was unsure what to do. The feather touch of it thrilled him.

Clearly no one had kissed her before. Yet beneath that innocence he sensed a ribald longing, and wondered if it was for him in particular or just a general interest in kissing. He wished it was for him. He longed for her. She was smart and strong, and, God, just the way she held a gun made his toes curl with lust. Having her in his arms, against his mouth, felt so good he almost could not bear it. But in the next moment, she would either swoon or stab him, so finally he drew away, and she swayed against the wall.

"Well, I never," she murmured dazedly.

Ned grinned. His pulse crashed as if he had scaled a mountain, which he supposed made a good metaphor for having kissed Cecilia Bassingthwaite, considering he'd been working toward it since the moment he saw her on the doorstep of Darlington House. He most definitely intended to do it again. But this was a smelly broom closet, and she was naive in ways he sometimes forgot, considering her cool gaze and ability to kill him with a hairpin. So he turned away, fumbling for the door handle, almost hitting himself in the face as he yanked the door open.

"We should probably hurry in case there are any other henchmen about."

"Yes. Right. True." She did not move.

Ned looked at her. The light streaming in from the corridor touched her face, illuminating its blushed mouth. The sight was so arousing, he had to take a deep breath to calm himself. "Are you all right?" he asked.

"I believe you have cured my headache."

He laughed. "I've never had my kissing described as medicinal before, but I'll take it as a compliment. Come on, let's go."

They made a cautious way through the servant's wing out to the stables. The horses she had earlier selected were saddled and waiting in the care of a young groom. Ned mounted, then noticed Cecilia staring unblinkingly at her stirrup.

"All right there?" he asked.

"Fine," she said in sterling British fashion, meaning that she was either fine or on the verge of complete internal catastrophe. She shook her head, regaining focus, and threw him a look that did not quite reach his face. He saw vulnerability in it, but mostly danger, and he rather wished he'd waited for a garden after all—if only so he could press her into a hedge afterward and kiss her again, and again, until her eyes were all softness and languor, with no suggestion of knife-edged revenge in them.

She hoisted herself up into the saddle, and Ned tossed a few coins to the groom. "We were never here."

"Who are you anyway?" the groom asked in bemusement.

Ned laughed. "No one."

"No one was not here," the groom said obediently, pocketing the coins.

"Wait! Stop!"

The shout came from the hotel's side door. The groom gasped. Ned and Cecilia turned, expecting to see one of several possible people. It was, however, Jacobsen, Morvath's officer. His scarred and pitted face contorted with emotion beneath a rough scrabble of gray hair. In his hand was a pistol.

"Go!" Ned shouted, and they urged their horses forward at a run as bullets screamed past their heads and somewhere nearby a rooster, announcing the day in high, proud notes of majesty, squawked and fell abruptly silent.

❊ 12 ❊

THE WOMAN IN BLACK—CANDY FROM A BABY—
THE QUEEN'S SILVERWARE—
NED PLUNGES INTO THE PIT OF HORROR—
THE PROBLEM WITH MEN THESE DAYS—
LADY ARMITAGE'S FORTRESS—TALLY HO!

If all else perished, and she remained, Lady Armitage should be content. And if all else remained, and Jemima Darlington were annihilated, the universe would turn to a mighty heaven, and Lady Armitage would become a source of visible delight to all around her!

But in the meanwhile, she walked the Cobb.

Day after day she walked, awaiting Signor de Luca. She had received an invitation to the Society gathering in Ottery St. Mary but could not tolerate the notion of sitting at a table with That Darlington Woman. Once Cecilia had been removed from the picture, they might meet again for tea and cakes. Red velvet cakes. Poisoned tea. And a knife in the back, in the manner of well-bred ladies.

Lady Armitage could not be easy until then. Life rubbed grittily against her skin. She could not even pick the pockets of her fellow pedestrians, so out of sorts did she feel. Instead, she paced the long harbor wall, black-cloaked, mysterious, her hair bending in the breeze as she stared wistfully out to sea—

Although the bright skies and calm waters rather detracted from the romance of it.

The man selling ice creams from a wheeled cart did not help.

And the breeze was so warm and gentle, she might as well have worn pink and stuck a bow on her hair.

Nevertheless, Lady Armitage sighed mournfully (and ate a small ice cream). Any moment now, Eduardo de Luca would stride toward her, his greatcoat flaring in the—er, his greatcoat hanging heavily about him, his blond head wickedly bare. He would grasp her hand with all the raw manners of a desperate-hearted rake, kiss it, and beg most pathetically to be her servant. That is, he was already her servant . . . *but he would beg to be the servant of her heart*, not just her purse!

And then, rising from his knees (for he had knelt in honor and devotion), he would present her with a small velvet bag containing the finger or ear of a young woman who had once given her a beloved toy dog because she thought Aunty Army might be lonely.

And so the great lady lingered beside the sea, until at last on Saturday she became bored (not at all troubled by gout, an affliction she certainly did not have) and retired to her sitting room with its windows overlooking the waters. A footman kept her supplied with tea, digestive biscuits, cocaine pastilles, and the delicious sight of his legs in tight breeches.

Still she sighed and lounged restlessly, albeit Vikingly, in an armchair. She was employing a pygmy leg bone to scratch beneath her starched wing of hair when the butler unexpectedly entered.

"Excuse me, ma'am. A gentleman is at the door. With which particular violence would you like him sent away?"

Signor de Luca at last! Lady Armitage sat up, tossing the bone aside. "Let him in. And, Whittaker, bring more tea."

"The special tea, ma'am?"

"No, no. At least, not yet. Some of that new Earl Grey concoction, I think."

"Yes, ma'am."

After he left, Lady Armitage arranged her skirts, smoothed her eyebrows, and experimented with several smiles before she decided upon the most suitable. She was thus elegantly situated when Signor de Luca entered the room. Her smile widened—

And then snapped shut.

She sat up so fast her hair reverberated. "You're not Eduardo!"

The man bowed. His shoulders bulged beneath his coat, and when he looked up, his hefty, scarred face puckered in a scowl that revolted Lady Armitage even more than the gun he pointed at her.

"Jacobsen," he introduced himself. "I work for Captain Morvath."

"Egads!" She leaned across to the side table and took another pastille.

"Is he here?"

"Morvath?" The pastille clattered among her teeth. "Tall man, gray-headed, really needs to pluck his nose hairs? Of course not. Oh please, sir, do put down the gun, it's ever so frightening." She poured herself a cup of tea.

"I meant Lightbourne."

"Who?" She frowned as she added sugar to the tea, but then her expression lit with understanding. "Ah, Signor de Luca. The boy with many names but no house. Why would you ask me that question? I am but a fragile woman come to the seaside for the sake of my health." She coughed unconvincingly—and then for real, the cocaine pastille having become stuck in her throat. Jacobsen watched in bewildered alarm as she hacked and wheezed and thumped her chest and finally swallowed the offending pastille. Then she frowned up at him. "Well? I haven't all day. I asked you a question: Why did you ask me that question?"

Jacobsen very nearly rubbed his forehead with his gun before recollecting himself. "I chased Lightbourne from Sidmouth but lost him coming into town. When I saw this pirate house I figured it was where he was headed."

"How on earth could you know this was a pirate house?"

"The skull and crossbones door knocker tipped me off."

"Observant of you."

"And the Jolly Roger flag flying from the eaves."

"Well spotted."

"And the fact the house is parked in the middle of Marine Parade, blocking traffic, with what appears to be a street lamp wedged beneath it."

"Yes, well, we are experiencing minor technical difficulties."

She picked up a fan that lay on the side table and began wafting it before her face. Jacobsen stared at her (no doubt entranced by her beauty and magnificence). "Lightbourne is not here," she said. "And this conversation has become tedious, Mr. Jigglesen. You are excused from my presence."

"Jacobsen. And I'm the one with the gun, woman. You can't tell me what to do."

"Of course I can. Don't you know who I am?"

"No," he said, and shot her.

Lady Armitage barely flinched. The bullet struck her fan with a sharp twang, rebounded, and hit Jacobsen in his shoulder. He shouted, dropping the pistol.

"You seem to be experiencing technical difficulties of your own," Lady Armitage remarked. "Ah, here is fresh tea."

Jacobsen spun toward the doorway and promptly fell backward, crashing to the hardwood floor. His eyes flickered shut.

"Good afternoon, Lady Armitage," Signor de Luca said, rubbing the fist he had just slammed into Jacobsen's brow. He bent, picking up the man's gun. "I apologize for interrupting your tête-à-tête."

"And so you should," Lady Armitage replied. "It was most uncivil of you, and you've left a mess on my floor. However, since the gentleman was intent on murdering me, I suppose I can forgive you this once. Where on earth is Whittaker with my tea?"

"I'm afraid he's unavailable, madam."

She narrowed her eyes. "Dead?"

Signor de Luca seemed offended. "Certainly not. What do you take me for?"

"A pirate . . . an Italian scoundrel . . . an assassin whom I hired to kill people . . ."

He flicked back his hair with an excess of dignity. "Your servants have been sent away with severance pay."

"What do you mean, severance pay? Did you cut off their hands?"

"No." A shadow of disappointment slipped across her face, and he frowned. "I paid them. In silverware, mostly."

Lady Armitage rose at once from her chair. "Surely you don't mean my Garrard & Co. sterling silver collection, given to me by the Queen?"

"Given to you?"

"Absolutely. She wouldn't have left it in her treasury guarded by only two soldiers if she hadn't meant me to take it."

"Fair enough. Yes, your sterling silver. But don't waste too much energy being upset about that. I'm stealing your house next."

She laughed. "What an entertaining fellow you are, Eduardo. Do you really think I have got to my age—er, that is to say, *my position in life*, without preparing for all contingencies? The steering mechanism of this house is locked, and the key is somewhere no man will ever find it."

She glanced down, then up again through long, thick, false eyelashes at him. Her mouth tilted like a sword raised in challenge.

Signor de Luca smiled in reply. "No man at all?"

"None whatsoever."

"Let me guess; many have tried, all have been poisoned." He stepped forward and removed the fan from her grip, tossing it aside, where it sliced unnoticed through a statuette of Artemis the Huntress and wedged itself in the wall. He aimed Jacobsen's gun between her eyes. "I do beg your pardon, madam, but I require you to kneel."

Her smug expression wavered. "What? You jest!"

"I'm afraid not. Do as I ask, or I'll shoot the legs out from under you."

The smile was sweet and gentle beneath his cold, cold stare. Lady Armitage swallowed dryly. It was not so much the wicked pirate with a gun that she feared, but the likelihood of her knees giving out halfway down, leaving her flat on her face with her gown's bustle bouncing above her. Perhaps Signor de Luca divined this, or perhaps he was a gentleman behind the weapon, for he offered her his hand to steady her descent. She took it gratefully, a little tremulously, and began to lower herself.

And then jolted forward, reaching with her free hand to take possession of his, er, personal jewels.

But he was less of a gentleman than he seemed, and he twisted her hand in his, almost yanking the arm from its socket as he pulled her off-balance and shoved her to her knees. Ruffles concertinaed around her. Something snapped in the scaffolding beneath her skirts. Lady Armitage deflated into a puddle of satin and injured dignity.

Down—but not out. Her view gave her a new idea. "It seems I am well positioned to suggest a renegotiation of terms," she said eyebrows dancing suggestively (albeit briefly; she had to stop as one threatened to fall off).

Signor de Luca rolled his eyes. Tucking the gun into the back of his trousers, he grimaced with disgust, took a deep breath, and reached into her bodice.

"Why, Signor!" Lady Armitage gasped. She slipped her fingers into her sleeve, where a knife was concealed—and then paused. Any minute now, she would stab the impertinent cad. Any minute.

"What is going on here?" came a female voice, the sort that suggests fingernails might be dragged down a chalkboard if people did not start behaving soon.

Signor de Luca, with his hand still rummaging inside Lady Armitage's undergarments, looked back over his shoulder. Lady Armitage tipped herself to one side so she could also see. Her eyes widened as she found Cecilia Bassingthwaite in her sitting room, holding a tea tray.

"Just stealing the house," Signor de Luca explained. He pulled from Lady Armitage's bodice a handkerchief, a sachet of white oleander, half a biscuit, and finally a long silver key. He grinned at Cecilia, but she only frowned as she set down the tray.

"That was unchivalrous of you," she said. "I'm sure Lady Armitage would have given you the key had you asked her nicely."

"Of course I would have," Lady Armitage agreed. She slipped the concealed knife down a little farther.

"I doubt it," the signor retorted.

"Did you even ask permission before you intruded upon her intimate presence? I imagine not."

"Words aren't required if the lady gives permission with her eyes."

Lady Armitage began to speak in defense of her eyes, but the conversation rushed ahead without her.

"What, even in the dark of a broom closet? Er, for example."

"Light was coming in through the crack at the bottom of the door."

"And a gentleman is adept at translating a lady's eyes, is he?"

"A gentleman of experience is, yes."

"Experience but no"—she surveyed the length of his body— "house."

The signor bristled. "I can assure you, madam, that my real estate is of substantial—"

"Excuse me," Lady Armitage said before this conversation became too titillating even for her. "Why is Cecilia Bassingthwaite standing in my drawing room?"

"You told me to bring you her finger," Signor de Luca replied.

"Yes, but not attached to the rest of her person!"

"Captain Lightbourne has difficulty understanding what a lady tells him," Cecilia explained, pouring tea into three delicate cups. "Tells him with words, that is, not some supposed look she gives when she has a headache and did not sleep well."

"It's a common fault in men," Lady Armitage said. She silently figured what angle the knife might take between her wrist and Signor de Luca's heart. "Modern patriarchy shows a shameful lack of respect toward women."

Cecilia nodded. "Only last month I robbed a man and tied him to his horse, and he did not bid me good afternoon as I sent him on his way."

"Shocking! I can't tell you how many men have insulted me over the years." (Actually, it was seventeen, but she only knew this because she kept her apothecary receipts.)

"What we need is female suffrage," Cecilia opined as she laid lemon slices, cut into the shape of flowers, atop the tea.

"I'm not so sure about that," Lady Armitage argued. "We suffer enough as it is."

"I meant voting rights for women, Aunty," Cecilia explained. "Too many men believe they rule the world."

"I think—" Signor de Luca began, but the women turned their gazes like weapons upon him, and he took a hasty, instinctive step back. "Never mind."

"Take this fellow, for example," Lady Armitage said, tipping her head toward Signor de Luca. "Can't even rob a house properly. Whereas if you or your dear, blighted Aunt Darlington were in charge, it would be halfway out of town by now, with me hanging beneath from my laces."

"I have your key!" Signor de Luca reminded her, holding it up as proof.

She grinned. "You have *a* key, Signor."

"I—what?"

"That is the key to the place where my actual key is kept."

He narrowed his eyes at her menacingly. "And where is that, madam?"

"You don't want to know."

"Yes, I do."

"No," Cecilia said, walking over to hand him a teacup. "You really don't."

"I—I demand—"

"Besides," Cecilia continued, returning to the tray. "Aunty Army will help us once she hears what has happened."

"Aunty Army?" Signor de Luca stared at her incredulously. "This is the woman who paid me to kill you."

"I'm sure Cecilia isn't offended by a little thing like that," Lady Armitage said.

"Help her up now, please," Cecilia added, "so she may have her tea."

"You're joking, Cecilia."

"Do I ever joke?"

He frowned, she sighed with exasperation, and they stared at each other. You could have cut the tension (both psychological and sexual) with a knife. Which is exactly what Lady Armitage intended to do. Taking advantage of the distraction, she tugged the blade from her sleeve and threw it at the signor.

The air seemed to flash and shout. Lady Armitage's knife cracked a plate Cecilia had flung like a discus toward it, then veered off course and impaled itself in the previously shot shoulder of Jacobsen, lying stupefied on the floor. He jolted up, screaming, his eyes flung open in shock, and Cecilia promptly returned him to unconsciousness with a brisk application of the tea tray.

The signor looked about to comment but drank his tea with a politic silence instead. Lady Armitage began reaching for the knife concealed in her other sleeve.

"We do not have time for this," Cecilia said. "Aunty, Morvath has kidnapped the Society and stolen their houses. You can imagine the terrible danger my aunt Darlington will be facing in Northangerland Abbey. Yours is the only battlehouse remaining. We need it to effect a rescue. Furthermore, I have a hangover from eating seafood and may die at any moment, leaving you the only pirate captain available."

"I'm—" the signor said, then sighed. "Never mind."

"Good heavens!" Lady Armitage declared. "Why did you not say so from the start? Of course I shall help." She began to lift herself from the ground, accepting Signor de Luca's rather cautious assistance (for she could have got up on her own, absolutely, her knees were as strong as a maiden's, but a lady does like to be given her due respect). Once standing, her hair quivering, she extended her hand, palm up. After a moment of reluctance, Signor de Luca surrendered the key into it. Turning away, she lifted her skirts, rummaging beneath them. Metal scraped against metal.

Ned looked at Cecilia, an eyebrow raised. *Chastity belt*, she mouthed, and his face contorted in horror.

Lady Armitage turned back, smoothing her skirts and holding up a small, golden, slightly damp key. "We sail at once," she pronounced in a ringing voice. "No one kills Jemima Darlington but me."

❊ 13 ❊

HELL ON EARTH—A LOST OPPORTUNITY—SEMI-STARVATION—
LADY ARMITAGE GETS A TASTE OF HER OWN MEDICINE—
A SHOT IN THE DARK—THE PSYCHOLOGY OF PNEUMONIA—
ALBERT AND VICTORIA, BIBLE STUDENTS, NOT MANNA
FROM HEAVEN—FADE TO BLACK

One can be happy in eternal solitude: a book, a cup of tea, and no company; that was Cecilia's idea of heaven. Having spent the past week surrounded by people, and thwarted at every turn in her efforts to locate a library, she was now feeling as if she had endured an upper circle of hell.

As a consequence, she stood at the window of Lady Armitage's dining room with her arms crossed and her mouth tight as she stared out across the lush green fields where they had finally moored for the evening. "Blackdown Hills," she said—alas, not for the first time. "Hills. We have seen nothing but meadows for hours now."

"There was that hill in Stockland," Ned reminded her as he set a plate of cold meats on the table. She glanced at it unhappily.

Without servants in the house, they had been forced to contrive a dinner from whatever they could find in the kitchen, so whilst Lady Armitage mapped out a plan of reconnaissance for the morning, and

Jacobsen shouted from the room in which they had him locked, Ned and Cecilia had searched cupboards and pantries for food.

This had presented an ideal opportunity for charming comic scenes that would increase their rapport—a little explosion of flour, a splashing back and forth of water, a bumping of hips and gazes as they maneuvered the small kitchen spaces and reached awkwardly for spoons—but since Ned was queasy from airsickness, and Cecilia had just about reached the end of her tether, they had wasted said opportunity and managed to lay a dinner table in sadly efficient time.

It was slim pickings, with only two types of sliced meat, cold roast potatoes, smoked fish, scallop fritters, bread rolls with sweetened butter, asparagus, artichoke hearts, and a braised apple dessert that Ned had whipped up while Cecilia prepared the guns for possible battle and Lady Armitage bunny hopped the house across farm fields before finally coming in to land.

Cecilia didn't think she had an appetite even for such meager offerings. Every time she tried to rest her thoughts, they turned into a sword slicing through sunlight, Cilla screaming at her to run, Morvath laughing as he ripped her world apart. She grew unbearably tense with memory and fear. Was Aunt Darlington being killed that same way, even now? Ned had promised not. And yet, which Ned exactly had promised? The charming assassin, the Queen's noble Captain Smith, or the man who had been working with her father? Could she trust anything he said? Her brain advised not, but her heart whispered otherwise. As for her stomach—it was more taut than Lady Armitage's hair.

She'd expected to have found the abbey by now. Although Ned had explained that Morvath kept on the move, and Jacobsen had confirmed this on pain of having the information seduced out of him by Lady Armitage if he did not speak fast, she'd still assumed a day would be enough to find a hulking great abbey accompanied by various battlehouses—especially considering the geography of the area.

"Only an Englishman would call that knoll a hill," she said. "The village's church tower was higher."

"That was because of the angle you were viewing it from," Ned replied complacently. "Besides, look at all that horizon out there, full of mystery and distant magic."

She gave him a long, cool look. Despite his mischievous grin, he appeared worn-out: unshaven, his eyes shadowed, his clothes dusty from the road. Cecilia supposed she herself was not much better. "Nevertheless," she said, "the name Blackdown Hills conjures a different impression than this." She indicated the view from the window.

Wandering over, Ned put his hands in his pockets as he looked out across sunset meadows of rural peace, speckled with sheep and trimmed with lush hedges of wild rose and brambleberry. "I will admit," he said, "it's not the typical location for a villain's lair."

Cecilia sighed. She felt tremulous—which was due entirely to worry, she told herself, and not the presence of the scoundrel so close beside her. After all, she was a strong, modern woman. A blackstocking, if you will. If Ned Lightbourne dared kiss her again, she would . . . she would . . . make him walk the plank! Although there wasn't far for him to fall in these so-called hills. Slapping would be better! Mind you, she did not want to gain a reputation as a slapper. Stab him! Yes, that was a lovely thought. She would thrust a long, heavy knife into him, penetrating—

"Goodness, it's very hot in here," she murmured, and tugged on the window latch.

Ned glanced at her sidelong, smiling as if he could read her thoughts. "Are you quite well, Cecilia?"

"Just worried, that's all." The window would not open. She muttered something as she tugged harder.

"Let me." As he reached over to fiddle with the latch, his sleeve brushed her bodice. His scent of road dust and apple peel slipped through her senses. Cecilia took a hasty step back, knocked into a chair, stumbled forward again, and found herself pressed entirely against his body. Her inner Miss Darlington gasped. Her inner pirate remarked upon how many weapons he had secreted in interesting places. And her inner Lady Armitage, which even the sweetest girl has somewhere deep inside, whispered that not all of those hard-edged items were weapons and if she pressed a little closer—

Cecilia leaped back as if scorched.

"I'm afraid the window won't budge," Ned said as if nothing untoward had just occurred. He tugged on his shirt cuff, which had been displaced by a ribbon on her bodice, but not before Cecilia glimpsed part of the anchor tattoo on his wrist. She fanned herself vigorously with a hand.

"Can I fetch you a glass of water?" he asked.

"No. No thank you. I am perfectly fine and composed."

"Not hot, then?"

He looked at her impassively, but the slow sweep of his eyelashes fanned her inner flames, making her wonder whether Lady Armitage would mind terribly if she smashed the window in order to get a spot of fresh air.

"It's only that you seem to be glistening—just here." He reached out, drew a finger gently down one side of her throat. He watched himself do it, then raised his eyes to hold her gaze without a word, without a breath between either of them.

"Oh my heart," Cecilia whispered. Then she realized what she'd said and blinked furiously. "I mean my *aunt*. If I am perspiring somewhat, it is merely because I am worried about my aunt." This justification strengthened her wits, and she nodded primly. "Besides, I thought I had explained to you that it's indecorous to mention any condition of a woman's—a woman's—"

"Body? I beg your pardon. But I must say"—he leaned close,

whispering—"if I was truly to speak indecorously about your body, you'd not be thinking of your aunt afterward."

His breath brushed her ear, but she felt it in her wrists, her heart, and certain other unmentionable places—hot, flickering, like the memory of his kiss. She tried to summon a response but he stepped back, turning to look out the window. "Don't fret about Miss Darlington," he said. "It's only been one day. Well, and another half day. And a full night. And we won't be able to go anywhere tonight either. But really, they will be fine. Perhaps uncomfortable in his dungeon, that's all. There's no need for panic."

"A lady should never panic," Lady Armitage said, sweeping into the room. Her bulging, old-fashioned skirts scraped the edges of the doorway and reverberated with a *twang* of steel from the crinoline beneath. Although garbed entirely in black, as befitted a widow, she glimmered with crystal sequins like stars, since she was after all a merry widow. A diamond tiara was wedged into her hair. "A lady stays tranquil and poised under all circumstances. Instead of panicking, she squares her jaw, protects her heart, and ensures that she has enough ammunition to gun down everyone in her path. I say, is this glazed ham?"

They sat at the table—pirate matron, evil mastermind's daughter, and the man hired by the former to murder the latter. "Please pass the beans," Lady Armitage said.

There being in fact no beans on the table, Ned passed her the asparagus, and she began forking them onto her plate. Cecilia watched her, since it meant looking in the opposite direction from Ned, and as Lady Armitage stabbed asparagus, sawed at ham, and ripped apart artichoke hearts, she felt herself grow calm once more. Captain Lightbourne was a wicked flirt, that was all, and she would ignore him in a perfectly dignified manner.

"Could you pass the salt, please, Cecilia?" he asked.

"Certainly." She threw it at his head.

"I have been interrogating that Jefferson fellow some more," Lady Armitage said, mindless of Ned's grin as he caught the salt canister and Cecilia's scowl in response. "He agrees with you, Signor, that Morvath roves through the area. But I suspect we are not too far from his current hideout."

"Interrogating?" Ned asked pointedly. Lady Armitage smiled and shrugged.

"I find myself quite undone lately," she explained. Ned recollected the hiding place of her house key and almost choked on a potato.

"Why do you think the hideout is near, Aunty?" Cecilia asked.

"There is an inordinate amount of smoke coming from beyond the woods to starboard."

"A farmer burning rubbish," Ned suggested.

"Maybe," Lady Armitage said. "Or a dangerous pirate in an abbey with many chimneys."

"We should scout tonight, under the cover of darkness," Cecilia proposed as she cut her ham into tiny, precise squares.

"Certainly not," Lady Armitage replied. "A Darlington does not go about at night like some cheap footpad."

Ned frowned. "But you are not a Darlington, Lady Armitage. In fact, you are the sworn enemy of the clan. So how can you tell her—"

Lady Armitage's look was silencing. "Since Cecilia's aunt is not present, and her poor mother is bewingèd in heaven, I must take on the responsibility of guiding her at this time."

"She is an adult," Ned pointed out. "And while I don't wish to be repetitive, you did ask me two weeks ago to kill her on your behalf."

"Ned," Cecilia murmured. "One does not discuss attempted murder at the dinner table."

"Cilla would be very proud to know her daughter was up for assassination," Lady Armitage said, waving an impatient hand to dismiss the topic.

Ned shrugged and ate his dinner without another word while the ladies talked about the weather. When the meal was finished and Lady Armitage retired to drink sherry and smoke a cigar in the drawing room, the younger pirates took the dishes into the kitchen.

"I shall investigate that smoke tonight," Cecilia reiterated as she stacked plates into the sink as preparation for a cleaning process she had no idea how to undertake, never having washed a dish in her life. "If it is Morvath, he might have noticed our approach and so by morning will be ready for us."

Ned paused in scraping leftovers into a bucket. "Don't you think it would be astonishingly convenient if, given the entire Blackdown Hills region, we chanced to land half a mile from where Morvath is hiding?"

"Indeed. It's the sort of thing that would happen only in a badly written novel."

"Or if Lady Armitage has betrayed you."

Cecilia frowned. "She wouldn't do such a thing."

"She paid for your assassination."

"Why do you keep raising that? We are scoundrels, Ned. We do not have polite, indoor disagreements. Besides, Aunty Army has always opposed Morvath. It would make no sense for her to betray me to him now."

"Oh, well, of course, everything Lady Armitage does is sensible."

Cecilia sighed but did not bother to argue. The truth was, she did not entirely possess the understanding to do so. The mix of immorality and manners practiced by not only Lady Armitage but all the Wisteria Society had long ago confounded her ability to think critically, requiring her to take constant refuge in dissociation. "I intend to investigate. You may stay here and guard the house."

"No," he said, taking a step toward her. "I'll come with you."

"We cannot go walking together at night unchaperoned."

He laughed. "How can you say that after having spent the past two days alone in my company?"

"Bad behavior in the past does not mean bad behavior must necessarily follow in the—" She paused, watching guardedly as he took another step closer, remembering his touch against her bare skin as they stood in the dining room earlier. The thought of it made her shiver, and her words scattered away. What had she been saying? Something about bad behavior in the—? "The bedroom," she said at a guess, and as he grinned in response she realized it had been a very wrong guess indeed.

"So I take it you mean no more kissing?" he asked.

"I most certainly do mean that!" She backed against the sink, but still he kept coming, and now she had nowhere further to retreat.

"But what about your eyes, Miss Bassingthwaite?" he asked. "What message do they give?"

He had moved so close she noticed a tiny, faded scar on his left cheek. So close she would not even have to extend her arm in order to—er, to slap him, of course! He was taller than her, and she had to tilt her head slightly to see that scar and the smiling blue eye above it. Suddenly she became aware how exposed her throat was, and worse, her lips. She looked down hastily.

This was a yet another mistake. The upper button of his shirt was undone, revealing tanned skin. Cecilia had never seen beneath a man's collar before; it was more titillating than she would have envisioned, had she been the kind of girl who envisions that sort of thing. She tried to look away, but he seemed to fill her entire view, so instead she laid a hand against his chest.

"My eyes are telling you to stand back, sir."

"Fair enough. But if you want me to do that, you should probably push me."

"I am pushing you." Her fingers traced the embroidery on his waistcoat.

He bent his head and murmured so near her ear it felt like a stroking touch, "Harder, Cecilia."

"But, sir," she managed to say, despite the fire burning through her wits. "A soft touch is more polite."

"Oh really?" He kissed her cheek softly. "Was that polite?"

All her nerves clamored to answer. But she contradicted them with determined calm. "I suppose it was."

He smiled. With a movement as soft as velvet, he kissed her mouth. "And was that polite?"

"Less so," Cecilia breathed.

"What about this?" He bit her lower lip so softly she gasped from the fierce gentleness of it. Immediately he took the chance to slip his tongue inside, sweeping its tip against the roof of her mouth until she moaned and clutched at his waistcoat. How rude he was! How disgraceful! She lifted herself on her toes to get closer, curving her tongue around his, not wanting him to escape.

But he drew back, and she caught her breath in regret before she could stop herself. He blinked at the sound of it, and for one small moment he looked as vulnerable as she felt. Then he took her face between his hands and kissed her again, long and deep and achingly tender. The softness filled her body, made her feel so boneless she had to lean against him to stay upright. He wrapped an arm around her, drawing her in more surely, moving his kisses from her mouth to her temple and brow. She wrapped a leg around his and, in an act that felt more daring than leaping from an airborne house, briefly kissed his jaw.

He tensed against her. His breath shook. So she kissed him again, even braver this time, at the corner of his mouth. He shifted, and their lips met, their hearts met; disarmed, she slipped with him into warm, lush bliss.

Slowly the kiss eased. The embrace of their bodies deepened until passion became comfort, mouths separating but hearts drawing closer. Their pulses felt like small, gentle kisses through their clothes. Cecilia sighed. This, now, was a softness more dangerous than any weapon. When was the last time anyone had held her in such a fashion? Not since the day her mother died. Cecilia hadn't understood until now how much she'd longed for it.

"I'm sorry for being impolite," he said.

"So you should be," she murmured, closing her eyes, wishing she could remain in his arms forever.

"When next we discuss hardness, it will be somewhere more conducive to a demonstration than Lady Armitage's kitchen."

Cecilia smiled dreamily—and then began to frown as her wits worked through that sentence. Their eventual comprehension shocked her, and she pushed him away with the fervor she really should have applied several moments ago. He stepped back, grinning rakishly.

But his eyes were heavy, and there was a depth to his grin she did not want to see. The man was a scoundrel, nothing more, and she must resist him! Turning away, she snatched a lantern from the kitchen bench.

"I'm going to search for Morvath's house," she said firmly.

"I'm going with you," Ned replied.

"No. Someone needs to stay and watch over Lady Armitage." And getting some distance from this man seemed like a wise idea right now.

"She's not a concern. I put a sleeping draft in her sherry."

Cecilia frowned. "Where did you get a sleeping draft?"

He crossed the kitchen to tap against a small cupboard set on the wall above the coffee grinder. Its door was marked with the word *Poisons*, beneath which was a delicate etching of a flower.

"I see," Cecilia said. "Well, in that case I suppose you may come." She glared at him, but in the depths of her mind she felt a fizzing, as if her traitorous wits had opened a bottle of wine.

Ned smiled sardonically. "Thank you, my lady."

"But you have to behave yourself."

His smile vanished. In three swift strides he was with her again and had his hand beneath her chin, tipping it up, before she could even catch her breath. She stared at him wide-eyed, pulse racing, as he bent toward her.

"Madam," he said.

"Yes?" It was more an exhalation than an actual word.

"Of course I will behave."

"You will?"

He began smiling again, slowly, like a finger slipping down her neck. "I give you my word as a scoundrel."

"Oh. Er, good."

He let her go, stepped back, his smile as crooked as his manners. Cecilia recalled Lady Armitage's advice and squared her jaw, looked away to protect her heart, and envisioned shooting Captain Lightbourne down on her well-swept inner path to tranquility.

Except then she had to return in imagination and minister to him, hiring a doctor to tend his gunshot wounds, making a bed for him in Aunt Darlington's guest room, feeding him soup spiced with herbal remedies Pleasance swore would not turn him into a vampire (although he might develop a craving for blood pudding), and lighting candles for his sake in church on Sundays. And as he lay sleeping, his long eyelashes casting shadows over his cheekbones, his muscular chest rising and falling gently beneath his damp, transparent night-shirt . . .

"Damn!" Cecilia swore for the first time in her life, causing Ned to jolt with surprise. He turned away from the door of Lady Armitage's drawing room and put a finger to his lips.

"She's asleep," he whispered. "What's wrong?"

"Nothing," Cecilia replied. "That is, I stubbed my toe."

"Inside your boots?"

"Yes. Stop looking at me like that."

"Like what?"

"With those eyelashes like that."

"Um, all right." He tried to wrangle his bemused expression into a smile. "Why don't *you* stay here and guard the house, maybe have a bit of a sleep? I'll go scout around and report back to you."

"No." She pulled black leather gloves from a pocket of her riding tunic and began to yank them onto her hands with such vehemence Ned expected her at any moment to break a finger. "Shall we proceed?"

He chuckled quietly, so as to not wake Lady Armitage, and gestured along the corridor. "Lead the way, madam."

By the dim light of a lantern, they crossed the field toward the oak woods. Ned took the lead then, being more familiar with the nocturnal hazards of a meadow. With his guidance they avoided cow pats, thistles, sudden ditches, murky dark puddles, and an iron rake someone had left lying about just waiting for a comic moment. They entered the woods. They had not gone far among the trees before a sudden noise alarmed them; dousing the lantern, Ned pulled Cecilia behind the shelter of an oak. Silently, barely breathing, they listened.

Someone else was creeping through the woods with a hesitancy that suggested stealth, although they were trampling fallen branches and leaves with a clumsiness that suggested a desire to be murdered by pirates. Ned and Cecilia looked at each other by faint moonlight. Ned pointed to Cecilia, raised his hand, then pointed beyond the tree. Cecilia nodded. Drawing the gun from his belt, Ned took a steadying breath, then leaped forth.

"Stop or I'll shoot!" he warned the stranger.

Or at least he began thus. He was, however, interrupted by Cecilia also leaping from behind the tree, gun rising as she, too, warned the stranger to stop.

"Excuse me?" Ned turned to her impatiently.

"What?" she said, glancing at him.

"I told you to stay behind the tree."

"No. You did this." She repeated the gestures he'd used, her gun waving as she did so.

"Yes, which means 'Stay behind the tree.'"

"That's ridiculous."

"Something's ridiculous," the stranger agreed.

They turned, weapons straightening, and stared at the gray-haired man before them in the moonlight. He was armed with a rifle.

"Jokerson!" Cecilia exclaimed.

"Jacobsen," he corrected through gritted teeth. "Drop your guns."

"No," Ned answered, and shot him.

Jacobsen screamed and flung backward, his rifle shooting at the sky. He smashed into the ground and lay abruptly silent.

Cecilia winced. "You didn't have to kill him."

Ned walked over to nudge a booted foot against the man. "He's not dead. I only shot his shoulder. He must have hit his head when he fell."

"Poor fellow."

Ned looked up from retrieving Jacobsen's rifle and stared at her incredulously. "He was going to kill us."

"Even so." She holstered her gun. "I don't like violence."

"Well, you're in the wrong profession, then, sweetheart." He emptied the rifle of its ammunition and threw bullets and gun in opposite directions. "We should probably return to the house. He might have killed Lady Armitage in his escape."

"I doubt that."

"Oh? Why?"

"Because he's still alive," answered a voice from the shadows.

Ned sighed.

"Aunty Army," Cecilia said as if meeting the lady on a London street in the middle of the afternoon.

Lady Armitage moved into view, stepping loudly on a twig as she did.

"So that noise was you," Ned said. "I thought it unlikely of Jacobsen. How are you even here? I gave you a sleeping potion."

"I appreciate your candor, Signor," Lady Armitage replied. "Strange quality for a pirate, but there you go. I, on the other hand, am not stupid enough to be honest. The potions in my cabinet are all mislabeled. You gave me something to cleanse my liver."

Ned could only laugh. "Touché," he said, bowing.

"But, Aunty," Cecilia said, "you shouldn't be out here. It's dangerous."

"I am a pirate terror, my dear."

"Yes, but it's also cold. You'll catch pneumonia."

"Nonsense. Pneumonia is only for young ladies whose aunts wish to repress them so that they never become independent and leave said aunts alone."

Cecilia gasped. Behind her, Ned nodded in agreement, but when

Cecilia turned to frown at him he shook his head instead, mouth hunched in firm disagreement.

"It's not your fault," Lady Armitage continued. "Jemima should have known better than to be so inhibiting. She saw what happened when her sister tried to keep Cilla on a tight leash. For that matter, she lived the consequences of her own wild youth. But it was obviously in your blood to break free and run off into the dark with a wicked boy."

"I'm not a boy," Ned interjected, but Cecilia spoke over him.

"Aunt Darlington had a wild youth?"

Both Lady Armitage and Ned looked at her with surprise.

"You don't know?" Ned asked.

Cecilia frowned. "Know what?"

"Never mind," Lady Armitage said firmly. "We should not stand here gossiping. If Morvath is out there, he will have heard you shooting that Jingelsen chap."

"How did Jacobsen even get free?" Ned asked.

"No idea."

"So he wasn't released by someone and sent out here to kill us?"

Lady Armitage gasped. "Of course not! What do you take me for, Signor?" Her smirk made a response unnecessary. "We must hurry now; there is much to do. If the abbey is indeed yonder, we must return to my house and prepare for battle in the morning—and assassinating Cecilia in the afternoon, Signor de Luca, if you please, or else I'd like my deposit refunded."

"Why don't I kill her now and get it over with?" Ned asked dryly.

"In a woods? She is not a peasant; have some respect!"

"Fine. But we go forth quietly—does everyone understand? No stamping on twigs, no sudden leaping out from behind trees. If that is Northangerland Abbey, we do not want to get caught."

"I agree," Lady Armitage said promptly.

Ned turned to Cecilia for her reply, but she was gazing off through the darkness with a thoughtful look in her eye. "Cecilia?" he said nervously.

She blinked and looked back at him. "What? Oh. Yes, I agree. We most certainly do not want to get caught and taken into the abbey."

Ned frowned at her. Lady Armitage frowned at her. She smiled brightly in return. "Are we going, then?"

"Just to look," Ned clarified.

"Of course." Her smile faded into a wounded expression. "Don't you trust me?"

Ned sighed. This was, after all, innocent young Cecilia, who had never gone more than a few hours from her aunt's guidance. Her big eyes gazing at him with hurt made him want to cringe apologetically. "Yes, I trust you," he said, smiling.

Lady Armitage made a snorting noise, but when they glanced at her she waved a hand beneath her nose. "Don't mind me. Allergies."

Ned sighed again and shook his head, then turned to lead a cautious way through the woods. Cecilia came close behind him, not at all smirking, followed by Lady Armitage. The old lady stepped on one twig and then, at a frown from Ned, became as silent as a rogue.

"I can't believe you don't know about your aunt and Morvath," Ned whispered to Cecilia.

"Know what?" she asked again.

"I'll tell you later."

After about fifteen minutes, the woods gave way to a bare field. The moon had passed behind a cloud, leaving the world heavy with darkness. They could see only the barest shapes of field, hedges, woods, and about five hundred feet away an innocent farmhouse hunched beside a few trees, light in one window, smoke rising from its chimney.

"No abbey," Ned whispered.

"That's strange," Cecilia whispered in reply. "I was so sure it would be here."

"Why?"

"Perhaps just wishful thinking. But Aunty Army did have me convinced."

"Hmm." He turned back to the old lady and stopped, suddenly cold.

"Shit."

"Captain!" Cecilia scolded. "You should not speak like that in the presence of ladies."

"Lady," he corrected.

"What?"

"Lady. Your Aunty Army is gone."

"Nonsense." Cecilia turned also, and her breath caught. "Aunty?" she called, but there was no reply. Lady Armitage had vanished.

Ned drew his gun. "We're in trouble."

"She must have tripped."

"Don't be stupid."

"Sir!"

"She's set us up."

"But there's nothing here. Besides, Aunty Army wouldn't betray me to Morvath. She must have got lost in the darkness."

"Only if you're speaking metaphorically." He indicated skyward, and Cecilia looked up to see Armitage House flying rather lopsidedly toward the eastern horizon.

"How rude," she said. "Never mind. We shall continue searching for the abbey."

"No, we shall steal that farmhouse and get out of here fast."

Cecilia frowned. "But—"

"Two of us on foot with only a pistol each will be no match for an entire abbey filled with cannons, armed servants, and a captive fleet of battlehouses."

"I also have a razor-sharp hairpin."

Ned laughed.

"I am not giving up on Aunt Darlington."

His expression became instantly sober. "I know. Neither am I. But we have to be sensible. We've almost certainly walked into a trap. That farmhouse is our only hope."

"But we can't fly it without a wheel and sextant."

"Have you never bodged a wheel together out of spoons and fencing wire? And we don't need to navigate, just get away." He grasped her hand and without further argument they ran across the field to the quiet, unsuspecting house. Darkness pressed heavily against them, as if rain was on the way. The air seemed to moan. Stumbling onto the rough mat of the farmhouse threshold, they caught their breath for a moment and then Ned knocked politely on the door.

"I've never stolen a house before," Cecilia confessed. "What is the etiquette?"

"Less direct than with a coach, and it's a little harder to get in. But once you do there's usually tea and a comfortable sofa."

The door opened and a man with profuse brown whiskers peered out suspiciously. "What?" he demanded.

"Good evening," Ned answered, all languid charm and innocent eyes. "My name is Mr. Albert, and this is my wife, Victoria. We were on our way home from Bible study when we broke the wheel of our carriage. We're hoping you might be able to point us in the direction of shelter for the night. We will happily pay for any advice you can offer. And perhaps, if you would be so kind, a drop of tea?"

The man's eyes narrowed. "You're not pirates, are you?"

"Do we look like pirates, sir?" Both he and Cecilia smiled broadly at the farmer.

"Well . . . Pay me, you say?"

"Absolutely."

"As it happens, my wife has just put on the ket—"

He stopped, his eyes growing wide as he stared with horror at something above and beyond Ned's shoulder. The pirates looked at each other and sighed. The farmer slammed his door shut. Bolts clattered into place.

"Well, at least we don't have to go to the trouble of house-stealing," Cecilia said.

"True. I say, have I told you how lovely your eyes look in the spotlight from an enemy's turret?"

"You're kind to say so."

They turned to watch the vast dark abbey descend from the sky in front of them.

Cecilia squinted up at the dozen windows bristling with cannons and guns. "Goodness, this is a shame," she commented mildly.

Ned stared at her openmouthed.

She shrugged. "I told you I wanted to get inside that abbey. If that means being captured, I really don't mind."

"You're mad. We need to run!"

But suddenly the great abbey door slammed open and three armed men dressed in black appeared.

"Lightbourne!" one growled. "Traitor! Do me a favor and try to escape, so I have a reason to shoot you."

Ned raised his eyes with amusement. "Don't be so dramatic, Randall. You're impressing no one. I'm here on Morvath's doorstep with his long-lost daughter, just as I was ordered to be. Far from being a traitor, I expect I'm due a pay rise for a job well done."

He winked at Cecilia. She gave him a vicious look and stepped back as if he was suddenly filthy.

"Oh, no, you don't," he said, catching her arm, pulling her back against him. "No trying to run away!"

"I wasn't," she began to say, but he clamped a hand over her mouth. She struggled, but his grip was serious and unbudging. "Randall, there's a bottle of chloroform and a handkerchief in my coat pocket. Get them out for me, will you?"

"Mmmph-mph!" Cecilia declaimed.

"Don't worry," Ned told her as Randall fumbled in his pocket. "It's not one of Aunty Army's potions. I always carry a little chloroform with me in case the need arises to kidnap someone." He grinned as her eyes widened. "That's right, I could have rendered you unconscious at any time and taken you to your father. Or prison. Or wherever I chose. So now will you be quiet?"

She responded by stamping on his foot. He did not even flinch. Taking the soaked handkerchief from Randall, he pressed it against her nose and mouth. "Have you had a busy day?" he asked Randall conversationally as Cecilia struggled in his arms.

"Oh, you know," Randall replied, shrugging. "Taunting prisoners, target practice, listening to the captain rave—the usual."

"Uh-huh," Ned said, and looked down at Cecilia. She was sagging against his shoulder, eyelids fluttering. "And there she goes," he said, smiling.

Cecilia felt herself falling, falling, even as Ned's arm held her up. Her last thought before the darkness overwhelmed her was that Aunt Darlington was going to be most annoyed indeed.

✻ 14 ✻

CONSTANTINOPLA LETS TOM TAKE THE LEAD—
FORBIDDEN CHOCOLATE—WINDSOR—HER MAJESTY'S LINEN—
HER MAJESTY'S PERSON—THE DANGERS OF TOAST—
AN ACCURATE PARROT—
THE PARROT HOPEFULLY GETS IT WRONG

Constantinopla did not think Tom Eames had any right to command her merely because he was older than her, or because he had seen more of the world than her. After all, one's claim to superiority depends on the use one has made of one's time and experience, and while Tom had been attached to his mother's apron strings for years, visiting boring museums (and robbing them), meeting boring aristocrats (and robbing them), Constantinopla had learned really important things, like how to make fudge over a Bunsen burner in a dormitory after lights-out and how much salt could be put into a teacher's tea before she noticed. Tom might be three years older, but Constantinopla was obviously his superior in meaningful ways.

However, she was not so far ignorant as to tell him this. When he put his manly foot down and insisted they return to Ottery St. Mary— "You are too young, Oply, to understand the consequences of your actions," he declared with all his new and unexpected authority as her fiancé—she grudgingly surrendered.

And yet they somehow managed to take a wrong turn among the country lanes, a fact Tom realized only when they were several miles toward London.

And when at Taunton he decided traveling by horse would be better than by train, Constantinopla agreed only moments before a male passerby snatched her purse and ran into the station, boarding a train for London. Tom gallantly chased him, with Constantinopla close behind, and he was on the verge of confronting the man at gunpoint when lo! she discovered she'd not lost her purse after all; it was merely in the other pocket. By then the train had pulled out from the station and there was nothing for it but to take seats in first class (stealing tickets from fellow passengers and tut-tutting judgmentally when those passengers were forced back to third class), to enjoy a dinner of roast pheasant, and to sleep until dawn ushered them into Windsor.

"Thank goodness I have you at my side to guide and protect me," Constantinopla had said as they ate the chocolate dessert Tom vetoed on the grounds it would make her sick but the waiter brought anyway, and of course one does not waste food. "How lucky I am that you proposed! We shall have such a happy marriage with you at the helm."

Although Tom could not actually recall proposing, he had smiled at this, and when she had curled up with her head on his lap to sleep, he'd felt nothing but adoration for her (literally: his legs went numb within half an hour and remained that way all night).

At Windsor, Tom determinedly took the upper hand. "We will not attempt to enter the castle," he declared. "Instead, we will inform the police about Morvath's plot."

"That makes good sense," Constantinopla agreed. "After all, what pirate doesn't seek help from the police in relation to her business? But perhaps we ought to change our clothes first, since we are rather dirty from our travels?"

Tom could see no harm in this. Therefore, Constantinopla followed him into a department store, where she modestly refused his offers of pink silk and creamy lace, choosing instead a simple black dress, which was less costly (not that Tom actually paid for them, since the store was not open for business at this early hour). They ate bonbons from the confectionery counter while changing clothes.

"But wouldn't you prefer a velvet hat with a feather?" Tom asked, perplexed, as Constantinopla set a white mobcap on her head.

"I want to be a good, frugal wife for you," she explained. "Let me help with your tie."

"I look like a butler," he said, scowling at his image in a glass cabinet as she reknotted the tie he was sure he'd got perfect.

"Not at all," Constantinopla murmured. "Not at all."

They left behind their own clothes and exited through a back door, politely locking it again behind them.

"Our clothes were worth far more than these ones," Tom said, "so it's not really stealing. In fact, the store is stealing from us."

"You are so clever," Constantinopla replied dreamily.

He smiled and puffed out his chest, and from there was easily persuaded that his idea of taking a shortcut along Queen Charlotte Street was an excellent one . . . then provoked in his protectiveness to enter a doorway when Constantinopla was sure she felt raindrops . . . and then inspired to climb a wall, follow a side path, duck out of the sight of a guard, turn left instead of right, and risk another door that would surely lead them out of this maze . . .

Whereupon they found themselves inside Windsor Castle's laundry room.

"Goodness me, what a surprise!" Constantinopla declared.

Tom frowned at her.

"I can see from your grim expression that you're thinking now we're here, and by pure chance dressed like servants, we might as well try to find the Queen. Very wise, my love."

She turned away from his darkening eyes, for if there's one thing midnight fudge-making teaches you (along with cunning, careful measuring, operating dangerous equipment in the dark, avoiding burns, and where to hide your sugar), it's how to not let things boil over. She heard Tom take a deep, calming breath, and by the time she turned back he was smiling with reluctant admiration for her machinations.

"All right, pirate girl," he said, bowing. "You win—this time. But understand for the future that I intend to be the head of my household."

"Of course, dearest. I defer to your greater understanding."

He grinned. "Since we're here, let's go find a queen."

Provisioned with stacks of folded clean linen, they made their way through the gorgeous halls of Windsor Castle. Tom's fingers itched to steal gold knickknacks and silver objets d'art displayed on the sideboards they passed, but Constantinopla had learned restraint (overindulge in fudge and you'd be too sick for Master Luxe's fencing class the next day) and she kept him on task. They saw only a footman, leaning half-asleep against the wall, a carpet sweeper, and a chambermaid who stopped them, demanding to know what they were doing.

"Been called to change the linen in Her Majesty's bedroom," Constantinopla said in what she supposed was an Irish accent, but which sounded more like a mix between Cockney and too much rum.

"Spilled her tea again, did she?" The maid sighed. "You'd better hurry, then, before she starts throwing food."

They walked on, glancing with relief at each other—

"Wait!" the maid called.

Their feet stopped, as did their pulses. Slowly they turned back. The maid looked at them with her hands on her hips.

"Where do you think you're going?"

"Um, I told you—"

"What is the matter with you, girl?"

"Um—"

"Are you new here or something?"

"Yes'm. Just over from Ireland. On account of being Irish, you see. Started yesterday."

"Well, that explains why you are going the long way. Take this corridor back here, then turn right, then left." She smiled warmly. "It's a big place, but don't worry, you'll soon learn all the shortcuts. Hurry now. She threw a triangle of toast at Belledy when he was late and nearly put out his eye."

"Cheers," Constantinopla said, and they hastily followed the directions. Once away from the helpful maid, Constantinopla grimaced.

"Mama will wash my mouth out with soap if she finds out I said *cheers.*"

Tom laughed. "I think she's going to be a little more concerned at you traveling unchaperoned to Windsor, breaking into the Queen's residence, and getting engaged without her permission."

"Well, we can only wait and see how she and Daddy react when they come back from excavating the Tomb of Minyas (and robbing it)."

They found the door to Queen Victoria's bedroom and were stopped by a guard.

"You there, servant fellow, let us in," Tom ordered, flapping a hand peremptorily. "We have clean sheets for Victoria's bed."

Constantinopla rolled her eyes. The guard flicked her a glance, then returned his impassive stare to somewhere just beyond Tom's face. "To clarify," he said in a voice as sharp as the sword he wore, "you—neither of whom I have seen before in the palace, and wearing nonstandard attire—seek to enter Her Majesty's bedchamber on the dubious premise of providing her with fresh bedding, although she has only now awakened and is enjoying her pre-breakfast meal?"

Constantinopla stepped forward before Tom could speak again. "They said downstairs it was urgent. She spilled her tea."

The man regarded her sternly. "No one has been in or out of her room since the tray was delivered, so how do you know this calamity has occurred?"

Constantinopla suffered one second of sheer blank terror before inspiration struck. "She telephoned down to the housekeeper."

"And what is the housekeeper's telephone number?"

"One-two-four-three," Constantinopla said promptly, guessing that he did not actually know himself.

He sighed, mouth flattening, as if disappointed. "Very well. You may enter."

Tom reached for the door handle.

"But—!"

They froze, staring anxiously at him.

"Be careful," he advised in a low voice. "Watch out for flying toast. And if she asks you to pull her finger, don't. Just—really don't."

They nodded and opened the door.

An odor of old dog wafted out.

Constantinopla and Tom glanced at each other nervously, then entered, the door swinging shut behind them.

Queen Victoria sat in an enormous four-poster bed at the center of the room, eating a buttered muffin. She was at once tiny (vertically) huge (horizontally) and terrifying (psychologically). Her round face moved as she chewed, but her small, dark eyes seemed fixed on a point in the mid-distance. Two dogs lay on the floor at the end of her bed, a large green parrot sat on a lampshade, and the long-departed Prince Albert reclined on pillows at the Queen's side—which is to say, in the form of a black-framed portrait.

Tom was struck insensible by the majestic, albeit domestic, vision of the Queen. But Constantinopla had been raised among women who considered themselves Victoria's equal, *at least*, and stepped forward undaunted. She laid her stack of linen on a nearby chair, then curtsied. "Your Maj—"

The Queen held up a silencing hand. Constantinopla waited as Victoria finished masticating. At last the Queen sighed with satisfaction and looked up.

"Yes?"

"Your Majesty, my name is—"

"Thief!" squawked the parrot. Constantinopla almost leaped out of her skin.

"I swear, I've stolen nothing," she said. "From—from the castle, at any rate. I am a pirate, it is true, but—"

"A pirate!" the Queen declared, not amused. "You warned me this day would come, Albert. The assassins have reached my inner chamber!"

"No, no." Constantinopla rushed forward two steps, then froze as the Queen grabbed for some toast. She curtsied again urgently. "I assure you, I mean no harm. My name is—"

"I could have been a pirate if I wasn't Queen," the Queen warned. She squinted as if calculating the best angle at which to take out Constantinopla's eye with a square of marmalade-covered sourdough. "One more step and I'll impale you."

"Death to thieves!" hollered the parrot, and one of the dogs lifted its head and barked.

Constantinopla's thoughts began to spin. But she was a pirate maiden, she had been trained for battle, and she could surely withstand a conversation with the Queen. "Your Majesty, my-name-is-Constantinopla-Brown-and-I-bring-you-urgent-news." She paused to take a breath, and Queen Victoria bit sharply into the toast. Marmalade oozed.

"Well? What news?" the Queen asked through her mouthful. "Hurry up, I don't have all day. As soon as we've finished here we have to go down to breakfast, don't we, Albert dear?"

Constantinopla glanced at the portrait and then back at the Queen, dazed. "Captain Morvath has stolen a dozen battlehouses and presents a serious threat to your throne!"

"Egad! Such horror! Who is Captain Morvath?"

"Er, a dreadful pirate, Your Majesty."

"As opposed to a nice pirate? You are all fiends! Do you know how much tax income I've lost because of you? How many ladies I've had come crying to me about stolen diamonds or stolen husbands?"

"Er, sorry," Constantinopla said meekly.

"And who is that?" the Queen demanded, waving toast at Tom. He cringed.

"Moron!" squawked the parrot.

Constantinopla repressed a traitorous corner of her mouth. "Your Majesty, may I present Mr. Eames, my fiancé. He is a pirate gentleman. Your Majesty, Captain Ned Smith sent us as his official emissaries to warn you about Morvath's evil plan." She eyed the parrot, praying it did not squawk *Liar!*

Silence, thank God.

More silence. Somewhat worrying.

Even more silence. Constantinopla held her breath.

At last, the Queen swallowed toast.

"Dear Ned. Such a charming fellow, looks awfully splendid in shirtsleeves."

"Hmm," Constantinopla agreed, her eyes softening. Tom scowled.

"But what is he doing? I sent him to deal with Miss Cecilia some-one. You might have heard of her father, a dreadful pirate, Captain Morris or Morepain or—"

"Morvath, Your Majesty?" Constantinopla suggested.

"No, I don't think so. But then, when you're surrounded by so many pompous men who think they can manage the realm better than you can, the names tend to blur together."

"May I ask what you mean by Captain Smith dealing with Cecilia, Your Majesty?"

"I don't think I shall tell you," the Queen said. "That's confidential Crown business. Don't you agree, Albert dear?"

The portrait of Prince Albert did not reply.

Constantinopla felt her heart, stomach, and life span shrink. Was Ned Smith, alias Teddy Luxe, commissioned to harm or imprison Cecilia? And Constantinopla had left her alone in his company! Miss Darlington was going to kill her.

If Queen Victoria did not do so first.

"Your Majesty, I—"

The Queen held up a spoonful of porridge with the same attitude as a pirate holding a grenade, and Constantinopla took a step back.

"Enough talking, girl. You have ruined my appetite. I almost cer-tainly won't be able to finish these oats before going down to breakfast."

"Your—"

"But I know just what to do with you. Adisa!" she called in a high, sharp voice, much like the sound a whip makes the moment before it connects with its hapless victim.

The door flung open and the enormous guard strode in, sword drawn.

Constantinopla blanched. Tom whimpered.

"Ha ha!" squawked the parrot. "You're dead!"

❈ 15 ❈

Cecilia had never wished to be a girl again, half-wild and hardy and free. Although she had been brought fairly late to propriety and self-restraint, she found they suited her. Indeed, if she were a bird, she would happily allow a net to ensnare her.

Granted, she might cut that net with her dagger, fashion a hammock from it, and lie in said hammock reading books and drinking lemonade someplace no one would bother her, but that is beside the point.

She remembered with discomfort her early years running barefoot and undisciplined through the forest of rooms in Northangerland Abbey while Cilla indulged in romantic ideas about parenting. "Frolic!" she had urged Cecilia. "Sing! Dance! Only don't disturb your papa when he's machinating evil in his study." Other pirate children were allowed to learn map reading, and write out the dictionary, and develop their posture by means of walking with a sword balanced on their head. But Cecilia had been forced to play with dolls.

Her father hadn't approved, which was one of the reasons Cilla left him (that and his penchant for trying to destroy the world). But he hadn't exactly been on Cecilia's side either.

"I will not have a daughter with a coward soul," he had declared, his eyes lit with the passion he felt whenever echoing one Brontë or another. He'd caught her reading a textbook in the sitting room, thus embarrassing him in front of the embezzler he was about to beat up. "Throw that book into the fire and go hunt for ghosts or draw eerie pictures on the wallpaper," he'd demanded.

"But it's arithmetic," Cecilia had said in a small, mournful voice.

Captain Morvath had rolled his eyes at the embezzler, who'd shrugged sympathetically. (He would have sympathized even if the captain had told Cecilia to go play with a crocodile, so desirous was he to appease Morvath and avoid a thrashing.)

"Arithmetic," the captain had scoffed. "What nonsense! I won't allow it. You need to live your life like wild poetry!"

He'd snatched the book, tossed it on the hearth fire, and given her a toy gun instead.

The memory tugged on her as she tried to haul herself out of drugged unconsciousness toward a familiar smell of old dusty wood. She felt cold against her face. She heard the wuthering of strange breezes through solemn corridors. Northangerland Abbey had been a spruce, well-lit, modern building until her father took possession of it. He spent years transforming it to a state of mournful gloom. It was, he liked to say, his tangible opus.

He was, everyone else said, a pretentious idiot.

A pretentious idiot with a whole lot of guns and the willingness to use them.

Whether Cilla had chosen to live with him or been forced into it, no one now would ever know. But there had come a time when, unable to bear the thought of yet another miserable day anchored on dreary, uninhabited moorland while her husband tried to find inspiration for a novel, she'd finally escaped.

Cecilia did not want to remember. She fought to wake completely, but memory got its scarred claws right around her and dragged her back down. She became a small child again, cold and frightened, clambering out a window into her mother's arms . . .

"We have to run, darling," Cilla had whispered, smiling despite the tears in her swollen eyes. "Don't be afraid. A whole world of fun and games is ahead of us!"

Little Cecilia had not liked the sound of that, but she'd obeyed. They had fled across the moors, their dark cloaks swooping, the moonlight plucking at them with long, ghostly fingers. If Morvath had seen it he would have run after them with pen and paper, begging them to describe their emotions as they went (and then dragging them home). But Morvath had been hunched over a glass of brandy in his study, feeling sorry for himself, and by the time he realized they had gone and made chase, it was too late. "We're safe now," Cilla had promised as they made their way to London and Miss Darlington . . .

She had been wrong.

Two years later, on a sunlit field in Greenwich, as Cilla blew dandelions and Cecilia danced laughing after them, Morvath had finally caught up.

"Run!" her mother had cried then too, much louder and wilder than before. So Cecilia had run again, run alone into a world that held no more fun and games, at least not until she met a half-Italian pirate with a sweet, wayward smile. She'd run until Miss Darlington found her crouched shivering behind the Greenwich Observatory, seeing nothing but her father's sword falling and her mother's fragile white wishes rising . . .

And Miss Darlington had enfolded her in calm, strong arms.

She gasped, opening her eyes, desperately shoving memory away. A hundred mad birds stared at her.

Blinking groggily, Cecilia realized she was in her old childhood bedroom. The yellow wallpaper, teeming with green and orange cockatiels, seemed to bulge and shrink as her vision adjusted. The dolls lined up along shelves leered at her. Cecilia turned over in the bed—

And found a young man seated at the bedside, watching her hungrily.

"I beg your pardon!" she admonished him, sitting up and reaching for a knife that was no longer up her sleeve. Nor in her garter belt. Nor under her waistband.

The young man leaned forward, his mustached smile slithering toward trim black sideburns. Cecilia moved as far from him as possible without falling out of the bed.

"Cousin," he said. His voice was as silky as oil on water. "I've been guarding you whilst you lay here the past two nights like Sleeping Beauty, deep in a forcèd slumber, your innocence dependent on a hopeful awakening."

Cecilia stared at him.

"You are," he said, pressing a hand against his breast, "as lovely as I ever dreamed, as dew bright and morning soft, with buds of womanhood unfurling in your eyes."

"What?" Cecilia said.

"You are a melody in form, a promise made real by the—"

"Who are you?" she asked. Her abruptness sliced through his effusions and left him silent, mouth agape. She watched as he regathered his superciliousness and slid it over his thin, jutting face. He was all gloss, from his slicked-back hair to his large, polished teeth; and yet, Cecilia noticed a scab of fear deep inside his gaze.

"I am your ardent servant and your cousin, Frederick Bassing-thwaite," he said, "imprisoned like you in this dour abbey under the cruel authority of Captain Morvath. Although we have never before met, dear Cecilia, I feel I know you intimately from the stories I've been told about your mother." He brought forth a silver locket and, opening it, showed Cecilia the tiny portrait it contained of Cilla Bassingthwaite. "I keep this in lieu of a picture of you, for I was told how alike you were. It is not true, forsooth! Thou art more lovely, more graceful in the eye of the . . ."

Cecilia clambered out of bed. Her body swayed to starboard and her mind to port, but she took a deep breath and shoved them back into alignment by sheer will. Although she was still dressed in her riding habit, the jacket had been unbuttoned and her boots were off. Her hair hung loose down her back. Clearly someone had attended to her comfort after having drugged and kidnapped her.

She frowned. He'd had that chloroform with him the whole time, yet had not taken her to the Queen's prison, nor to her father's house until it landed right in front of them. He'd supported and protected her—and kissed her too, although she didn't want to think about that. But then he'd declared himself Morvath's servant all along and had chatted with Randall as he rendered her unconscious.

It did not matter. Ned Lightbourne did not matter, not even in the slightest. All that did was rescuing the Society and assassinating her father. Taking her boots from the floor, Cecilia shoved them on and buttoned them as fast as she could.

"When your father approached me," Cousin Frederick was saying, "I felt disinclined to accept his hospitality. He brought me here anyway, determined to secure in my person your best happiness. Although I have been a wretched prisoner, fed only three times a day, and allowed no liberty but what is available within these dozens of walls, I care not! All I do, I do for you! Captain Morvath's assurance that you would make for me a perfect bride has been answered with the most joyous proof. Think, my dear cousin, how the wounds of the past shall be repaired between our families when we are united in matrimonial bliss!"

By the time he ended this speech, Cecilia had climbed over the bed, crossed the floor in three strides, discovered that the door was locked, and then turned to survey the room. It seemed everything had been left as it was when she lived here twelve years ago.

"You will love Starkthorn Castle just like your mother did," Frederick continued, oblivious to both Cecilia's mood and Cilla's. "The orchard is rich with nature's bounty, the same as your own Venusian form . . ."

Returning across the room, Cecilia began pulling dolls from the shelves, inspecting them closely before tossing them onto the bed.

". . . Thou art a blushing apple, and I the worm of love . . ."

She found what she was seeking in a porcelain doll dressed as Olga the Ogre, an émigré pirate rumored to have bathed in the blood of virgin boys. (It was actually pomegranate juice, excellent for the skin, but Olga saw no need to ruin her reputation by advertising this.)

". . . We shall populate the family tree with our sunlit fecundity . . ."

Olga had died being trampled by the cattle of a mad Scottish baron she had been trying to ride (er, the cattle, not the baron), but her doll still contained beneath its scarlet dress a vicious little knife seven-year-old Cecilia hid there in the days before she and her mother escaped the abbey. She hastily tucked the knife into her garter belt, causing Frederick to almost swoon at the sight of her leg.

"I say," he gasped. "Even knowing your breeding, I did not expect such a fine filly! You remind me of my sister; she has the same ravishing calves . . ."

Cecilia stared narrowly at the wall for a moment, then tapped against one of the birds. Nothing happened. She tried another, then another. Finally, the wall shifted as a secret door came ajar. Hinges groaned. Mustiness wafted out. As Frederick continued to wax eloquent about his sister's figure, she stepped into the darkness beyond the wall.

Twelve years was a long time, but Cecilia had never forgotten this particular hidden passage, having taken it scores of times as a child. Walk straight for a minute, follow a bend to the right, go three steps down, and open a door into Morvath's library.

"It's very dark," Frederick said, trailing behind her. Cecilia stopped, swallowing an impatient word.

"Why don't you wait in the bedroom?" she suggested, turning back toward him.

"But I would follow you into the pits of hell, dearest Cecilia."

"I'm not going there. I'm going to the library, and thereon to kill my father. You'll be safer in the bedroom. I'll come back for you afterward."

"Kill Morvath? How I love your kittenish humor. When we are married—"

"I'm not joking," Cecilia interrupted him. "I never joke. Allow me to be plainer, Cousin Frederick. Either wait in the bedroom or be stabbed here, now."

"But I—"

"Just listen to the lady," came a suggestion from the darkness behind Cecilia. She sighed. At this rate, she would be older than Lady Armitage before she got to set foot in a library again.

"Captain Lightbourne," she said wearily.

She did not need to see him to feel his grin; the heat of it burned into her spine. "Miss Bassingthwaite. We meet again. Again."

"Fiend."

"I'm glad to see you too. The chloroform should have worn off hours ago. It was almost as if you didn't want to wake up."

"Cad."

"And yet you woke still so eloquent."

She tried to think fast. The situation was not good: caught in a lightless passage between a sniveling jellyfish and a smirking scoundrel, with only knife enough for one of them, and a library just out of reach.

"You can't spin around and kick me in the unmentionables," Ned mused, answering her thoughts. "The passage isn't wide enough for that. You can't run; Freddy's in the way. And the weapon you almost certainly have hidden somewhere is useless, since your back is to me. There's also the aggravating factor of this gun I have pointed at your head. Go back into the bedroom, Cecilia."

"I say!" Frederick pouted. "You can't call me Freddy in that manner, Lightbourne. I am a scion of the noble pirate family Bassingthwaite and you are a homeless nobody!"

"Actually," Ned replied, "in Portugal I am known as Duarte Leveport, Baron of Valando, a title gifted to me after I—er, did a favor for Princess Maria Amélia. Therefore, I outrank you, *Freddy*. Now, get out of the way so the lady can return to her room."

"She's not a lady."

Ned cocked his pistol. "I beg your pardon?"

"She's an angel." Frederick flung out his arms expansively. There was a crack as his wrists smacked against the walls. "Ow! See the pain I suffer on your behalf, dear Cecilia? *Lady* is too meager a term for one so—"

"Just shoot him," Cecilia said.

"I would, but I'm worried about ricochets in this small space," Ned answered.

"I don't mind risking death if it means shutting him up."

"Very well."

Frederick scurried off, muttering something about the insignificance of Portugal. With a sigh, Cecilia began to follow. But Ned caught her arm and pulled her back, and she turned to scold him. He pressed the hand holding the pistol against her mouth.

"I'm sorry for the chloroform," he whispered, "but I didn't know what you might say. And if they doubted I was Morvath's man, they'd have killed me and taken you anyway."

The explanation made sense, and she felt her heart hug itself with relief. But her mouth still tasted like bitterness and gunmetal. "It's fine, don't worry," she whispered back. "I'm glad they didn't kill you."

She gazed up at him big-eyed through her eyelashes, and he swallowed dryly. His hand dropped from her mouth and she smiled. Leaning closer, she whispered near to his ear, "Because I want to kill you myself."

She yanked herself out of his hold, but he caught her again before she could turn away. "Please believe me, Cecilia. I'm on your side."

"Then why are you standing here with a gun pointed at me, forcing me back into imprisonment?"

He frowned as if the answer was so obvious he could not believe she'd even asked. "This is the lair of the villain. Evil abounds in every corridor: pirates, mercenaries, creepy spiders. Good God, woman, you can't run around like it's Mayfair on a Sunday morning. I'm trying to protect you from yourself."

"Are you calling me weak and stupid?"

His frown buckled; he blinked a few times. "No, of course not. I'm calling you—" He hesitated, and her eyes narrowed.

"Yes?"

"I'm— Look, this is not safe. There are probably spiders above us at this very moment, waiting to pounce." He glanced at the dusty beams overhead, and Cecilia huffed a laugh. Looking at her again, he held her gaze so intensely that the sardonic tilt to her mouth slipped. "Please," he whispered. "Just go back into the bedroom."

"Fine," she relented. "But only to save you from the hideous fanged arachnids that are even now lowering themselves toward your face." She lifted her chin imperiously and began to turn away, but he abruptly drew her so close their heartbeats knocked against each other.

"The Society are being held in the cellars. Be wary of Frederick."

"And don't turn your back on me, Captain, unless you fancy a knife in it."

When she pulled away this time, he let her go. She marched into the bedroom.

Ned came behind. "Your father wants to see you at breakfast," he said. "A bath is being prepared for you now."

"I'm not—" she began, but then Frederick was rushing over, grasping her hand in both of his.

"Fear not, dear cousin," he urged. "Lightbourne is a brute, but I will keep you safe with me, your tender limbs and gentle heart ensconced in my protection despite—"

Cecilia turned, took Ned's gun from his hand, and smacked the butt of it into Frederick's forehead. He gave a little scream and collapsed among the dolls on the bed.

"Much better," Cecilia said, handing back the gun.

Ned grinned. "Listen, Cec—"

"Miss. Bass. Ing. Thwaite."

"But—"

The door opened, admitting a footman and two henchmen carrying guns and soft, folded towels.

"Your bath is ready, ma'am," said the footman. "If you will follow me."

Ned dropped his words into grim silence. On the bed, Frederick groaned. Cecilia shook her head in disgust and walked away without a backward look.

Far below, in the musty gloom of the abbey cellar, Pleasance stood chewing her thumb knuckle unhappily. She'd spent years dreaming of being captive in the dungeon of a madman, but the reality proved not as deliciously woeful as she'd expected. It was, in fact, plain uncomfortable. And boring, too. The Wisteria Society ladies had taken the opportunity to catch up on gossip, but as a mere housemaid Pleasance was ignored, even if she did know how to fly a house and seven ways to rob a duchess of her diamonds. She hoped something interesting would happen soon, before she lost all faith in melodrama.

If only the guards would enter. All they needed to do was take three steps into the cellar. Three little steps. The prisoners had been stripped down to their underwear and divested of enough concealed weaponry to supply a battalion, so what harm could it do to walk three steps inside?

(There was of course an extensive trap awaiting anyone who tried, since pirates needed only their underwear and a few old wine crates, a stray nail or two, to create something lethal. Pleasance did not dare to even think about it. Thoughts were not safe things. The mind was no sanctuary.)

Nearby, Miss Darlington perched on an overturned box, eyes closed, as if she meditated peacefully in a summer garden instead of a damp, barely lit cellar. The rest of the Society watched her cautiously and whispered behind their hands. Everyone knew about Morvath's hatred of the Darlington clan, which was equaled only by his hatred of the Bassingthwaite clan, his adopted family the Morvath clan, the Hanoverian clan currently represented by Queen Victoria, the Chapman and Hall publishing clan, and the company that made those caramel cream profiteroles that ended up tasting like fish. No one could believe she was still alive. Morvath must be planning something particularly slow and vicious for her, and several conversations were taking place, in the spirit of professional curiosity, as to what it might be.

Pleasance, however, remained unconcerned. Miss Darlington had survived seven decades of turmoil (admittedly, most of it caused by herself), and no sulking crybaby of a man would defeat her.

"Psst," said a ghost. Pleasance frowned, determined not to listen.

"Psst," they said again. She shook her head.

A pebble hit her arm. Looking around wildly, she saw that it had not been the tormented spirit of a murdered princess hissing at her after all but a figure in the deep shadows behind an empty bottle rack. She sidled over.

"Pleasant?" the figure asked.

"Begone, foul spirit," she whispered from the corner of her mouth.

"What?" it whispered back.

"My thoughts are guarded by the archangels; you will not corrupt me."

"Er, all right. But I'm not a spirit. My name is Ned—"

"I am not so easily deceived, O evil apparition! Only a spirit could appear out of nowhere in this way."

"Actually there's a secret door—"

"As if I'd believe something so bizarre!"

The spirit was quiet a moment. Then it relented. "You're right. I am the ghost of Emily Brontë."

"Really?" Pleasance glanced in its direction. "I cannot see you through the shadows, but you sound like a man."

"I had a very gruff voice, people always said so. Oh how the heights do wuther."

Pleasance gasped. "You are Emily Brontë!"

"I am. After all, where else in the world would I haunt but the cellar of my deranged bastard nephew's flying abbey?"

"That makes sense."

Ned rolled his eyes. "I need your help, Pleasant. I need you to tell Miss Darlington that her niece is on board, and if she wants to keep her safe, she must do as I ask so that together we can overcome Captain Morvath."

"Why don't you ask her yourself? I'll bring her over."

"No, wait! Miss Darlington does not have your psychic sensitivity. She will not hear my ethereal voice."

"That is true." Pleasance shuffled closer. "You smell a lot like soap for a ghost."

"Er, well, cleanliness is next to godliness, you know, and I am in heaven."

"Except when you are haunting an old Gothic abbey, of course."

"Of course. Warn Miss Darlington to be ready for my return. When the time is right, I will help her and the Society escape, if she follows my instructions."

"It seems like a trap, Emily."

The silence following this sounded tight, as if it was frowning with impatience. "Why would I trap people already locked up, Pleasant?"

"Because—"

"But it is a test! A test of your soul, to find out if you are worthy of being a true heroine! Are you worthy, Pleasant?"

She drew in a sharp, trembling breath. "I pray so, Emily!"

"Then tell Miss Darlington what I said."

"I shall!"

"I'll return in a while."

"Fare thee well, noble spirit of the moors."

"Right. See you soon."

There was a shuffle and a scrape in the darkness, then a faint creak as if from hinges. Pleasance saw a glance of soft golden light, just as she imagined must infuse the holy netherworld. She clutched her hands together against her heart. Then, with a carefully unhurried gait, she crossed to Miss Darlington and crouched down.

"That Italian assassin was just here, miss," she whispered to the old lady. "He came through a secret door behind the wine racks. It looks like it leads to a servant's corridor. Kitchens beyond, from the smell of it."

"What did he want?" Miss Darlington asked without opening her eyes.

"To buy your cooperation with Miss Bassingthwaite's life."

"So the lackey plans to overthrow his master. Thus go the inevitabilities of men. What did he say about Cecilia?"

"That she was in the abbey, miss."

Miss Darlington opened one eye. "Is that so? What a troublesome development. Gather the troops, Pleasance."

"With respect, miss, I don't think they'll all get through the secret door without being noticed."

"Nonsense, gel. There are three secret doors leading out of this cellar, not to mention a secret hatch in the ceiling. We have remained here only to rest and get our meals served to us. But if Cecilia is on board, there is no more time to waste. Tally ho."

"Tally ho," Pleasance whispered, and hurried away to spread the word.

⤞ 16 ⤝

BREAKFAST WITH THE DEVIL—LADIES' DUEL—A REUNION,
A RECOLLECTION—EXPLOSIONS (PORCELAIN, HEROINE)—
ESCAPE (FAST, FUTILE)—NED THROWS CECILIA INTO DANGER

Cecilia was mortally sorry the breakfast room door was not worth knocking down. But she would rather be dignified than happy, so she gently pushed it ajar, then stepped back in order that her armed escort might enter first.

He shook his head and indicated with his rifle that no, no, she should precede him.

"Thank you," she murmured, and he almost smiled in reply before remembering he was a hardened thug. She entered the breakfast room—

And came face-to-face with her greatest foe.

"Jane Fairweather," she said, her eyes darkening as she regarded the tight-haired woman standing before her with a plate of food. "Good morning."

"Cecilia Morvath," Jane replied. Her mouth shifted to one side in an approximation of a smile. "My dear, how lovely to see you. And looking so youthful with your hair down. Why, no one would guess you are any more than sixteen."

The other people in the room held their breath.

"That is a charming example of the graciousness one can always expect from you, Jane dear," Cecilia said. "In return, may I offer that age is treating you well? I imagine not having robbed any banks is good for the complexion."

Jane paled but nevertheless managed to sharpen her smile. "I do declare, you yourself appear in excellent health, despite your aunt's regular concern. Those few extra pounds you've put on suit you."

A gasp went up from the witnesses.

"How kind," Cecilia said. "And I'm glad I needn't have feared for your own health after all, as I see you now quite safe and unfettered in my father's lair, partaking of his hospitality—and his toast and marmalade and eggs and ham and kippers and, goodness me, steak cutlets. I envy one with such a hearty appetite who can yet remain so exceedingly thin."

"You must tell me where you procured your dress. I've not seen such a style in decades."

Cecilia brushed a hand down the white muslin skirts. "It was my mother's. I did not take you for having an interest in fashion. You're always so discreet with what you wear."

"Discretion is the better part of valor, as *my* family have always exemplified."

"What admirable self-awareness, to call your wardrobe choices pusillanimous."

Out of the corner of her eye, she saw Frederick mouth that word, trying to guess what it meant. Jane was more clever. Her mouth snapped back into a hard white pinch. "At least they're my choices, and not forced on me by my overbearing aunt as if I am a child."

Cecilia smiled languidly, having worked Jane into this most satisfactory degree of aggravation; she swept a disinterested glance down the young woman's form, then turned away. Jane scowled, for there was no comeback to silence, and recollected too late that Cecilia had, after all, been educated by Miss Darlington. No one bested that grand lady in the deadly martial art of polite conversation.

Cecilia glanced around the room. To her relief, Morvath was nowhere to be seen. Ned leaned back against the wall beside the food-laden sideboard, attending to his cuticles with a dagger. His black frock coat was embroidered with silver and gold, he had a ruby in his ear alongside the loop earring, and the buckles of his tall black boots were so polished, lantern light flashed and flared against them. The extravagance should have made him look like a dandy, but somehow it only honed the sense of danger about him, like a flower luring victims into its poisonous core. He appeared to have been highly entertained by the ladies' parley, and as he caught Cecilia's eye he raised his eyebrows in a manner that made her want to grab the nearest butter knife and stab him.

Nearby, Frederick cowered over a plate of kippers and jam toast. Cecilia tried not to stare at the smear of butter in his mustache. And at the end of the table the senior Miss Fairweather was holding a fork defensively, her gaze flickering from Cecilia to the open door and back again as if begging for rescue. Poor lady, forced into Morvath's clutches by her traitorous granddaughter! Cecilia took a seat beside her.

"Madam," she said, laying a hand next to Miss Fairweather's on the white-clothed table. "Are you well? Have you seen my aunt? Is she alive?"

Miss Fairweather seemed taken aback. Obviously she was unused to kindness. How cruelly Jane must treat her! Cecilia offered a gentle, encouraging smile.

"I am doing as well as I can," Miss Fairweather replied, her voice trembling. Jane gasped a contemptuous laugh, but Cecilia pointedly ignored her.

"These are difficult times," she told Miss Fairweather, and even went so far as to pat the woman's hand. The lady stiffened, then gave a great shuddering sigh. "But my aunt?" Cecilia persisted.

"Your aunt is fine," Ned said from across the room.

She threw him a scowl. He smiled wryly in reply.

"She was in good health when I last saw her," Miss Fairweather said. "Have you come to reunite with your father, my dear?"

"Miss Bassingthwaite was kidnapped, Grandmama," Jane said, her tone suggesting that being kidnapped showed a failure of character on Cecilia's part. "She did not wish to be here at all."

"Oh dear," Miss Fairweather murmured. "That is difficult indeed."

"But we are blessed with her company," Frederick said, his buttered mustache quivering above the words. "With all her loveliness she shines a gentle, beatific light into the dismal—"

"I was disappointed to be betrayed by someone I thought I could trust," Cecilia said, absolutely not dignifying Ned with a glance. "But there is a certain convenience to being here. All the better to rescue you and the rest of the Society."

Miss Fairweather perked up at this. "True, true. But how will you do so, my dear? Do you have a plan? Tell me all the particulars."

"Well, I thought—" Cecilia began, but was interrupted by Jane taking a sudden coughing fit. Cecilia looked at her with a fierce blankness, then turned back to Miss Fairweather. "I thought—" she repeated, raising her voice, and was interrupted again by Ned's dagger slamming into the wall beside her head.

Frederick squeaked. Jane choked on her coughing.

"Oops," Ned said with false innocence. "Sorry, my hand slipped."

Cecilia smiled apologetically at Miss Fairweather. Then she stood, smoothing her skirts, and turned to pull the dagger from the wall so she might return it, point first, to Captain Lightbourne.

She could not budge it at all.

She stared across the room at him, wide-eyed with disbelief. He stared back inscrutably. As tension flared between them, Frederick squeaked again. Jane covered her mouth with a napkin. Miss Fairweather looked from one to the other as if trying to decide which of them was best for her to settle her gaze upon.

And then someone laughed.

Cecilia turned to see a handsome silver-haired man thrust himself into the room. She dropped abruptly back into her chair.

"Cecilia!" he exclaimed, spreading his arms and smile wide as he stepped forward to greet her. "My lovely daughter! My, how you've grown."

Cecilia swallowed a scream. She rose again from the chair—

And memory swept her away.

It had been a beautiful day.

She and Cilla had arrived early for the Wisteria Society summer gathering at Greenwich, and while they'd awaited the other ladies Cecilia had danced after the dandelions Cilla blew for her, seeing nothing but tiny white wishes until suddenly, inexorably, a shadow had blotted them out . . .

"Patrick!" Cilla had reached for a sword she remembered too late she'd left on the picnic blanket. Cecilia, acting on sheer piratic instinct, had drawn her own small dagger from a secret pocket in her dress, eliciting a grin from Morvath.

"Hello, my little buccaneer," he'd said. The grin had been as sharp as the long, bright sword in his hand. His eyes had burned with a fervor

Cecilia remembered from nights when he recited his poetry at her bedside, making her reluctant to sleep for fear of nightmares.

"No!" Cilla, with no shield but her own body, had pushed Cecilia behind her. "Leave her alone, I beg you."

"But she is my child. My wild-hearted daughter with eyes like the northern sea. She deserves to know her heritage."

"Darlington is her heritage, Bassingthwaite is. Go away, Patrick. We're not yours anymore."

"Go away!" Cecilia had brandished her dagger from behind Cilla's hip, making Morvath laugh.

"See, she has the Brontë fire. Don't worry, Cilla, I'll raise her well. Under my guidance, she will become one of the greatest scoundrels England has ever known."

"We will never go back with you!"

His smile had deepened with hideous amusement. "You misunderstand, my love. I'm only taking her. You, I'm going to kill."

The words had struck Cecilia so fiercely, she'd dropped her knife. Cilla had reached back without taking her gaze from Morvath and grasped Cecilia's bodice, clutching on and shoving away in the same confused, anguished moment. "Baby," she'd said in a voice that would make tight bands around Cecilia's heart for years afterward. "Run! Run as fast as you can, and don't look back."

Morvath had only shrugged languidly. "I'll catch her if she does."

"But, Mama—"

"Go!"

She'd run, obedient as ever. A moment later terror had broken through, spiking her breath and her muscles, making her stagger. She'd looked back, crying—and had watched her father drive his long, bright sword into her mother's body.

Ten years later, in Morvath's house, under his hot, dark eye, Cecilia felt her own body shudder violently as if she had been the one stabbed, reopening a wound that had formed deep scars on her soul. She was half herself and half Cilla falling to the summer grass, thoughtless, blind with the memory of blood. She tried to detach from it, as was her mind's habitual defense—throwing horror and rage into the wild moorland behind her consciousness. But she heard someone shouting, heard the crash of heartbeats, the thump of boots on hard ground.

"*Run!*" her mother whispered again, screamed, sighed.

And so she ran, ran, all her life she ran, leaving love behind.

Ned watched amazed as Cecilia shouted curses and threw plates, cutlery, a dish of marmalade, at the dread Captain Morvath.

And the captain, his affable paternal smile faltering, could seemingly do no more than hold up his arms in defense as a pat of butter smashed into the wall beside him, followed immediately thereafter by a steak knife. The Misses Fairweather stared aghast. Frederick tried to crawl under the table. The armed guard standing at the door hesitated, being under orders to treat the captain's daughter with all gentleness and respect, and not knowing how to translate this into stopping the captain's daughter from killing the captain with a teapot.

"Put that down," the guard said experimentally—

Tea and china exploded at Morvath's feet.

The guard gave up on words and lifted his rifle instead. Seeing this, Ned hastily stepped forward, grasping Cecilia's arm. She looked at him for a stunned moment, and he winced at the eerie stillness in her eyes. Their wintry color had turned as vivid as summer, and it terrified him. Then she pulled away and ran from the room.

Silence fell, disturbed only by the small, shuddering sound of a plate coming to rest on the floor. No one moved.

"Goodness me," Miss Fairweather said at last, shrugging her mouth, as if Cecilia had just committed a mild faux pas.

"Is it safe to come out?" Frederick inquired from beneath the table. No one bothered to answer.

"Somebody go get her," Morvath said. "She has the passion of Catherine Earnshaw, but she needs to eat breakfast for the sake of her health."

Ned happened to catch Jane's eye at that moment and saw it darken with the same understanding he had of Morvath's words. "I'll go," he said before anyone else could speak. He was almost out the door before Morvath called to him.

"Don't hurt her!"

Ned glanced back. The captain stood with slumped shoulders, marmalade in his hair and butter freckling his face, looking like a defeated, regretful, slightly ridiculous father—*don't hurt my precious, troubled girl*. But the set of his jaw spoke more honestly—*because I want that right for myself*.

Ned did not answer, mistrusting his voice. Instead, he simply nodded and hurried away.

Morvath's roar followed him out.

Cecilia was fast for a woman in a long dress and petticoats. She made it down a flight of stairs, along two corridors, past an astonished henchman whose thereafter unconscious body Ned had to leap over as he ran, and partway down the portrait gallery before he finally caught up with her. "Look, a bookshelf!" he shouted, and as she glanced up she stumbled. Her foot caught in the hem of her dress and she fell.

Ned hurried over, ready to restrain her should she try to jump up and attack him. But she seemed defeated at last; she swayed as she sat up. Ned lowered himself to his haunches beside her.

"Go away," she muttered.

"I'm afraid I cannot oblige," he replied. "Captain Morvath wants you back in the breakfast room. For God's sake, girl, didn't your aunt teach you that it's bad manners to throw food at the table, especially when it hits the most dangerous man in all of England?"

"It's only bad manners if you miss."

He laughed, despite himself.

She glanced sidelong through the fall of her hair. "Did the steak knife get him?"

"No, but he'll be sneezing marmalade for a week."

She nearly smiled, but then all expression vanished from her face. "Someone's coming."

Ned heard the footsteps and hurriedly rose, pulling Cecilia up with him. When she struggled, he held her tighter. "Be smart," he whispered. "Do what I tell you."

"Knave!" she retorted.

"Sure, but—"

At that moment the guard with the rifle appeared in the gallery. Seeing them, he raised his gun.

"Caught her," Ned called out, grinning, as he began to shove Cecilia back along the gallery. "And I didn't even have to use the knife in my coat pocket."

"I'm surprised you resisted," the guard said.

Ned's smile dipped into a mockery of sorrow. "Why does no one trust me? You'd almost think I went around stabbing people as soon as they got close to me."

"What, you mean like an assassin?"

"I would never stab a lady. At least, not in the house of her very dangerous father. I do stab men, of course, probably in the arm or maybe the throat if I'm being serious, and only when I can't shoot them because the noise would cause a problem. I'd have to use a fair bit of force, though, to make sure I disarmed them before they could react."

"God you talk a lot of nonsense," the guard said. "I myself don't mind stabbing ladies, if you know what I mean." He slid a lewd gaze over Cecilia's body.

"By all means, have at it," Ned said, and pushed Cecilia at him.

The guard yelled, then gurgled, and then his gun clattered to the floor. He stared idiotically at the knife Cecilia had thrust right through his arm. She twisted it, and as he collapsed with a cry, Ned met his forehead with a knee. Bone cracked against bone, and the guard slumped unconscious to the floor.

"Nicely done," Ned told Cecilia as he bent to retrieve his knife. Blood poured from the wound, and he grimaced, wiping the blade on the guard's coat. "I think we make a good team, don't you? I appreciate that you trusted me."

He turned to smile at her—

And sighed as he watched her run away down the gallery.

⚹ 17 ⚹

A HEARTY DISCUSSION—DEATH AT A SÉANCE—TWO ALEXANDERS—
INTO THE DARK—NED SILENCES CECILIA—
NED IS ASSAULTED—A TRAITOR DISCOVERED—
POX AND OTHER INFESTATIONS—
THE DEAD MOTHER'S SECRET GARDEN

L ife was too short to not be spent in nursing animosities or register-
ing wrongs: thus Miss Darlington had educated Cecilia, accord-
ing to the ideals of the Wisteria Society. So Cecilia had spent the past
several years planning for the moment she encountered her father. The
speech she would give. The explanations she would demand from him.
And the weapon she would introduce to his toxic heart.

Then she actually saw him, and all those careful, precious plans
shattered like a teapot at his feet.

As she ran, she imagined what her mind had contemplated so
coolly over the years—his body beneath her boots, his voice crying out
and then breaking into breathless silence. She envisioned beating him,
hanging him, throwing him out a high window while flying above a
very pointy mountain. Violence swelled the muscles in her body and
heated her breath. She liked its feeling. And yet, the thought of turning

around, going back, doing those things to him, made her want to cry like an anguished child.

When Ned caught her again, halfway along the portrait gallery, she spun about, raising her free hand to hit him. But he snatched her wrist and pulled her against him in a tight embrace.

"It's all right," he said. His voice was rough yet consoling.

Cecilia leaned against him. "I'm not returning to that room."

"I know."

He laid his chin on the top of her head, and she tucked her foot around his left ankle. "I'm serious, Ned," she said, and twisted her foot. He stumbled, his grip easing; she kneed him in the stomach and stepped free.

"I appreciate your feelings," he gasped, snatching the back of her skirt so she couldn't run again. She fell forward, the sudden unexpected movement causing her skirt to rip from his fingers. Tucking her head beneath her, she rolled over her shoulders on the ground, jumped to her feet again, and was turning back to him with a tiny knife in her hand before he could blink.

"I don't think you do," she said. "I watched him kill my mother."

She lunged with the knife and he sidestepped, grasping her arm and yanking her around. "And I watched him kill mine," he said as the knife dropped to the ground. He kicked it away and in that tiny moment of distraction she ducked under his arm, twisting it and ramming her fist into his side.

"I'm sorry to hear that," she said.

His breath burst. He pulled from her grip so hard she staggered, and catching her around the waist, he flipped her onto her back. "Thank you," he said, straddling her hips.

"Were you very young?" Without waiting for a response, she grasped his thighs as leverage and slipped through his legs. Retrieving her knife, she scrambled up and, before he could fully turn around, leaped on his back.

"Thirteen," he said, his voice constricted by her arm around his throat.

"I'll kill him for both of us." She wrapped her legs around his hips so she had more force for strangling him. He ran backward, slamming her against the wall. She groaned.

"That would involve returning to the breakfast room," he said as her grip loosened and she slid to her feet. He turned, snatching her wrists, pinning them to the wall on either side of her head. The knife protruded helplessly from her fist. "And it would involve becoming just what he planned for you all along—a heartless replica of himself. He'd win, even as you stabbed him. No, I'll kill him, and save you from being despoiled."

"That's thoughtful of you," she said, and brought her knee up sharply.

He blocked it with his thigh. Pressing against her, he wedged her tightly between himself and the wall. They stared at each other with bright eyes, their breath mingling, burning. He could feel her heart pound. She could feel something that was not his heart budging against her. The awareness of it clashed in their gaze.

"Your mother," she said. "How did it happen?"

He blinked. A shadow slipped beneath his lashes and disappeared again. "Morvath stabbed her. She was a famous seer, she held séances, and every month he'd come to talk to the Brontës. When he found her secret table-knocking device, he murdered her right then and there. I wanted to fight him—"

"You were only a boy."

"I was weak. I ran. It was Cilla who found me. I'll never forget her striding out of the London fog in a long scarlet coat, with all that golden hair and a gold-handled gun. She looked like the queen of pirates." He gazed at Cecilia unfocusedly, seeing her mother instead. "When I told her I owed her my life, she made me repay it with a promise."

Cecilia nodded. "It's the pirate's code. Never give something without a return."

He smiled. The memory of Cilla's ferocious beauty was vivid in his mind, as if he hadn't gazed upon her insipid, sentimentalized portrait only the other day. She'd been so much more than paints could capture. He remembered, too, the way she'd hugged him, gentle yet fierce, while he wept in anguish. It was entirely different from how he held her daughter in this moment, eleven years later, a man now and strong in body and mind. He'd been awestruck by Cilla Bassingthwaite, but it was Cecilia's coolness that paradoxically warmed him; her implacability that made him hot in dangerous places; her shadows, so deep beneath the still surface, that burned right through his heart.

He had made his promise to the mother, but he lived it for the incomparable daughter.

"We have to get out of this house," he said.

"So you really are Captain Ned Smith."

He grinned. "No. But I am an agent of the Crown. And I am on your side. Cilla bade me work to make the world a safe place for her child." He paused, releasing one of her hands so he could draw a strand of hair from her brow. The gentle touch made her shiver. She laid her free hand against his cheek, but he caught it, pressed it instead against his heart.

"From that day, everything I've done has been for her. For you. I used money she gave me to become a pirate so I'd be strong and cunning. I took Lady Armitage's contract so a real assassin did not. I endured Morvath's poetry so as to know his plans and protect you from them. I thought surely he would recognize me, but he never did. I thought more than once I'd kill him, but he has always been too well defended.

"So I stayed, spying on behalf of the Queen but in my heart motivated by that promise to Cilla. Then I met you and grew to realize you didn't need me after all. You could protect yourself well enough. So the promise became an excuse just to be with you. Not because you're Cilla's daughter, but because you're you."

"Oh," she whispered. "Thank you."

"You're welcome. Does this mean you might finally trust me?"

The wistfulness in his voice shook her—made her think of how he'd gone through all those years without fierce pirate aunts to warm him, scold him, or overprotect him, every time he was chilled by the memory of his mother's death. "Maybe," she said, smiling into his beautiful, shadowed eyes.

"I wouldn't if I were you," someone else replied.

They leaped apart, turning with weapons raised—

And Ned sighed.

"Damn it, O'Riley, what the hell are you doing here?"

Cecilia stared in bemusement at the man standing before them. With his dark, roughly cropped hair, unshaven jaw, and sardonic smile, he was the most piratic pirate she had ever seen. His tall, scarred boots alone were enough to make a law-abiding citizen tremble; they would have fainted dead away at the guns and knives half-hidden behind his long black coat. He swung his large sword with the laziness of someone who knows how to swing it with deadly accuracy when the time comes, and Cecilia sensed that, if she made one wrong move, he'd knock her down without thinking and refuse to apologize afterward.

She did not like him.

"I'm here because you're an idiot, Lightbourne," he said.

Well, perhaps she'd judged too hastily.

"A fool," he continued. "A dunce, determined to get yourself in trouble."

Actually, she'd been entirely mistaken: this was a fine fellow indeed.

Ned laughed curtly. "Go away, Alex."

"I really don't understand why you have a reputation for charm. I'm staying."

"I suppose you want my thanks."

"No."

"In that case, you have them. How did you even find me?"

Alex shrugged. "I knew you were working with Morvath, and I read in the newspaper that his battlehouse had been sighted at Blackdown Hills. So I came here and asked around the locals. It didn't take long to find the place."

Ned and Cecilia looked at each other. "Asked the locals," Ned said blankly.

"I'm not sure what astonishes me most," Cecilia replied, "that we didn't think of it, or that a man on his own actually asked for directions."

"Ha," Alex said dryly. He pointed his sword at Cecilia. "Is this her?"

Ned sighed again. "Miss Bassingthwaite, may I introduce my friend Captain Alexander O'Riley, an Irishman abroad. Alex has a particular interest in flying fast and aggravating the hell out of me. Alex, Miss Bassingthwaite."

The pirate bowed. "Pleased to meet you, madam."

Before Cecilia could reply, a hard, hot voice echoed from some nearby corridor, making them all jolt.

"Cecilia! Where are you?"

The pirates stared wide-eyed at one another. "Morvath," Ned said unnecessarily.

"Cecilia!" the voice called again. "Come back before the tea gets cold. And, Ned, come back too. I have a special breakfast for you."

The air seemed to crack as a gun was cocked.

"Shit." Ned began to run, tugging Cecilia with him, despairing of the gallery's stark length but needing instinctively to get Cecilia as far as he could from her father.

"There's a staircase at the end of the gallery," Alex said, hurrying alongside. "It goes down to the kitchens and a back door."

"Lead the way," Ned ordered him, but then staggered as Cecilia suddenly wrenched her hand from his hold. Before he could catch her again she hurried over to the gallery wall.

"I know I'm uncultured," Alex said, staring at her incredulously, "but is this the best moment to appreciate art?"

"Secret passages," Cecilia said. Frowning up at the portraits, she muttered as she rapidly sidestepped beneath them, tapping the wall under each frame. Ned heard fragments of names—"Zenobia, Mary, Arthur"—and recognized them as characters from Branwell Brontë's early writing. He'd tried to read those stories once as part of his preparation for infiltrating Morvath's mad brain but hadn't got far. They were dense, strange, and altogether disturbing. One thing he did remember was Morvath's favorite character, the great pirate and rogue Alexander Percy.

And there he was, all bright ringlets and snazzy collar, gazing poetically along the gallery from within a gilded frame. Ned dashed over to the portrait. Surely the most likely place for a secret doorway would be beneath this original, albeit imaginary, lord of Northangerland. But Cecilia shook her head.

"Maria Henrietta," she whispered, and shoved at the wall beneath a small ink sketch of a woman. The wood parted, and Cecilia turned to flick her hand at him, urging him to hurry. Ned glanced along the gallery, ensuring they were unseen, then slipped after her through the opening. An intense odor of rot made him grimace, but it was more appealing than being murdered by a lunatic pirate. Alex entered after him, and as he eased the door shut as silently as possible, a pitch blackness shrank the world into nothingness.

"Does he know this passage?" Ned whispered.

"Yes," Cecilia replied, so close her voice brushed warmly against his throat. "But it originally opened under Percy like you thought. My mother switched the portraits; I just couldn't remember which one. If we—"

Ned clapped his hand over her mouth. Footsteps knocked slowly along the gallery floor.

"Cecilia," Morvath called. "Don't hide from me. It's not a nice way to treat one's father."

The steps drew closer. The three pirates huddled back from the door, unwilling to move through the narrow passage in case Morvath heard them—but anxious he would hear their breathing, their heartbeats, if they stayed still.

Tap. Tap. He was testing for the secret door. *Zenobia—Mary—*

Cecilia thought she would suffocate. She bit Ned's hand and he yanked it away with a hiss. But it did not help. The old, stale darkness was pressing against her, forcing her breath back into her lungs. She felt a scream building inside.

"Come now, daughter," Morvath called. "Where is your loyalty? I know you're with that two-faced Lightbourne. Don't listen to him. Don't trust a word he says. He's no scoundrel; he doesn't have a truly bad bone in his body. You'll be so much happier with Frederick. You and he will be the prince and princess of thieves, and I will be England's king."

He thumped the wall barely inches from where they stood. Ned shifted closer against Cecilia; beside them, Alex made the tiniest sound as he unsheathed a weapon. Cecilia bit her lips desperately to keep silent.

"Damn it, girl! You're going to be sorry. For every half hour you stay hidden, I will slit the throat of a pirate lady." His voice shuddered through the timbers. His smile cut the dark. "I'm sure you don't want that, do you?"

Cecilia moved instantly to open the door. Ned caught her, pushing her against raw wood and spiderwebs. She struggled, but he was gentle, confusing her instinct to resist. He brushed back her hair, soothing her, calming her, until she eased beneath him.

"Cecilia!" Morvath shouted again, but his voice was fading, and his footsteps moved away. Finally he was gone.

Ned shifted back, but Cecilia pulled him to her again with unthinking need, her arms and her heart clinging to the comfort of his steady self-assurance.

"Pardon me," someone whispered in a high, fine voice. "I don't like to interrupt, but you are blocking our escape."

Ned immediately stepped away from Cecilia. "Who's there?" he demanded.

A sharp scratching sounded in the blackness, then light flared. As the pirates squinted against it, the light bloomed, filling the passage. Their eyes adjusted; they saw a rotund woman holding up a lantern.

"Who are you?" Alex asked, raising his sword.

"Captain Anne Brown, at your service," she said archly. "Who are you?"

"Miss Brown!" Cecilia sidled past the men to grasp the woman's hand. "You're safe! You're free! Is my aunt also?"

"Ah, Cecilia, so good to have found you. Your aunt is about six people to the rear of me."

Cecilia felt a rush of relief so powerful, she might have wept from it had Miss Brown not been watching her with sharp, cynical eyes. "Morvath said he would kill you if I didn't return to him."

"Yes, dear," Miss Brown replied, patting Cecilia's arm. "We heard him. But we have all escaped. Except Miss Fairweather and her granddaughter Jane. They were taken from us yesterday and we fear the worst."

"The worst indeed, Miss Brown," Cecilia replied. "Jane Fairweather is a traitor! Captain Lightbourne can tell you all—"

"Actually . . ." Ned interjected.

"It was she who aided Morvath's kidnapping of the Society. I never trusted her myself. What kind of person scrapes the icing off a bun before eating it? As for her tastes in literature— But are you otherwise all here? The children?"

"No, they and the men are being held elsewhere as hostages for our good behavior. And so we must not delay! The guards will soon realize we have gone."

Suddenly a tumult of footsteps filled the gallery. People were running from both directions; someone shouted. The pirates froze, barely daring to breathe.

"You lot, to the upper floor!" a man called. "Leave no door unopened. The girl must be somewhere. Jack, find that Bassingthwaite landlubber as well. He'll probably be cowering in a corner, but in case he's trying to escape, catch him."

"Dead or alive, boss?"

"Alive, I guess. Although I doubt anyone would mind if you cut out his tongue. Now, don't just stand there! Go, go, go!"

The footsteps swarmed away, and in the secret passage everyone breathed.

"We'll try for an exit farther along," Miss Brown whispered.

The young pirates turned about. Ned took three steps in the shadows and collided with a body that squeaked like an oversize mouse.

"Who the hell?" Ned hissed.

"It is I, Frederick Bassingthwaite."

"Good God, is half the bloody abbey in this crawlspace?" Alex muttered.

"I was trying to hide behind a cabinet," Frederick explained, "and fell through the wall. Someone came into the room shortly thereafter, so I followed this malodorous tunnel, hoping for an escape from the devil's pit of—"

"Turn around and lead the way back, there's a good chap," Ned told him.

"I? But you are the one with a weapon; you should go first. I'll accompany Cecilia and protect her from harm."

"What with, a sharp-edged handkerchief?"

Frederick huffed. "Blaggard!"

"Dandy," Ned retorted.

"Rake."

"Sure. Better that than a twit."

"You aren't fit to tie her laces."

"I've already untied them. Try again."

Frederick gasped. "Be glad I don't have the ancestral Bassing-thwaite sword with me, sir, or I would challenge you to a duel this very moment!"

"You can borrow my sword if you like. I'm sure I have a butter knife somewhere I could use myself. It might hurt a little more when I cut out your heart, though."

"At least I have a heart!"

Alex leaned forward. "Ned? Fred? Small word of advice? You might want to stop fighting about which of you is taking the lead, considering Miss Bassingthwaite has already taken it and is about fifty feet ahead of us by now."

The men promptly turned and, with a brief skirmish of elbows, hurried along the passage after Cecilia. Alex strode after them, and the Wisteria Society, resembling nothing so much as a smirk in the darkness, followed.

Occasionally they heard voices or footsteps, or knuckles bashing against the wall, and they stopped until silence returned. Finally they came upon a sliver of light and, after listening against the wall, agreed to risk it. Ned hooked his fingers in the slight gap and cautiously pushed the door ajar.

Immediately before him stood a drinks cabinet. Ned hunkered down behind it, listening. Silence reassured him, but even so he peered around the cabinet's edge, gun poised. He was in a sitting room. Its lamps were doused, drapes closed, and the darkness clung damply to the silence like a ghost. No one was inside.

With a sigh of relief he stood and was opening his mouth to call the ladies out when something soft but heavy whacked him in the head. He spun about, dazed, and was whacked again. He had no opportunity to aim his gun at the assailant before he was pounded to his knees, and all he could do was cover his head with his arms in futile self-defense against what appeared to be assassination by pillow.

"Ow!" he cried—albeit quietly, so as not to attract the attention of Morvath's henchmen. "Ow! Stop it!"

Suddenly the object was yanked away and Ned looked up carefully through hands and hair to see Cecilia holding a knife to the throat of Jane Fairweather.

"Cecilia," the girl said, blinking behind the spectacles that hung askew on her face.

"Traitor," Cecilia replied.

"Now, see here!" Jane exclaimed—but then faltered as Frederick emerged from the passage, draped in cobwebs like a maudlin bride. "I—" she began again, but was silenced once more as the daunting figure of Alex O'Riley appeared, followed by fourteen ladies in various states of undress. Jane blushed at Miss Brown's chemise, gasped at Millie the Monster's drawers (pink, with cheerful little yellow bows), and almost fainted when Miss Darlington emerged in a camisole and petticoat.

Soon the room was packed with half-naked women, and Cecilia had all she could do to keep Jane upright.

"Cecilia!" Miss Darlington snapped, and immediately Cecilia's shoulders straightened, her chin lifted, and her knife hand moved to a more refined angle. "What on earth are you doing to Miss Fairweather?"

"She betrayed us to Morvath," Cecilia explained.

"She attacked me with a pillow," Ned added.

"Cushion," Jane said pedantically, and Cecilia pressed the knife a little firmer against her pulse. Jane winced. "I'm sorry, I assumed you were one of Captain Morvath's men. I was hiding from them behind the drapes. I am no traitor, I swear!"

"If you aren't," Cecilia asked, "why are you running around free in Northangerland Abbey, breakfasting with Morvath?"

"I cannot say," Jane mumbled.

"I can," Ned interjected. "And in fact have been trying to say it all along. It's simple. Miss Fairweather is not the culprit, Miss Fairweather is. The senior Miss Fairweather. Miss Fairweather's grandmother Fairweather: Miss Muriel Fairweather, not Miss Jane Fairweather, to be clear."

"Egads!" Millie the Monster exclaimed. The rest of the Society muttered among themselves. Cecilia hesitated, looking at Jane's delicate face and taut mouth, which was always so fond of quoting Wordsworth. She wished there was another reason to continue holding the girl at knifepoint, but dislike based on an old, vague jealousy and the sorrow of faded friendship did not seem enough. She lowered the knife and stepped back.

Jane straightened her spectacles, then curtsied to the women. "I apologize on behalf of my grandmother. Would you believe it was an affair of the heart?"

"No," said fifteen voices.

"Would you believe Morvath preyed on her sensitivities as an elderly woman?"

"No."

"Oh. Well then, would you believe he promised her five thousand pounds and the Heppingworth Diamond?"

"That sounds more like it," Miss Darlington said, and the others nodded in agreement.

"I did not approve of her choice. But I am a Fairweather. Loyalty is all to us."

Mrs. Rotunder snorted a brusque laugh. "Your aunt had your uncle arrested because he stole the Rembrandt she stole from Prince Edward's mistress."

"Loyalty is second only to the craft of piracy to us," Jane amended. "I dared not expose the false theft of our house, and I hadn't the courage to foil your kidnapping. I did urge Cecilia to leave the teahouse, to save her from her father." She smiled at Cecilia, who stared back impassively. The smile faltered. "I thought rumors of his wickedness were surely exaggerated. A few days in Captain Morvath's company changed my heart. He made us listen to his 'Ode to Pensiveness.'" She shuddered. Ned and Frederick shuddered. Even Miss Darlington shuddered, although that may have been due to wearing almost no clothes in a chilly, shadowed room.

"When I heard Cecilia had been brought on board the abbey, I was determined to help her escape, despite my grandmother's trust in me. I stole the key to the secret garden where the Society houses have been moored."

"Jolly good!" cheered the pirates in enthusiastic whispers. "Well done! Brava! Fine work!" They elbowed Cecilia aside to pat Jane's back, shake her hand, and mortify her thoroughly with a close view of their bare ankles and uncorseted breasts. Cecilia turned away with pursed lips and caught Ned smirking at her. She scowled.

"Cecilia," Miss Darlington said, emerging from the throng like a battlehouse hoving into view. "Are you all right? Have you seen your father?"

Everyone turned to look at Cecilia in anticipation of her reply. She noted the unspoken third question in their eyes: *Have your instincts awoken to the moldy, dark heritage of villainy that stalks these halls in which you were raised?* (Or, as they would more likely put it, *Have you gone off the rails yet?*)

"I met him briefly, but we did not speak," she explained, her voice tight. "I'm fine."

The ladies, being British to the core, were not fooled by *fine*. They looked more closely at her mother's dress, as if it was her mother's ghost; they turned their suspicious stares then to Ned, who grinned in response.

"Your eyes are bleary," Miss Darlington continued fretfully. "I fear you have caught chicken pox in this damp place. And you should not wear your hair down; you never know what vermin you might attract." She gave Ned a pointed glare. Her expression stiffened as she noticed Frederick standing beside him. "I say, who is that?"

Frederick bowed. "Allow me to introduce myself, O madam of magnificence, whose august name—"

"That is my cousin," Cecilia said. "Aunt Darlington, please meet Mr. Frederick Bassingthwaite. He is late of Starkthorn Castle and has a keen interest in ladies' calves. Mr. Bassingthwaite, Miss Darlington."

Frederick stepped forward to take Miss Darlington's hand, but she did not offer it. "A Bassingthwaite in Northangerland Abbey."

"Cecilia and I are to be married," Frederick explained. "I am the happiest of men! Our fates have aligned and for as long as—"

"We must go at once to the garden," Miss Darlington declared. "Cecilia, do you remember the way?"

"I'm not sure," Cecilia admitted. She could envision her mother drifting through the walled courtyard lavishly filled with greenery and flowers, but its location was beyond her power of recollection.

"I know it," Ned said.

Miss Darlington threw him the sort of look she usually bestowed upon an unsanitary surface. "Well, I suppose there is no help for it. Cecilia, keep him by your side and see that he stays out of trouble."

Ned frowned. "I am a cap—oh, never mind."

Miss Darlington patted Cecilia's arm in an effusion of emotion, then frowned. "This muslin is far too flimsy. Why are you not wearing a shawl? Do you want to languish and die? Pull yourself together, girl! And if anything happens that *actually* threatens your life, you must run away, do you understand?"

Cecilia nodded wearily. It was, after all, the story of her life.

"Run away to find some guns and shoot the place up," Miss Brown amended with a wink.

"Hm," Miss Darlington said. "Let's call that Plan B."

"And look, ladies," Gertrude Rotunder said cheerfully, holding up a bottle of whiskey. "Weapons!"

"Hurrah!" whispered the pirates.

❖ 18 ❖

A LADIES' CRAFT-MAKING SESSION—FIRST IMPRESSIONS—
THE VILLAIN'S DENOUEMENT—A NEW THEORY—
EXPLOSIONS (INFORMATIONAL, LITERARY, GARNISHES)—MELEE—
THE RIDDLE OF THE DOOR—SCRAPED—THE TELLTALE HEART

Observe a lady when she has some woman's work in hand, and you will see the image of peace, calmly intent on her task. Thus were the matrons of the Wisteria Society; holding themselves in humble, feminine focus, they smashed bottles between cushions, sharpened swizzle sticks, and handed out corkscrews. Olivia Etterly fashioned a knuckle-duster from teaspoons, and Millie the Monster took the drapes' braided cord as a garrote.

Cecilia stood guard at the door as they worked. She stared out at a corridor that formed a shadowed groove in her memory, its tallow candles smoking dolefully on sconces along the walls. She tried to envision herself as a little girl dancing its length but could not do so. That part of her was so distant now, it seemed to be a different girl in a different life, as if Cecilia herself had always lived with Miss Darlington, reading aloud from moralizing works in the mornings, training to rob and swindle people in the afternoon, and never daring to dream in case she encountered in her heart a sad-eyed little ghost hugging a math textbook.

"Are you all right?" came a quiet male voice at her shoulder. Cecilia turned and was momentarily alarmed to see Alex O'Riley standing beside her. Candlelight flickered in his dark blue eyes and against the silver hook earring hanging from his left ear as if trying, but failing utterly, to haunt him.

"You look rather melancholy," he said, his voice tinted with a slight Irish accent.

"I am perfectly cheerful," she replied, and gave him a smile to prove it. He winced.

"Any more cheerful-looking and you'd be in a coffin."

Cecilia snapped her smile back. "Your perception is confused, Captain O'Riley."

"I won't disagree with you there," he said, leaning back against the doorjamb. "Having grown up with stories about the infamous Wisteria Society, I did not expect to see a group of old ladies in petticoats. My perception is very confused indeed."

"Only a man would feel that way," Cecilia retorted.

"No doubt. I'm also confused about you, Miss Bassingthwaite. You look nothing like your mother."

A sudden dizziness of emotion swamped her, and she drew herself more erect, eyes tightening. No one had ever said such a thing to her in all her life. She was ~~outraged~~ ~~annoyed~~ astonishingly pleased.

"How do you know?" she asked.

He took a ring from his thumb, tipping back its ruby to reveal a secret compartment wherein was set the portrait of Cilla Bassingthwaite. Cecilia swallowed a sound.

"I stole this from Ned some years ago. I thought he was too obsessed with the ghost of a woman he'd only met once. I didn't understand at the time. She's magnificent, to be sure, but you are—" He regarded her with an almost professional interest. "If I may say so, your beauty is more considerate."

"Er," Cecilia said. "Thank you?"

"You're welcome. Would you like the ring?" He held it out.

Cecilia shook her head hastily. "No, I have my locket . . . and a portrait in my bedroom . . . and a sketch . . . and an embroidered likeness in a frame."

"Goodness," he murmured, returning the ring to his thumb. "So are you going to marry Lightbourne?"

"What?" She was so startled she almost shouted the question. "Certainly not! Why on earth would you ask that?"

He shrugged. "No reason. Except I've known you for ten minutes, and for a lot of that time you've been touching each other. Even now, he's caressing you with his eyes."

"He is not," Cecilia retorted, and glanced across the room at Ned. He stood with Frederick, teaching him to make a weapon from silver toothpicks and knotted ribbons, but his attention was not on Frederick's bewildered efforts. He stared at Cecilia with a heat that made her immediately blush. She looked away, saw Alex's sardonic expression, and scowled.

"He's an idiot."

"He is," Alex agreed. "And if you hurt him, I will be most displeased indeed."

He left before she could reply. Frowning after him, she happened to rest her gaze, purely by chance, on Ned once more. She watched him slide a gold fob watch from Frederick's coat pocket, and her pulse flickered in unusual places within her body.

He had kissed her twice now. Outrageous! Indefensible! Would he kiss her in the sunlight next time? My goodness, she hoped not! Would he hold her close, his hand stroking her back as if she was something to be handled with care, cherished? Heaven forbid!

She clutched her little childhood knife so fiercely that her finger-nails dug into the palm of her hand. Life had been much more tranquil before that nom-de-plumed pirate barged his way in. Well, there had been escapades, heists, assassins, ghastly memories to repress, tea parties, tigers, and the lingering thought of her father out there somewhere haunting her sense of justice. But there had been none of these *smiles*.

Once this Morvath business was over, Cecilia intended to collect a stack of books and lock herself in her sitting room until Captain Light-bourne went away.

Was he still watching her? Uncouth rogue! She glanced over, and he winked at her, and she snapped her gaze back to the corridor with such speed she saw stars.

Felt stars beneath her heart.

"Tally ho," someone whispered. Cecilia turned with relief to see the pirates were finally armed and ready. She checked the corridor both ways, listened a moment, then indicated it was safe for them to proceed.

The floorboards creaked mournfully as the group followed Ned's directions along several corridors toward the secret garden. Cecilia had a flash of memory—Morvath pulling up the floor tiles, having old warped boards laid instead. She despised him all over again.

Miss Brown and Bloodhound Bess were in the lead, jagged bottles at the ready, with Miss Darlington and Cecilia directing the rear. Suddenly Miss Brown came to a halt, holding up her fisted hand. Everyone stopped. She pointed at the corner ahead, then spun her finger. The group turned around—

"Eek!" Frederick squealed.

Morvath was striding along the corridor, a long-handled pistol in his hand, several grim-faced men accompanying him. His black great-coat swooped as he walked. His eyes flared with dark fire. Half the

Wisteria Society turned to flee but were stopped by another group of armed men appearing around the corner.

"Well met, Mother," Morvath said as he came to a halt, raising his pistol. Astonished, Cecilia looked around to see whom he meant. Miss Brown, long widowed and happy to pull up her skirts behind some bushes? Bloodhound Bess with her luring scar-smile? Millie the Monster because you just never knew with some people?

"Son," Miss Darlington replied impassively.

Cecilia stepped back as if the revelation had physically struck her. Aunt Darlington was her grandmother?

Life seemed to both expand and implode all in one astonishing moment. She collided with Ned and he put a steadying arm around her.

"Life is a downward journey, madam," Morvath said, "and you are about to reach the bottom."

"The words of Branwell Brontë, I believe," Miss Darlington responded. "But intelligence is an upward curve and does not involve plagiarizing one's supposed father."

"Rather my father's words than my mother's regard!" Morvath retorted. "Rather the echo of a man than the living breath of any woman! Our sex will always be superior to yours!"

"Tell that to the publishers of *Jane Eyre*."

The captain's face burned scarlet. "Had my father lived, he would have far surpassed his sisters in greatness. But women dragged him low. And you broke his heart, refusing to marry him."

Miss Darlington shrugged. "I would gladly have broken his heart, or even better put a sword through it, had I been able to find him."

"Question," Essie said, raising her hand. "What do you mean by 'supposed father,' Jem?"

Miss Darlington lifted her chin with a surfeit of dignity. "A lady does not lower herself to mathematics. Branwell Brontë might have been his father." She paused for dramatic effect. "Or Chubber Darwin."

"What?" exclaimed the entire company.

She shrugged. "Chubber Darwin. Nice chap, rather bookish; I think he went on to do something with animals."

"You don't mean Charles Darwin, do you?" Ned asked.

"Yes indeed," Miss Darlington replied.

Morvath choked on a cry. He swallowed it with difficulty, his mouth twisting. "My father was a *scientist*?"

"Or Branwell," Miss Darlington added. "Who really knows?"

The captain growled incoherently.

"I would have married either of them, but Chubber had just become engaged to his cousin and Branwell disappeared. I had no choice but to adopt you out."

"Discard me," he spat.

"Give you to a worthy couple who swore to love you with all they had."

"All they had? Country peace, summers at the beach, rest on Sunday! What kind of life is that for a poet or pirate? I could have been captain of the infamous Darlington House!"

"Actually," Petunia Dole put in, "Darlington House is entailed to the female, I believe? Unless you were a woman, it was never going to be yours."

"Silence!" Morvath shouted. "You ruined my life—all of you! Depriving me of my birthright, stealing Cilla away from me, refusing me entry into your society."

"Our *ladies'* society?" Olivia asked.

"But I will triumph!" Morvath went on. "I have all your houses. And soon the throne of England will be mine. No more queens! All women will return to the hearth where they belong, and men will once again be the masters!"

"Do you think he's revealed his plot enough?" Petunia asked, slapping her jagged half-bottle against her hand.

"Yes," Miss Darlington said. "Patrick, I'm sorry if you were hurt by me adopting you out, but the world makes love impossible for women sometimes, leaving us with no choice but loss and grief." She shrugged. "Or rampant piracy. But I don't want to hurt you, lad. I love you, always have, despite everything. Can't we sit down over tea and—"

"No!"

"Very well. Cecilia, Plan B."

Cecilia's pulse stammered. She knew it was her duty to follow a senior member's directive but could not so easily leave her aunt, or for that matter the old dream of defeating her father. Stepping from Ned's hold, she reached into a pocket of her dress, pulled out the deadly item therein, and smashed it to the ground between Morvath and the Wisteria Society.

Everyone leaped back.

"Nooo!" Morvath howled. He raised a furious gaze from the cracked, rumpled volume of *Wuthering Heights* to glare at Cecilia. "How dare you!"

"I have evolved beyond the point of wanting to read it," Cecilia said.

"You—you are just like your mother—such a disappointment to me!"

"Thank God for that," she replied.

Miss Darlington nodded briskly to her, and Cecilia almost smiled at such an effusive demonstration of approval.

"En garde!" Petunia shouted.

And Morvath shot her.

His pistol exploded in a cloud of hot gas and metal fragments. With a scream, he threw it from him and clutched his burned, bleeding hand against his chest.

"Did I mention," Ned mentioned, "that I tampered with all your guns?"

"Traitor!" Morvath roared.

Ned shrugged. "It depends on who's saying so."

The air hissed as Morvath drew his sword. Behind him, guns clattered to the floor and the henchmen pulled out swords, knives, truncheons.

Petunia stepped back, hands on her hips. "Everybody sorted now? Shall we try again? En garde!"

"For England!"

"For Cilla!"

The sexes rushed forward to battle.

"Come on," Ned murmured, pulling Cecilia away.

They shoved through the rush of hollering women and cursing men, ducking swords, cowering as a jar of cocktail onions exploded nearby. A man grabbed Cecilia's hair and she kicked his shin, then kneed him in the unmentionables. As he collapsed howling to the ground, she gathered up her skirts, leaped his body, and twisted the arm of another man who was about to stab Essie in the back. Ned reached past her, snatched the knife from the man's hand, and used it to stab a third in the thigh, while Cecilia forced the man to his knees. A swift application of Ned's boot heel to his head rendered him unconscious. Thus they cleared passage for themselves through the melee, and within moments were around the corner and running hard along a corridor.

"Wait for me!" Jane cried out behind them.

"Oh, lovely," Cecilia muttered.

"I have the key to the garden door!" Jane said breathlessly as she reached them. "The Wisteria houses are still fully armed."

"We'll give the ladies air support," Ned said, grinning.

"Fine," Cecilia agreed. "But keep up. This will be even harder than robbing a bank, you know."

"I would have robbed a bank," Jane retorted, "but there are few of us who are secure enough to commit such a crime without a bad influence encouraging us. With my parents off selling fool's gold in America, and my grandmother too busy conspiring against the Society, I've been forced to be sensible."

"No pirate should have to be sensible," Cecilia conceded reluctantly.

"Wait for me!" came another cry. They glanced back to see Frederick stumbling and gasping along behind.

"Wonderful," Ned muttered. No one waited, but Frederick managed to keep up nevertheless, driven by terror. Behind him came Alex, blood dripping from his sword.

"Anyone else?" Ned asked dryly.

"Oh, I'm not coming with you," Alex said as he ran. "I'm heading out for my own house. I just got a new thirteen-pounder field gun and I'm keen to try it."

"Aim for the west wing," Ned told him. "That's where they keep their artillery store."

"Will do. Break a leg, old chap."

Alex veered off. The others reached the end of the corridor, rushed down a flight of stairs, made short work of two henchmen they encountered there, and turned into another long, murky corridor that dwindled into shadow. Ned led them past one door but stopped at the next.

"This one," he said, tugging at its rusted knob handle. "Jane, bring that—"

He stopped, staring at the knob, which had just broken off in his hand.

"Key," he said limply.

"Try to fit it back on," Jane suggested.

"We're going to die!" Frederick wailed.

"It's completely broken," Ned said, trying without success to reattach the handle.

Cecilia frowned. "Are you sure?"

"Kick the door down," Jane suggested.

"I don't want to die a virgin," Frederick wailed.

"For God's sake!" Ned rolled his eyes.

Cecilia stepped forward, nudging him aside. With her tiny knife she began levering the exposed locking mechanism.

"Gently!" Jane suggested.

"I feel faint," Frederick wailed.

"Marry me," Ned whispered to Cecilia.

"Over Freddy's dead body," she muttered in reply.

"This afternoon, then," Ned said. "The poor chap is about to expire from hysterics."

"That's what happens when you live in a luxurious ancestral castle instead of a house that someone pushed off a cliff."

"I'm going to kiss you for saying that. I'm going to kiss your mouth and your throat and your brea—"

"Language, Captain Lightbourne." She looked up to frown at him; then her expression slid into a sly, half-sided smile. She pushed the door open. Ned grinned, his eyes bright with admiration.

"Quickly," Jane urged, flapping her hands at them.

"Huzzah!" Frederick cheered.

Ned and Cecilia stepped aside to let them go through first. "What do you think?" Ned murmured. "Should we shut the door on them and run away, steal some offices, become lawyers?"

Cecilia sighed and shook her head. They entered the secret garden.

꧁꧂

Cilla's garden was the literal heart of Northangerland Abbey—and the psychological one too, judging from its dark, dripping tangle of overgrowth. The shadows were clammy, the walls black with mold. From somewhere among the dead roses, an owl hooted. Or perhaps it was the ghost of a long-lost arborist, drifting mournfully through his ruined heaven. The pirates shivered.

"Alas, your mother would surely be heartbroken to see this," Frederick whispered to Cecilia.

"Why?" Cecilia asked. "It looks exactly as I remember it."

"Oh."

The houses of the Wisteria Society loomed silently about them. They had been crammed in however they could fit: some angled against a wall, others piled three deep. Darlington House sat like a throned queen atop Millie the Monster's cottage.

Ned stated the obvious. "We're going to have to climb."

"I don't think I can," Jane admitted, growing pale as she eyed the heights.

"I shall remain here with you, dear maiden, and protect you with my very life," Frederick declared, his own face so white he looked like one of Pleasance's ghosts.

"That house is on the ground." Ned pointed to a narrow four-story Georgian town house with pink lavender growing in its window boxes.

"I'll take it," Jane said promptly.

"I'll accompany you," Frederick added. "A lady should never be alone in this dangerous world."

"Excellent!" Ned slapped Frederick on the shoulder. Frederick winced. "Good luck to you both."

Jane and Frederick hurried off. Ned turned to ask Cecilia if she needed assistance, but she had vanished. He looked around urgently and saw the door to Millie's house was ajar. He ran through the cozy little rooms, calling her name in a loud whisper, nearly leaping out of his skin when she reappeared suddenly carrying a ladder.

He pressed a hand against his hard-beating heart. "You shouldn't keep going off like that without telling people."

"Why not?" She frowned with confusion.

"Because people care about you. They worry when you disappear."

Her confusion deepened. Ned sighed, and without further word he took up one end of the ladder and helped her carry it from the house.

"Where are Jane and Freddy?" she asked as they emerged into the garden.

"Why, are you worried about them?" Ned replied facetiously.

"No. I'm merely in a hurry to be getting aloft."

"They found a house they didn't have to climb into." As he spoke, the town house began to shudder and rise. It scraped against a villa, and lavender buds fluttered gently through the garden.

"Freddy went with Jane?" Cecilia said. "Finally, some good fortune."

"So you don't want to marry him, then?" Ned asked as they extended the ladder and propped it against the cottage wall.

"I don't want to marry anyone."

"But what would Lady Victoria do without her Lord Albert?"

"Employ a Scottish gillie. You go up first."

"I should go beneath you in case you fall."

"I am wearing a dress, sir. I don't want you to look up and see my underwear."

"I've seen it before," he reminded her with a grin. But she merely looked at him expressionlessly until he shrugged and began to climb. She tucked up her skirts and followed behind.

Upon reaching the cottage rooftop, they trudged over thatch to the front door of Darlington House. Cecilia opened it.

The foyer was a mess. Flower vases had tipped, spilling their contents. The Duke of Kent's crystal bowl lay shattered on the floor. A trail of lace and ribbon emerged from the sitting room, only to end with pearl-handled scissors lying in a pool of blood on the parquet floor.

"Wipe your feet," Cecilia told Ned. "The wheelroom is upstairs, at the end of the corridor. I'm going to check the doors are shut, then prepare the guns. You get us aloft."

"Your wheel isn't locked with a key hidden somewhere interesting?" Ned asked, eyeing her drawers.

Cecilia frowned, rearranging her skirts. "No. And stop smiling like that or I'll make you walk the plank."

Ned laughed and jogged up the stairs. Cecilia hurried into the Lilac Drawing Room, where a cataclysm of scrapbook paper and floral decals confronted her. Mr. Etterly had not been taken without a fight. She made certain the porch door was closed, then ran through the rest of the ground-floor rooms until she could call out to Ned, "Secure for flight!" Immediately the house began to rise.

Cecilia dashed to the attic. Darlington House had a fine selection of artillery, including a multibarreled gun, cannon, and harpoon. Cecilia chose the cannon without hesitation, even knowing the danger it presented to the Wisteria Society still within the abbey.

"God be with you, Aunty," Cecilia whispered. Her heart clenched—but she had spent ten years repressing love even more fiercely than a patriarchal system could, and this was not the moment to stop doing so. She hauled the cannon to the window and began to load it.

✳ 19 ✳

EXPLOSIONS, YET AGAIN—THE HEIR OF BOUDICCA—
EMPRESS OF THE SKIES—BLOOD AND GHOSTS—
PLEASANCE BECOMES A HEROINE—
PLEASANCE BECOMES A MAD BARONESS—
AN INTERLUDE—CECILIA DECIDES

A scientific woman ought to have no wishes, no affections, a mere heart of stone (and a good supply of ammunition). Constantinopla Brown prided herself on being scientific, piratic, a feminine creature; even so, she winced as the cannonball struck Northangerland Abbey. Somewhere inside that building were the venerable ladies of the Wisteria Society. Perhaps they'd even been in the corner of the west wing that had just exploded in a cloud of smoke and debris. Had Constantinopla brought the royal troops to rescue them, only to doom them instead to a horrific death?!

"Pass the chicken."

Constantinopla was jolted from her troubled thoughts by Queen Victoria's demand. "Yes, Your Majesty," she said, and reached into the picnic basket for a leg of fried chicken. The Queen, seated on a stool invisible beneath her vast black dress, laid down her paintbrush to take the chicken. As she munched, she contemplated the watercolor she was painting.

"I'm not sure I've managed to capture the deep red of the fire in that gable. What do you think, Albert dear?"

The portrait of Prince Albert, propped on a chair beside her, advanced no opinion.

"It's lovely, Your Majesty," Constantinopla said. And winced at yet another explosion. This one sent dirt and grass in an eruption terrifyingly close to the royal troops. Northangerland Abbey was fighting back. Although the Queen had brought two cannons and fifty armed men, and although three battlehouses swooped and dove above, firing on the abbey, Morvath was well stocked to fend off assault. If he got his premises in the air, there would be little hope of stopping him.

Mind you, if they got Windsor Castle in the air, he would be defeated within moments.

Constantinopla had been stunned when Queen Victoria offered her castle for the rescue effort, declaring that she'd seen enough uprisings for one reign and would put a stop to this one herself.

"But, Your Majesty," Constantinopla had said, curtsying apologetically, "I don't have the qualifications to lift a building of this size. I am but nineteen."

Tom had shot her a dark look but said nothing.

"Pish," the Queen had replied, waving a fork dismissively. "I am Queen; it will rise for me."

"You know the pirate's flying incantation?" Constantinopla had been shocked out of Your-Majestying.

"Of course I do. You simply haven't taught it to me yet."

Constantinopla had blinked, trying to parse this logic. She could only conclude that royal time operated differently from that of ordinary people.

Tom had pulled Constantinopla to one side. "We can't teach her the incantation," he'd whispered. "Think what your grandmother would say!"

"If she is alive to say anything at all," Constantinopla had replied, "then I will be pleased to hear it. You know Morvath is going to kill the Society. I will gladly teach the Queen if it means getting troops to the rescue."

And so Tom and Constantinopla had tutored the Queen in sorcery. They'd been surprised to find Her Majesty an apt student.

"We are descended from the great warrior queens of yore," Queen Victoria had reminded her. "It is in our blood to ride into battle and destroy the enemy."

She had paused to sip tea from a delicate porcelain cup, and Tom had taken the opportunity to ask Constantinopla in a whisper where Yore was. She'd sighed. If only she could be a lesbian and yet still have a grand public wedding.

The Queen caught her expression and waved her over. "My dear," she whispered. "Some advice from a long-married woman: every time he speaks, close your eyes and think of England."

A wheel had been procured, cannons and troops brought in, and the Queen had intoned the flying incantation in a voice that sent shivers through all who heard it. Windsor Castle had moaned and shuddered, then rose ponderously into the air. Constantinopla's legs had trembled beneath her and she'd clutched Tom's hand so tightly her knuckles blazed white. She'd been born a pirate; the idea of flying houses had always seemed ordinary to her. But standing now in a stone behemoth of one thousand rooms as it hauled itself into the air, she had felt the bend of gravity against sorcery, and had been horrifyingly aware that all that came between her and a crashing demise was one old lady's ability to maintain a rhyme.

Suddenly the castle had tilted, making everyone gasp. But Victoria had stomped a tiny foot, roaring the incantation less with the power of a queen and empress than with that of a mother of nine children. The castle had meekly righted itself and gone on rising, and from there it had been smooth sailing. Servants had brought tea for the Queen's parched throat, and Constantinopla had found herself getting her flight practicum in the grandest way possible, helping to navigate England's literal battlehouse on a course to Blackdown Hills.

Unfortunately, no one present had the skill to maneuver a hulking great castle in aerial battle. The captain of the troops had suggested simply landing on top of the abbey, thereby getting rid of Morvath and the Wisteria Society in one foul swoop. He had then proved his mettle by not flinching when the Queen threw a vase at him.

"There are ladies inside that abbey," she'd reminded him. "Have better manners!"

The captain, who often had been sent by the same queen to try arresting those ladies as they smuggled untaxed tea into England and jewels into their own purses, had felt disinclined to be polite toward them now. However, he had bowed in surrender to the Queen's changed opinion.

And so they could only moor Windsor Castle beyond the range of Morvath's guns and sit out front beneath large parasols, drinking lemonade served by dispassionate servants and watching the skirmish unfold.

"That smaller town house darts like a wasp," Queen Victoria commented. "I never thought to see such grace and speed in an edifice."

"That's Darlington House, Your Majesty," Constantinopla told her. "Miss Darlington is one of the greatest lady pirates. They say the spirit of Black Beryl rides her."

"I should like to meet her," the Queen declared.

"Oh, she's been dead almost two hundred years," Tom said.

The Queen gave him a look that suggested she would have taken off his head if she really was like her ancestresses. "I meant Miss Darlington."

"I'm sure it can be arranged, Your Majesty," Constantinopla said.

"She may attend our Jubilee Banquet," the Queen proclaimed airily.

If she survives, Constantinopla thought, and winced again as the cannons roared.

It was not altogether certain that Miss Darlington would honor the Queen with her presence at the banquet. Not only did she suspect Victoria was rather unhygienic, considering all those children the Queen had conceived, but there was also the slight impediment of Miss Darlington herself being half-dead.

Pleasance huddled with her in the tiny bedchamber they had limped into after an agonizing escape from the melee. Pleasance's knee was gashed, her ribs bruised, and a serrated knife protruded from her left bicep.

Yet she had carried her mistress along several corridors, up a flight of stairs, and into a room where they could hide behind a narrow, rusting bed. Miss Darlington was deathly pale where she was not deathly blood-soaked, but still she strained against Pleasance's arms, wanting to rejoin the fight.

In fact, Pleasance had no idea where the fight had gone. After Morvath stabbed his mother and then barely escaped the skirmish himself as a dozen enraged ladies descended upon him, people scattered and the melee spread into smaller private battles. The clash of metal and flare of sudden, brief screams echoed through the abbey as henchmen pursued pirates and pirates pursued henchmen, depending on who happened to be in the lead at the time. Explosions rang out, causing the whole building to shudder. Pleasance could smell smoke, and she knew if fire was headed their way, they would have no escape from it.

She had always thought that, when she died, she would like to haunt a nice cobwebbed attic or perhaps a mysteriously locked cellar in a duke's country house. She would be the moan that chilled an otherwise stoic man, the whisper that drew children into eerie games, the last thing a forlorn wife saw before sliding into death from heartbreak. The idea of dying in Northangerland Abbey distressed her. Here, she would need to get in a very long line of ghosts, wights, and strange-glimpses-of-something-white before being allowed any haunting opportunity.

"Pleasance," Miss Darlington murmured through blue lips. "Leave me, dear girl. Save yourself."

With a cry, Pleasance grasped the elderly lady more closely to her bosom. "I will never leave you, miss," she vowed. "We will die togeth— Um, that is to say, we will survive together, and be rescued, and later this evening drink a cup of tea together in the comfort of your own home. At least, I shall serve the tea, and you shall drink it, and I shall wash the cup afterward."

Miss Darlington reached up weakly to touch Pleasance's humble, shining face. "I would drink tea with you any day," she whispered.

Pleasance flushed with pride. She clutched the bed to haul herself up, then stood for a moment trying not to swoon as several ghosts came close to gibber at her. She blew them away with a determined exhalation. Miss Darlington would not die in this dismal chamber! Pleasance would rescue her even if the cost was her own paltry life.

In the back of her mind, several ghosts rubbed their spectral hands with gleeful anticipation. Pleasance ignored them. She needed a weapon if she was to secure freedom for Miss Darlington, and there was only one available in this room. So she clenched her teeth, her limbs, her very toes—and with a sudden, harsh movement she pulled the blade from her arm.

Pain almost threw her to the ground. But Pleasance was a heroine, and she remained standing. Brushing back her wild curls, ignoring the blood pouring from her arm, she took the rotting blanket from the bed, lifted Miss Darlington as gently as she could onto it, and began dragging the elderly lady toward the door.

She almost made it.

Suddenly the door crashed ajar and a rough-faced man with a heavily bandaged shoulder charged into the room. His pistol lifted, and before Pleasance could even think of the knife in her hand, he snatched it from her.

"Well, well, what have we here," he said with grim delight. "Miss Jemima Darlington."

Fury erupted within Pleasance. It blazed through any last barrier she had between reality and interesting fiction and smoked her inner mad baroness out.

With a bloodthirsty scream, she leaped at Jacobsen.

Northangerland Abbey was breaking apart. Houses rose from its courtyard garden as pirates escaped the fight to join the greater action beyond. The abbey's cannons roared and its machine guns clattered, but they could not angle up to shoot the houses swarming above, nor could they reach the royal troops, whose own cannons had a longer range. Fires grew. Gables shattered. Henchmen began running out, hollering their surrender, hands held high.

In the attic of Darlington House, Cecilia watched the destruction with a cold gaze. Almost everyone she knew in the world was in that building. Nonetheless, she dutifully aimed the cannon once more and fired—

A corner of the abbey's west wing erupted. It was her most successful shot so far; with such a gaping hole in its side, the stabilizing component of the flight incantation would never hold. Northangerland Abbey was going nowhere. Cecilia took a deep breath of relief—

And her relentless composure finally cracked, sending emotion slamming through her mind. She stumbled back, gasping.

Had she just killed Aunt Darlington? What if the old lady had left the fight, crossed the abbey, climbed several stairs, and entered the west wing?

"Oh God," she breathed. "Oh God."

God, however, did not respond, and the ingrained dictates of piracy pulled her out of black panic. With a further deep breath, she forced down the terror, loaded another cannonball, and took aim.

And shook so violently she could not light the fuse.

Fire flew across her vision. Smoke poured out of the abbey's facade. She might not be shooting, but other pirates were, in addition to the troops on the ground. It was all beyond her control. She could not stop trembling. Turning away from the cannon, she grasped the copper trumpet and shouted into it.

"Land the house!"

There followed a moment of astonished silence; then Ned's voice echoed up from the wheelroom below. "Cecilia? Are you all right?"

No, she thought, scrubbing her forehead with both hands. No, she was not all right. She was frightened and lonely, and her heart ached with an unbearable longing for her mother's wild and gentle smile. She wanted the shooting to stop. She wanted a cup of tea.

"I'm fine," she said into the trumpet. "I need to go in and rescue my aunty."

"But that's—"

He stopped, but she heard it in his silence. *That's like walking into a deathtrap.* Her heart thundered, panic surging once more. A deathtrap holding Aunt Darlington. And Pleasance. And all the mad, magnificent ladies of the Wisteria Society. She should never have left; she should have remained to fight at their side, regardless of what they ordered.

She should have remained with her mother, so that Cilla had not died alone.

All her life she had run away, doing as she was told, escaping into emptiness and leaving death in her wake.

Suddenly the house swooped to avoid gunfire from the abbey, and Cecilia almost fell. She caught herself against the cannon, but her stomach seemed to keep falling, and she knew if she stayed in this room she would devolve into hysterics. So she gathered up her skirts and ran again—in the right direction this time.

Ned had done an excellent job with the stabilizing magic, but even so Cecilia bashed against the wall and the balustrade as she made an unsteady course downstairs. She stumbled into the wheelroom, and Ned looked at her with calm eyes that suggested he'd been expecting her arrival.

"I'm not letting you go back in there." His tone was conversational, but final.

"Move away from my wheel," she replied.

"Your aunt wouldn't want you to risk— Wait, what is that?"

He stared at something out the window. Suspecting a trick, Cecilia grasped the wheel. But he did not let go, and his grip was so strong she could not move it even a degree.

"Look," he said, nodding at the window.

Cecilia squinted through the bright morning light. "It's a house," she said dismissively. "Give me back my wheel."

He shook his head. "Too small for a house."

She tried to shove the wheel again but failed. The flying object caught her eye as it flashed with sunlight. She looked more carefully and identified it. "That's a garden shed."

"I think you're right," Ned agreed. "Someone's escaping."

They stared at the shed for a taut moment, then turned to each other.

"Morvath," they said in unison.

"It could be anyone," Ned added reasonably.

"But it's him," Cecilia countered. "I can feel it."

"That's a very Brontë thing to say."

Cecilia arched an eyebrow. "Well then, allow me to consult my possible Darwin heritage instead." She took the spyglass from a nearby shelf and held it to her eye. The world was a vast black emptiness, echoing like the mordant spaces between soul-wrought words . . .

Ned leaned across and removed the lens cap, and poetry became science again.

Cecilia adjusted the focus and saw a tiny window on the garden shed. More adjustments brought her through that to see a silver head inside. She immediately recognized her father.

"Er, are you all right?" Ned asked hesitantly.

Cecilia blinked and the world expanded. She realized she had thrown the spyglass across the room, shattering Countess Ambury's stained-glass lamp.

"It's him," she confirmed, and pointed out the window. "Follow that shed, Ned."

They flew after it, Ned muttering the incantation's third stanza under his breath to increase their propulsion as the town house strained to keep up with the speedy little shed.

"Faster, if you please," Cecilia said; and tapped her boot heel against the floor; and crossed her arms, then uncrossed them. *"Faster,"* she reiterated.

Ned did not answer, for he was still chanting the stanza, but his frown was eloquent. Cecilia paced away; rearranged a few books on the shelves; tapped her heel again. "Really," she said, pacing back, "this is your top speed? A tongue-tied schoolboy translating from the original Latin could do better."

"Why don't you steer?" he suggested, stepping away from the wheel. She grasped it immediately and, alas, officiously. Ned tried not to laugh. "I'll man the guns," he said.

Cecilia stopped, tripping over the first word of the stanza. "Wait—what?"

Ned looked at her blankly. "The guns. To shoot him down. I assume we want to do that? What with him being an evil villain who must be stopped and all."

"Of course," she said, but her voice was as blanched as her face had become.

"Or perhaps not?" Ned added gently.

Cecilia hesitated. She watched the garden shed tilt and veer as it raced for the horizon.

His hair had been red when he was young.

Cecilia remembered him telling her that, although she'd never actually seen it herself, for he'd gone gray before she was born. Her mother told her he'd been so vain about those Titian curls, and worn little silver spectacles although his eyesight was perfect, and read literary papers he barely comprehended, all to be as much like Branwell Brontë as possible. His adoptive parents had named him George, after the old king, but when he learned the truth of his origins he changed it to Patrick, in honor of his Brontë grandfather, and found a sense of belonging at last in that noble lineage. Poet . . . pirate . . . dastardly villain.

One night he had shown Cecilia a portrait of himself as a youth, and he'd laughed delightedly at her wide-eyed reaction.

"But you're prettier now," she'd said, touching the silver strands of his hair.

He had laughed again, but this time it sounded sharp, like a sword brushing against skin. She had upset him, just like that. "Sorry," she'd murmured, lowering her eyes.

"Men aren't pretty," he had explained. "Men are handsome or distinguished. And red hair is my Brontë heritage, as it is yours. That heritage is something to be proud of, Cecilia Patricia."

She'd had no idea what he meant. She had been so little, her knees did not reach the edge of the sofa. So little she should have been in bed, with her dolls and her maniac cockatiel wallpaper, and her nursemaid embroidering the veil she planned to be married in just as soon as her fiancé returned from visiting a mysterious count in Transylvania. But Morvath, having drunk a little too much brandy that night, had been in a talkative mood.

"What is heritage?" Cecilia had asked him, the private dictionary in her mind waiting excitedly to add a new word.

"Heritage? Why, it is everything! My father, the great poet Branwell Brontë, has bestowed upon us all that is best about us. His imagination, his passion, his wild Irish spirit. It flows through me to you. I know that you will grow up to be a storm!"

Cecilia had tried to be tempestuous for him, but it always gave her a headache. She'd been relieved when Aunt Darlington took her in hand. Even reading *Wuthering Heights* had proven a trial—she'd kept wanting to edit it.

But in this moment, standing in the Darlington House wheelroom watching Morvath escape the consequences of his evil yet again, she felt a tempest raging through her. The man deserved to die! He had slaughtered her mother—Ned's mother—perhaps even Aunt Darlington. He had kidnapped the Wisteria Society and plotted to overthrow the rightful queen. She turned to tell Ned yes, shoot him down.

Ned waited quietly for her response. His face was wan, his eyes tired, but Cecilia saw him for a moment as she had when he first knocked on her door in Mayfair, dressed in a ridiculous coat, trying to make her believe something impossible. The mix of sweetness and danger was still there now, tilting his smile even though he was trying to keep his expression gentle. And she felt the same certainty she had all along—that despite calling himself an assassin, he wanted to make the world better, a little brighter, a little more amusing, if he could.

She smiled back at him.

"No," she said. "Shoot him down for yourself if you will, to avenge your mother, but I won't ask you to be a killer."

For the briefest moment his complacency fractured, revealing the grief, loneliness, vulnerability, beneath. And then he shrugged.

"I'm in favor of not wasting ammunition," he said. "Let's just follow. He'll have to land sooner or later."

Their gazes held, their souls reaching out to share a moment of deep, wordless understanding. Then Cecilia nodded.

"Good," she said briskly.

They turned back to the window and watched the shed slam into a hillside and explode in flames.

✳ 20 ✳

TRIUMPH—A LACK OF SPIRITS—THROUGH THE LOOKING GLASS—
INCONSOLABLE—NEAR DEATH BY DOOR SLAMMING—
SPECIAL HUGS—LITTLE DEATHS—THE FIRST GOOD-BYE

If Ned had his life to live over again, he would have made a rule to never read Morvath's manuscripts or listen to his poetic accounts of his various murders, not even once a week. The past two years had been excruciating. But it was over now. As he flew Darlington House back toward the battlefield, he could see in the distance houses cluttered on the ground between Northangerland Abbey and Windsor Castle. Ned smiled. Morvath's grand misogynist dream to conquer the world had met the full force of ladies and collapsed in less than an hour. Morvath himself was dead.

That's natural selection for you.

We got you justice, Mama, Ned whispered to the long-departed spirit of his mother. He heard nothing in reply but his own old grief and was not surprised—after all, he'd been the one to mix the corn flour and water to make ectoplasm for her séances, so he didn't actually believe in ghosts—yet at the same time it saddened him more than he could quite bear. And somehow tangled in with that was a sadness for

Morvath too, at least for the confused man with a heart full of poetry and a deep yearning to be valued. But thinking about it made Ned want to cry, which made him want to curse, and so he focused on simply flying.

Beside him, Cecilia looked out through the telescope. She had said little since the explosion. Her calm was brittle, eerie, and Ned waited nervously for her to begin crying. But as they approached Northangerland Abbey she merely laid down the telescope and took a deep breath.

"Turn the house around," she said.

Ned frowned at her, certain he'd misheard.

"I have seen my aunt through the telescope," she explained. "I cannot ascertain her condition, but she is out of the abbey and alive. Now turn the house around and land it beyond the woods, if you please."

"But—" Ned said, and would have added further expressions of bemusement had Cecilia not taken a pistol from a nearby shelf and directed it at his head.

"Kindly do as I ask."

He laughed. "Are you hijacking your own house?"

"I am hijacking my life, at least for a little while. Please, I don't want to shoot you. It would make kissing you decidedly unpleasant."

Ned promptly wheeled the house around and muttered so fast through the landing stanza, the house trembled. As they glided down over treetops toward a meadow that lay between woods and hills, Cecilia alternated between scowling and hyperventilating. Ned did not know whether to be frightened of her or for her. He decided his safest option was simply to focus on setting the house down and reciting the anchoring stanza in the correct order.

"We cannot stay in this room," Cecilia declared once they had landed. She gestured with her pistol at the elegant furniture and polished floor. "It will be far too uncomfortable. You will have to come into my—er—where I sleep—"

"Your bedroom?" Ned asked, more confused than ever.

"Exactly." Her expression was so rigid it might at any moment crack. "Although you will have to excuse the mess. I was not expecting company."

"Why are you even inviting company into your bedroom?"

She glared across the room at a book slightly misaligned on a shelf. "Soon we must return to the battlefield. I will reunite with my aunt, and I suppose you will report to the Queen. Since you have confessed yourself not truly an assassin, I won't see you again. My life will resume its normal pattern. Tea parties. Bank robberies. Long evenings spent reading to my aunt until she falls asleep. This is—"

She stopped, swallowing some unspeakable word. But Ned had no intention of letting her get away with it this time. "Is what, Cecilia?"

She shrugged one shoulder, still not looking at him. "Regrettable."

"I see." And he did see—behind her stringent manner she was frightened. Within the taut, bristling posture of her body, she was trembling with vulnerability and grief. He stepped forward, took the gun, and tossed it on a chair. Then wrapping his arms around her, he drew her close.

"It's all right to cry," he whispered. She tried to pull away, but he went on holding her, determined not to let go even if she turned into a sea monster, a screaming mare, a Lady Armitage spitting poison. He stroked her long, beautiful hair. She smelled of roses and cannon smoke, and his body ached for her in a way he knew he could not satisfy.

At least, not yet. But soon. He'd marry her in the quadrangle of the Bodleian Library, he decided. He'd take her on a honeymoon to Biblioteca Marciana. They could name their firstborn William, in honor of the incomparable Shakespeare. Or Wilhelmina, he supposed, if they were lucky enough to have a daughter. Not Cecilia, though. Heritage ended here.

But his romantic dream shattered as she stomped on his foot, pulling herself from his hold so forcefully he stumbled. "Ow," he said, scowling. She shook her hair from her face and scowled right back. "Why did you do that?"

"Because I don't want to cry, Ned. And I don't want your *consolation*."

"You don't?" He had never been so confused in all his life. Even now, he could see the shyness in her eyes, could practically feel the ache emanating from her body. Or maybe it was his own ache, growing so powerful in some places that he feared he might—

Oh.

His scowl faded as he finally understood. Hers flared into a blush. She lifted her chin with exquisite hauteur, almost but not quite disguising her embarrassment, and began to turn away.

He grabbed her hand. Without another word, he pulled her from the cockpit, marching so decisively along the hallway she had to run stumbling to keep up. He paused at one doorway, shot her a demanding look. She shook her head.

"Next one," she muttered with a mix of determination and mortification.

He strode to the door, thrust it open so enthusiastically it banged against the wall—and then nearly got his face broken as the door flung back at him and slammed shut. The sound of Cecilia trying not to laugh did not improve his patience. He opened the door again more carefully and hauled her into the room.

He groaned. Facing him was the most alluring bed he'd ever seen. Simple white blankets tucked in without a crease; two pillows so thin even a pauper would disdain them—it was a bed that spoke so much of Cecilia he could barely breathe, looking at it. She slept in that bed, her body shifting against its sheets, her nightgown tangling up to her waist . . .

He hastily turned away. The rest of the room was as calm, although with feminine touches that eased its prim austerity—pearls, shawls, a polished Winchester rifle. On one wall, a black-draped portrait of Cilla gazed down, her painted eyes focused directly on him as if she knew what he was planning to do. Ned winced. He was as degenerate as the next man, but he could not debauch a girl while her mother's portrait looked on.

"Tsk," Cecilia said. Pulling her hand free, she strode across the room and arranged the mourning drapery so Cilla was veiled. As she looked back at Ned, she winked.

A laugh broke from him then, a sudden lighthearted delight he had not felt in years. The sexual heat scouring his body deepened into a richer, more sincere warmth. *Oh damn*, he thought. *I love this woman.* He went to her, laid his hands on her shoulders, gazed into her wintry eyes.

"Tell me what you're thinking."

"I'm thinking I'm a scoundrel," she said, cool-voiced despite her inflamed face, "so I'm going to take what I want. If—that is, if you'll give it to me."

"Gladly, sweetheart." In fact, he was struggling not to throw her on the bed and give it to her without further delay, as he had been for quite some time now. But he lowered his hands, allowing her space. "Are you sure, though? Because it will ruin you forever."

"Only if people find out." She smiled with such intensity, Ned forgot nice allowances. Grasping her hand, he turned it, kissed her soft, fine-veined wrist, stroking tiny circles against the skin with his tongue. She shivered.

"I meant," he said, looking up through his eyelashes at her, "you'll be ruined for any other experience."

She laughed.

The sound of it sent a rush of fire through him. Putting his hand behind her head, he pulled her toward him and kissed her with all the passion and desire he'd felt for her since she answered the door to him in London. She seemed to melt in his embrace, her protective rigor finally giving way, her heart and body surrendering. But as she swayed, clutching at his coat to stay upright, Ned felt the weight of her inexperience and his own wish to protect her from harm. He needed to calm himself the hell down. Easing back, he smiled, brushing the hair away from her beloved face.

"I'll try to be careful," he promised.

"Oh God," she said huskily, "that's the last thing I want you to be."

He swung her up into his arms, carried her to the bed, tripped on a cudgel lying on the floor, and dropped her onto the mattress. So much for being careful. Thankfully she was wearing an old-fashioned dress with no bustle, so she did not bounce back.

"I did warn you about the mess," she said, smiling up at him from a tumult of white muslin and long rosy hair, and he almost expired on the spot from adoration. He crawled onto the bed, boots and coat and all, and she swallowed nervously, her smile shivering away.

There was no time to undress her, to explore each revelation of bare, creamy skin with his hands and mouth; if they did not return soon, a search party would be sent for them, and then she really would be ruined. But Ned thought he'd not have undressed her anyway, not this first time, when it took all her courage to lie fully clothed beneath him, her breath shaky and her eyes like a storm. He loosened the buttons of her bodice, kissed her throat and décolletage, and she stirred with a wildness that spoke truly of her innocence.

Reality struck him then like a physical blow. "Damn," he cursed, falling back against the ridiculous pillows. "I don't have any protection."

"That's all right," Cecilia said kindly. "You can borrow the gun in my side-table drawer if you want."

He laughed. Turning onto his elbow, he looked down at her with such fondness, her eyes filled with tears. Frowning, she blinked them away. He kissed her frown, the corner of each eye, her mouth. "I meant protection against pregnancy."

She gasped. "Language, sir! But you need not worry. Pleasance has certain herbs I can steal."

"In that case——" He turned away again, causing her to make noises of confusion; he removed his boots, coat, knives, and gun, then returned to her side with a smile he'd perfected over the years, a smile to make her squirm even before he set one finger on her. She responded just as he'd hoped, her body restless, her tongue slipping across her lips to wet them. It was such an erotic sight, Ned could only be grateful he'd left his trousers on or else they'd be finished a whole lot quicker than necessary. Gathering her skirts up to her knees, removing her shoes and drawers, he slipped his hand along the length of one thigh, swallowing dryly as his touch moved from silk stocking to soft skin. This was secret, sacred territory. He'd been here with other women, but none so precious to him as the one who lay with him now. Inexplicably, he began to feel frightened.

"Hurry," she whispered.

"Sweetheart," he said, "let me take you out of time for a while."

And he kissed her until even he forgot there was a world beyond this room.

Cecilia stared at the ceiling in bemusement. She knew nothing of how this procedure should go, apart from having overheard Mrs. Rotunder say it was a convenient time to work out her weekly budget. She did not expect Captain Lightbourne would be touching her thigh in that highly discombobulating manner, or——

Oh! That wasn't her thigh he just——

Oh!

She might have leaped from the bed were he not leaning over her, supporting himself with one arm while the other was occupied beneath her dress. His fingers were being decidedly rude, but before she could reason that this was acceptable under the circumstances, her body reached its own opinion. It rose toward him with wicked piratic abandon, legs spreading, hips moving in concert with his stroking fingers. The sensation was—

Alas, every possible adjective disappeared from mind, taking the mind itself with them. She reached for Ned, brushing back his hair, cupping his face, finding anchorage in his calm, steady gaze.

Then he slipped a finger inside her body and she lost it again, her hands falling back helplessly to the bed.

"Yes?" he asked, making sure.

She wanted to answer yes, or at least tell him to not waste energy talking, but all she could do was moan. He apparently translated this correctly, for he moved down and his tongue made a reply of its own where his fingers had been. *Disgraceful!* her wits declared in titillated horror. *Shut up*, her body replied.

Even as he kissed her, Ned crooked the finger within her, moving it slowly at first but then more decidedly, tightening all her nerves until Cecilia was certain she would not survive the pleasure of it. He added another finger, pressing in deeper as his tongue worked faster. The raw intimacy, after days of watching him out of the corner of her eye and dreaming of how he might feel in her arms, became overwhelming. Suddenly her nerves broke apart, shooting sparks of ecstasy through her, from her curling toes to the cry leaping out of her throat. Her entire being felt like one great pulsing heart.

Ned moved up to kiss her open mouth. He tasted wicked, and she would have blushed were she not already vehemently doing so. His fingers remained inside her, holding her to his calm as she shuddered down into softness.

"Oh, I say," she murmured, looking at him rather unfocusedly.

"Are you all right?" His smile was tender, as if he knew the answer perfectly well but wanted to hear her say it. His fingers slid out, and she sighed.

"Yes, I think so. I beg your pardon for my indecorous behavior."

"Cecilia. Don't apologize for orgasming."

She frowned. "I suspect that is a rude word and you should not say it to me."

"Fine, I promise never to say it again." His smile became roguish. "But I shall do it to you as often as I can manage."

"Oh. Er, well, I suppose that is in the bounds of good manners."

"The best manners, I should think." He began kissing her again along her jawline, stopping only to take her earlobe gently between his teeth. She turned her head wantonly to encourage him. She'd wondered sometimes what it would be like to fly without the protection of a house—a witch, boundless; a dream of herself. Now she suspected it would feel like this, here in his arms, under his gorgeous smile. The thought of gathering herself together into a stiff, careful posture for the world again was almost a physical pain, scouring her heart and making her want to weep. But she knew it must be done. This was only ever meant to be one beautiful moment.

"Thank you," she said rather formally. "I hope that was also pleasant for you."

"More than I can express," he murmured against her cheek.

"It went quicker than I supposed; we should not be missed at all."

Ned lifted his head, blinking at her through the fall of his hair; he frowned in bemusement. "Er, sweetheart, you do realize we haven't finished yet?"

"We haven't?" Her eyes widened.

Ned's grin returned, even more wicked than before. "We're not even halfway through." Taking her hand, he held it against the hard swelling in his trousers. "Do you see?"

Cecilia blushed. His fingers were damp against hers; his eyes were growing dark in the most heart-stirring way. "I did wonder—that is, I wondered if—er, the gentleman's accoutrement was involved in proceedings—"

He laughed. "You are too perfect," he said, and as she took a deep breath to argue the semantics of that, he lowered himself to kiss her into a hot, urgent silence.

She felt anxiety rising again as she imagined what might happen next. But he kissed her face and whispered silliness and soon she was giggling, squirming with delight beneath him, forgetting everything but the loveliness of him and the rightness of their being together. Then he straightened so he was kneeling between her legs, drawing them wider with firm hands, pushing up her knees, and Cecilia caught her breath. Her bunched dress protected her from an immodest view, but *he* could see everything.

Egads. Really, they ought to address this sort of thing in etiquette class. Cecilia had to restrain herself from pulling down her dress and begging his pardon again. Her sense of vulnerability, and his clear mastery of the situation, presented an affront to all her piratic sensibilities—and yet were at the same time utterly arousing. She had never guessed being unshielded to another person would thrill her so. If only he would *not actually look.*

He did not look. He held her gaze with a cool serenity while he began to unbutton his trousers. As the last fastening came free and he slipped the garment down his hips, Cecilia closed her eyes and thought of England.

Lush, flowering England laid open to the gasping, caressing winds.

And then he was moving into her once more, not his fingers this time, and she could have wept for the feeling of it—so right, so perfect, as if all her life she'd suffered an emptiness only this man could fill. It ached a little, stretching her despite the earlier work of his fingers, but somehow that was part of the wondrousness. Ned hooked his hands around her thighs, lifting them over his hips and moving in deeper as he lowered himself onto his elbows. Her eyes flung open at a shock of sensation. He caught her gaze, and they stared at each other entranced as their bodies came together, their spirits already there.

"You're fully ruined now," he murmured, smiling wryly.

"No," she breathed. "I was ruined the moment I laid eyes on you. Utterly ruined for everything else, evermore."

"Told you so."

"Fiend." She frowned with mocking severity.

"Rake?" he suggested.

"Oh, yes, please."

His smile tumbled. He moved back, then slid in slow and deep again, and they disappeared together into their own secret universe.

Damn, Cecilia thought as she rocked against his thrusting body. *I love him.*

His heart was going to break. Ned knew it, but could do nothing about it. His longing for her blistered him, even though he was inside her body. He wanted to see her naked. He wanted to kiss her breasts and navel and every other inch of her. He wanted to pour her tea in the morning while she read him amusing stories from the newspaper.

All his life he was going to ache for this woman, no matter how close they got.

The desperate need might have robbed him of his gentleness, but he loved her, and so he was as careful as he'd promised her, never mind what she'd said. She was far too naive to appreciate what would happen if he abandoned caution. One of these days he'd set his passion free—and the last of her inhibitions along with it. But today was—was—

He gave up thinking about it. He yielded to the wordless, rhythmic pulse of his body. It felt like gliding in sunlight.

And then Cecilia slipped a soft, gentle hand under his shirt. She stroked his back in wonder, trailing sparks behind her fingers. "I can't believe I'm getting to touch you," she whispered, and the words stroked his heart in a way he'd never felt before. Control fraying, he moved in her harder, and she rocked against him faster, and the world began to burn.

Suddenly, her breathing fell apart. Ned held her close, wanting to have it all in that moment—her breath, heartbeat, soul. She clung to him just as urgently, fingernails digging into skin, and as her most intimate muscles clenched around him he, too, climaxed, finding his heaven with her.

"Cecilia," he whispered in the scorched darkness.

"Ned," she breathed.

It was the simplest truth of them. It felt like everything.

Afterward, they sat together on the side of the bed, holding hands. "Well, I never," Ned murmured, looking at Cecilia's delicate fingers entwined in his.

"We should get back," she said.

Neither of them moved.

"Are you all right?" he asked, tipping his head sideways toward her.

"Yes." She leaned her head against his shoulder. "A little concerned my aunt will take one look at me and know what I've been doing, lock me in my bedroom, and have me marry Cousin Frederick as a precaution against willfulness. Otherwise, fine, thank you."

"You're an adult, my darling. You could always lock your aunt in her bedroom and steal her house."

"Ha ha."

"Or steal a house of your own."

She sighed. "That's the dream. A pretty cottage, too many books, and—"

You. She did not say it. After all, he'd given her his body for the moment; she could not take his heart as well. Not even years of pirate training had made her so ruthless.

Ned sighed. "I guess we do have to get back."

"Yes. But at least—at least now I know."

He did not ask, assuming no doubt she meant her physical experience and not the bittersweet recognition of love she could never share with him. He turned, lifted her chin, kissed her soft and slow with love and sorrow.

It felt to her like good-bye, and her heart cried and shredded its damp handkerchief. To Ned, though, it was a promise—a way of saying he'd marry her as soon as he could, except first there were queens and aunts to manage. But they were pirates, used to shaping the world however they decided. They were motherless children. Neither thought for a moment to stop and actually properly talk.

"Ready?" Ned asked, smiling into her eyes.

Cecilia shrugged. "Tally ho."

❧ 21 ❧

POST-TRAUMATIC HOUSEWORK DISORDER—
HER MAJESTY'S SPECIAL SERVICE—A ROYAL HANDSHAKE—
NED'S TROUSERS—A ROADBLOCK—THE GHOST OF MISS DARLINGTON—
DEGENERATION (METAPHORICAL AND LITERAL)—
MORE OF HER MAJESTY'S SPECIAL SERVICE—
A BLOODLESS VICTORY

Nothing is easier than to admit the truth of the universal struggle to find a good parking space. After some hovering and maneuvering, Ned was finally able to set Darlington House down not far from where Queen Victoria sat picnicking in grand state with Tom Eames and Constantinopla Brown. Oply's presence explained why the Queen was there, but Ned could not imagine either her or Tom having the skill to raise a castle and fly it all the way from Windsor. Curious, worried, he muttered the anchoring stanza, then hurried downstairs.

Cecilia looked up from sweeping the foyer floor. She looked as implacable as a stick of dynamite. Ned eyed the broom warily as he approached, not altogether sure she wouldn't hit him with it just to relieve her nervous tension.

"I'm almost finished," she said. "I have to get this floor done, dust the side tables, clean the kitchen, and hang the bedding out to air. Then everything will be tidy again."

He stepped close. His quiet, unblinking gaze caught her, held her still, so that he could take the broom uncontested from her grip. He set it against a wall that was actually nowhere near, and as it clattered to the floor he put his arms around her.

For a moment he thought she would protest. But she only sighed and relaxed against him. He whispered nothing in particular, kissing her hair. She nestled closer, and then he was the one to sigh. He was on the verge of begging her to marry him when a sudden knock on the door prevented it. Cecilia moved away, leaving him oddly bereft, and crossed to open the door.

"Yes?" she said.

Two dozen armed soldiers stood at the threshold.

"Good morning," said the man in front. "Could we interest you in an unconditional surrender?"

"By all means," Cecilia replied. "I do not know who you are, but I am most happy to accept your surrender."

"Er." The man grimaced with embarrassment. "I referred to your surrender, madam. I am Lieutenant Fluthian of Her Majesty's Special Service. And you are under arrest."

"Oh, for goodness' sake, Fluffy." Ned opened the door wider and scowled at the lieutenant. "Don't be such a twit."

"M-Major Candent." The lieutenant flushed scarlet. "I did not realize."

"Major?" Cecilia echoed, raising one eyebrow.

Ned shrugged.

"You outrank us all," she said, amused.

"I'm also a colonel somewhere or the other. It doesn't signify. Get out of the way, Fluffy. We're going to talk to the Queen."

"Oh. I—well—I—can you—well, yes—certainly, sir." Lieutenant

Fluthian stepped aside, and his troops echoed the movement with flawless synchronicity. Ned offered Cecilia his arm, she took it, and they exited Darlington House.

They had gone two steps when Cecilia stopped. "Just a moment," she said, and with a meaningful glance at Lieutenant Fluthian she returned to lock the front door.

Ned grinned. "Her Majesty's Special Service are not prone to thieving," he chided.

"Then return my amethyst ring," she replied.

Laughing, he drew the ring from his jacket pocket. Cecilia reached for it but he clasped her hand and held it steady as he slipped the ring onto her middle finger. The slow, heavy slide of it made his heart stir. Looking up through his eyelashes, he smiled as he watched a blush color her lovely face.

"Are you ever going to return my heart?" he asked softly.

She shrugged. "Maybe for a ransom. Good heavens, is that Constantinopla Brown?"

The young pirate girl was running toward them, her dress a maelstrom of flounces, her massive hair bow flapping as if she was attempting personal liftoff. "You're here!" she cried happily. "Do you see what I did?"

"Is my aunt Darlington safe?" Cecilia asked at once.

Constantinopla waved a hand at the question. "Of course! Master Luxe, do you see I brought the Queen to your rescue?"

Ned nodded with mild amusement. "I do see, Miss Brown. I also recall telling you to stay in Ottery St. Mary."

She flushed, but her smile did not falter. "Oh, that was Tom's fault. He practically dragged me to Windsor."

"Where is my aunt?" Cecilia asked.

"Somewhere," Constantinopla replied, not taking her shining gaze from Ned's face. "In the castle or somewhere. A doctor is attending her. Look at the dress the Queen gave me!"

"A doctor?" Cecilia almost shouted, and Ned squeezed her hand in comfort.

"It's nothing, just a scratch," Constantinopla assured her blithely. "You should have seen the other fellow! Master Luxe, the Queen herself let me help fly her castle! I finally have my wings!"

"Is that so?" Ned murmured. He glanced over her shoulder and grinned. "Hello there," he said.

"Incorrigible lout," came the reply.

Constantinopla spun about and nearly tripped over herself, curtsying. "Your—Your Majesty," she stammered.

"Yes, yes," the Queen said at the end of a weary sigh. "Young lady, would you run and fetch me a parasol while I have a word with Major Candent here."

Constantinopla was intelligent enough not to glance at the large Chinese paper parasol the Queen was carrying. She bobbed another curtsy and fled. Queen Victoria gave Ned a blank look that twitched at its edges and sparkled in its eyes. His grin deepened. Out of the corner of his eye he saw Cecilia staring at him incredulously.

"I never knew a girl more determined to remind me of my majesty," Queen Victoria said. "The constant curtsying made me quite dizzy." She looked then at Cecilia. "You, however, are not curtsying at all."

"Ma'am," Cecilia said, and held out her hand. Queen Victoria stared at it as if it was a bishop's wig.

"Your Majesty," Ned said smoothly, taking a step forward. "May I introduce Miss Cecilia Bassingthwaite, niece of Miss Jemima Darlington, who is a pirate of some ill repute. Cecilia recently resided in Mayfair and has a particular interest in literature. Miss Bassingthwaite, Her Majesty Queen Victoria, Queen of England and Empress of India."

"Pleased to make your acquaintance," Cecilia said.

"I see you are one of those *educated* girls who believe they are equal to everyone else," the Queen commented archly. "I cannot abide the subject of women's rights. It is alike in folly to the notion of marriage. The only woman with personal agency should be me, and the only man worth marrying was my dear Albert." However, she reached out reluctantly and touched her fingers to the back of Cecilia's hand in the manner of bestowing a blessing.

Cecilia turned her own hand, grasped the Queen's firmly, and shook it. The Queen's eyes, nostrils, in fact entire face, widened. Ned bit his lips to prevent himself from laughing.

Victoria snatched back her hand. "Major," she said, turning to scowl at Ned. "Where is this Morvath creature about whom everyone has been pestering me?"

"Dead, Your Majesty," Ned reported. "He attempted to escape in a garden shed but it crashed."

"You are certain?"

"There was a rather persuasive explosion, ma'am. The world and its publishing industry are safe at last from Captain Morvath's machinations."

"Excellent. Come and drink tea with me, you pretty young rapscallion, and tell me all the details. Did you gut anyone with your sword? Were you forced to seduce any women to gather information?" She held out her arm and Ned released Cecilia's hand to take it instead. He brushed a fingertip against the Queen's bare skin and she huffed with amused disapproval. Leaning near to Cecilia, she said, "His fashion sense is intolerable, but I do declare there is a fine figure beneath it. What a shame men no longer wear tight breeches. I say, do you think he dresses to the left?"

"I'm afraid I don't know what you mean, ma'am," Cecilia murmured, but the look she gave Ned turned his face scarlet. The Queen chuckled.

"Excuse me," Cecilia said, "but I must find my aunt."

"Darlington?" Queen Victoria asked. "My physician is attending to her in the thirty-second guest bedroom. Have a footman show you the way."

"Thank you, ma'am," Cecilia said, and ran off without a backward look.

Ned sighed as he watched her go. "I am so glad you are back," Queen Victoria was saying. "I declare you shall never leave again."

"Your servant, ma'am," he said, and smiled down at her with all his pirate charm.

She laughed. "What a lie!"

"You're the first to ever doubt it, ma'am."

"And that," she said, marching him toward the picnic site, "is why some are merely pirates and I am Queen."

Cecilia was almost to the castle when Alex O'Riley stopped her. Stepping directly in her way, six foot tall and bristling with weapons, he gave her a look that was effective as a knife to her throat.

"May I help you?" she inquired.

"That was a long time you were gone," he said pointedly.

Cecilia straightened her back and presented him with a stare so Darlingtonesque, he paled and took a step back.

"We were experiencing technical difficulties," she said, daring him to argue.

"Is that what they're calling it these days?"

"I do not know, Captain O'Riley. But if you don't get out of my way, they will be calling it murder, plain and simple."

He laughed. "I like you, Miss Bassingthwaite."

"And yet here you are, still standing in my way."

He hurried back, bowing to her, and she strode off without another glance. *Men!* she thought irritably as she went. Their hysterical nature was a trial to any rational creature.

A footman met her at the castle door, and after another cold stare and a few choice words from her, he humbly begged to escort her to the thirty-second bedroom. But they never made it that far. Halfway up the wide marble staircase of the castle's main hall, they found Miss Darlington coming down. At first Cecilia thought it was a ghost, for her aunt was dressed in a voluminous, blood-spattered white night-gown, her hair floating about her shockingly pallid face, her eyes wide and staring as she descended at a precipitous rate; furthermore, Pleas-ance chased her, crying, "Don't go! Don't go!" in the same tone she'd used when the Darlington House parlor ghost had taken a new, more distressing job with Baroness Reve.

But Miss Darlington exuded vitality as she budged past Cecilia. "Don't just stand there, girl!" she said in a decidedly unspectral voice (although it did send chills down Cecilia's spine). "We must leave at once!"

The fear and tension eased from Cecilia's body in a long breath. She had a wild, uncouth inclination to hug her aunt, but then tension abruptly returned. Would Miss Darlington guess what she had been up to beyond the woods?

Apparently not. Her aunt stormed down the stairs without a back-ward glance. Cecilia hurried to follow. The footman who had been ac-companying her kept pace with a crisp, professional stride, being well used to the dramatics of elderly ladies.

"What is wrong, Aunty?" Cecilia asked as they went.

"I have been assaulted!" Miss Darlington declared. She flung an arm out in emphasis and the footman only just caught the antique vase she knocked over. "I will not remain in this den of iniquity a moment longer!"

Cecilia glanced questioningly at Pleasance.

"There was a doctor," Pleasance explained.

"Oh dear."

"After he tended to her wounds he wanted to inject her with morphine for the pain, and she called him a pervert."

"Degenerate!" Miss Darlington specified. She swooped onto the polished floor of the grand entrance hall, then abruptly stopped, causing the others to collide in a jumbled halt. She glared at a set of knight's armor.

"It's not a real person, Aunty," Cecilia assured her.

"*Tsk*," Miss Darlington replied. With one firm tug, she yanked the knight's lance from his grip, then cracked it across her knee. The footman moaned. Miss Darlington tossed aside half the broken lance and proceeded to use the other half as a cane to support herself as she strode along the strip of red carpet that ran down the length of the hall.

"Oh, my poor bones," she moaned unconvincingly.

The footman opened his mouth to protest this treatment of Her Majesty's antiquities, but Cecilia caught his gaze and he wisely silenced himself. They hurried to keep up.

"What happened with the doctor?" Cecilia whispered to Pleasance.

"He told her not to be a silly old woman and to take the morphine," Pleasance whispered in reply.

"So he had a death wish, then?"

"Apparently. The blood on her nightgown belongs to him."

"If he is dead it's his own fault," Miss Darlington said, proving herself to have the hearing ability of bats and elderly aunts everywhere. "I merely used his own injector on him."

"In his—er—" Pleasance lowered her gaze, waggling her eyebrows eloquently.

"Oh dear," Cecilia murmured again.

"Yes, well," Miss Darlington said, "if you are going to threaten to stab me with a metaphorically phallic instrument, prepare to be stabbed yourself in your actual—"

The castle doors slammed open. Everyone staggered to a halt as a bulky, gray-haired figure loomed in the exposed sunlight.

"You again?" Miss Darlington huffed with exasperation.

"Jehovahsen!" Cecilia gasped.

He strode toward them. His face was smoke-stained, his arm bandaged from shoulder to elbow. Cecilia pushed the footman protectively behind her. Pleasance gnashed her teeth. And Miss Darlington swung her cane around so its jagged end was pointed at Jacobsen.

"I have had a tiring morning," she said, "and would be obliged if you stopped right there, my good fellow. Any misbehavior shall compel me to disembowel you, and I really just want to go home for a cup of tea."

"Please don't fight in the entrance hall," the footman begged with the tone hand-wringing would have were it a voice. "We'll never get the blood out of the carpet."

Everyone looked down at the carpet on which they stood.

"It's red," Cecilia said. "Exactly blood colored, in fact."

"There's a stain here," Pleasance added, shuffling her shoe against it.

"I can kill him without drawing blood," Miss Darlington offered.

"Kill me and you will hang," Jacobsen said. "I am a captain with Her Majesty's secret service, but—"

"What, another one?" Cecilia shook her head. "It seems that lately a lady cannot go a day about her peaceful felonious business without being harassed by secret service agents."

Jacobsen stared openmouthed at her for a moment, then shook his wits back into order. "I am Sergeant Jacobsen, employed by Colonel Williams to spy on Major Candent, who has been spying on Captain

Morvath," he said, then paused while they worked this through. "When I learned you were caught up in this matter, Miss Darlington, I tried to contact your niece so she could furnish me with your whereabouts, for you owe me—"

"Oh, for heaven's sake." Miss Darlington swung her makeshift cane, smashing the sergeant on his bandaged arm and making him scream. Then she flipped the cane, thrust its blunt end into his stomach, and whacked him over the head. He collapsed, landing with a sickening crunch on his much-abused arm. With one groan, he was lost to consciousness.

"This is what happens to debt collectors who are rude enough to call without an appointment," Miss Darlington said. A splinter of pain pierced her dignified expression, but she straightened her shoulders, brushed back her wispy aureole of hair, and marched toward the open door, cane swinging like a baton from her hand. "No blood, I'll have you note."

"Er, thank you," the footman said tremulously.

"Cecilia! Hasten your pace! I am inclined to faint and wish to do so on my own premises before Anne Brown or that Rotunder woman sees me."

It was too late. At that very moment Gertrude Rotunder came bustling toward them as if made manifest by the speaking of her name. A maidservant rushed behind trying to keep a parasol above the lady's head while also carrying a shawl, spare gloves, reticule, and rifle.

"Jem, found you at last!" Mrs. Rotunder exclaimed. "Is it true your son is dead, blown to bits by your granddaughter?"

Cecilia and Pleasance cringed, but Miss Darlington showed only an expression of mild, polite interest. "I have not been informed of such developments," she said. "Cecilia dear, is Mrs. Rotunder correct?"

"No," Cecilia replied. "That is, I am sorry to tell you he is dead,

Aunty, but it was not my doing. He accidentally flew into a hillside. I assure you his end would have been immediate and therefore painless."

"I see."

A pregnant pause ensued, through which Mrs. Rotunder watched hopefully for any sign of emotional collapse, and Cecilia and Pleasance watched anxiously for the same. But Miss Darlington merely sniffed. "Pleasance dear, run ahead and put on the kettle. And light the oven, if you would be so kind. I do not recall what day this is, but I think venison for lunch would suit me. Cecilia, you look pale. Allow me to support you for the walk home."

Cecilia promptly stepped forward and held out her arm. Miss Darlington managed to lean on it without her spine losing any of its imperious rigidity.

They edged around Mrs. Rotunder and followed Pleasance toward the house.

"The hostages have been rescued," Mrs. Rotunder said, persisting behind them. "Olivia is planning a celebratory party for this evening."

"We shall not attend," Miss Darlington replied. "Cecilia's health could not withstand such excitement. Kindly convey our apologies to Olivia." (In modern parlance: "Fuck off.")

Mrs. Rotunder huffed so vehemently, the satin flowers on her hat quivered. Cecilia supposed a new assassin would present himself at their door in the days ahead. She tried not to smile. But Miss Darlington, catching her gaze sidelong, winked, and she found her mouth twitching despite herself.

"Good day, Mrs. Rotunder," Miss Darlington said explicitly, and the former spun on a sharp boot heel and stalked away.

Miss Darlington scrutinized the chaos around them with a narrow, disapproving eye. Pirate ladies and soldier men were bustling about with the good cheer (or sheer relief) that arises from a victorious battle. Morvath's henchmen huddled together under guard—for which they appeared grateful, as several of the Wisteria Society were advocating their dismemberment, and only the stoic professionalism of the Queen's soldiers kept them safe. Miss Darlington shook her head.

"Disgraceful behavior for ladies," she opined, "shouting like that for the torture of captives. In my day we would have knocked those soldiers down and had the captives whipped without squawking about it first."

"I do believe it is still your day, Aunty," Cecilia assured her.

"Ah, but these bones do ache, my dear," Miss Darlington admitted in a whisper. "And that doctor stitched me up as if I was a roast ham. How can a wound breathe fresh clean air if it is sewn shut? Should I die overnight, the house is yours, as are the emeralds I have hidden beneath my bed. Make sure Pleasance doesn't read too many horror tales."

Cecilia swallowed a rush of sentimentality. "You'll be fine, Aunty. Death wouldn't dare approach you without your advance permission."

Miss Darlington snorted, but in fact she had been angling the conversation toward a different point. "So he really is gone?"

"I'm afraid so," Cecilia murmured.

"Ah. At least now, after all these long years, I may grieve his loss fully. Although it will be difficult to do so without a lock of his hair or a photograph of him sitting dead in a chair, holding a book and with a pipe between his lifeless lips. The scar he has given me will have to suffice. Here we are at home, thank goodness. Why is there water and blood on my foyer floor? I can verily see the germs swimming in it! Egads, we shall all perish from diphtheria. Now, close the door, Cecilia—let us have some peace."

※ 22 ※

TRANQUILITY—A ROUSING GAME OF FOOTBALL—
THE QUEEN OF BOHEMIA'S SMELLING SALTS—A SHINING WIGWAM—
INVASIONS—THE MISSES FAIRWEATHER RECEIVE JUSTICE
APPROPRIATE FOR THEIR CRIMES—A VISITATION—KINDRED SPIRITS

It is not the strongest of the species that survive, nor the most intelligent, but the one most equipped with helpful servants and unmarried nieces willing to do their bidding. Miss Darlington was within the half hour in a fine state of well-being, despite her several wounds and the inconvenience of age in her aforementioned bones.

One might not be immediately cognizant of this, however, due to her moans and sighs. Cecilia and Pleasance were expert at translating that sublanguage—although they still fussed over the lady, out of training and love. Shawls were procured, a footstool moved into place, handkerchiefs fetched from a table comfortably within Miss Darlington's reach. All the ladies washed in warm perfumed water, then dressed in fresh clothes. Outside, the cacophony of voices went on, but within the Lilac Drawing Room of Darlington House, tranquility reigned.

"A splash of sherry in the tea," Miss Darlington whispered achingly to Pleasance. "Just to sweeten the pot."

Pleasance dripped sherry from Countess Brabinger's crystal decanter into Lady Askew's teapot. An explosion from Northangerland Abbey shook the house.

"That's not a splash; that's a speck," Miss Darlington said. "Add more, if you please."

Pleasance continued to pour until Miss Darlington deemed the amount splashish—about half a cup.

"Cecilia dear, will you read aloud to fill the silence?" Miss Darlington asked.

As gunfire scattered in celebration and soldiers began singing, Cecilia took up the volume of *Hiawatha*. Memory stirred in her heart. She saw again a wickedly endearing smile, a lock of hair falling over a bright eye, a brochure about auks. She remembered the feeling of his fingers sliding up her thigh and—

"That is an awful lot of throat clearing you are doing," Miss Darlington observed.

"Forgive me, Aunty. Don't worry, I'm quite well."

"You are on the brink of laryngitis! Pleasance, fetch Miss Bassingthwaite some lemonade."

"Yes, miss," Pleasance said. She began to cross the room but stumbled as the backwash from a rising house shook theirs.

"Someone is leaving?" Miss Darlington said with surprise. "Olivia will be displeased if she doesn't have even numbers for her party table."

Cecilia leaned aside to look out the window. "No, it appears some people are playing football," she said.

"And how would that create"—Miss Darlington paused as the house trembled again—"a backwash?"

"They are playing with houses."

Miss Darlington pursed her lips in disapproval of such youthful high spirits. "Football is not a suitable pursuit for ladies. But this is a sign of the times, alas. I fear as the new century looms we will lose the dignified feminine habit of gentleness."

"Perhaps," Cecilia replied. "Oh dear, you have dropped the Queen of Bohemia's bottle of smelling salts for which you kneecapped two guards and seduced another before pushing him out the window. Shall I pick it up for you?"

"No, don't bother. Useless thing. It is far too small for its purpose. Read to me, dear. Soothe my troubled mind."

Cecilia turned to *The Song of Hiawatha*. She had just found her place beneath the level moon when a fervent knocking came upon the front door.

Pleasance entered to inform them of a caller in much the same way a doctor informs a Romantic poet of their tuberculosis.

"Ignore it," Miss Darlington murmured from her cozy state.

"Ignore it?" Pleasance's mouth fell open. For her, an unanswered knock was equivalent to having to put down a book three pages before the ending. She threw Cecilia a pleading look.

"Ignore it," Cecilia reiterated, although with a sympathetic smile. " 'And before him on the upland, he could see the Shining Wigwam—' "

"Who? Where?" Pleasance peered around anxiously—as if, having been neglected at the door, Miss Wigwam had forced another entry.

"It is in the poem, dear," Cecilia explained. "Hiawatha sees the magician's tent."

There came again a knocking, only this time it was heels against the foyer floor, accompanied by a trilling voice. "Yoo-hoo! Jem! Anyone home?"

Miss Darlington sighed. "Anne Brown," she muttered.

And indeed Miss Brown entered the room, her propulsion so determined, and so assisted by her bellows-like skirts, that Pleasance had no option but to scurry before her or be trampled.

"The door was open," Miss Brown said. "I mean, it was shut and locked, but *in essence* it was open, if you understand me. I say, Jem!" She stared aghast at Miss Darlington. "You do look rather done in."

"It is but a scratch," Miss Darlington replied dismissively.

"It is several cuts and one stab wound," Cecilia corrected. "I'm afraid Aunty is not able to entertain visitors at this time."

Miss Brown gave her a cool, penetrating look. "My how you've grown since I last saw you, Cecilia."

"That was two hours ago, Miss Brown."

"Exactly. Amazing what flying off unchaperoned with a knave, defeating one's villainous father, and meeting the Queen can do for a girl's stature."

Cecilia held her breath. This was it! Finally! The moment of her promotion!

But then Anne Brown turned away. "Don't worry, Jem, I won't trouble you for long. I merely have a small matter upon which I seek your advice."

"It's fine," Miss Darlington said, frowning briefly at Cecilia, who had given a loud sigh. "What matter?"

Miss Brown looked over her shoulder. "Bring it in, girls!"

Several Wisteria Society ladies trooped into the sitting room, shoving the wretched figure of Miss Muriel Fairweather. She hunched within her torn, smoke-stained dress, making no effort to repel the ladies' hands. Contempt squatted in her eyes—but as Cecilia met that heavy, dark gaze, she realized the contempt was directed inwardly. Miss Fairweather was very sorry indeed for getting caught.

"There is a dispute as to what we should do with it," Miss Brown explained.

Miss Darlington endeavored to sit taller in her chair. Pleasance dashed forward with a cushion to place behind her back; Miss Darlington took said cushion and threw it at Miss Fairweather.

"Traitor!"

Miss Fairweather shrugged.

"Have you nothing to say for yourself? No excuse for betraying your fellow Wisterians?"

Miss Fairweather shrugged again. "It made me rich."

"I see." Miss Darlington's eyebrows angled together as if to discuss the matter between themselves. She glared at Miss Fairweather for a moment, then her expression eased. "Makes sense."

"What?" Miss Fairweather blinked with bewilderment.

"I would have done the same myself," Miss Darlington said. "You, Anne?"

"Probably," Miss Brown agreed.

The Wisteria Society ladies looked at one another and nodded. A few of them patted Miss Fairweather on the back in congratulatory fashion. "How rich?" Millie the Monster asked.

"Several thousand pounds and a rather nice diamond," Miss Fairweather said with a triumphant smile.

"Ten percent into the kitty," Miss Darlington decreed. "That should buy tea and biscuits for the next few reunions. And let that be a lesson to you!"

"Don't betray your friends?" Olivia Etterly suggested.

"Don't be there when it all comes crashing down?" Bloodhound Bess contributed.

Miss Darlington shook her head. "Don't ever trust a man who flies a ridiculously large building. He's obviously compensating. Now everyone get out."

The ladies bustled away, although Olivia paused to say she was sorry the Darlington household could not attend her modest victory soiree that evening.

"As you can see, Cecilia is in no fit condition," Miss Darlington said, and sucked in a sharp breath through her teeth as the stitches beneath her breast pulled.

"But we will see you at the Jubilee Banquet?"

"You have an invitation?" Cecilia asked, trying to keep the surprise from her voice.

Olivia and Miss Darlington laughed. "Of course not," Olivia said, and left.

Quiet was restored to the house. Miss Darlington sagged back in her chair. "More tea," she requested, "and a bigger splash this time. A dollop. In fact, just put a splash of tea in the sherry."

Pleasance set about making a new drink. Cecilia returned to *Hiawatha*. " 'The Shining Wigwam,' " she read, " 'of the Manito of Wampam—' "

"Man-eater?" Pleasance squeaked, dropping a teaspoon.

"No, dear," Cecilia reassured her. "It means—er—"

She was saved from being exposed in a literary ignorance by another knocking on the door.

Miss Darlington sighed. "One would think there'd be more peace in the countryside. Pleasance, send them away."

"Yes, miss," Pleasance said, and exited the sitting room door—

Only to return immediately, running backward so as to prevent her demise by stampeding gentleman. Frederick entered the room with a full-bodied flourish, Jane Fairweather scurrying in his wake.

"Miss Darlington!" he effused. "Cecilia! And—er—unknown woman who is staring at me quite alarmingly. I bring you tidings from the fond heart of Bassingthwaite, i.e., yours truly, on such a propitious—"

"Who is this?" Miss Darlington demanded.

"It is I, O venerable aunt who—"

"Frederick Bassingthwaite, miss," Pleasance belatedly announced.

"Who?" Miss Darlington asked, taking up a pair of opera glasses to scrutinize him more closely (albeit blurrily, as the glasses were a recent acquisition from the Duchess of Argyll, who was shorter of sight than our lady).

"Your nephew Frederick," Cecilia explained.

Miss Darlington looked at her blankly.

"You were introduced to him this morning."

"Doesn't ring a bell."

"Your sister's grandson?"

"Aloysius darling?" She smiled with sudden sincere affection.

"No," Cecilia said patiently. "Aloysius was killed attempting to steal a gold chalice from St. Paul's Cathedral. Struck by lightning, I believe. This is the younger son."

"Oh." Miss Darlington put the opera glasses back on the table with a sharp little clink that made everyone in the room wince. "What do you want, lad?"

Frederick swallowed nervously. "I wish to invite you to the wedding." He glanced at Cecilia with a limp smile.

"No," Cecilia said before she could stop herself.

"Whyever not, dear?" Miss Darlington asked. "I like a good wedding. The pretty dresses. The flowers. The rich purses to nab."

"Frederick," Cecilia said gently. "I am sorry, but I can't marry you."

"Oh," he said, grimacing with embarrassment. "Oh dear me. I do beg your pardon, cousin, but I meant that I am marrying Miss Fairweather."

Cecilia's mouth fell ajar. She blinked from Frederick to Jane, whose demurely lowered face did not quite hide its smirk, and then back to Frederick again.

"But—but—"

"It is true, we only just met," Frederick said, "but I was struck immediately through the heart by her golden darts of starlike beauty.

There was no defense against it. 'Mightier far than strength of nerve or sinew, or the sway of magic potent over sun and star, is love—' "

"What is he saying?" Miss Darlington demanded, her face creased with bewilderment.

"He is quoting Wordsworth, Aunty," Cecilia explained.

Frederick heard the contempt in her voice and misunderstood. Striding forward, he grasped her hand. "My dearest pearl of a cousin, please do not be distressed!" he implored, enlarging his heavy, oil-colored eyes until they bulged. Cecilia noticed his mustache still bore a dab of butter, and she tried not to smile. "It is all utterly beyond my power! I have been kidnapped away from you by my own true queen of pirates, and if only—"

"Please, do not concern yourself," Cecilia murmured, releasing her hand from his with little effort, for he had a soft, dainty grip. "I am glad for you and Jane. In each other you have met with perfect justice. Er, I mean, perfect joy. Jane, I offer you all due felicitations."

Jane scowled from beneath her eyelashes. "Thank you, I shall take them in the same spirit they were offered," she answered, "and wish you all the tranquil blessings of your maiden days, dear Cecilia. You must come to stay at Starkthorn Castle once I have settled in as its mistress."

"Jolly idea!" Frederick enthused.

"I will have—how many is it, Frederick, thirty bedrooms?—at my disposal to offer you. Of course, as a wife, it will be my special pleasure to provide comfort and hospitality to all my single visitors."

Cecilia found herself too tired to think of a cutting reply. Miss Darlington came to her rescue.

"Frederick is a lucky man to have you to wife, Jane dear. Your talent for making the best of a bad situation continually proves itself. Considering the Bassingthwaite estate is nearly bankrupt, they will benefit greatly from your shrewdness."

"Bankrupt?" Jane repeated sharply.

"Was that before or after Captain Morvath stripped the castle of all its munitions, Aunty?" Cecilia asked.

Jane gasped. That Frederick did not perish immediately from the daggers she threw at him was not because they were only metaphorical, but because he was smiling idiotically into the middle distance and failed to notice.

"I am indeed a lucky man," he said. "My heart has been endowed with the best fortune, its coffers overflowing with Jane's charms—"

"But not your actual coffers," Jane muttered thunderously.

"So it was a matter of love at first sight?" Miss Darlington surmised. "How romantic. I am always suspicious of love earned by familiarity—it shows a lack of imagination. Of course, a quick inspection of financial records can only prove true love's value. But who am I to comment? Only an old maid who knows nothing of the joys of being dominated by a man, living self-reliant as I do in my own small home." She sighed, glancing around at the treasures cluttering her sitting room. "Now, go away, you two. My head is beginning to pound."

Frederick and Jane withdrew, and Cecilia could hear Jane hissing at Frederick all through the foyer. The door slammed behind them. She added a drop of medicinal strychnine to Miss Darlington's sherry tea in aid of her headache, and as she replaced the cap on the medicine bottle, her hand trembled slightly.

Miss Darlington immediately noticed. "Cecilia," she snapped. "You are becoming quite hysterical. I believe when we return to London we shall have to employ a doctor for you. A brisk pelvic massage will be the very thing to restore your nerves to tranquility."

"Thank you, Aunty," Cecilia said. "I am but a little tired." As the house shook again and someone hollered "Score!" she retreated into poetry.

" 'The mightiest of Magicians—' "

A knock sounded on the front door.

Miss Darlington ejected a forceful sigh. Cecilia shut the book with an audible clap.

"We are not home," Miss Darlington told Pleasance.

"Yes, miss," the maid said, and hurried to convey this message to the caller. A moment later she returned, pale-faced and tremulous.

"It—it—it—your—"

"Tsk," Miss Darlington said.

"Tsk," a new voice said.

The ladies turned to see Queen Victoria bustle into the room.

Pleasance, who had survived ghostly encounters, pirate ladies, and enough internal demons to populate a circle of hell, threw her apron over her head and hid behind a chair.

Cecilia looked past the Queen to Ned loitering behind. As their eyes met, she felt a rush of love and longing, and it was all she could do to not leap up and run to his side. He smiled at her and then looked away, his expression becoming opaque.

"We are minded to meet the lady of whom everyone speaks so warmly," Queen Victoria intoned as if there was a crowd of parliamentarians before her, not two exhausted pirates and a chair concealing a housemaid.

"Warmly, hey?" Miss Darlington was unimpressed. "I can't say I wouldn't prefer anxiously, or respectfully, or with a fearful glance over their shoulder."

"That certainly is more satisfying," the Queen agreed.

"Have a seat, if you please," Miss Darlington invited.

Cecilia rose to offer hers to the Queen. Victoria sat, the vast billows of her dress overflowing the chair. Her dolorous visage did not alter as she contemplated the elegantly crammed sitting room—until all at once her eyes widened, flaring with excitement. "I say, is that Spanish sherry?"

Cecilia poured her a glass. While she was doing so, Queen Victoria and Miss Darlington shared a cool, professional stare.

"We have heard your son stabbed you," the Queen remarked.

"We have heard your son gambles and squanders his days and keeps mistresses," Miss Darlington replied.

The sherry glass shook as Cecilia handed it to the Queen.

Victoria gave Cecilia a penetrating look and then shrugged and smiled ruefully, as if having won a silent argument with herself. "Major Candent left an item of some personal value in your cockpit," she said. "I presume he has your permission to retrieve it?"

"Of course," Miss Darlington agreed. "Major Candent, hey?"

Ned bowed.

She regarded him keenly for a moment and then sighed, as if having lost her own inner argument. "He may not go alone," she stipulated. "After the day I've had, I do not wish to be burgled as well."

"I wouldn't burgle you," Ned said, but everyone ignored him.

"Pleasance," Cecilia said, "please accompany the gentleman upstairs."

The chair concealing Pleasance trembled.

Miss Darlington and the Queen exchanged a loaded glance. "You need not fear stairs, girl," the Queen said. "Why, I have been walking them unassisted for several years now, and never tripped yet. I'm sure you will be entirely safe and not tumble to an unsightly demise."

"Neck broken," Miss Darlington said.

"Brains dashed out," Queen Victoria added.

The chair shuddered.

"You need not fear the gentleman either," Miss Darlington said. "He has proven himself an utter failure as an assassin. I'm sure he won't harm you in any way."

"Throat cut," Queen Victoria said.

"Heart impaled," Miss Darlington added.

The chair rocked violently on its feet.

"I'll go," Cecilia said.

"Only if you insist," her aunt murmured.

"Most kind of you," the Queen added.

Cecilia frowned, suspecting foul play, but Miss Darlington and Queen Victoria merely smiled in unison and sipped sherry.

❊ 23 ❊

GREAT BALLS OF FIRE—ITALIAN KISSING—EXPLOSIONS (SENSUAL)—
A SHOCKING SIGHT—CECILIA IS NOT UNWELL—DEPARTURES—
ALLERGIES—A BECHDEL TEST CONVERSATION—
ALAS, BACK TO MEN AGAIN

False requests to locate lost property are highly injurious to the progress of science, and Cecilia was determined to take a scientific approach to her association with Ned Lightbourne. She knew perfectly well he had not left anything in the cockpit, and she intended to chastise him as soon as they were beyond earshot of Miss Darlington, Queen Victoria, the royal bodyguard standing alert in the foyer, the ladies-in-waiting leaning tiredly against the balustrade, and the downstairs ghosts.

But the moment he opened a random door along the upstairs hallway and pulled her through it, science went the way of the dinosaurs. Which is to say, obliterated by sudden overwhelming fire. All that remained were a few birds fluttering madly in her stomach. Ned shut the door, pushed her back against it, and was kissing her before she could utter a single word of stern advice.

Cecilia knew she ought to resist, but every good sense in her had melted into a pool of heat. She put her arms around him, grasped his coat, and as his tongue stroked into her mouth she heard bells.

Church bells.

She gasped and shoved him away.

He blinked at her dazedly. "What's wrong?"

Her own eyes were dazed too, in addition to her limbs, heart, brain. "The bells are ringing and I cannot marry you regardless of what convention may demand following our wanton behavior, for although I may be inclined to follow that course upon the merest further persuasion, I am also bound to the loving service of my dear aunt, who needs me for her comfort and—"

"Cecilia." He laid a finger against her lips. "It's only the clock chiming."

She looked over his shoulder at the clock on the wall, its pendulum knocking methodically against the hour. "Oh my God," she blasphemed, and pushed Ned even farther away. He stumbled slightly, and his brow lined with bewilderment.

"What is the matter?"

"This room," she breathed.

He glanced about at the brown wallpaper, the bed plumped high with quilts, the dressing table and washbasin. "It's a bedroom," he said.

"It's Aunt Darlington's bedroom," Cecilia elucidated. "You kissed me in Aunt Darlington's bedroom." A shudder went through her whole body.

Ned smiled wickedly. "And I'm going to do it again."

"No." She tried to back up but the door behind her was unrelenting in its material properties. *Damn science*, she thought. At least the Brontës would have had the door swing open or a madwoman burn the house down.

"No?" he asked, stepping toward her.

"Absolutely not," she declared. The heated look he was giving her did not bode well for calm, reasonable discourse.

"All right," he conceded, stepping back again, and she grabbed his coat lapels, pulled him to her, and kissed him until he tipped forward, pressing his hands against the door. Then, ducking beneath his arm, she slipped away, leaving him staring with frustration at the decal of a cherub Miss Darlington had pasted to the door. With luck, his internal calm was now restored and they could have a measured conversation.

Her own internal calm had disappeared somewhere she could not find it, but that was of no account—she was a woman, and therefore stronger willed.

Although perhaps not stronger boned. It felt like the only thing keeping her upright was that aforementioned will. My goodness, and Aunt Darlington had kissed *two* men?

(Cecilia was disinclined to think of Aunt Darlington doing anything more than *kissing* men, despite the evidence otherwise. Even that was disturbing enough. It was akin to recollecting where milk came from. Cecilia glanced at the bed, and her internal calm leaped onto a boat and sailed for the West Indies.)

"Cecilia—" Ned began, his hand in his hair, his voice heavy.

"No." She shook her head, trying to convince herself. "No. If I married you, Aunt Darlington would dwell in a constant state of terror that I'd contract lunacy or some other marital disease."

"She could come and live with us. Or I could live here."

Cecilia gave him a wry, sad smile. "She'd eat you alive. Besides, *any day now* the Wisteria Society are going to make me a senior member. I'll be presented with a black flag and given permission to fly my own house—"

"Given permission?" Ned repeated dryly. "Um, aren't you a pirate? An unscrupulous lawbreaker?"

"Yes. And?"

He laughed. "You really don't see the irony?"

"All I see is that I'll at last be fully accepted by my family—er, my Society. But if I take up with a handsome and mysterious man, they will never trust me enough. It's not you. It's not even me. It's my mother running away with my father and betraying the Society, and then him killing her, and no one ever quite recovering from that . . . It's my inheritance."

"I'm not planning to kill you, Cecilia."

"I know. But I'm sorry, I can't risk doing anything like her, not now, after waiting and working so long for this." And yet, oh, she did secretly wish—

For tea. That is what she wished for. Tea. And a nice biscuit.

And maybe a cold bath.

She sighed. Ned sighed. He leaned back against the door. His breath was heavy and his eyes dark behind the fall of his hair. Glimmering dark. Hot dark.

Oh dear.

Cecilia swallowed dryly and smoothed her skirts. "The only conclusion one can make," she said in a cool voice, "is that we must pretend none of this ever happened."

"Falsify evidence?" he said, giving her a wry, half-wild smile. "Rewrite the story?"

Excellent, he understood both possible sides of her heritage. That was going to make this easier. "Yes."

He laughed, and she realized he understood nothing at all.

Or perhaps just didn't care. It was clear from his expression that the only reason he was not kissing her again was because he feared what she might do to him if he tried. And yet—violence was not his worry, she realized with a strange clenching sensation. It seemed to her he feared rather how she would soften him, disarm him, hurt him in ways deeper than any knife might. She remembered how he'd looked only two hours before—the vulnerability in his eyes as he lay down with her. But now he grinned, a swaggering gesture, and he blithely brushed back his hair. She watched unbreathing as it fell strand by strand again.

"Cecilia, you're a pirate," he said. "Your entire job description involves naughty behavior."

"For a man, maybe," she replied. "But we ladies must adhere to social codes."

"Even while robbing and cheating?"

"Especially while robbing and cheating."

"I see." He tipped his head, regarded her quietly. "You are a conundrum."

"And you are endangering my reputation."

"I suspect it's already extinct, madam."

"Well, I—"

"—never. Of course."

They stared at each other. To continue the paleo-archeological simile, it was like the Yellowstone Caldera eruption, only with embroidered clothing. Eventually, Ned sighed. "I can't just walk away from you, Cecilia."

"And I can't walk away with you. Besides, you are an agent of the Crown. I am a pirate. Sooner or later, you'd have to arrest me."

"I'm not really an agent of the Crown, you know," he confessed. "I merely stole Queen Victoria's trust. (And certain other small items of value, not worth mentioning at this moment.) I've been a pirate since the day my mother died and yours rescued me."

"A pirate without a premises," she teased.

"A premises is easy to steal. Your heart, it seems, is harder."

Cecilia frowned. Had she not been obvious enough? "You don't have to steal my heart." Her voice broke, and she had to swallow heavily before she could speak again. Even then, it was only a whisper. "I would give it to you freely if I could."

"Oh." He closed his eyes, laid a hand against his breast, savoring the words. " 'Thus much I at least may recall, it hath taught me that what I most cherish'd deserved to be dearest of all.' "

"Byron," she said with some surprise. "Now, that's a poet for pirates. And spoken correctly, too. I fear I get to know you even as I must farewell you."

He opened one eye to look at her, half a smile beneath it. "And no argument at this time will persuade you otherwise?"

Her heart rose with a desperate reply, but she repressed it as surely as Aunt Darlington might have done. "None, sir."

"Then may I at least kiss you *alla prossima?*"

"You want to kiss me outside?"

He laughed. "No, it's an Italian way of saying something like goodbye."

"So you are Signor de Luca."

"No," he said softly. "Just Ned. Just me."

She shrugged one shoulder, pressing her face against it. "Very well. A farewell kiss."

Ned smiled. It was not a wicked pirate grin, nor a seductive tilt of the lips. It was gentle, sad, and it melted right through Cecilia until she almost said no—*no, don't kiss me, don't farewell me, stay forever by my side.* But ponderous, polite silence filled her throat, and she could only watch as he stepped toward her again and took her hand.

He tipped it over, and bent his head, and very gently kissed her wrist.

Dinosaurs, mountains, worlds, disappeared as the sun exploded into darkness.

Cecilia felt ashen as they returned downstairs. She was almost to the foyer before she realized she could hear swords clashing in the sitting room. The royal staff were crowded around the doorway, craning their necks anxiously to see what was happening within. Cecilia and Ned pushed their way through.

And then stopped, staring in astonishment.

Miss Darlington stood, wrapped in a silk shawl, with one hand pressed against her wounded ribs while the other held a sword pointed at Queen Victoria.

"Oh dear," Cecilia murmured.

And the Queen stood with hips swiveled, one hand in the air like that of an opera singer, the other holding a sword pointed at Miss Darlington.

"Oh dear," Ned sighed.

"You need to move your left foot forward a little more," Miss Darlington was saying, "and lower your right hand."

"Like this?" the Queen asked, shuffling about to no effect whatsoever.

"Exactly," Miss Darlington replied.

"Pardon me, ladies," Ned interrupted sternly. "I do not think this entirely proper. Your Majesty, she is a pirate."

"Nonsense," the Queen scoffed. "A cat may look at a queen."

"And a queen may look at a pirate maven," Miss Darlington added.

"Yes, but they shouldn't raise swords to each other. Someone could get hurt."

"Oh, don't be such a fusspot," Victoria replied. She rolled her eyes, shook her head at Miss Darlington. "Men these days. Albert was the same. 'Don't ride in an open carriage for fear of assassins.' 'Don't have parties.' 'Don't hit me with the furniture.' They need to develop more spine."

"True," Miss Darlington agreed. "And yet."

Queen Victoria sighed longingly. "And yet. Ah, Major Candent." She lowered the sword, shaving off the edge of a side table as she did. "Did you find what you were missing?"

"Yes, ma'am," he said, "but it didn't belong to me after all."

The Queen stared at him confusedly. "But then—surely you simply demand it?"

"I do not have your kind of authority, ma'am."

"Then you steal it," Miss Darlington said.

"You told me not to burgle you, ma'am."

Miss Darlington huffed. Queen Victoria shook her head.

"Dear Miss Darlington, bring your niece to my Jubilee Banquet," the Queen said.

"Dear Queen Victoria, will it be well guarded?" Miss Darlington asked. "Cecilia has a poor constitution and I worry about her heart."

"I understand. My baby, Beatrice, also had fragile health. I protected her as long as I could, until that rogue Liko snatched her out from under me. Now I see her only three-quarters of the day, Miss Darlington. Three-quarters!"

"Tragic," Miss Darlington agreed.

"Nevertheless, we senior ladies cannot prevent young ones having their enjoyment. At least not forever apparently, despite all our resources and determination. Therefore you may have no fears for Cecilia's heart. Major Candent shall direct security at the banquet."

"Ah. Excellent. I can see you are a woman after my own mind."

"No, you are a woman after *my* own mind."

Cecilia watched her aunt's eyes narrow and she stepped forward promptly before an argument could explode. "Won't you sit again, dear Aunty?" she said, taking the sword and carefully lowering Miss Darlington into her chair.

Ned had also entered the fray. "I suggest we leave now, Your Majesty," he said, taking her sword and setting it aside. "The area is unsecured and I would like to see you safe again in Windsor."

The Queen scowled. "I suppose this means I shall have that curtsying girl at me again. She may be able to fly a building, but if she Your-Majestys me one more time I will be tempted to throw her in a dungeon."

"Don't worry," Ned said as he steered the Queen gently from the room. "I'll fly the castle back for you."

"You can fly a whole castle on your own?"

"Sure."

The Queen glanced over her shoulder at Miss Darlington. A conversation of eyebrows ensued. Cecilia liked it even less than the sword fighting and stepped between them on the excuse of pouring her aunt another cup of tea. When she looked up again from the teapot, the Queen, her staff, and Ned Lightbourne were gone.

Just like that.

And her heart, it seemed, had wandered off with them. Dullness lay heavy, clammy, in its place—but she had felt this kind of loss before, and she knew it would soon become tranquility. An endless winter-colored pool of tranquility. So she set a smile to her still-tingling lips and handed the tea to Miss Darlington.

"You look forlorn," her aunt said.

"I fear I may be sickening," she replied.

"Nonsense."

Cecilia blinked. "I—I—beg your pardon?"

"You are fit as a fiddle, my girl. We will have no malingering here! Now, take Pleasance and hie upstairs, if you please. I want us to be in the air before that castle. A Darlington follows behind no one."

Early afternoon sunlight emblazoned the world. The sky was all possibility—or all emptiness, depending on your perspective. As Pleasance murmured the incantation, Cecilia navigated Darlington House up into its serenity. Her eyes were watering from the light— "Or possibly allergies," she said when Pleasance looked at her dubiously. "The countryside is full of pollen, after all."

Golden pollen over laughing blue eyes—er, skies.

Once airborne, the two young women stood at the cockpit window, looking down on the Devonshire field wherein Northangerland Abbey had met its doom. A pirate flag fluttered smugly from the abbey ruins. Her Majesty's soldiers were being rounded up with military precision, although they tipped their hats and bowed at pirate ladies as they trudged back to the castle. Several houses continued to kick around a football, while children danced beneath with practice swords and toy wheels. Constantinopla Brown could be seen chasing them merrily, skirts hoisted to her knees, and Tom Eames chased her in turn.

"Indecorous," Cecilia said.

"Hooliganism," Pleasance agreed.

They sighed wistfully.

Cecilia leaned on the wheel as she gazed out at the long, pale sky. "Where would you go, Pleasance, if you could go anywhere? What would you do?"

"Why, serve you and Miss Darlington, miss," Pleasance answered promptly.

"Of course. And now your candid answer?"

Pleasance considered the horizon. "I'd like to tour abandoned castles. Kidnap a few authors. Attend a lecture series by a mad scientist. You know, get myself an education."

Cecilia's heart warmed at this vision. "What would you do with your education?"

"Improve whatever part of the world I could touch upon."

"Yes," Cecilia said dreamily.

"Maybe write some books myself, experiment a bit with lightning. But not to create monsters, you understand. I'd respect people. And maybe get some respect for me too."

"Respect. Yes. And equal rights."

"And a voice in government."

"And Lady Coffingham's emerald tiara."

"Ooh, that sounds pretty, miss."

"It is, and doesn't suit her in the least."

"So you'd be doing her a favor."

Cecilia smiled. Then frowned. "There is blood on your sleeve, dear."

Pleasance glanced at it. "The bandage must have soaked through. I'll replace it soon."

"Bandage? Pleasance, were you injured?"

Pleasance shrugged, then winced. "Only a scratch, miss. I can still serve you well."

"I'm not worried about you serving me. Go downstairs, please, and tend to your injury. I am fine here alone."

Pleasance gave Cecilia a look at least as deep as her stab wound, but Cecilia was staring at the horizon again.

"I thought he was a very handsome chap," Pleasance remarked.

"Tolerable, I suppose," Cecilia replied.

"He'll come back for you."

"I'm the one who left. Not that I—not that there was any leaving, in that sense, of course. Merely departure from an acquaintance. A temporary business associate. A—"

"Friend?"

Cecilia blinked. "Blasted allergies," she muttered, knuckling first one eye, then the other.

Pleasance handed her a handkerchief, then went downstairs to sew her own arm. Cecilia flew on alone toward the white magic of the eastern skyline, Windsor Castle following some distance behind.

❋ 24 ❋

TAKING THE LOW ROAD—BUCKINGHAM PALACE—
PRINCE ALBERT OGLES CECILIA—ACCIDENTAL ROBBERY—
THE KING OF BELGIUM'S BEARD—DR. LUMES—
THE OBLIGATORY ROMANTIC WALTZ—A PROPOSAL OF THEFT

A man who dares to waste one hour of time has not discovered the value of making a grand entrance. Miss Darlington and Cecilia approached Buckingham Palace at what seemed to be a leisurely pace, as befitted their general social superiority; in fact, it was timed to the minute so they were exactly the right degree of unpunctual.

Through the windows of their (i.e., Lord Bacomb's) carriage, they could see the city in a dreamlike blur of darkness and golden lamplight. Cecilia had gazed out at it for a while, entranced, but grew queasy from the motion and had to sit back. Miss Darlington never varied from her stiff posture. The carriage rocked around them, and they gripped the cushioned seats, unused to such an ungainly, primitive mode of transport.

"Seldom have I lowered myself in this fashion," Miss Darlington said. "I hope we are fed well for our sacrifices."

Cecilia regarded her aunt, resplendent in blue silk (and a black cloak, brown muff, gray scarf) with sapphires at her throat and ears, looking as magnificent as a queen—and surmised she would be happier at home by the fire, dressed in a flannel nightgown, drinking tea. Her wounds still irritated her, although she gave no complaint. And her thoughts were little better, judging from the serenity of her visage. Miss Darlington's serenity was her iron shield, forged over a lifetime of scoundrelry: not even the merest regret penetrated into the world. And yet, there were lines on her brow that had not been visible a week ago, and a shadow of weariness in her eyes. Cecilia knew her aunt was old, but for the first time began to perceive her as elderly. It was a painful realization.

"I am sure the Queen's menu will prove adequate," she said. "Although I doubt it will surpass Pleasance's chicken pie."

Miss Darlington chuckled at this tepid joke, but in fact Cecilia was serious. Despite the pearls, she, too, would have preferred flannel worn beside a cozy fire while she read her latest book (*On the Origin of Species*) in peace. The idea of mingling with kings and queens offered her no excitement. Miss Darlington had forbidden thievery for the evening, and Cecilia could not think of anything interesting about royalty other than their jewels. After all, they did little more than sit around in stationary houses, aggravating their ministers and marrying one another.

Besides, Major Candent would be present at the banquet, and presumably for the ballroom dancing afterward. Cecilia did not want to see Major Candent. She did not want to think about Major Candent. Or Ned Lightbourne. Or Teddy Luxe with his skintight breeches and pink dancing shoes, sliding her across the floor in a tango.

"Are you all right, dear?" Miss Darlington asked. "You gave the most remarkable shudder."

"Fine, thank you, Aunty," Cecilia replied.

"I fear it was a mistake to come out this evening. You will perish from dengue fever before the night is done."

"Not unless I am bitten by something," Cecilia said—and then had to fan herself rather urgently with her gloved hand.

"Hmm." Miss Darlington rummaged in her purse, then handed a lozenge to Cecilia. "Take this, my dear. It will offer some protection."

Cecilia eyed the lozenge warily. "What is it?"

"Merely a dose of cocaine. I keep it handy in case of toothache, neuralgia, or syphilis."

"Thank you." Cecilia pretended to swallow the pill. She then discreetly slipped it into her purse, alongside her handkerchief, powder box, and pearl-handled revolver. It was unlikely any medicine could cure what ailed her. Had a floral-scented envelope arrived at any point containing an invitation to tea with the Wisteria Society's senior members, she might be feeling better now. But having sacrificed love for the sake of her career, she still awaited promotion.

Perhaps it would happen tonight!

Or perhaps never.

"You have been out of sorts all this week," Miss Darlington observed. "And I never did get around to employing that doctor for you. Maybe what you need is a good assassination attempt to invigorate your blood."

Cecilia envisioned Signor de Luca creeping into her bedroom, blade unsheathed, and tried not to moan.

"I myself have been disturbingly untroubled by Lady Armitage," Miss Darlington mused. "Not a single poisoned apple or missile. I hope she is all right."

"Perhaps her house finally broke down," Cecilia suggested.

"Hmm," Miss Darlington said again, and stared out the window as if wishing for a red-doored town house to suddenly swoop down, guns blazing in an effort to murder them.

Buckingham Palace glimmered like the jewelry box Cecilia stole from Lady Diana Hollister when she was eleven years old (and sold back to her for a profit when she was fifteen). The ladies were assisted down from their carriage and escorted into the magnificent Bow Room, where royalty, aristocracy, and several incognito pirates mingled in a display of wealth so ostentatious that Cecilia had to link her fingers together to keep them from business.

People turned to stare as they entered, and Miss Darlington strode through the parted throng as if she was the Queen herself. She had left her cane at home, and although Cecilia suspected her of maintaining a stable gait only through determination and the aid of several cocaine pills, she gave no indication of frailty.

Following behind, Cecilia absolutely did not glance about in search of Ned Lightbourne (nor did she see him). Murmurs rippled through the company—"scoundrels"; "dangerous ladies"; "those sapphire earrings look just like the ones I lost." Gentlemen bowed. But none of them had blond hair falling piratically over one eye, nor silver hooped in their ear, nor a bewildering effect on her pulse that might have caused Cecilia to stumble, had they done so.

She passed Olivia Etterly in discussion with the King of Denmark—

("Oh yes, it's an excellent opportunity, Your Majesty, I bought land there myself only last month, such divine views of the jungle, I'd be pleased to introduce you to my agent, who just so happens to be present this evening."

"What is their name?"

"Miss Fairweather, Your Majesty. A widow of integrity and excellent repute.")

—and glancing away with a smile, caught sight of Bloodhound Bess laughing heartily with Prince Wilhelm of Germany as she slipped a gold medallion from his breast.

She and Miss Darlington came before Queen Victoria, and Cecilia was astonished to see Miss Darlington curtsy to the Queen. She followed the example and as she rose found the Queen staring up at her.

"Ah yes, the conundrum," Victoria said. Cecilia smiled politely, but her wits turned inward, rummaging through old boxes, tossing memories hither and yon, trying to remember where they'd heard that word before. "We are pleased to see you here tonight," the Queen continued. "One must do what one can for the younger generation, don't you agree, Albert dear?"

She applied this question to a marble bust of Prince Albert that stood on a small, black-clothed table beside her chair. The bust had nothing to say, but it did stare at Cecilia with such intensity that she wished she was wearing a coat over her ball gown.

"Thank you, Your Majesty," Cecilia said.

"Not that we actually *want* to do anything," the Queen added, "but the mournful sighs got too much for us."

"I know what you mean," Miss Darlington said wryly.

Cecilia, who had no idea what she meant, watched the two ladies smirk at each other and began to worry. Perhaps she ought to have taken that cocaine pill after all: she suspected she would have a headache before this night was done.

The company dined in an opulent room surrounded by high, overwrought walls and the glare of so many candles Cecilia could barely see the food on her golden plate. She was seated between the King of Belgium and Princess Louise, and if the princess's bracelet happened to fall into a surreptitious pocket of Cecilia's skirt, that could be fairly described as an accidental collision between fingers and gold chain; and if the king later could not find his signet ring, well, anything might have happened to it—there must be a dozen innocent reasons why it ended up in Cecilia's purse.

Besides, *no thieving* was obviously more of a guideline than a rule, since there might be circumstances in which thieving was essential—for example, if King Leopold's life had been endangered by his signet ring (due to a spontaneous allergy to gold)—and everyone knew it was morally acceptable to ignore guidelines.

The mealtime was as tedious as Cecilia had expected. She spent the entire first course listening to the king boast about all the buildings he had commissioned to be raised (albeit not literally, Belgian people being too sensible for piracy), and he mistook the glazed look in Cecilia's eyes for shining interest. Alas, she somehow managed to knock over a candle and the king's beard caught fire, which at least broke the tedium for a few minutes; after this, she turned to her left and for the remainder of the meal discussed the weather with Princess Louise.

Afterward, they trooped into yet another grand room, where a band played and the company danced in a sparkling, dizzying swirl of color. Olivia Etterly stopped her along the way to ask in a whisper whether she had seen Lady Armitage that evening. "No," Cecilia whispered in reply. "Is she here?"

"That's the thing," Olivia said. "No one knows. No one has seen or heard of her all week. No assassination attempts, no newspaper warnings to the general public, no children running in terror along the street while her house chased them. It's as if she's disappeared."

Cecilia thought of the last time she had seen Lady Armitage—standing in the dark forest, laughing as she realized Cecilia intended to be captured by Morvath if possible.

Hearing that laugh, Cecilia had felt a moment's pride. Lady Armitage had considered her dangerous and had admired her for it, run away back to her house because of it. Not like the other Wisteria Society women, who had done everything they could over the years to repress her, keeping her on the sofa, ensuring she did not turn out like Patrick Morvath or, worse in a way, Cilla.

As they repressed her still.

A sudden strange love for the wily old Lady Armitage rushed through Cecilia's heart. She found herself giving Olivia a smile like a scimitar. The older woman took half a step back, and there it was—that caution darkening her eyes, seeing Cecilia's ghosts rather than the woman she was herself.

Oddly, it didn't hurt. She just felt the sharpness in her smile and her eyes. "Never mind," she said. "Knowing Lady Armitage, she's probably off somewhere getting married. I wouldn't worry, at least not about her, if I were you."

Olivia swallowed dryly. "You're right," she murmured, then ducked her head and hurried away so that Cecilia would stop smiling at her like that.

Cecilia found herself a quiet space at the edge of the room where she could scrutinize the crowd. Perhaps it was just her own sudden fierceness, or perhaps the mention of Lady Armitage, but she felt a sense of danger that had her nerves tightening and her wits coming to armed attention.

But apart from a spiked fern that gave her a moment's concern, swaying as someone knocked against it and reminding her of Aunty Army's perpendicular hair, nothing suggested a need for alarm. In fact, danger seemed impossible among such gentility. Princesses glimmered; princes laughed. Alex O'Riley, in an elegant dinner suit but unshaven, was sharing an intense conversation with Prince Wilhelm and the King of Belgium. Glancing up, he winked at her before the German prince tugged on his sleeve, demanding all his attention. Even Miss Darlington was trotting along in a two-step with Prince Edward as if she hadn't a week ago been knifed by her long-lost maniac son; the prince was struggling to keep up. Cecilia sighed.

"Why so sad?" came a voice in her ear.

Cecilia nearly (and unscientifically) spontaneously combusted. She glanced sidelong at Ned Lightbourne's wicked smile before hastily looking ahead once more. Any thoughts of Lady Armitage were immediately lost to this clear and present danger. Ned was not dressed as an officer of Her Majesty's forces, instead wearing impeccable white linen beneath a black tailcoat, his black trousers so tight it was dangerous to her blood flow, his hair brushed back in suave style. He looked like he was planning to steal the castle and every lady in it. Cecilia instinctively felt for the comfort of the knife tucked among her skirts.

"It seems you are just where you wished to be," he commented. "Standing alone at the sidelines, watching over your aunt so she does not feel lonely or mournful."

They observed Miss Darlington swirl past, batting her eyelashes at the English prince.

"Go away, Ned," Cecilia muttered.

"Ned? Who is this Ned of whom you speak? Madam, may I have the honor of introducing myself? Dr. Edward Lumes at your service. Just back in town from a sojourn in the countryside and available to—um, service you."

"Dr. Lumes," she echoed scathingly. "I suppose you are going to suggest giving me a complete physical inspection."

"Oh, I'm not that kind of doctor," he replied in a languid voice, and leaned even closer to whisper, "I'm a doctor of literature, madam."

She nearly swooned into his arms.

"Have you missed me?" he asked.

"Oh God yes," she answered before she could prevent herself, and then blushed violently as he grinned. She opened her fan with such vehemence that its concealed blades dropped to the floor with a clatter. She began to employ it with the vigor of one whose nostrils (or in this case, hormones) are ablaze, but to no discernible effect other than sending a breeze through Ned's hair. One strand slid over his forehead and Cecilia's internal heat grew so intense she gave up on the fan and reached for a glass of lemonade instead.

A long, unladylike gulp informed her too late that the cordial had been mixed with wine. She hastily set down the glass and, anticipating a dreadful headache, retrieved the cocaine pill from her purse. She swallowed it without further hesitation, sipping alcoholic lemonade by necessity to wash it down. Then she turned to favor Captain Lightbourne with a censorious glare.

He appeared to be standing next to the specters of Signor de Luca and Teddy Luxe, but when she blinked he resolved into one, slightly blurry, figure. "While I am pleased to make your acquaintance, Doctor," she said coolly, "I believe myself to be literate enough without any service you may provide. Thank you and have a good Easter. Er, evening. Where did I put my fan?" She opened her fan to fan herself while futilely searching purse, table, and floor for the fan.

"Dance with me," Ned whispered, stroking a gloved finger down the bare skin of her upper back.

She shrugged him away. "The music has stopped."

"It's going to start again. I've put in a special request with the band."

He took the fan from her and tossed it over his shoulder, where it fell into a grand display of roses. Then he held out a hand, and Cecilia's good manners (or inebriation) saw her taking it before she even knew what she was doing. Almost immediately she tried to relinquish her grip, but he had her now and would not let her go.

"Very well," she relented. "One dance. But this is most impertinent of you, Captain Lightbourne. We have said our farewells."

"You said farewell," he countered as he led her toward the dance area. Behind them, the roses exploded into a shower of smoke and petals, sending bystanders scattering with screams and horrified gasps. "I said *alla prossima*. That's Italian for 'until next time.'"

"Oh, if you are going to speak Italian at me, what hope do I have?"

He smiled and, tugging gently on her hand, turned her toward him. He caught her waist with his free hand, shifted his other hand so their gloved palms lay together. "No hope at all, Miss Bassingthwaite," he said cheerfully, and as music filled the room again he drew her even closer.

"A waltz!" she gasped. "It is too decadent."

"Maybe seventy years ago. And you are not so old as that, my dear," he added, looking appreciatively at her décolletage. He moved his left foot forward and Cecilia moved her right back in self-defense. Before she was conscious of it, they were gliding around the floor.

"You are a scoundrel," she whispered furiously.

"Yes," he agreed. "I'm thinking of starting a Society of Gentlemen Scoundrels."

"You're millennia too late. It already exists and is called the patriarchy."

He laughed. "Touché. Alas, I will never best you in conversation, will I?"

"No."

"Although I have rendered you wordless several times now, and that's even more satisfying."

She stared at him aghast.

"And I see I've done it again. Yes, very satisfying indeed." He grinned, and as he lifted their hands she spun away beneath his arm and returned. He slipped his hand around her waist again and she tried not to shiver. Summoning her wits, she demanded from them a suitably acerbic comment—

But her wits had dressed themselves in pink sparkling tulle and danced away with their eyes closed, their faces turned up to the starry chandeliers, blissfully ignoring her. Cecilia was left mute (and a little dizzy).

Ned was a magnificent dancer. Lithe and confident, he held her with a firmness that made her feel delicate in his arms. But she was not delicate, she reminded herself. She could kill him with one swift movement should she choose.

And yet—the intoxicating lemonade, or the intoxicating gorgeousness of the occasion, convinced her for once to let go, to let herself feel—to surrender in this dreaming moment to the handsome, seductive, and altogether dangerous man who led her in the dance. She closed her eyes and joined her wits in bliss, waltzing the night to freedom.

"While I have you quiet," Ned murmured, "I must make a confession."

"No, don't talk," she whispered. "You'll ruin everything."

He dipped her, and when she came up, her mind full of stars, he sighed. "I must, I'm afraid. Forgive me, Cecilia, but I've stolen Pleasance."

She opened her eyes, the dream wavering. "I beg your pardon?"

"I've stolen Pleasance," he repeated. "You know—young housemaid, deceased vampirical baroness, and a few subsidiary ghosts too, I suspect? I thought it would take some doing, but as it turned out all I needed was to mention I'm friends with Robert Louis Stevenson, and she fell immediately in with my scheme."

"What scheme?" Cecilia asked, and he lifted their hands. She spun a little too fast, her skirts whipping about, her wits staggering. "I am going to kill you," she warned upon her return.

"I hope you do it slowly," he said, grinning with such heat that all the words in her throat burned away and she could only gasp in outrage. "Will you use that knife you have tucked in your garter, warm against your thigh? Or will you use your bare hands?"

"I shall dismember you," she said pointedly, and he winced.

"You might find that hard," he replied.

"I'm sure it will only feel like a small prick."

"Temptress."

"Libertine."

They danced past Prince Wilhelm and the Queen of Hawaii, who were waltzing ponderously, and nodded a smiling acknowledgment to them.

"Rogue," Cecilia continued, hissing the word through her smile. "Profligate."

"Yes, yes, I know," Ned replied. "Knave, rakehell, et cetera. But back to the matter at hand. I stole Pleasance, and she stole a premises, and together we are going to steal you."

"What premises?"

"You'll see."

He waltzed her to the edge of the crowd, among fern shadows. His steps slowed, and his hand pushed her gently closer until she could feel his heartbeat through her bones. He was not smiling now. The charm, the pleasant easy cheer, had disappeared. Raw, vulnerable longing darkened his eyes.

"I love you, Cecilia Bassingthwaite," he said. "Please marry me. Please say yes."

"Oh." She stepped on his foot, but neither of them noticed. "I— but—my aunt—"

"And this is why I'm stealing you. Pleasance agrees. It's like you've caged yourself in duty and guilt. You won't let yourself go."

"I can't." She had left her mother, and her mother had died. Besides, Aunt Darlington was so old now, so fragile—

Crash!

All right, so Aunt Darlington had just knocked over a chair in her exuberance as she danced poor Prince Edward half to death, but that was beside the point.

"You don't have to leave her," Ned said. "You simply have to let me take you away instead."

She stared up into his beautiful, solemn eyes, and her wits held their breath—hands clutched to their fast-beating hearts, eyes wide, as they awaited instructions. But she did not need them for an answer. Opening her mouth, she said—

"Excuse me," came Captain Morvath's voice behind her. "May I cut in?"

And she felt a long, sharp knife at her throat.

❋ 25 ❋

NO ZOMBIES, I ASSURE YOU—THE SEEDS OF POETRY—
BAD TIMING MAKES AN ASS OF THE VILLAIN—
A NAME FROM THE PAST—
THE CONSEQUENCE OF NOT EDUCATING WOMEN—
A DIABOLICAL PLAN—THE WEIGHT OF THE CROWN—
CECILIA IMPERILS HER REPUTATION—THE CINDERELLA HOUR

In the struggle for survival, the fittest win out at the expense of their rivals because they keep a parachute in their escape garden shed and employ it in timely fashion to avoid colliding with their environment. Thus Patrick Morvath was able to circumvent extinction and, after a brief detour to a London tailor, arrive at the Jubilee Banquet in order to exact revenge upon Queen Victoria (and possibly read his latest poem aloud to the gathered royalty, since such a discerning audience would surely appreciate his genius, especially if he was standing over the dead body of the English queen as he orated).

But when he arrived in Buckingham Palace and saw Jemima Darlington among the crowd, his plan imploded in white-hot flames. He had stabbed her with all the grief and fury within him, and yet here she was—dancing! Laughing on the arms of some popinjay with a ridiculous mustache!! It was as if he hadn't impacted her at all!!!

A cry broke out of his soul but he swallowed it down, since howling with all the loneliness and shame of a small boy was not quite the done thing at a royal ball. He would write it out later, he told himself, as was his habit—blistering page after page with the poetry of his wounded psyche. Thus, in the way of all creative masters, he would draw great art from his tragedy . . .

Smother made an excellent rhyme with *mother*.

He began stalking toward Jemima Darlington (having to zigzag because she was dancing so fast) but halted when he caught sight of Cecilia with that treacherous Lightbourne. In the crystalline light, her hair was gold, and she looked more like Cilla than ever before. Morvath's heart clenched. Suddenly, a new plan cooled his mind. A way to kill two birds with one knife.

Jemima Darlington could watch Cecilia die before she died herself.

He smiled and licked his lips with anticipation.

Despite the crush in the ballroom, he thought he would have trouble catching his prey unawares, but in the end it proved absurdly easy. Cecilia and Lightbourne were so intent upon each other, they didn't even notice his approach.

"Excuse me," he said. "May I cut in?"

And he grabbed Cecilia, pressing his knife to her throat.

Morvath pulled Cecilia from Ned's hands before either of them could fully comprehend the situation. Stepping back, he knocked into a large potted fern, which rocked loudly against the floor; he shuffled aside, dragging Cecilia with him, and dancers screamed as they rushed away from the scandal. Ned drew his gun but could not shoot without endangering Cecilia, and Morvath laughed at him.

"Foolish boy!" he scoffed.

Ned frowned and cupped a hand to his ear. "What? The music is so loud. Say that again?"

Morvath snarled. "Foolish boy!" he shouted. "I am going to cut off your limbs, drag you to a pit of vipers, and throw you to the very bottom!"

The music ceased abruptly, and *bottom* resounded through the sudden silence. "Language," an anonymous woman hissed, and Morvath's face flamed.

"Shut up!" he screamed. "Shut the hell up! I have heard enough from women to last me for a lifetime! You will all be silent!"

"Who is this conceited fellow?" Prince Wilhelm demanded. "What does he think he's doing, invading our banquet and spoiling the peace in this belligerent fashion? What kind of man does that?"

"It's just Patrick Morvath," Bloodhound Bess called out. "An unpublished poet."

"I said shut up!" Morvath roared, and Cecilia winced from the force of it. "No artist is truly appreciated in his lifetime! And one more word from any female and I'll cut Cecilia's throat open in front of you all!"

"You wouldn't kill your own daughter," Ned said tersely. He held his gun with both hands, aiming it between Morvath's eyes. His own eyes were resolutely focused on the captain; he did not dare glance at Cecilia.

"How do I know she's my daughter?" Morvath retorted. "Cilla probably cuckolded me. God knows women are fickle, unfaithful beasts. Look at my own mother. Jemima Darlington!" he bellowed. "Step forward so you can be introduced as the trollop you are."

A gasp arose from the company.

"I say, good fellow," declared Prince Edward. "Even if she is your mother, you can't talk about her like that."

"What do you know about it?" Morvath spat.

"My mother is the Queen," Prince Edward replied inexpressively. He paused while people came to their own conclusions about his statement. "Apologize to the lady at once."

"Never! She is the one who should apologize to me! Her lewd, immoral behavior—"

"Silence!" roared a furious male voice. Everyone stared, mouths agape, as a large man in dusty clothes and with a bandaged arm shoved his way through the crowd to stand near Miss Darlington. He was white-faced but his eyes blazed with a dark fire of passion. Miss Darlington looked at him with astonishment, and he returned the gaze grimly, as if he had come to collect a debt from her and not even the hijacking of a royal banquet would prevent him from doing so. "Say another word about this fine lady and I will see you dead, sir!"

"Jaggersen?" Morvath said, incredulous.

"Jacobsen! Jacobsen!" The misnomered man stamped his foot in frustration. "Jake Jacobsen from Coventry, son of Joe Jacobsen, officer in Her Majesty's royal guard."

"Pleased to make your acquaintance," called a wit from the crowd.

"Oh, *Jake* Jacobsen," Miss Darlington said unexpectedly. "I remember you now."

He laid a hand to his heart. "I have never forgotten you, madam."

"The hair tricked my eye. It used to be red, didn't it?"

"Quite a while ago now," he said, bashfully running a hand through his gray locks.

"No!" Morvath screamed.

Miss Darlington shrugged. "What can I say? If society wanted me to keep track of my illicit lovers, they should have educated me better."

"But he's nobody!" Morvath raged. "Just some half-witted copper probably raised on a farm."

"Pig farm," Jacobsen agreed.

Morvath hauled Cecilia back two steps, pressing the knife so hard against her throat she could feel her pulse bash urgently against the blade. She tried to think of how she might break his grip, disarm him, but the wine and cocaine were swirling heavily through her body, weighing her down, making her feel as though she might at any moment take a nap in her father's arms. She stared at Ned, at his grim mouth that was usually smiling, his cold eyes that had warmed her so many times. She tried to impress the vision of him on her brain so that when Morvath killed her she could carry her own secret heaven beyond the grave. Somewhere out there stood Aunt Darlington, but Cecilia already had her tucked into her heart. It was Ned she wanted, here in these last moments—Ned like a mystery, a flare of magic, a horizon.

"You!" Morvath shouted abruptly, causing her thoughts to shatter. The King of Portugal tapped a finger to his own chest and mouthed, *Me?* in horror. "Yes, you. Find something to tie the hands and gag the mouths of the pirate women I can see in this crowd."

"Why?" Olivia asked, feet akimbo, hands on her hips. "What is your plan?"

"Yes, reveal it to us," Bloodhound Bess urged.

Morvath turned purple with rage. "I will not be mocked!" He hauled in a long, deep breath, trying to calm himself. As he exhaled, he began to intone the pirates' flying spell. The castle jolted; people screamed, grasping at one another as they stumbled; some fell to their knees.

"Don't be stupid," Ned warned. "You don't have the strength to fly a castle like this on your own, especially without a wheel."

"I don't need a wheel to merely lift it to a great height and then drop it," Morvath retorted.

"But then you'll die too."

"Ha! I'm not as stupid as you, Lightbourne. I always have a premises on hand. Cecilia and I are going to the roof, where a tool shed awaits my escape. Anyone tries to follow me and you'll have to clamber over her dead body."

"Well, that's a fairly reasonable plan," Miss Fairweather said to Bloodhound Bess, who nodded.

"Don't do it," Ned said.

"Shut up, you—you—mummy's boy!" Morvath sneered in reply.

Ned rolled his eyes. "I wasn't talking to you."

"What—?"

Morvath looked behind, but he was too late. With an inarticulate cry, he crumpled to the ground and was still.

Queen Victoria hoisted the emerald crown with which she had bashed the villain over the head. "I told you these things were heavy," she said, handing it to a lady-in-waiting.

A relieved exhalation went through the crowd. Alex O'Riley holstered the gun he'd been silently pointing toward Morvath. Several pirate ladies turned to shrug at one another and then look around for another drink. Ned hurried forward, taking Cecilia in his arms, but she struggled to break free.

"Sir," she whispered. "Not over my father's dead body."

"I don't think he's dead," Ned reassured her. "I can hear him moaning. That was always Morvath's problem—never knew when to shut up."

"But my reputation!"

He laughed. "Cecilia, your father tried to kill the royalty of several countries. I expect your reputation is entirely lost." He drew back, hands shifting to either side of her head, gun handle pressing against her ear. "My love," he said, and kissed her.

The assembled crowd cooed and whistled in most unregal fashion.

Cecilia tried to push him away but her wits captured her nerves and forced her to sag against his body. He held her close, and yet she felt as if she was flying to a wild horizon. Finally he let her go, and she stumbled back, confused by gravity.

"You'll have to marry him now," Queen Victoria said with a chuckle. Then she grimaced down at Morvath's unconscious body. "What a repulsive fellow. And his waistcoat is far too long. Someone clear this mess away."

Two red-coated guards rushed to drag Morvath from the dance floor. Ladies moved back, pulling their skirts against their legs so he did not sully them as he was hauled past. Gentlemen murmured to whoever would listen that they of course would have attacked the fiend themselves, foiling his dastardly plot, if only they had been close enough . . . wearing their sword . . . not protecting the lady at their side . . . not suffering from a terrible nameless malady that slowed their movements. When the body neared Petunia Dole, her foot suffered an unforeseen spasm and kicked him in the head. Olivia Etterly was so astonished by this, she stumbled, and only by stepping heavily upon his groin was she able to restore her balance.

Morvath was then taken from the palace into the custody of the police force. (Charged with disturbing the peace, attempted murder, and upsetting the Queen on her special day, he was shipped off to Afghanistan, where they put him to work in a copper mine. But he escaped, developed an addiction to opium, and wandered the southern mountains orating epic poetry about the poppy—*rhymes with floppy*—until eventually meeting his doom at the hands of a prospective bride and her pet weasel.)

Cecilia finally steadied herself, recollecting her inner resolve. "I'm sorry," she told Ned whilst smoothing her dress, straightening her gloves. "I do thank you for the kind offer and, er, the generous expression of your ardor, but I can't marry you, Captain, regardless of my heart's conviction. As we previously discussed, I am bound in duty to my aunt."

"Miss Darlington?" the Queen called.

"Huh? What's that?" Miss Darlington turned from smiling at Jacobsen, her eyes blinking, her expression trying to settle into seriousness. "Did someone want me?"

The entire company laughed. Ned holstered his gun at the back of his waistband and smiled down at Cecilia's flushing face until she sighed.

"It's not amusing," she said. "I am trying to do the right thing."

"Oh good heavens!" Miss Darlington threw up her hands impatiently. (Countess Feodora's pearl ring slipped from her glove and rolled across the floor.) "This has gone far enough! Did I not raise you to be a proper scoundrel, Cecilia? Have you not been educated in the correct ways of ladylike piratism? Why are you even *thinking* of trying to do the right thing?"

Cecilia blinked, confounded. "I—er—"

"Run away with the boy. Abandon your duties. Live in sin. Or else your bad name will be utterly redeemed."

"But—" Cecilia began.

"So long as you promise to drink your daily tonic, wear a scarf in all weather, and not go after the Bevelrede fortune, which I have my eye on—"

"What?!" shouted an alarmed Count Bevelrede from within the crowd.

"—I will give you my blessing for an elopement. But of course it's up to you."

Cecilia frowned. What would a heroine do in this moment? How might she best fit herself to this evolution of events?

"Then again," Olivia said momentously, and Cecilia pivoted

toward her. "If you stay, we do have a seat for you at our senior table. Almost everyone's agreed. You've proven yourself to be a good girl, and we're confident you will obey our laws. Congratulations!"

Cecilia blinked, swaying slightly in astonishment. Ten years of dreaming rushed into her throat, and she drew a breath to answer—

"Wait!"

The Queen had spoken. Everyone turned to stare at her in silent anticipation. She held her hand raised and head slightly tilted as if listening. "It will be midnight in a minute," she said. "Now is your magical moment, Miss Bassingthwaite. The decision is yours. Will you run away and be a wild woman, or will you stay and dance with the prince? We have several here for you to choose from."

Cecilia looked at Miss Darlington. The old lady scowled, and Cecilia felt her heart leap with love and gratitude. *"Hiawatha—"* she tried to say, but Miss Darlington waved a disdainful hand.

"Was boring me horribly. Those Americans have no idea how to be swashbuckling. I recall that Mr. Jacobsen here used to read aloud to me from the works of Byron."

Queen Victoria and several nearby ladies sighed dreamily.

"I shall read from them again every day, my dear Jemima," Jacobsen declared. "And lay your feet in my hands every night."

"How romantic," murmured the ladies in the crowd.

"Is that a metaphor?" asked the gentlemen in the crowd.

Ned leaned forward to whisper smilingly to Cecilia, "It appears you have been made redundant."

Cecilia frowned. "I could choose the seat at the senior table."

"That is one possibility," he agreed.

"I could steal my own house, live alone."

"You could."

"Be independent."

"Yes."

"Read anything I wanted with no one commenting."

"That's certainly true."

Suddenly the clock struck midnight. Its stentorian tones reverberated through the excited silence of the ballroom. Cecilia took a deep breath. Ned took a deep breath, watching her. Miss Darlington yawned.

And then Cecilia grinned. The decision wasn't so hard after all, here inside the unbounded magic of love. Curtsying to her aunt, nodding briskly to the Queen, she gathered up her skirts and turned to give Ned an imperious look.

"Well?" she demanded. "Are you coming or not?"

And with that, she strode from the ballroom.

Ned glanced at Queen Victoria, shrugging his mouth in apology. She flapped a hand at him. Behind her, and languidly stealing a pearl bracelet from Princess Louise's wrist, Alex tossed him a sardonic smile, then nodded sidelong to indicate Ned really ought to hurry after Cecilia, considering she was almost out of the room. Ned did not run—but almost.

But just before she reached the door, Cecilia turned. "You said almost everyone," she called out to Olivia. "Who dissented?"

"Two members," Olivia said. "Lady Armitage sent in a postal vote. And—"

"And I said no," Miss Darlington interjected. She gave Cecilia a long, fierce look. "Fly free, my dear."

Sudden tears filled Cecilia's eyes. "Oh," she whispered, overpowered by emotion. "I love you, Aunty."

"Yes, yes. Just come back next Wednesday, you know I can't do the *Times* crossword without your help."

Cecilia laughed. "I'll see you then."

And putting her hand in Ned's, she left the ballroom.

"Is that it?" demanded the Queen, glaring at the crowd. "Anyone else want to attempt mass murder or elope with a rakish pirate? No? Then can we please get back to celebrating me?"

The crowd curtsied to her. "Your Majesty," they murmured gratifyingly.

And the band began to play.

✳ 26 ✳

A WOMAN'S LIBERATION—BENEATH AN ACHING MOON—
BOOKISH—CECILIA BECOMES A FALLEN WOMAN—
STRIPPED NAKED—GENRIFICATION—HOMECOMING

And so Cecilia made her own way forward. Which is to say, holding Ned's hand, and advised by ushers as to the correct exit from the castle, and followed by guards who seemed to think she might steal the royal treasures if they took their eye off her even for a moment—but independent in heart, where it really counted. They stepped out into the moonlight.

Not that the moonlight was apparent, considering all the gas lamps blazing in the courtyard and the lights shining through the windows of the palace; but Cecilia could sense the moon up there somewhere. It shone like the crooked grin of Cilla Bassingthwaite, the lost pirate queen, blowing wishes that freckled the sky and flared gently in Cecilia's memory. She never had to look to sense her mother's light.

"Do you think Cilla would approve of me?" Ned asked as if he'd known her thoughts.

"I approve of you," she answered. "That's all that matters."

He smiled, and she looked at him instead of the high, bright horizon. His formal elegance was ruffled around the edges, and the wry, overconfident gleam in his eye had returned. She thought of the gun he had tucked in his waistband, and her blood warmed. Suddenly she wanted him out of that fine coat and into a broom closet.

"Well," he said, "I hope you approve of this also."

She followed the gesture of his hand and her eyes widened as a building sank to the ground before her. She heard guards' footsteps come running, saw out of the corner of her eye Ned reassuring them with a wave. But she could not look away from the edifice.

"Do you like it?" Ned asked.

"Um," Cecilia replied eloquently.

"It's my gift to you." He squeezed her hand gently, and she responded in kind—testing his balance, reassuring herself she could flip him onto his back any moment she needed to, before relaxing and letting him be there beside her in partnership.

The house he had brought her was a brown stone cottage with a steep roof and white-framed windows that shone lamplit in the darkness. Roses clambered over its frontage, framing the pirate-red door. Smoke wafted fragrantly from its chimney. Looking up at the gabled window set into the roof, Cecilia saw Pleasance draw aside a white lace curtain to wave to her. Dazed, she did not wave back. Instead, she lowered her gaze to the front door. Stepping toward it, drawing Ned with her, she read the plaque on the lintel.

"Pucklechurch Community Library. No!"

Ned smiled. "Yes."

She turned to stare at him. "You stole a library?"

"Well, I made the arrangements, but Pleasance did the labor. As soon as you left for the banquet tonight, she flew to Gloucestershire in an outhouse and back again at top speed in order to arrive in time."

"She did that for me?" Cecilia was deeply touched. And excited to think of this first theft from Aunt Darlington—her housemaid. "But won't Pucklechurch seek justice?"

"I imagine they'll be more than happy we took the building off their hands. They wanted to expand their cemetery to accommodate all the picnicking tourists, so this library was slated for destruction and its books were to be sold or burned."

Cecilia gasped.

"There are twenty thousand of them, give or take. It used to be a private house so it has a kitchen and bathroom, but we'll need to renovate, and to acquire some furnishings and munitions to make it homey. I hope you don't mind."

"Mind?" Her eyes lit up. "Think of the fun we shall have, shopping for sofas and guns and lamps."

"Stealing them, you mean."

She lifted her chin regally, and Ned had a premonition of what the rest of his life with her was going to be like. "Attaining through discretion," she said.

"Breaking and entering," he countered.

"Visiting without disturbing the occupants."

He laughed. But as she looked at him with her beautiful luminous eyes, his laughter faded. His smile became deep, heavy. She reached out, touching his heart, and he felt a thousand defenses of charm, cunning, carelessness, shattering beneath her gentleness, leaving him at last with the clarity of truth. He loved her. He needed her.

Lifting a hand, he laid it gently against her cheek. She was warm, soft—not like a marble princess or fierce pirate, just Cecilia, opening her silence for him. He could have wept then, for the trust she gave him, the vulnerability in her winter-colored eyes.

Suddenly the library door opened, slapping away their intimate peace. They turned, hands instinctively reaching for weapons, and Pleasance grinned at them.

"Welcome home, miss," she said, curtsying.

Cecilia reached forward to awkwardly pat the maid's arm. "Thank you, dear. Are you quite all right after your hurried journey?" For Pleasance's curls bristled even more than usual and her eyes shone as if she had skimmed the edge of heaven to get to Pucklechurch and back in time.

"I do feel a little consumptive, miss," Pleasance answered cheerfully. "But such is the way of life. A shadow hangs over all of us, claiming our souls even from the moment of birth, and all we can do is surrender or succumb to screaming madness. Please come in."

She drew the door ajar. Cecilia was about to take a step forward when Ned tugged her hand. Before she could chastise him, he swooped her up in his arms and proceeded to carry her over the threshold.

Then backed up and turned sideways so her ball gown would not jam the entrance.

And then shoved a little.

And tripped on her long, flowing skirt, tumbling them both to the tiled floor of the entrance hall.

"Oh my," Pleasance said. "It's bad luck to fall when you first enter a house. It disturbs the ghosts." She sounded excited at the possibility.

"Not bad luck, just women's bloody ridiculous fashions," Ned muttered. He stood, brushing a stray thread from his sleek velvet coat and straightening his bow tie.

"Or men's irrational customs," Cecilia retorted. Ned reached out a hand and she tsked as she looked at it. "Etiquette demands that a gentleman remove his glove before helping a lady up from the floor onto which he has so recklessly tossed her."

"I beg your pardon, madam." Taking hold of the glove's hem, he slowly slid it forward over his hand, revealing the skin beneath. His eyes never left hers, which Cecilia considered fortunate as it meant he would not see her throat move as she swallowed heavily.

"Er—um—I should just go—" Pleasance stammered, and yet she did not take her presence from the room, nor her wide-eyed stare from the scene before her.

The glove removed, the fingers naked, Ned presented his hand again. Cecilia blushed as she took it. He gripped her own gloved fingers firmly and pulled her to her feet. She swayed a little but he held her steady, touching her nowhere but her hand—somehow making her feel like he touched her all over. Their gazes locked in a highly indecent stare.

"So are you happy, miss?" Pleasance interrupted, bouncing a little, causing Ned to smile tightly and Cecilia to almost giggle. "Do you like your new house?"

"I do," Cecilia said. "It is most agreeable."

Pleasance turned her bright, flushed face to Ned. "That's such very high praise from the miss, sir. You did well."

"I could not have achieved it without you, Pleasance my dear," he replied charmingly.

"It was the least I could do for Miss Bassingthwaite. She's our own true heroine."

"Oh, I wouldn't say that," Cecilia murmured.

"But you rescued the Society from Northangerland Abbey, miss."

"Actually, they rescued themselves."

"You fired the Darlington guns to make the abbey unstable for flight."

"But it was Jane Fairweather who found the houses in the garden," Cecilia corrected with painstaking care. "Without her, we couldn't have gone anywhere."

"You defeated his henchmen."

"That was the royal troops, whom Constantinopla Brown organized."

"But you shot down Captain Morvath!"

"Actually, he crashed into a hillside. And then reappeared tonight at the banquet."

"Egads!" Pleasance gasped.

"It's all right," Ned assured her. "He took Cecilia captive, but—"

"But she wreaked vengeance upon him for her tragically murdered mother?" Pleasance suggested, pointing to the portrait of Cilla, which had previously hung in Cecilia's bedroom but now presided over this entrance hall.

Ned shook his head.

"She foiled him with her usual cleverness?"

Ned winced.

"The Queen hit him over the head with her tiara," Cecilia explained. "I'm afraid I've done nothing at all to advance the plot."

"You chose to come away with me," Ned reminded her.

"So this is merely a romance?" She frowned disapprovingly. "I was hoping for an epic adventure, or a Gothic mystery at the very least."

Ned laughed. "Darling, don't worry. The story has just begun."

Cecilia grinned and took his hand, and if Pleasance was watching, or was discreetly slipping away, she did not notice. She leaned forward to kiss him.

The building rose, or perhaps it was just her heart.

"I love you," she whispered.

"Of course you do," he replied wickedly.

And together they walked into the library.

Acknowledgments

One quiet, sunlit afternoon, I was minding my own business when suddenly two elegant ladies holding teacups and pistols appeared in my consciousness. From that moment on, everything else came to a halt as I worked to find out who they might be. Thus Cecilia and Miss Darlington literally kidnapped my imagination in true piratic fashion. They then went on to change my life, as pirates are wont to do. I give them not only their due but my endless gratitude.

Hugs and wholehearted thanks to Taylor Haggerty, dream-maker extraordinaire. Your kindness, steadiness, and good cheer have uplifted my anxious heart more often than you know. Cheers also to the ladies of Root Literary, who have created an agency full of sparkle and loveliness. I still pinch myself with amazement that I'm part of the Root Lit family.

Getting to work with Kristine Swartz has been a real honor. Thank you so much, Kristine, for your graciousness, patience, and humor, and for helping me take my lady scoundrels further than I ever dreamed they could go. Thanks also to the entire fabulous Berkley team, including Bridget O'Toole, Jessica Brock, Stephanie Felty, Lindsey Tulloch, and Eileen Chetti. You've all contributed toward making this experience a delight. Swooning gratitude to Katie Anderson and Dawn Cooper for the truly gorgeous cover, and Laura K. Corless for the book design of my dreams.

Thanks and blessings to Raquel Vasquez Gilliland, Renee April, Kate Gillard, and all my online chums, for your support, friendship, and general egging-on. May your tea always be the perfect temperature when you go to drink it. Special love to my first teachers, Mrs. Milne and Mr. Robson. You were so kind, and so bolstering of the little girl who spent her days half-lost in stories. This book wouldn't have existed without you. Thanks also to the west wind and old hills that godmothered my imagination throughout childhood. Wherever I am, I carry you with me.

I raise a teacup to the Brontë family and Charles Darwin, whose works provided the misquotes at each chapter beginning. No offense intended!

My deepest gratitude goes to my family, Amaya, Julie, Dale, Steph, Simon, Anya, and Myla. Without the solid foundation you gave me, I couldn't have gone flying with mad pirates. Dad, you nurtured my love of stories. Mum, you've bravely read everything, from badly spelled epics about pink horses right through to kissing scenes, and deserve a medal for it. Amaya, without your insistence I might never have written this book, so with all my heart I thank you for that, and for the joy you bring me always.

Finally, hugs to my readers. I wish you a life blessed with fair winds and fabulous hats. Tally ho!

Photo courtesy of the author

INDIA HOLTON resides in New Zealand, where she's enjoyed the typical Kiwi lifestyle of wandering around forests, living barefoot on islands, and messing about in boats. Now she lives in a cottage near the sea, writing books about unconventional women and charming rogues, and drinking far too much tea.

CONNECT ONLINE

 IndiaHolton

India.Holton

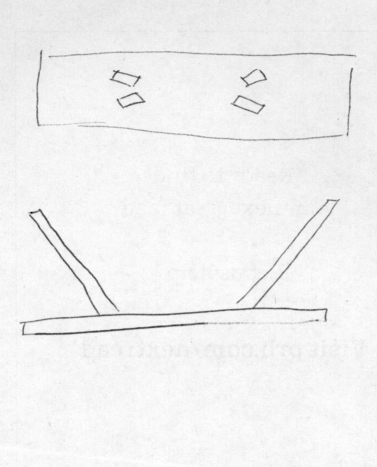